Emily Barr is the well-loved and bestselling author of *Backpack*, the original backpacking novel, and many other highly acclaimed novels. A former journalist, she has travelled around the world and written columns and travel pieces for the *Observer* and the *Guardian*. After living in France, Emily and her husband (whom she met backpacking) have settled in Cornwall with their three children. To learn more about Emily and her novels, you can visit her website www.emilybarr.com.

Praise for Emily Barr's novels:

'Thrillingly sinister . . . *Single White Female* with a twist, only far, far less predictable'   *Glamour*

'Barr has come up with the goods again: a buzzy, exciting work that refuses to bow to convention'   *Sunday Express*

'This gripping novel will have you gasping in sympathy' *Company*

'Barr's fluid, assured descriptions of India afford a vivid and convincing sense of place'   *Guardian*

'Brilliantly written, tense and refreshing, you'll devour this fantastic read'   *Closer*

'This dark but funny tale is full of shocking twists, making it a terrific page-turner'   *Cosmopolitan*

'She has a nice line in black humour and the travel details seem absolutely authentic'   *Daily Mail*

'Compelling'   *Heat*

'A great read from start to finish . . . believable characters that are variously biting, insightful and sympathetic'   *The Times*

'One of the most compelling page-turners around' *B* magazine

'Bright and breezy with a nasty little twist'   *Mirror*

By Emily Barr

The First Wife

Emily Barr

headline
review

First published in 2011 by HEADLINE REVIEW
An imprint of HEADLINE PUBLISHING GROUP

First published in paperback in 2011 by HEADLINE REVIEW
An imprint of HEADLINE PUBLISHING GROUP

1

Cataloguing in Publication Data is available from the British Library

978 0 7553 5137 4

Typeset in Garamond ITC by Palimpsest Book Production Limited,
Falkirk, Stirlingshire

Printed and bound in Great Britain by
CPI Group (UK), Croydon, CR0 4YY

Headline's policy is to use papers that are natural, renewable and recyclable products and
made from wood grown in sustainable forests. The logging and manufacturing processes
are expected to conform to the environmental regulations of the country of origin.

HEADLINE PUBLISHING GROUP
An Hachette UK Company
338 Euston Road
London NW1 3BH

www.headline.co.uk
www.hachette.co.uk

For James, Gabe, Seb and Lottie,
as ever, with lots of love

Thanks to Aidan and LeEtta of Trevithick School, Camborne, for donating their names to two of the characters in this book after winning the writing competition with their fantastic and intriguing imaginative feats.

Thank you to Samantha Lloyd for a research trip to Barcelona that took an unexpected and delightful turn thanks to a cloud of volcanic ash, and to everyone who helped hold the fort at home until we got back.

I feel incredibly fortunate to have both Jonny Geller and Sherise Hobbs in my corner, and this book would not have reached fruition without their input and encouragement. Huge thanks to both of them: they are the best.

And thank you to the teachers at St Francis School who look after my children while I write, and to everyone who puts up with the swings between obsessiveness and despair that are all part of the process. Finally, thanks to my family for providing the necessary counterpart to the life spent writing; making me go for walks on beaches, take them to the cinema, and scrabble around doing 'creative homework' at the weekend.

prologue

August

It rained all day, the day of her funeral. A few of her friends showed up for the service, but when it ended, they huddled under black umbrellas talking about who would be next, and wandered off together, and nobody went on to the crematorium but me.

The crematorium was familiar from the previous funeral. It was blank, boring and terrible at the same time. Confronted by rows of expectant seats, I sat in the middle of the front row. For once, there was nowhere to hide. I was out in the world.

Only a few weeks earlier, I had been here for his funeral; but that time I had taken her, leading her by the hand and trying to keep her from saying inappropriate things. She shouted out something about a baby as his coffin slid away, and she had no idea that she was saying goodbye to her husband. I had been her carer. She was, even then, my protector, in all her crazy randomness.

1

Today the world was new. Its edges were sharper. For a few disorientating seconds, I felt I was on a stage set, that behind these fake walls was darkness. The reality was worse than darkness: there was a world of which I knew nothing, in which I had no place. I gripped the edges of the seat with both my hands.

Sombre music was piped in from somewhere, and a man arrived and pretended he was speaking to a crowded room. I hardly heard his platitudes, because he had not known her, and nothing he said meant anything. I tried not even to think about her. I was glad we had decided on no hymns.

Her coffin was in front of me. I stared at it, imagining the body in there, knowing I should be displaying a few tears, if only to prove to the man in the suit ('Joy led a long and fulfilled life') that I really was her granddaughter.

I was a terrible person. Once I started crying, I could not stop, and he had to raise his voice to get his words to carry over my sobs. Yet I knew that my tears were not just for her. They were also for myself. The rain hammered on the flat roof.

The man in the suit did not mention my tears. He said she was a beloved mother, without remarking on the fact that her only child had not bothered to turn up. He did, however, seem to be very interested in muttering his way through the words as quickly as he possibly could, and walking out of the door.

I set off down the road, heading for home automatically. I was following the ancient family solicitor's advice: the cottage was going on the market in the morning, I would pack up all my stuff, wait for the place to sell, and then leave.

At that point, my plan skidded to an abrupt halt. The two old people I had spent years caring for were dead. They had been my world: I had no friends. I knew I had no family any more; at least, I had to act as though I had no one. I had hardly dared to hope they would come back for this. I had written them a postcard, in my most careful calligraphy with my purple fountain pen. I was worried about scaring them off, so I just wrote this:

Joy and Ken both died this month. Please come home for a while.

I posted it to the last address Grandma had for them, a place called Mount Eden.

They would not have received it, booked their flights, and got back in time for the funeral. I had never expected that. I did half-hope that they would show up in the next few weeks, though, while I was still at the cottage.

They might come. I did not write my name on it, in case I scared them off. Even now, I half-expected that every person I saw on the street would be one of them. I lived and relived a scene in which they appeared from around a corner, looked at me, looked again, and smiled. It happened again and again, in my dreams and in my daydreams. I would know them at once, either of them, and I would forgive everything, in half a second.

I walked home, three miles, through the downpour. Puddles gathered as I watched, on our track, and I stepped straight through them, soaking my black ballet shoes. Rain cascaded down my face. My dress, which I had hardly had time to iron since the previous funeral, clung to my body, cold and clammy. My hair turned to wet string and stuck to my neck and back. By the time I reached the cottage, I was soaked through. I looked deranged, but that did not matter, as there was no one to see me.

I had come to live in this cottage when I was a child, and it seemed inconceivable that I would ever think of any other house as 'home'. It was a pretty, deceptively large house, with thick stone walls and a climbing rose up the wall. There were four bedrooms (three upstairs, one down), a big kitchen with a table, and a sitting room filled with ancient furniture. Everything was old and made to last. It was a delightful, comforting time-warp.

I opened the heavy wooden door, and tried not to look at the spot at the bottom of the stairs where both of them had fallen – first him, and then, fatally, her.

Almost all our stuff was already packed away. Without telling either of them, I had been sorting it into boxes for years. Neither of them had been upstairs for a long time. In that time, every single thing up there, with the exception of the contents of my bedroom and bathroom, had been either thrown away, sent to charity, or boxed up. I had been so scared of them dying, for so long that, perversely, the only way to hold the terror at bay was by making horrible preparations for the day on which I would find myself alone. That had seemed to make it less likely to happen.

The fact that they *would* both die, one day, had always been there, though the three of us existed right up to the end by pretending that we would carry on the way we were for ever. It had seemed distasteful even to think about what would happen to me when they were gone.

Ever since I was eight, I had lived with Grandma and Granddad in their cottage in this Cornish village. They were everything to me, my rock, my stability, and I loved them furiously, clinging on tight and never quite relaxing into the belief that they would not abandon me. And now, finally, they had. Grandma could have gone on for decades more, though she had been losing her mind for over a year. It had happened suddenly, unexpectedly, and it was all my fault. She must have wandered upstairs in the night. I had vaguely heard a cry and a bump, but had not properly woken. I would never know for sure, but I was certain in my heart that she had seen the upstairs rooms in her house – her old bedroom, the spare room that had housed her fabulous clothes, my mother's childhood room – empty and packed up in anticipation of her death, and had fallen down the stairs in horror and confusion.

My packing up to ward the moment off had made it happen.

When I contemplated the world outside these walls, I grabbed the table to keep myself upright. I had not the faintest idea of what to do.

I had been an anxious child, and when I came to live with them I was eager to fit in. I embraced every aspect of life in this cottage with gusto. It was only when I was eleven that I realised that my grandparents were the local eccentrics. When I had friends over, I saw that their habit of walking around naked was odd and apparently alarming and scary. They meant nothing sinister by it: it was just what they did, just as they started each day with a cup of hot water with a chunk of ginger in it, and recited one of Shakespeare's sonnets before every meal because it was 'better than Grace'.

The friends went home and told their parents about the nudity, and after that, no one was allowed to come to play. I became the Weird Girl. Grandma and Granddad descended slowly into incapacity, and by the time I was fourteen I was looking after them more than they looked after me; helping them up the stairs, keeping the cottage clean. I managed to care for them when they needed it and do my GCSE coursework without too much trouble, until Granddad fell downstairs. That was the beginning of the end for him, and it marked the moment at which they both gave up.

And now they were dead. I skirted the fated tiles at the bottom of the stairs and headed to the kitchen, where I put the kettle on. It would take me a day to pack up the rest of the house, and I would sell it. I would take the money, and with my funds in the bank, I would do something.

Oh, I thought, yet again. If only I had the faintest idea what that *something* might be. The house was going on the market for three hundred thousand pounds. They would have paid the mortgage off years ago. With that money, I could do anything I wanted. I had already applied for a passport, just in case. It was simply going to be a question of working out what normal people did, how they did it, and doing that. It was a straightforward question of courage.

In the back garden, I picked some sprigs of mint from

the pot next to the wall. I rinsed the mint in the ceramic sink, and stuffed it into the teapot with a teaspoon of sugar, because we drank mint tea, rather than commercial rubbish that was crammed full of chemicals. We drank home-made herb tea, or proper coffee, or water. On Sundays we had a glass or two of sherry.

I hated being here without them. I could not stay here, living their life on my own. It was time for me to go out into the world, like one of the Three Little Pigs.

As I poured the boiling water into the hand-painted teapot, I allowed myself a few minutes to contemplate the hard truth of the fact that Grandma and I would never again sit in front of the roaring fire brushing each other's long hair. Granddad would never heave himself to his feet to declaim Edmund's soliloquy, from *King Lear*, ending with a triumphant: 'now, gods, stand up for bastards!' Those things were gone. Other things would fill the gaps they left, but I could not begin to imagine what those things might be.

I was on my own in the world. I was twenty, with a clutch of GCSEs and a pretty yet overgrown cottage to my name. I knew most of Shakespeare's sonnets by heart, but I had no idea how people lived. My hands trembled as I poured a stream of dirty hot minty water into my cup. There was no one to care whether I used a saucer or not. My days were no longer to be spent washing and cleaning and escorting elderly people to the loo. Time stretched ahead, blank and unknowable.

part one

chapter one

September

'Guys!' she yelled from the bottom of the stairs. 'Downstairs now! All of you!'

I stood up, remembered she did not mean me, and sat back down.

'Coming!' called a child's voice much closer to me.

'All right,' added another, and there was the sound of several sets of feet hurtling down the stairs. I tried to imagine a world in which children were called 'guys'; but in fact, I did not have to imagine it. I was living in it.

I had a bed, in a house. It was a tiny single bed with a Barbie duvet cover on it. I did not care about the size of the bedroom. It was clean and warm and I had no complaints. I sat on my bed, grateful for its softness, and rocked to and fro. I felt like a spy. I was not from this world, but I needed to pretend that I was. There was a time when I used to come to homes like this, as a child. Proper homes, normal ones, with strange rules that were

11

so obvious to everyone else that no one would ever explain them. There was a time when friends at school would invite me over to play. This could have been one of their houses: it was modern and clean and filled with people who did things differently. It had been strange enough visiting these places. Now I had come to live in one.

I was back from the precipice. It was important to get this right.

This was a family home, and everyone who lived here was already squashed before their lodger arrived. The two girls had moved into bunk beds so that I could have a room of my own, and the older one of them, Mia, had hung around as I arrived, shooting me fierce looks when our eyes met. I supposed she did not like me because I was taking up her space. The younger children did not seem particularly interested in me. Twins Jessica and Zac were eleven, and there was another boy, Tommy, who was six.

John was father to some of the children and stepfather to the others. The mother (of everyone except Mia) was Julia, and I liked her, which was why I had taken this room. In fact, I took this room partly because I liked Julia, and partly because I was absolutely desperate for a roof and some walls, and terrified of what might happen to me if I stayed where I had been for a moment longer.

I sat on the bed and stretched my legs out. There was a little fabric-covered wardrobe next to the window, and it tipped sideways into a rhombus if I so much as breathed on it. A couple of shelves higher up on the walls were empty at the moment, and there was no floor space at all.

When you opened the door, it hit the bed as soon as it reached a 90-degree angle.

I clenched my eyes tight shut, and told myself I was home. The room was, perhaps, one third of the size of my bedroom at the cottage, and that had not been particularly big. I allowed myself the luxury of going back there, just for a few seconds, just to draw strength.

At the cottage, I had slept on a lumpy double bed, high off the ground, with a brass bedstead. There was an old pinkish carpet, a varnished wooden dressing-table, two little windows, one looking to the front and one to the side. The side one looked over trees and grass, and the front window gave a view of a distant flat horizon of the sea. My clothes hung in an enormous polished mahogany wardrobe that just touched the ceiling. Along one wall, there were two huge bookcases, filled with books. When I was ten, I had cleared one shelf, and piled the books beside the bed to use as a little table for my clock and a glass of water. I liked it because I could 'read the table' whenever the fancy took me, and change its genre regularly.

The emptied shelf became a display place for my precious things: mainly, a picture of me aged about two, holding hands with both my parents.

Grandma would knock on the door and make sure I was awake for school. She would bring me in a cup of milky coffee, because from the age of nine I made myself like it, and she would set it down carefully on my book-table. Her blue fleece dressing-gown was fastened tightly over her white nightdress, and her morning hair was thick down her back, just like mine. After her coffee, she would pin it up in a chignon, using hundreds of hairpins, which she would shed around the house over the course of the day. Wherever she went, they would fall on the flagstone floors of the downstairs of the cottage with melodic little tinkles.

'Good morning, Lilybella,' she would say with a smile, and she would open my curtains, the front window first and then the side window, and report on the weather.

'Glorious day,' she would say, or, 'Great weather for ducks!' or else, 'You know, I rather think these clouds are going to blow right out to sea.' Whatever was going on out there, she found its bright side.

I was clutching my head in my hands. Each hand was hanging onto a clump of thick curls. I missed them both so much. I had no idea what to do, and my grief was tempered with fury at them. I had been completely wrong about the money. When I accepted an offer on the cottage, Mr Jackson, the doddery solicitor, had sat me down and gently explained that there would be no money. There was only a black hole of debt that had to be paid with the proceeds of the sale of the cottage. I had no idea where these debts had come from, only that I had been left with nothing. Just a few hundred pounds from under my grandmother's mattress, which had got me this far. I was grateful for that, at least.

However hard I tried to make the sums add up, they did not. We had a little old Mini, that no one had driven for years. We never went on holiday: I had not left Cornwall once, not in my entire life. Grandma bought us nice clothes and shoes, and we got new books all the time, but it was simply not possible that we had spent all that money, just existing from day to day. They had done something else with it. I was steeling myself to ask the bank to give me details of all the transactions they had made.

I wiped a tear from my eye and started unpacking the books from my box (I had had to select a very few of them to bring with me, and had chosen mostly poetry) and building my book-table, all over again. It meant the door would open even less.

I had moved to our nearest town: Falmouth. It seemed like the least worst of the limited options ranged in front of me. I needed a job, and there were hundreds of bars and restaurants and shops here, plenty of houses and schools that might need cleaning. It also had a university, and although I had failed miserably at my exams, I must have had enough qualifications to get me onto a course of some sort, one day, when I was settled. For now, I had applied for housing benefit and Jobseekers' Allowance, thanks to the advice of the only person I had met who seemed even slightly interested in me, a man called Al at the Citizens' Advice Bureau.

I met Al when I forced myself to cycle into Falmouth, and track down his office because I had it at the back of my head that the 'Citizens' Advice Bureau' was a place to go for help. I was a citizen, and I certainly needed advice.

The truth about my financial situation had knocked me out. The cottage sale went through, and I was unable to make any plans or do anything; because how can you do anything when you have hardly any money? The day arrived when the new people were due to move in, and

I had still done nothing. They were letting me keep our boxes of stuff in the shed for the moment.

When I walked into the Citizens' Advice Bureau, my limbs were aching, I was horribly dirty, and since my hair was unwashed, it had formed greasy ringlets that gave me away at once as a rough sleeper.

I had woken in the dankness of dawn, in the dust and dirt of the shed that Granddad had liked to tell me he built when my mother was a little girl. The wind blew straight through it. I got up quickly, folded my old duvet, which still had its floral cover on it, and stuffed it back into the box. I had to balance the mattress back up against the wall and creep away, pulling the door shut behind me.

It was my lowest point. Today, I said to myself, you must make something happen. There is no alternative. If I did nothing, the house's new owners would spot me sneaking into their shed in the dead of night, or sneaking out at sunrise. They would call the police.

I edged into the CAB, trying to look inconspicuous. A man with big black eyes and a tired face looked up at me, then smiled. Without a word, he ushered me into a room so small it was more of a cupboard, sat me down and did his best to disentangle my complicated situation. He made me apply for benefits straight away, and told me that I would be all right.

'People like you don't need to sleep rough,' he said, looking at me hard. He was mixed race, and his head was shaved. He was, I thought, somewhere in his thirties. 'Seriously, Lily. That's what we're here for, to stop someone like you slipping through the net just because you don't know what to do. Believe me, my dear, I've been there. I slept on the streets in London for years. I did it so you don't have to.'

I stared at him. 'You slept on the streets in London?'

His eyes were warm. 'Can't recommend it, I'm afraid. But then you know that already. Is it a comfy shed?'

I looked down, feeling myself blushing, and shook my head. I liked him. I wondered whether I 'fancied' him. That was what people did, in the real world. I decided I probably ought to, but I didn't. He was hardly going to reciprocate, anyway.

'The new people said I could keep my stuff in there,' I said quietly, 'until I found somewhere to live. So I still have that key, and I've got all the old bedding in there. I just sit on the beach and read a book until it's dark, and then creep into the shed with a torch and make myself a little place to sleep.'

'Like a hamster.'

'Then when it gets light, I get up again, pack away the bed, and creep off before they wake up.'

'It's boring,' he said, 'isn't it? Waiting for hours to pass.'

'Yes!' The fact that he knew this made the wretchedness recede, a little. 'Waiting! Just waiting all the time. That's why I came here today, so I could go and sit in the library, because it's getting too cold for the beach. And also, today is kind of the deadline I set myself. For doing something.'

He nodded. 'Right. We can sort this out, you know. You've come to the right place.' He held out his hand, and I shook it. 'I'm Alan. You can call me Al. If I can call you Betty, that is.'

I frowned. 'Why do you want to do that?'

He laughed. 'Don't worry. It was a joke. Simon and Garfunkel. I was trying to get in there before you said it, but I see that was an unnecessary precaution.'

Al seemed to have so much experience of situations that were worse than mine that it was impossible not to follow his advice. Things changed rapidly. He told me to go for every menial job I could get my hands on, and save as much money as I could. He told me to cycle to the university campus and have a look around, to inspire myself and give me something to aim for.

'It's totally within your grasp,' he said. 'We'll torch the bloody shed. Metaphorically. You're young, you'll scrub up nicely, and you can get everything going your way. Have a look at the noticeboards while you're there. There'll be rooms to rent in houses. That's what you want. You probably won't get one in a student house, because of council tax. They don't have to pay if everyone in the house is a student. But there'll be families looking for a lodger, and I think that's the kind of set-up you want. A family situation will mean you're less lonely. While you're up there, pop into the gym or something and see if you can grab a shower.' He looked up at me and smiled. 'Go there right now before you think up reasons not to. I'd go with you if I wasn't needed here.'

It took me a while to realise that no one on campus was giving me a second glance. All around me, confident boys and girls of my own age were laughing, chatting urgently, making lengthy arrangements into phones. They looked as though they knew where they were going, both in the next ten minutes and for the rest of their lives.

They looked happy, and carefree, like people who had two ordinary parents. None of them sniggered or stared. None muttered complaints about the Weird Girl invading their space. If I had been here with my grandparents, they would have whispered about us. People always did. On my own, I seemed to fit. Slowly, I started walking tall, the way Grandma had taught me, with my head held high. I walked properly: shoulders back, chin up. I knew I smelled horrible, and my hair was worse than ever (it was perhaps, I thought, time to cut it off), but nobody noticed. Nobody could see that I was crumbling inside, that every step I took was a triumph. I did not dare seek out a shower, but I locked myself in a disabled toilet cubicle, and did the best washing I could, using the soap from the dispenser. I even rinsed my hair with soap: it was a start.

And when I found the accommodation noticeboard, buried amongst the student houses was this sign: *Small room in friendly family home. Avail immed. Reduced rates for babysitting*.

Without stopping to reflect, I wrote the number on my hand, found a payphone, called it, looked at the room, and moved in. Everything was strange, from now on. I did what Al wanted me to do, because he was the only person who had given me a plan. I knew I would always be grateful to him for that.

My new home was in the suburbs, half an hour's walk from the town centre. It was a boxy house with cardboard walls, on a street of similar houses. My window looked out on a tiny square of front garden, a road (a steep hill) and an identical house opposite. I knew I had done well to get here, but this was only the first step. Tomorrow I was going to go out, again, and this time I would be looking for a job. I was properly clean now, wearing clean clothes, and I was as ready as I could possibly be to face the world.

There was a washing machine in the kitchen here. Grandma hated washing machines in kitchens: she said it was unhygienic, but I was going to have to get used to it. There were two televisions and a Wii. Nothing was quite the way I was used to things being.

There was a tap on my bedroom door. I made a noise that was supposed to be 'Come in?' but just came out as a scared grunt. The door swung open and bumped the book-table, and Mia, the teenager, stood there. She was slight and blonde, and was wearing a tiny skirt and leggings, with her white-blonde hair pulled across her face so it was half-hidden. As I understood it, John was her father, but Julia was her stepmother. One day, perhaps, I would find out what had become of her real mother. Motherless people were interesting.

'Hey,' she said sulkily. 'Julia says, do you want to come down and have a cup of tea?'

I shot her my best smile.

'Yes, please,' I said. 'That would be lovely.'

I sat up and tried to iron out my features, to make myself look normal. Smoothing down my hair, I looked at myself in the mirror. I, Lily Button, was about to start my new life.

I took a deep breath and headed for the stairs.

chapter two

A week later

'Bathroom's free!'

I jumped out of bed and grabbed my towel. I could not be late. I had a big thing to do today: this was the day on which I was going to work, for money. I had decided to dress as I felt a student would, if she had a cleaning job in her spare time. That was the person I was aiming to be.

My wardrobe was not exactly crammed with disguises. Most of my clothes had been bought by Grandma, and she had liked floral dresses, velvet capes, and quirky hats. I managed, in the end, to achieve more or less the look I was going for, by combining a pair of black trousers that were fairly tight, with a maroon satin tunic embroidered with silver flowers at the hem. Both items were a bit odd for normal people, but from a distance I thought it would be OK.

I laid the outfit out on my bed, and ran for the shower as soon as I heard John's voice.

He smiled back over his shoulder, as he disappeared into his and Julia's bedroom, which was right next to mine. He had a towel round his waist, and his chest was hairy in a greyish, wiry way. John was forty-six, and as he had already told me twice, he was 'an apple' – exceptionally round around the middle in a way that boded ill, he said, for his future health.

'Heart attacks on legs,' he would say cheerfully. 'That's what "apples" are.'

He had left the window open, but it was only a tiny window of frosted glass that opened a fraction, and it did almost nothing. The air was foggy. My hair started dripping as soon as I closed the door. There was a strange intimacy in coming straight into someone else's bathroom. I could smell him, and his shower gel, and his farts.

When Grandma and Granddad moved into the downstairs bedroom, I had the upstairs bathroom all to myself. This one was smaller, and it was full of toothbrushes and different shampoo for different people, and smears of toothpaste.

I tested the water with a hand. It was almost warm: it would do nicely. I smiled to myself as I borrowed Mia's shampoo again. For the first time in my life, I was going out to work. Cleaning was something I knew I could do, because I had scrubbed our cottage ruthlessly for years, anxious to meet Grandma's standards. I was going to do it well. It helped that I was not going to have to talk to anyone while I was there. I was resolutely looking forward, not back. Al had told me that if I made myself a life, good things would happen to me.

'Get work of some sort,' he said. 'You'll meet people. Things will happen to you that you will never be able to predict or imagine. Everything you get to do, do it well, and you'll open up new horizons.'

I was hanging onto this as I dried myself and wrapped one of Grandma's towels around my hair. I had no other option. I made a conscious effort and poured myself into my new persona. I was going to act like a cheerful, confident person and, sooner or later, perhaps reality would catch up.

I smiled and bounced down the stairs, copying the careless strides of the eleven year olds.

'Morning, Julia,' I chirped.

'Well,' said Julia. 'Good morning, Lily Button.'

'Morning!' I said again, even brighter this time. I took my black lace-up boots from the rack and stood them next to the door, ready for departure. They were not brilliantly practical shoes for a cleaner, but they were sturdier than my ballet shoes. They were like Victorian riding boots, and I knew they had been expensive. I had stupidly high-quality clothes and shoes, and no actual money whatsoever.

'Where you get that energy . . .' Julia said, shaking her head. 'When you got here I was quite worried about the way you seemed to lie on your bed all day with a book. So pale and thin, like a girl in a ghost story. Now, suddenly I can't focus on you, you move so fast.'

Julia was forty-something, but she looked good. I

thought of a saying that both my grandparents had liked to recite. It was Coco Chanel: 'Nature gives you the face you have at twenty; life shapes the face you have at thirty; but at fifty, you get the face you deserve.' Granddad had liked to say that, while admiring himself in the mirror. Although Julia was not going to be fifty for several years, I thought it was right. Her face was kind and her eyes were sparkly, but most of all, she looked wise.

She was dressed now for work: she did not have a uniform, but wore a pair of black trousers, with a loose floral blouse over the top with a name badge on her chest that read *Julia Hobson Health Visitor*. I liked to see her ready for work, because I loved to imagine her checking that all the babies in Falmouth were all right, making sure their parents were looking after them properly, testing their hearing and their reflexes. If I had a baby (which I would not) I would want Julia to be my health visitor.

'I'm off to work this morning,' I reminded her, and I nipped into the kitchen, put the kettle on, and stuck two pieces of toast into the toaster. I only wanted one, but there was bound to be someone who would devour the other. Sharing a slice of my 86p loaf of bread was a grand gesture, in my way, and one that would probably pass unnoticed.

The twins were sitting at the tiny kitchen table, looking wholesome in burgundy uniforms, listening to their iPod with one headphone each, and nodding enthusiastically along with it. Jessica was eating a bowl of cereal, and Zacary was spreading Marmite on toast. Both their faces were covered in light brown freckles, and they had matching wide smiles. Zac's dark hair was carefully spiked upwards, and Jessica's was pulled forward over her face, in an imitation of Mia's.

'I know!' Julia said, following me. 'Jess and Zac, you have to leave in less than five minutes. Jess, you have to do something with your hair. At least take a hairband on your wrist for when they tell you off.'

They pretended not to hear, even though they each had a free ear. This was their second week at secondary school.

'Coffee, Julia?' I asked, and started measuring it into the cafetière. Left to herself, Julia made instant, but Granddad had been vehemently anti-instant coffee, and I could not bear to desecrate his memory even by trying it. I had used five of my precious last pounds to buy four packs of real coffee, on a special offer at the supermarket. I liked to imagine him approving of this impractical allocation of my resources.

I looked at Julia and waited for her to tell me not to bother.

'Oh, don't feel you have to bother,' she said. 'Instant would be fine, unless you're making anyway. Where's Tommy?'

'Watching telly,' the twins said, in unison. I knew she knew it really: the jaunty music that I had now learned signified a programme called *Charlie and Lola* was providing the soundtrack to the entire house, and probably the house next door, too.

'Did John give him breakfast?' She took six lunchboxes from the fridge and put three of them into school bags, one into her own backpack, and left the last two on the table.

'Yep,' they said together.

'He had a boiled egg,' Zac added, with some distaste.

'Mia up?'

They both shrugged. Julia looked at the clock.

'She's cutting it fine, but I suppose it's her business.'

'Here you go.' I passed her a mug of black coffee, and poured milk into mine. I spread some peanut butter on my toast and ate it standing up.

Julia took the second piece.

'So, Lily,' she said, as she started spreading it with Utterly Butterly, 'are you in tonight? I'm going to need to hear all about your day.' She whisked the twins' dishes away and dumped them in the sink. 'I can't believe who you're going to be cleaning for. I saw them both once at a council reception. He was very dishy and she was like a film star. I've told you that before, haven't I? A hundred times.'

'I won't see them.'

'Yes, but you get to look at all their things! It'll be better than seeing them. Right, if I'm dropping Tommy on the way, I'm out of here. Jess and Zac, you too.'

They left in a whirlwind. Tommy doubled back to hug my legs, which took me aback. I patted his head, confused, but feeling strangely warm inside.

Seconds after the door slammed behind them, Mia drifted into the kitchen, smiled a watery smile, pulled her blonde hair across her face, and opened her lunchbox. She took out a packet of crisps, two biscuits wrapped in clingfilm, and some granary-bread cheese and tomato sand-wiches, piled them up on the side, and clicked it shut with only an apple left inside, before putting it into her bag.

'Can I have these?' I asked, picking up her rejects. I could not bear to watch her throwing good food away.

'Course,' she said. 'Saves me having to dump them. She goes through the bins, you know, to check up on me. Through the bloody bins!' She poured an inch of black coffee into a Noddy mug, drank it quickly, smiled and left the house. John came into the kitchen, grabbed his lunchbox, wished me luck, and followed his daughter.

The door banged behind them with a delightful finality. I exhaled and sat down. The pace of life in this house exhausted me and made my head spin; but I was getting better at joining in. That had been my best breakfast-time yet. I had not hung back waiting my turn. I had just gone in there and done what I needed to do. I had excelled.

I had ten minutes spare, to sit by myself, and it felt luxurious. I ran upstairs to fetch a book. War poetry, I thought, would steel me for the day ahead.

chapter three

The people I was cleaning for lived in the smart part of town. This job had come to me thanks to an advert in the local paper, placed by a cleaning agency. It appealed to me partly because I knew all about cleaning, and partly because I thought I would not have to banter with people if I worked as a cleaner. The idea of banter put me off applying for any job in a café or bar. I knew I would never have the confidence for that, or any idea what to say. But I had a job. At least, I had some work. I wanted to tell Al about this success, but I had picked up the phone and tapped in the CAB's number twice, and both times he had been busy. I had not liked to leave a message because my news was not important.

I had expected a 'cleaning agency' to have sparkly offices with rows of buckets and mops and disinfectant sprays lined up like artillery. Instead, it had been one, abrasive woman.

'As it happens,' she said on the phone, in her scratchy voice, 'I have an excellent job for somebody, and everyone seems to have buggered off. Let me have a look at you, and if you seem the right sort, it might be your lucky day.'

'Be careful,' said Julia, before I went to meet Mrs Keast at her house. I was secretly thrilled at how over-protective she sounded. I was meeting a woman, about a job, so of course I would be fine, but it was nice to know that Julia cared.

The house was not far from Julia's, and everything in it looked pathologically clean. Mrs Keast was heavy-set, with short grey hair and a red face. Every time I answered one of her questions ('so how would you tackle a bathroom?') she took three steps back and looked at me through narrowed eyes as I stuttered out an answer about doing the floor last. Although I had never cleaned a house professionally in my life (or done anything whatsoever professionally in my life), I seemed to pass the test, because I did, after all, know my stuff.

'The reason for the Spanish Inquisition,' she said, in the end, 'is because this is about Harry and Sarah Summer's house.' She paused – reverentially, I thought. 'You seem like the right type for them, and I'll take it as read that you can get things spotless.'

She looked at me, and I knew I was supposed to react. I took hold of a strand of my hair and pulled it roughly around my finger. I had no idea what to say. Her house smelled of chemicals, and I noticed an air freshener plugged into the wall, behind the sofa.

'Harry and Sarah Summer?' I echoed.

'You know!' She was cross. 'Harry Summer – everyone knows him. Looks like a movie star. Used to be on the telly . . . ?'

I shook my head. She rolled her eyes, then instructed me on exactly what she wanted me to do. I was astonished to be trusted with a set of keys and the burglar-alarm code.

When I got back to the house, I tried the names out on Julia, and then I saw the reaction that Mrs Keast had wanted. She clapped a hand to her mouth.

'Harry Summer?' she echoed. 'Seriously? You're cleaning *their* house? My goodness, Lily, you're certainly going in at the top. You'll have to have a poke around and tell me everything.'

It turned out that Harry Summer was the local celebrity. Julia filled me in on his background: a trained lawyer, he had acted in a soap opera for five years, until, at the age of about thirty, he had suddenly quit, got married and moved to Cornwall. Julia seemed to think that there had been abundant rumours about what had actually gone on to make him leave London and the television, but she could not remember quite what they were.

'And they're probably not true anyway,' she added. 'He's a lovely man. He went back to the law and he's ever so respectable. We all love him.'

As soon as I stepped through the garden gate, I gasped. This was a different world. Behind the small trees that screened the house from the road, the garden path twisted, and there were lavender bushes and roses and other plants on either side of it. The path was covered with tiny pebbles, and my footsteps crunched, too loudly. I could smell the scent of all these plants, and the sea in the air, and it was like being in an enchanted kingdom.

I thought of the little cottage that I had assumed would be mine. Although this was a different sort of house altogether, it was the same, too. There was something magical about both of them.

The house itself was white and smooth, with three storeys. I stood in the porch and rang the bell at first, but when nobody answered, as I knew they would not, I put the big square key into the first of the three locks.

My fingers shook as I punched the code into the burglar alarm. I was so terrified of getting it wrong that I almost did. But the agitated beeps became one long tone, and then it finally stopped. I closed the door behind me and listened to the stillness.

The hall floor was covered with old-looking terracotta tiles, with a red patterned rug on top. The upper part of the walls was painted a mushroomy colour, and then there was a dado rail, and the bottom part was papered with wallpaper with huge green and brown flowers on it. I pushed the nearest door, and found the sitting room. Silence hung heavy all around. This room had a chaise longue, two dark leather chairs, and a huge sofa. The floor was polished wood, and there was a tapestry-style rug. A big canvas hung over the mantelpiece, with blue like the sea, and a different blue like the sky, and white here and there. I spotted a vase full of deep red flowers. Gerberas. These were my favourite flowers, because they were proper flowers, with a middle bit and petals, and they came in wonderful colours. They had been Grandma's favourites, too. She would buy seven bunches at a time (things always came in sevens, with her) and we would arrange them, cramming them into vases all over the cottage, making gerberas the first thing you saw in every room.

Everything seemed to be planned. There was no chaos, although there was plenty of clutter. The next room had a piano and an expensive-looking Apple computer, and shelves and shelves and shelves of books. I looked at their spines with approval: there were a lot of novels, many of which I had read, a mixture of heavy and lighter ones, and Nelson Mandela's autobiography and a collection of sailing books. There were *Private Eye* annuals, and there was a lot of stuff about the law.

I picked up a photo from the desk. It showed two people on their wedding day. It must have been a long time ago, ten years at least, because Julia had said Harry Summer was about forty now, and in this picture he was definitely not. His wife looked like one of those Hitchcock blondes, all icy and perfect. They were beautiful, both of them: the sort of otherworldly people who inhabited glossy magazines.

His wife had a sister with some children, I concluded: there was a photo of them. Her sister had short dark hair, but they were very alike. I knew almost nothing about the wife, except that she was called Sarah. Julia claimed to hate her for being beautiful with a desirable husband, but I knew she did not mean it.

I found the vacuum cleaner in the cupboard under the stairs, and decided to start at the top of the house and work my way down. I lugged it up the stairs.

It took me more than my allotted four hours to get every part of the house sparkling, and to do it in that time,

I had to hold myself back, at every turn, from poking around. I had never felt a curiosity like this before. When I looked closely, the whole place was strangely dirty: the loos were stained, the fridge was filthy with dried-on splatters of food, and their bedroom had a pervasive smell of bodies and sweat and feet to it. It was satisfying to have proper dirt to clean away.

I changed the sheets on their bed, as instructed, and tidied their cupboards. Their sheets and duvet covers had labels in them saying *Laura Ashley*, and just seeing the words, embroidered on such lovely things, made me catch my breath. Grandma had adored Laura Ashley, and before she was ill, she used to drive her little car into Truro twice a year to do a big shop for both of our wardrobes. I sighed. I missed them so much.

As a distraction, I started reciting Granddad's favourite poetry. At first I spoke quietly, running through a few sonnets that were drowned by the sound of the hoover. 'My mistress' eyes are nothing like the sun', 'Like as the waves make towards the pebbled shore', and so on. By the time I reached the kitchen, which was huge and light, at the back of the house, I was declaiming Macbeth's best speech: 'a tale told by an idiot, full of sound and fury, signifying nothing.' I finished with a flourish, hoping there was no security surveillance in the room.

The bleak truth of the words cheered me, slightly. Neither of the grandparents had believed in an afterlife, and I was pretty sure that everything they had ever been had vanished. All that was left of them, now, was me. It was difficult, getting by in this world while being partly-them.

I sprayed all available surfaces with eco-spray. I tried to assimilate the fact that the people who lived here had five bedrooms and used only one: they slept in the biggest bedroom on the first floor, with a bay window looking out to the front. If I were them, I would have chosen the room in the attic.

It was a wonderful room, a retreat from the world, which took up the whole of the top floor. It was a place from which you could look without being seen. There were windows to the front and to the back, and a sloping ceiling. It seemed to be a spare room (there was a bed made up in pale blue sheets with a patchwork blanket over the top, and it didn't look as though it had been slept in lately).

When I finished the kitchen, I ran back up there and lost ten minutes standing at the front window, gazing at the panorama. I allowed myself to be the lady of the house, just for a moment.

'And this is the view,' I said casually to my guests. 'Yes, it is quite impressive, I suppose.' I brought my grandparents back to life, and gave them the big bedroom on the first floor. 'Grandma and Granddad are perfectly happy down there,' I confided to my imaginary friends, 'but I spend most of my time up here. You know, it's hard to step away from the window sometimes. I'm in my own little kingdom.'

It was easy to live in Cornwall without appreciating it, particularly as all I had to compare it to was what I had read about in books or newspapers. To the left, I could see Pendennis Castle, standing high above the water. It was an old castle, built by Henry VIII, and had been used in the war. I knew that much, but I had never been to visit it. I had been to the ice-cream van that was parked on the headland below it, years ago, with the grandparents. They bought me an ice cream with a flake, and we sat on a sea-battered rock while the wind blew my hair into tangles.

I could see the boats far out at sea, huge tankers just sitting there. There was the glassy sloping roof of the swimming pool on the headland, the green fields of Flushing across the estuary. There was the Atlantic Ocean. We were perched on the very edge of the continent.

I finished, and put away all the paraphernalia, hoping that the job I had done was good enough. I longed to come back here week after week after week. I could construct an entire alternative life, based in this house.

I made sure all the doors were closed, and I left my bag outside, in the porch, while I went back in to set the burglar alarm. I punched in the eight numbers carefully: it went 81181825, and I wondered whether there was any significance to the digits. All those ones and eights must have meant something. I closed the door behind me, double-locked it, triple-locked it, and took in a deep breath of fertile, pollenated air.

Now I could see the life I would aim for. I could not really see how I was going to get from where I was now, to a house like this, but I would give it my best shot. I would have to find out how someone my age would go about getting a couple of A levels. Then I would be able to get myself into university, and perhaps I, too, could become a lawyer one day. If this was a lawyer's house, I would become a lawyer.

I had made a start, at least. I had just done the first half-day's paid work of my life.

chapter four

Queenstown, New Zealand

Jack Baker was unhappy. The kids were at school and nursery, the sun was shining, Rachel was at home and he had a job to do at one of the hotels, out of town. This was the part of the day he usually liked. Him in one place, his family scattered over various different locations. All of them doing their own thing. The radio blasting out rubbish music from ten or twenty years ago.

His utility vehicle bumped along the track. He had no excuse for not being happy, but it was harder to come by these days.

He reached the tarmac road and indicated left. He was going to one of the ski lodges, to fix the hot tub. His toolbox was in the back of the truck; the mountains were ahead of him. What was there not to love? The sun was shining, so the snow on the peaks shone and shimmered. The sky was huge, and deeply blue. People fantasised about his bloody lifestyle: wife, three kids, comfortable house, plenty of work. Total security. And all that in the most beautiful place on earth.

The trouble was, how could he be sure that this was the most beautiful spot on the planet when he hadn't seen any of the others? He told himself again that he was a lucky sod. It was becoming harder and harder to remember that. It seemed to keep slipping his mind.

LeEtta, the youngest of the kids, was three. Perhaps things would start to change. This was probably the hangover from the sleep-deprived years. He and Rachel had been married before they were eighteen, had three children over the course of seven years, and now he was twenty-nine years old, and sometimes he felt he was living the life of a man of forty, fifty, sixty. At least if he was sixty, he'd be close to being able to give it up and travel the world. That was what he had always said he would do. Rachel laughed at the idea, just because he had never left New Zealand. He'd been to the North Island, though: he was not completely tragic.

On days like this, he wanted to keep driving. The trouble was, he'd drive for half a day, and then he'd reach the sea, and then what? Jack was a Kiwi through and through, but that didn't mean he had no interest in the rest of the world. It just seemed like a bigger thing to get on a plane and leave your family behind, than to be in a car already, and keep going. If he lived in Europe, he could be in Spain in half a day, he thought, no matter which country he lived in. It was Spain he'd head for. It had always been Spain, since he was a teenage kid.

As the road twisted around a corner, the sun hit him straight in the eyes, half-blinding him. There was something on the road, a shape, although it was blurred by the dazzling light. Jack jammed his foot onto the brake.

The road was dry and clear, and the car screeched obediently to a halt, but before it stopped it hit the thing, whatever it was, the thing that was in front of him. If the ute had had airbags, they would have inflated. That went through his mind at the point of impact. Jack heard himself gasping for breath, sucking the air into his lungs until his head went dizzy.

'All is not right in the rib area,' he said aloud, because it wasn't. He seemed to be pressed right up against the steering wheel, to the point where it now felt that the bottom of the wheel had decided to become his extra rib. He had no idea how many ribs there actually were, but now he had one more, and it was made of hard plastic.

Minutes passed, many of them, and he saw that nothing was going to happen unless he did it himself. The radio was still going, but no one would be anywhere near close enough to hear. The music stopped and the news came on. There was a war, thousands of miles away. Most things that happened were thousands of miles from here. 'The Monsters of Auckland' – a couple who had killed their own little baby – had lost their appeal. That was a bit closer to home, but those sick bastards were still on a different island, thank God. And Jack was stuck behind the wheel.

Not many folks used this road. The hotel was shut, up there. He needed to get himself out of the truck, see what the damage was, all round. Otherwise he could be here for days. Then he'd hit the radio news, maybe. The local news, at least.

Jack winced as he stood up, but the door opened, and he managed to get himself onto the tarmac. He stretched, then doubled over, in agony. Stretching had been stupid. All the same, as he was on his feet, it couldn't be that bad. He had no idea how much time had passed, but he could not believe he was only just remembering that there was something he had hit. He had run his truck into something, and that was why he was here.

Please don't be a kid, he muttered. *Or any kind of person at all, for that matter*.

When he saw it, he laughed, in a bit of an hysterical manner. He soon stopped that, when someone rammed a blunt spear through his ribcage. It was not as bad as he had expected. What else was it going to be, really, but a sheep? A former sheep, at that, and a big one. From what he could see, it had been lying in the road and hadn't bothered to shift itself when three-quarters of a ton of metal came speeding straight into it. Natural selection in process, he supposed, or else it had been dead to start with.

The ute looked OK. It was a bit dented at the front, but nothing he couldn't hammer out himself. As long as the engine started, he'd be able to turn it around and head back home, get Rachel to take him to the doctor.

As he performed a careful three-point turn, keeping his torso facing straight ahead, he thought that he must remember to call the hotel and tell them he wasn't coming today. He could send someone else up there in his place.

He would be glad to see Rachel. She'd let him lie down while she took care of those sorts of things. She did not always like him, that was true, but when there was a crisis, as there was now, she came through. That, he reminded himself, was all a man could ask for in life.

chapter five

October

I woke on Saturday morning with anxiety eating me from the inside. Despite my busy weekdays, this always happened on weekend mornings. There was nowhere to go today, no one to see, nobody who would be remotely interested in my company. I lay in bed, eyes wide open, staring at the dappled light on the ceiling and wishing I were back in my own bed, in my haven in the cottage.

A car passed by outside, and I could tell from the noise its tyres made as they cut through the puddles, that it was either raining now, or it had been recently. The younger children were up, shouting to each other downstairs, the television turned up loud. There was no sound of John or Julia. They must still have been asleep.

I was struggling with the television. We had never had one, and the children seemed to watch it all the time. It was hard not to disapprove, but I knew that it was part of modern life, and that everyone enjoyed it. They all talked all the time about things like *X Factor* and *I'm a Celeb*, and I was trying hard to join in, to sit and watch them and pretend to be captivated. Perhaps one day I would get there.

I was only truly happy when I was at Harry and Sarah Summer's house. For four hours every Tuesday morning, I scrubbed it from top to bottom, then walked around admiring my handiwork. It was so peaceful there, and I loved imagining it was mine.

I had three cleaning jobs, now: the other two were family homes, one with teenagers and the other with toddlers, and I spent all my time at both of them picking up clutter and piling it neatly on windowsills and chests of drawers, before vacuuming the space where the mess had previously been.

I heard John grunting on the other side of the wall. That got me out of bed.

Five minutes later, my hair still wet from the shower, I was downstairs. Mia looked up at me with her sullen expression. I gave her a smile and headed towards the kettle, needing coffee after tossing and turning for most of the night. I slipped out of the house without uttering a word to anyone: the three younger children were watching *The Sarah Jane Adventures*, and when I looked into the room, they were hunched together contentedly on the sofa and did not look round, so I crept away. I clicked the door shut behind me as quietly as I could.

The rain had just about stopped, but everything was wet. The pavement was a deep, dark black. The sky was looming and low. There was even a little trickle of water dripping into the drain at the side of the road. The house opposite had rain stains down the front of it, dark patches on its exterior wall, which was not, I imagined, a good sign.

I kept my bike chained to a lamp post a little way up the road. The sky was so heavy, this morning, that I switched my lights on, just to be safe, and I heaved myself onto the saddle and felt the wind in my hair as I free-wheeled down the hill, past boxy house after boxy house, until I reached the shops. The row of shops at the bottom of our hill consisted of a chain convenience food shop, filled with bags of crisps, expensive-yet-nasty loaves of bread and chilled sandwiches, a chip shop, a hairdressers and a Post Office. I pedalled past it all, and my legs burned as I went up the hill. There was still moisture in the air, and I was glad I hadn't bothered to borrow Mia's hairdryer. My hair was going to frizz no matter what.

I was fighting off something that was scaring me. Being all alone was horrible. In the last years of my grandparents' lives, I had never been alone for a moment, had never had time for self-indulgent navel-gazing. Everything I ever did was about them. I washed them, cooked for them, made endless cups of herbal tea, using the enormous variety of plants from the garden. I helped them into bed, washed up everything, scoured the bathroom for them. When Granddad died, in his sleep, less than four months ago, I kept going by turning all my attention onto Grandma, even though she hardly knew who I was, by then. I suspected she had Alzheimer's, or dementia (I had no idea whether they were the same thing or not), and because both of them had been vehemently mistrustful of the medical profession, I had never called a doctor until she was actually dead. Now that I lived in the real world, I realised I should have done it sooner, but back then I had been so caught up in doing what they wanted that when they forbade it, I took them at face value.

But now, I had no focus. I could clean people's houses, but nobody cared. I was invisible: even if the people I cleaned for were at home, as the family with the young children often were, they did not look at me, and they only thought of me as 'the cleaner'. I could swerve, now, into the path of a bus, and get myself run over, and nobody would mind. It would be worse for the people on the bus than it would be for anyone else.

As I reached the top of the hill, where the houses became bigger and older, I heard myself inhale, loudly. I was losing everything. With my head down, I carried on, trying to hold myself together. The rugby club was here, at the top of the hill. I was going to cycle past it. That was my goal. I could barely see the road. A car, behind me, honked its horn, though I had no idea what I had done wrong. I supposed I might not be cycling straight. I went straight across the roundabout, weaving randomly between cars, and down the long hill into town, and I threw my bike to the ground outside the library.

I had no idea what to do. I was slipping away from myself and I could not handle it. When I looked wildly around, I could only see a world in which I had no place.

The harbour was just down the hill. Light rain blew into my face as I leaned against the railing and looked at the dark water. There was a massive ocean out there. I could be a part of it. No one would miss me. I was not exaggerating, or being dramatic. This was the truth: nobody in the world would miss me. Julia and John would have to get a new lodger, but next time they would get someone who slotted in properly.

It was still early. A few people were wandering around and most of the shops were shut. The emptiness inside me was so huge, so gasping, that there was nothing I could do. It was stronger than I was. All I could do was to climb over this railing, and go to wherever the only people who had ever cared for me might be.

I climbed over the rail, first with one foot, then the other. I did not look back. The water was several metres below me, and there were rusty ladders that led back up to the banks. Little boats bobbed around in the choppy waves, and the water was slatey grey, its surface rippled by a wind that seemed to be growing stronger.

This would solve it all. I had no idea why I had not thought of it before. Far ahead of me were the green fields of Flushing, with big houses that were rumoured to belong to proper A-list celebrities over to the left, along its water-front. There were sailing boats and the ferry to St Mawes, out in the water. There was plenty of space, and there were, I was sure, currents and watery treachery aplenty. Everything I needed was here. I breathed out as far as I could, so that I would sink quickly, and focused on the leap with grim satisfaction.

'Lily!' a voice shouted. Then again, with a question: 'Lily?'

I tried not to look round. This was my moment. But my concentration was gone, and I turned. He was running towards me, across the paving stones, his black eyes wide, his shirt flapping.

'Lily, what are you doing?' he yelled, when he got close enough.

I should have flung myself into the water then, before he reached me. Yet I knew two things, as I watched him. The first was that I was delighted to be rescued. The second was that even if I had done it, Al would have had me fished out of the water at once, so I would just have got cold and wet, and looked silly, and nothing else would have changed.

I looked at him, still gripping the rail behind me with both hands.

'Al,' I said, and my smile was appropriately watery.

'For God's sake, Lily,' he said. 'What the hell are you doing? You're not admiring the view.'

'No.'

He took my arm and held it tightly. 'Climb back, right now.'

I did as I was told, inelegantly hoisting myself back into the land of the ordinary. A few people were standing a little way away, watching.

'Sorry,' I told him. My knees were trembling.

'Come on,' he said. 'I'll buy you a coffee. And a cake or something. Look at you. Like a fucking ghost. Lucky I was taking the scenic route to buy the paper.'

Ten minutes later, I was in a chain café on the main street, cradling a hot milky coffee and feeling sheepish while Boccherini's string quintet played in the background.

'It just came over me,' I managed to say. 'It was the only thing I wanted to do.'

'Yeah,' he agreed. 'You feel like your life's so shit that you've got nothing to lose.'

'Exactly.'

'You wouldn't have got away with it, you know. I wasn't the only one who noticed you. You'd have hit the water and been hoisted straight back out and given a good telling-off.' I smiled. 'Maybe that's what you want?' he added. 'Someone to care whether you were around?'

I nodded, embarrassed now. 'I was just thinking how gorgeous it would be to be away from it all.'

'Not going as well as you hoped?'

I shook my head. This café was warm, and pleasingly bland. 'It's not exactly that,' I said. 'I haven't had any hopes at all. It's just that I don't know how to live.' I looked into his eyes. He seemed as if he might understand. 'My grandparents,' I said slowly. 'We had a good life, a lovely cottage, a sea view, a vegetable garden, loads of books. No telly. We were totally cut off. Grandma had a few friends, but no really good friends. I had no one.' It felt strange to be talking to someone. I was not used to it.

'You can't really have had no one at all. You went to school, surely? Even if you don't fit in at school, there are the other misfits to hang with?'

'No, I really had nobody. I was looking after them, so I would dash into school, do what I had to do, and dash home again. I didn't want friends. I had everything I needed at home. I thought I did.'

Al smiled. He was, I could see, a very handsome man, in spite of the fact that he had shaved all his hair off, which I found rather intimidating.

'Can I ask what happened to your parents?' he said gently. 'I'm assuming you're an orphan?'

'An orphan? I don't think so. I could be.' I looked down at the table.

'You don't want to talk about it?'

'Not really. So, tell me how you went from sleeping rough in London to working at the CAB in Falmouth. That's got to be a more interesting story.'

It was. Al had grown up in foster care, run away, lived in hostels and on the streets, got involved in drugs: 'the standard downward spiral. At the time you think you're the only one in the world it's happening to, but believe me, Lily, it's a well-trodden path.' He had been saved by a volunteer at a night shelter one Christmas. 'You know,' he said, 'all those people who volunteer at a night shelter because it's Christmas, as if that's a different day from all the others if you don't have a home. It makes them feel better about themselves for one day of the year. So I was all cynical about it, but then this woman walked in. There was something about her. It was like I knew her. Turned out she'd taught me for a couple of years, at primary school. She was horrified because it turned out she thought I was bright, and she'd been imagining me doing all right for myself in the world, getting educated and doing worth-while things of some sort. Then she met me at rock bloody bottom, drunk and, honestly, horrible and abusive. She helped me out.'

'How did she do that?'

'Well, she took a massive gamble on me. Took me home with her, because she was on her own, and gave me her spare room.' He looked at me, his eyes wide. 'I mean, can you imagine? A drunk off the streets? Not the most sensible course of action on her part. But it paid off for her, probably because I'm a conformist at heart. It's a longish story, even from that point, but I'm here. Sometimes I wonder how long it'll— But I'm here, and I want to try to do the same for others as Mrs Jennings did for me.' He put one of his large hands on top of mine. 'I'm talking about you, young lady. OK?' He looked at me hard. I concluded quickly that I was not attracted to him at all, even though I would have liked to be. 'I'm giving you my mobile number. Call me any time. I mean it.'

I cycled home, and it was still raining. When I came in through the front door, I could hear that everyone was still there. The television was still on. The adults were downstairs. I thought of Al, getting himself together at Mrs Jennings's flat in London. I had nothing to overcome, not compared to him. His old teacher had taken him in because she wanted to help. These people had taken me in because I was paying them, or at least, for the moment, the state was paying them. As I stood on the doormat and pulled my silly boots off, Julia appeared. She looked confused.

'Oh,' she said. 'Lily. You've been out?'

I smiled at her. 'I had coffee with a friend,' I said, savouring the words.

'Oh, that's nice. I was just trying to make some of your real coffee. You've given us a bit of a taste for it. I don't suppose you want another . . . ?'

'I certainly do,' I said. 'Shall I make it?'

She grinned. 'Would you? I have no idea how much to spoon into that thing.'

This house was warm, because a house like this was so

much easier to heat than the cottage had ever been, and it smelled nice, like clean washing drying on radiators. Al wanted to help me. Julia wanted me to make coffee. I could hear the twins playing on the Wii, jumping about, snorting in their exertions, and laughing so hard that they were almost hysterical. Tommy and John were watching TV in John and Julia's bedroom. There was no sign of Mia. Julia and I sat in the kitchen. I was not sure what to talk about, but I thought if I went back to attempting to act like a normal person, I might at least exert a positive force on Julia's day. She might be fooled, though a part of me hoped she wouldn't be, because I could imagine depressed mothers trying to pull the wool over her eyes and make her think they were looking after their babies properly: I hoped she could see through a bit of bravado.

She took the cup I handed her, a huge mug with a baby's handprint in paint on the side, and sighed.

'Ah,' she said. 'Lily, this is bliss. It really is. You make better coffee than they do in the shops, I swear.' She smiled at me, her eyes crinkling at the corners, her dark hair sticking up around her head as though she had just stumbled out of bed. She sipped her drink and closed her eyes. 'So you're settling in?' she asked, without opening them.

'I'm fine,' I told her, busying myself with my own drink, not looking at her.

'Were you thinking of doing a course? You found our card at the campus, didn't you? Were you looking at studying?'

I nodded. The future was unimaginable. The fact that I had come this far was weird enough.

'Maybe. I haven't got A levels. I'm not quite sure what I could do,' I managed to admit.

She frowned slightly. 'Now, isn't that funny? I would have thought you'd have had lots of academic qualifications. All those books you have around you. You're such a bright girl. If you want us to help you get set up with a course or something, I have a fair idea of how it's done. Just say the word. You know, Mia's talking about doing English in the sixth form now, even though she's never been interested in books before, and I'm sure it's because of you.'

'Because of *me*?'

'Oh yes, she looks up to you enormously. Well, you would, wouldn't you? There she is, fifteen, seething at the world. There you are, twenty, with your beautiful hair and your lovely clothes and all your books. She has a curfew – you get to arrange your life how you like it.'

I had to laugh at this. 'She has a curfew, and I never go out.'

Julia smiled. 'It's the principle of the thing. You know, when we decided to let out the room, I was afraid we'd have a student living with us, coming back at all hours, being sick in the garden, all that. That'll teach me to stereotype the younger generation.'

I had no idea what to say to that. After a few awkward seconds, I decided to tell the truth.

'I've never been drunk in my life,' I said. 'I lived with my grandparents and we had two glasses of sherry on a Sunday. Apart from that I've never had alcohol.'

'No! You've never had a glass of wine?'

'Never.' I anticipated her next few questions. 'Or beer, or champagne, or, I don't know, vodka or whatever else there is. No. Never. If you look in my food cupboard, you'll see I've got a bottle of sherry in there. It's the only tipple I know.'

'Well,' said Julia, 'we'll have to remedy that. Will you have dinner with John and me tonight, Lily? I was going to try to make an effort and cook something nice anyway.'

This threw me. I tried to say the right thing, but it came out very primly. 'Thank you,' I said. 'Only if you let me cook for you next time.'

'You've got a deal.'

Over dinner, Julia asked me about Christmas. I had just forced down half a glass of wine, so I was less guarded than usual. White wine was not the nectar that popular culture seemed to promise. I hated it. However, John had insisted on presenting me with a glass of red as well, upon hearing the shocking news about my inexperience, and that was even worse. In fact, I knew at once that it was beyond me. It was soupy and indigestible. White wine, therefore, looked almost palatable in comparison.

Julia had cooked a vegetable lasagne. It was not the sort of food that Grandma would have sanctioned in her kitchen, because everything we ate had to involve a piece of protein, a piece of carbohydrate, and vegetables, ideally from the garden, though when my grandparents became incapacitated I stopped the vegetable patch and started a local box delivery.

I closed my eyes, out of habit, waiting for 'grace'. I was ready to recite my sonnet. It was going to be 'From you I have been absent in the spring' – 'Sonnet 98'. I only just stopped myself in time.

'So,' said Julia, passing me the garlic bread (a novel and pleasing taste sensation), 'what are your Christmas plans, Lily?'

'Christmas?'

'I know it's still a way off, but will you be visiting relatives?'

John was chewing hard, as if he wanted to swallow quickly and say something. 'Annual family duty?' he managed to get out, in the end. 'We all have to do it.'

'I don't think I even know where the rest of your family are,' Julia added. They looked at me expectantly.

'Oh, there isn't any,' I told them. Normally I would have left it at that, but the wine was making my head spin, and I felt reckless. 'Not that I know of, anyway. The grandparents I lived with; they were it. They were my mother's parents, and she was their only child. I'm an only child too. There probably are people out there related to my dad, but I wouldn't have the first clue who they might be, or where to look for them.'

'Oh,' said Julia, knocking back her drink and holding her glass out to John. 'You poor thing!'

'Mmm,' I agreed, gulping down my white wine glass and holding that out to John too, since he had the bottle in his hand. It seemed to be the polite thing to do. 'I knew I would be on my own at some point, but I didn't have any plans, because . . . Well, because it was easier not to, I suppose.'

'And were you very young when you lost your parents?' John asked, putting the bottle down.

I drew a deep breath, and took another large gulp of wine before I replied. It made me dizzy.

'I didn't exactly lose them,' I said. I looked at my plate. There were fatty globules on the cheese sauce, and I suddenly felt nauseous. I decided to see what the truth would sound like, if I said it out loud. 'They . . . Well, as far as I know, they never intended to have a child, and when I came along, they never really managed to be parents. They weren't particularly young or anything. They were just bad at it. It was always Grandma and Granddad who took care of me, and then my parents decided they'd really had enough. When I was eight, they moved away. I think they live in New Zealand now, but I've never heard from them.' I carried on talking, to cover the shocked silence. 'When my grandparents died, one after the other, pretty quickly, I found an address in the cottage. I knew Grandma would have one for them. I wrote a note, and I asked them to come back, but they didn't reply. And now I suppose they wouldn't be able to find me even if they wanted to.'

Julia banged her glass down on the table and opened her mouth, but did not say anything.

'Should be shot,' John suggested.

'Oh,' said Julia. 'Absolutely right they should be shot.'

I tried to smile. 'It's OK. I don't have them in my life, do I? I don't have to deal with them any more. I've blanked lots of it out, but when I remember my early childhood, it's not specific events, it's just trying to get these people to want me, when they don't. That's all I see.'

'Thank God for your grandparents,' said Julia.

'Yes,' I agreed. 'They saved me. Without them, I'd probably be a psychopath.'

They both smiled, as though I had made a joke, although I hadn't.

'So,' said John, 'you'll spend Christmas with us, if you can bear the noise. Will you do that?'

'Thank you,' I said, hoping he meant it. 'That would be lovely.'

I woke late the next morning, with a pounding headache. At first I thought I was ill, and was quite looking forward to spending the day recuperating in bed with a book. Gradually, it dawned on me that this might be what a hangover felt like. I had read about hangovers. I could feel the individual veins pulsing at my temples. My throat was dry and painful. My stomach heaved and gurgled. I drank all the water I had by the bed, and waited until it sounded quiet before I scurried out to the bathroom for a refill, and to brush my teeth because they felt furry.

I didn't go downstairs until midday, and when I did, feeling pale and wobbly, I was surprised to see Julia peeling potatoes, listening to the radio, and helping the twins with their homework, all with a smile on her face.

'Oh, hello Lily!' she said, all brightly. 'We weren't sure if you were in or out.'

I put the kettle on. 'In. Feeling a bit rough, actually.'

'Oh no, are you ill?' She gazed into my face. 'You do look terribly pale.'

I glanced at the twins, who were sitting at the table comparing drawings of parallelograms. I swallowed hard. The two of them looked so wholesome, and both of them were so like Julia. I wanted to be a child like them, with a mother, rather than an adult with a hangover.

'I think it was the wine,' I managed to say.

'The wine? But you only had, what, a couple of glasses?'

She smiled. 'Yes, I suppose you're not used to it. There's some paracetamol in the bathroom cupboard. Take two. Eat something. You'll be fine.'

'OK.' I looked out of the window. It was a sunny, crisp-looking day. 'Then I think I'll go for a walk, down to the beach. Clear my head.'

I walked back to the harbour, leaned on the same railing and stared out. I had no urge to climb over today. I had lots to think about. I should probably never drink wine again, but at some point, when I had recovered, I would try beer. There was plenty of food I had never eaten. I wondered, for instance, what curry would taste like.

The boats bobbed around on the waves. The cold air nipped my nose. My head had cleared, and I felt so much better that I decided to buy a pasty and eat it on the way home. A Cornish pasty had been a treat that Granddad used to produce, still warm in a paper bag, occasionally, when I was younger. Now, with my tiny income and my continued reliance on benefits, it was still a treat, but I had two pound coins in my pocket, and I was going to spend them.

I bought my pasty from a shop on the corner of the main street. They were almost sold out: even though it was Sunday, Falmouth was busy with people walking, shopping, talking, as though it were Saturday. The bells of the church were ringing complex tunes in the background, and I considered diverting my route home to see if there was a wedding to look at. Seagulls squawked overhead, and I felt a couple of them swooping close, interested in the pasty.

I turned left up a steep side road. There was no way to get home without going up two steep hills and down one, no matter which route I took. I set off up the first one, a lane that was mainly used by forklift trucks belonging to Trago Mills, the local department store, as they brought things down from the warehouse. Not many people used this lane. As I walked, I took a huge bite from the pasty in my hands, and then I looked up and I saw him.

As he came towards me, I frantically tried to chew and swallow my mouthful of meat and pastry. I gulped it down, a painful lump travelling slowly down my throat, and looked at him. He smiled. It must have been a casual smile to a passing stranger, but I had never seen a more intense, a more generous smile. With one look, he seemed to stare straight into my soul. I winced to myself even as that clichéd thought flitted across my mind.

Harry Summer was different in the flesh, because no wedding photo, no magazine spread, no website (I had sat with Julia as she showed me his image on the computer) could possibly have captured the charm of the man. He was handsome like a film star, his face impossibly proportioned to be the perfect, ideal face for the male of the species, his hair glossy, his shoulders broad.

We grew closer. I could hear the thud my boots made on the tarmac. A seagull took flight in front of me. I stepped back slightly, and felt stupid.

He was still looking at me, still smiling.

'Hello,' he said, as we passed, but he didn't slow down. I had a sudden urge to grab the sleeve of his jacket (a jacket I was pretty sure I had removed from the dry cleaner's plastic cover, less than a week ago) and announce myself, but I resisted.

'Hello,' I said back, in a voice that came out too quietly. My legs were trembling. For some reason, I felt different. I was glowing, just from the way he looked at me.

He was like that with everyone: I knew that. It was why he was a celebrity. All the same, I walked home with my hangover gone, and a small smile on my face. Now I knew for sure that I did not fancy Al.

chapter six

Queenstown

He would, he decided, stop the car right outside the house; he wouldn't even bother to turn into the car port. His ribs were really aching now. Maybe Rachel would be able to get the doctor to pay him a visit, or perhaps she would take him straight to the hospital. Maybe he should have gone directly there himself, but it was too late now.

As he turned the corner, he was relieved just by the sight of their little one-storey house, the front lawn littered with bats and balls and a rickety plastic slide. His space in the car port was taken by two trikes, anyway, carefully parked by his younger children, no doubt. This was home, and any other thoughts he had, about seeing Europe for instance, were stupid. Good thing he'd never said them aloud. Not often, anyway.

Rachel's car was here. Jack smiled at that. Her minibus, more like. He would have thought you could get three kids across the back seat of a normal car, and two parents in the front: job done. That was the way it had been when he was a kid, but apparently this was no longer the case.

These days, the moment your second child was born, you had to upgrade to a 'people carrier', a hulking great thing with flip-down seats in the back, so you could transport a five-a-side sports team everywhere you went. LeEtta was three, Aidan was five, and their eldest, Sarah-Jane, was eight years old, but they were still paying off the bloody car.

Still, he was glad to see it, because it meant Rachel was home. He needed his wife. It was a basic thing, and probably all of this was karma, serving him right for the things he'd been thinking just before he crashed. He had everything: craving travel and adventures was just stupid. It was his secret fantasy, the way other blokes looked at porn. That was all. He knew, as he rubbed his aching ribs, that he never, ever wanted actually to act on it. The National Geographic channel would be enough for him.

There were a couple of other cars parked on their stretch of road, which was unusual, because normally it was empty. He actually had to reverse park between them to get himself as close to the house as possible. Twisting in his seat was agony, so he just did it using his mirrors, and although he ended up a fair way from the kerb, he did not suppose it mattered. At least he hadn't clipped either of the others.

The sun was hotter than he'd realised. He walked gingerly up to the door and pulled back the screen. He was just about ready to collapse. Some ice-cold water would, he thought, be good.

'Rach?' he rasped. 'I'm back. Had a bit of a mishap.'

He pushed the wooden door, the actual door, but it was locked. This was unusual: they normally only locked it when they were out. She must have gone to the shop or over to one of her friends' for coffee and a gossip. He fumbled in his pocket, got out his keys. Put the key in the lock, turned it. Pushed the door open, and stepped in. Listened to the scuffles inside.

He did not get a bad feeling until he heard the whispering. There was a definite edge of panic to the sound, although he could not hear the actual words. As he walked, taking long purposeful strides that were bloody agony to his ribs, he had the distinct feeling that there was something heavy and bad hanging right above his head, by a thread. A thread that was shortly to be cut by one of those imaginary swords, whatever they were called.

She was in the bedroom, and although she was dressed and looking at him with that defiant expression of hers, her T-shirt was inside out and her hair was all over the place. Rachel was twenty-eight, six months younger than him, but she could easily pass for twenty-three, and she was asked for ID all the time. Her long blonde mane was normally arranged so that every hair was in its appointed place, but now it was messed up so much that he almost laughed. Her face was so sweet and innocent, but that innocence was rather belied by the presence of a member of Jack's rugby team, over by the window, looking as if he might be about to exit through it. And also by the presence of the local physio, on all fours, as if he might be about to climb under the bed.

'Rachel,' Jack said, and he could feel that it was ending, right here, right now.

Of course he wasn't happy. He'd been trapped in this stupid marriage for years. She wasn't happy either – he could work that out from the scene in front of him. While he had been gazing at the horizon and dreaming of Europe, she was finding her own escape rather closer to home. He barely even blamed her.

Before anyone said a word, his mind leaped ahead. He could get his own place, have the kids at weekends or whatever divorced dads did. He could go away, do some travelling, bring them out to stay with him for a week in the holidays. He would be free.

All the same, this was not an ideal scenario. The three of them were looking at him, waiting. He tried to find the words.

'The three of you?' was all he managed to say. Then, when they still stared, he started shouting. 'Get out of my house! Out! I was so bloody careful not to clip your cars, you bastards, and—'

Sam, from rugby, heaved the window open and clambered out without a backward glance. Mark, the physio, chose to edge past him to the door. Jack heard the cars starting, and waited until they had driven away.

He turned back to his wife, who had preemptive tears in her eyes.

'Jesus, Rachel,' he said. 'How long's it been . . . ?'

She shook her head. Her crying grew louder, building up into proper sobs. He wondered whether he ought to comfort her. When he took a nervous step closer, unsure of the etiquette, she flung herself at him, against his chest. He winced, put an arm on one of her shoulders, and another arm on the other, and drew her gently away from his sore ribs. He knew he should be shouting, furious, calling her all sorts of names. Yet he could not feel anything but a resounding sense of relief. He realised he had been waiting for something like this, for a drama. He could overlook the details (two people he would have counted as vague mates of his, the use of his bed).

'It's OK,' he said, and he kissed the top of her head, an old habit. 'Hey, Rach – it's all right. Look, maybe you've done us a favour here. It hasn't been right for a while, has it?'

She pulled away and glared at him.

'You're not even going to bother to fight? Jesus, Jack. For fuck's sake. Pathetic! No wonder I take my thrills where I can bloody find them.'

He looked at her and, in spite of themselves, they both began to grin. They were so pleased with the future that Rachel's extravagant infidelity had opened up to them that soon they were giggling, and not long after that, they were clutching each other, roaring hysterically, until it occurred to Jack that he was in agony. He sat down suddenly on the bed and held his side.

'Rachel,' he said, still giggling in a rather mad way, 'I came back because I crashed the ute a bit. Need you to take me to a doctor. Then I suppose we'd better talk.'

'Sure,' she said, and she looked more like his old sweetheart than she had in years. Some cloud that he had never noticed had lifted from her face. 'Actually,' she said, 'there's probably a lot we need to be talking about. A lot I need to tell you, now we've got this far.'

chapter seven

November

I ran to their house with my anorak on and my flimsy hood pulled up over my head. I tried to jump over, or skitter around, the puddles, but it did not work. My tights were wet, my feet were wet. My hood blew down, and my hair was soon as drenched as it would have been after a lengthy swim, though I had, of course, never learned to swim. I was wearing the black trousers I always wore for work, and they were now going to stick to my thighs, heavy and cold, for hours.

I didn't have an umbrella, because I had never even owned one. There was no point: the branches of even the biggest trees were bent and whipped around by the wind. I saw someone on the other side of the road, struggling as hers turned inside out, trying to pull it back into shape. The rain was almost horizontal. There was nothing to do but get your head down, hurry to your destination, and long for a warm and cosy shelter.

In their porch, I jumped up and down and shook myself like a dog. I let myself in, but when I put the first key in the top lock, it would only turn in the opposite way from usual. It took a lot of fumbling with all three locks before the door swung open, and I realised that it had not been double-, let alone triple-locked, at all.

This meant there was someone at home. Someone who had either not heard me fiddling with all my keys, locking and unlocking with each in turn, or someone who had heard and not bothered to come and help out.

As I stepped inside, the alarm did not beep. It had not been set. I had been cleaning here for two months, and this had never happened before.

I called a tentative, 'Hello?', but there was no reply. As noisily as I could, I put my wet shoes and my socks on the hall radiator, and hung my coat in the porch outside so it would not drip all over the floor. Then I closed the front door, stood still, and listened.

I might be in this house with Harry Summer. Or with Sarah Summer. Or with someone else, or no one.

'Hello?' I called again, into the silence. My voice was too loud and I felt self-conscious and silly.

There was no sound at all. They had forgotten to lock up properly: that was all.

I pulled myself together, got out everything I needed from the cupboard under the stairs, and set off to start, as always, at the top of the house. I told myself that it made sense to do this, to end up back downstairs, but really I did it this way because I could not wait for my first look at the view.

* * *

There was a black leather bag on the floor of the top bedroom, with clothes spilling out of it. The duvet was hanging half-off the bed. One of the pillows still had the imprint of a head on it. The room had a different smell: it smelled, I thought, like men's toiletries, deodorant and things like that.

I stood still in the doorway, taking it in. When I was certain there was no person anywhere in the room, I knocked on the open door, stepped gingerly in, and looked around.

A pair of pyjama bottoms was crumpled on the floor. There were, I saw, men's clothes in and around the bag. I pulled the duvet straight. There was half a cup of coffee beside the bed, and a folded-over section of the *Guardian*, so I supposed that this guest, whoever he was, had come back to bed with coffee and the paper (I happened to know that the Summers had the *Guardian* delivered by the paper boy, who was Zac's friend Simon, who said they gave him a ten-pound tip last Christmas). I touched the side of the coffee cup. It was still warm.

Like me, the guest had spent some time standing at the window. I could tell, because he had rubbed several viewing-areas into the condensation. They were too high for me. I put my feet where his must have been, and rubbed the rest of the insides of the windows with one of my cloths, which was instantly drenched. The view from this room was different every time I looked. Today there was mist rolling in from the sea, and I could barely see the castle or swimming pool. The sea faded away, just a few metres out, as if it were a stage set. I could not see the tankers, but I knew they were out there, lurking close to the horizon. I always wondered about the sailors who lived on them. They came ashore sometimes in little boats, and I had seen a couple of them, once, in the Tesco at Events Square, buying bags and bags full of tins and cheap bread and rice. People said they just had to wait, living on the boats, until someone in charge called them home again.

I knew that the visitor stood here with his coffee, because there were brown drips on the carpet that I would try to get off in a minute. Before that, I cleaned the insides of the windows properly. Then I folded the clothes that were scattered on the floor next to his bag, and put them on the chair. I felt more comfortable, once I had imposed some order.

As I was reassuring myself that he must have gone out without bothering with the double-lock and the alarm, I heard a splash of water. A tap, I thought. A tap had been left on. I knew I had not imagined it. It came from the little bathroom that adjoined this room. I stood still. There was another splash, louder this time. I bit my lip, edged towards it, and knocked. When there was, again, no response, I grabbed the handle, turned it, and opened the door.

He sat up in the bath, his mouth open, his expression horrified. My heart leaped into my mouth. It was him: Harry Summer. Harry Summer was naked in the bath, and I had just walked in.

I managed to say, 'Oh, sorry,' before closing the door firmly. I heard the water sloshing around as he got out. 'Um, I'm Lily, your cleaner,' I called, from the other side of the door. 'Sorry, I had no idea you were here, otherwise of course I wouldn't have—'

'No, don't worry,' Harry called, in a gruff voice. He chuckled. 'Tell you what, Lily-the-cleaner. Pop downstairs and make us some coffee, will you, while I get myself decent?'

'Yes!' I yelled gratefully, and I set off down the stairs, as quickly as I possibly could.

I cleaned the kitchen frantically while the kettle boiled, even though it put my system completely out of sequence. It was a huge, light room at the back of the house, and the chrome oven was still spotless from last week: they did not seem to cook very often. I washed out the cafetière and found a tin of coffee in the fridge, an old-fashioned-looking tin with *Mother's Coffee* emblazoned on it and a picture of a fifties-style housewife. As a cleaner, I felt I did not have a right to make myself a drink, but at the same time, Harry Summer had asked me to make him one. I would only have a cup if I were offered one.

I wondered why he was in the upstairs bathroom, and why he was not at work, and whether he was sleeping up there.

'Lucky I went for the "bubbles" option!' he said, standing in the kitchen doorway and laughing. I looked at him, confused. He was nearly Harry. He was tall and good-looking, but now that I looked at him properly, I could see that he was someone else. 'Otherwise you really would have got more than you bargained for,' he continued. 'Fergus Summer. Nice to meet you, particularly in such entertaining circumstances.'

I forced myself to smile. 'I'm Lily,' I told him again. He was definitely someone who would have laughed at 'Button'. I tried to be brave. I had barely ever even spoken to a man one-to-one like this and I was not sure how to be. I clasped my hands behind my back so that he would not see them shaking. 'I'm, er, so sorry. I called out and knocked and . . . in the end I thought someone must have left a tap running. And I came in. Sorry.' I took a breath.

'Please,' he said, and I saw him looking me up and down. My trousers were still wet, and they felt all clammy on my thighs, and my hair was half-straggly, half-frizzy. 'Don't think anything of it. It's made my morning, to be frank with you, Lily. In fact, it's made my week. I had my ears underwater. Didn't hear a thing. I see you straightened out my disgusting mess while you were up there. No need to, but thanks.'

'Milk?' I said. 'Sugar?'

'Cream. It's in the fridge. Join me?'

I hesitated. 'Um, I would love a coffee, if that would be OK, but I have to clean at the same time.'

'They work you hard, my darling brother and his wife?'

'I work. They pay me. I have a few jobs but this is my best one.' I found a tub of double cream and held it up. 'This?'

'That's the baby. Why on earth is this your best job?'

'It's the nicest house and they don't have children,' I said, as I handed him the tub. I was horribly embarrassed by this entire encounter, but I liked this man, too.

'Well, those things are both true. Children do make a vile mess, don't they? I've got two of my own, for my sins.' He looked cheerful as he said this, as if he did not really mean it. 'So, you like them? They treat you well?'

'Um,' I said, 'I haven't met them.'

'Oh,' he beamed, taking the pot of cream, his hand brushing mine as he did so. 'Now this is getting better and better. You have met me, naked – me naked, not you, admittedly – while my brother has no idea that his house is ordered by a beautiful young lady with enormous choco-latey eyes, if you don't mind my saying so.'

I felt myself blushing, and I looked at the floor. I could not think of a single thing to say, so I kept quiet.

'Sorry, I didn't mean to embarrass you,' he said. 'That's the last thing I'd want. Look, this is the way you do it.' He was holding the cream tub high above his mug, letting a narrow stream of thick liquid swirl into his coffee, twirling it around to form a spiral. I was vaguely aware that he was showing off. 'Want me to do yours?'

'No, thanks,' I said. 'I'll stick to milk.' I tried to think of something to say. 'So,' I muttered. 'You're staying a few days?'

Fergus sat down at the chunky wooden table. 'I am indeed, Lily. Not necessarily out of choice. There are, to be honest with you, more harmonious households in which to take one's vacation. But . . . well, trouble in Paradise, rather than a holiday. Steer clear of the Summer men, that's my advice. We're not good with women.'

I opened the fridge and started taking things out so that I could clean the shelves. I piled artisanal cheese, a tub of olives, two bottles of white wine, and lots of bottles of beer onto the counter, wondering, as I did so, how they could stomach all the wine they seemed to drink. There were different bottles in there every week.

'Trouble?' I said politely, without looking up.

'How old are you, Lily?'

I looked over my shoulder, my guard up.

'Twenty,' I said.

'Boyfriend? Husband? Kids?'

'No.'

'Lucky you. Sensible girl.' I cleaned the inside of the fridge for a while, before he spoke again. 'Just a bit of marital trouble,' he said eventually. 'Been married since I was two years older than you are now. I was just a puppy, you know, a fucking puppy. She had my best years.'

'Did you have her best years too?'

'I did. She could have done a lot better for herself than me. That's for sure.'

I was hesitant over how much I should ask.

'Have you left?' I tried tentatively.

He laughed. 'Not so much "left" as been evicted. We'll sort it out – we always do. But in the meantime, I thought I'd come down here and give her a bit of breathing space. Sarah seemed to think that looking at the sea would cheer me up. So did my mother. When those two agree on something, you have to do it. You have no choice. I mean, looking at the fucking sea? What's that going to do?'

'Sometimes it's nice,' I said, forgetting my nerves. 'Don't you think? Sometimes you can look at the water and the waves, and it can make you forget about other things. Because it just carries on, no matter what.'

'Oh, Lily,' he said, and he stared at me. I was tongue-tied all over again, and desperate to end this conversation, so I knocked my coffee back and went upstairs, without a word, to carry on with my work.

chapter eight

December

It was dark outside the carriage, by the time my train drew into Penmere, and I could see the trees whipping around in the freezing wind. Much of the rest of the country had snow, and I was hoping we would, too. Most years, everyone else had snow and we had rain, but for the past couple of winters, even Cornwall had managed enough snow to get the gardens populated by oddly-proportioned snowmen, and the schools closed for a day or two.

I was cold, through and through. The train, a little one-carriage one, was warm and a bit smelly, because it was crammed with people, most of them students, but it was going to take more than a sweaty train to warm my bones up again. I smiled to myself, and thought back to the strangely normal, amazing day I had just had. Yesterday, I had bumped into Al in the library. I was picking up an armful of Russian novels, while his hands were full of children's picture books.

'You've got a child?' I asked, enormously surprised.

He laughed. 'Jesus, no way! Lily, you'd know if I had a child. No, my friend Boris has two kids. I'm going to see them this afternoon, said I'd take some books along. Can't afford to buy them, so I'm providing a mobile-library service.'

I smiled. 'You've got a friend called Boris –' I said, pleased. 'And I'm getting out Russian books. Is Boris Russian?'

Al shook his head. 'Not even slightly, I'm afraid. Real name Stanley Finnigan.'

'So, why's he called Boris?'

'He's the spitting image of Boris Becker. Who, come to think of it, does not look at all the way a Boris ought to look. Not at all brooding or Russian.'

'Oh.'

'Want a coffee?'

'Can't,' I told him proudly. 'Got to get back to the house because I'm looking after Tommy this afternoon. Julia's got to drive the twins to see their dad, and he lives in Launceston, so I said I'd have Tommy – he's the youngest – while she does it. "Reduced rates for babysitting" – remember?'

'Hey,' said Al, understanding at once how pleased I was. 'Look at you, doing your bit. Are you feeling more at home?'

'I'm getting there. The strange thing was, I was acting cheerful and normal, but secretly I was miserable. Now, though, I'm almost starting to believe my act. I've started talking to Mia and once you get to know her, she's not as grumpy as all that. She actually seems to look up to me, bizarrely. I mean, who could possibly look up to someone who's spent all their life taking care of old people, and who has never even tasted beer?'

I was aware that we were standing in the middle of the library, and people were having to walk around us. No one seemed to mind. This, I told myself, was because standing in the library chatting was a normal thing to do. I was successfully passing myself off as someone ordinary.

'Of course she looks up to you, you idiot.'

'Only because I'm older than her. She's exactly the sort of pretty, cool girl who would have hated me at school. God, nothing gives people like that a laugh better than a teacher doing the register and coming to the name Lilybella Button. Lily Bellybutton was only the start of it. The worst thing was when the teachers colluded with them. You know, all snigger together to get in with the cool kids. Everyone's happy, apart from one – pretty good strike rate.'

He winced. 'I can imagine. Right, what about tomorrow? Why don't we go somewhere – have an adventure?'

And so we caught the first train this morning, changed at Truro, and then at St Erth, and ended up in St Ives. I had hazy memories of going there once, years ago, on a summer's day. We had parked the Mini in a car park on a hill by a church, and I had run down a steep hill towards town and fallen over and grazed my knees. I remembered Grandma helping me up, cleaning my grazes, and buying huge plasters to cover both injuries. Granddad bought me an enormous strawberry ice cream to cheer me up. I could recapture the feeling of amazement that they cared enough to do that, and that told me that it must have happened soon after I went to live with them.

Today had been a different matter altogether. We stepped off the train under a leaden sky, and walked to the beach, where there were a few people, a lot of jumping dogs, and waves that were massive and hostile. We walked along the sand, quickly, to warm up, and stood on Porthminster Beach and looked across the bay.

'That's Hayle,' Al said. 'And that long beach is Gwithian. See the lighthouse over there? Godrevy.'

'That's Virginia Wolf's lighthouse, isn't it?' I said. 'Her book – *To the Lighthouse*?'

'Trust you to know that, Lily Bellybutton.'

St Ives was quiet, and as we walked through the town, it felt almost ghostly.

'This place is insane in the summer,' Al said. 'So busy, you can't do anything. It's much better to come at this time of year, when it's cold and grey and the light is so other-worldly.'

I looked around. We were on a lane called Teetotal Street, lined with little terraced cottages. The light was shifting all the time, and right at that moment, a black cloud moved, and the sun came out. The sky was dark, but the light was, briefly, bright.

'I'm frozen,' I said. 'What do we do now?'

'Now,' said Al, 'we go and shelter in a pub, and you have half a pint of beer.'

I walked with him, but I was not keen. 'I'm not drinking half a pint. I can't take the hangover.'

The pub was tucked away in a back street, and it was warm and busy. I stepped across the threshold, onto a brightly-patterned carpet, and wrinkled my face.

'What's the problem?' asked Al, turning and looking back at me.

'It's a bit smelly,' I confided.

'Oh, come on, Princess,' he cajoled. 'Find us a table and I'll get you a drink. We'll have some crisps too, to line your stomach. You can't live in the modern world without being able to put away a modest amount of alcohol. Consider it part of your ongoing education.'

Although it was still the morning, just, there were plenty of people in here. No one looked at us. Al was soon leaning on the bar, holding out a ten-pound note, waving it at the barmaid.

When he came to sit down next to me, he put the small glass of beer in front of me with a flourish. I smiled at him. I felt as though I had known Al for a long time. Unlike Harry Summer, he did not make my knees go weak. Unlike Fergus Summer, I was pretty sure he never flirted with me. He was, I was starting to think, a proper friend.

'Thank you,' I said. He lifted his own glass, which was filled with clear bubbly liquid.

'Cheers,' he said, and we clinked glasses. I looked at his. There was ice and two thin slices of lemon in it.

'What's that?' I asked. 'Is it gin and tonic?' I knew about gin and tonic because it featured in books a lot, and because Granddad had always reminisced about it. If it was gin and tonic I was going to ask for a sip.

'No, it's not,' Al said, laughing at me in a nice way. 'I'm impressed at your keenness to learn, though. It's lemonade. Bog-standard kiddies' lemonade, I'm afraid.'

'Seriously? Why?'

He answered straight away.

'Because when I was down on my luck, I drank enough lager to last me a lifetime, that's why. Got myself a bit of a problem with it. The first thing Mrs Jennings did was to get me off it. She got me some stuff that made me sick whenever I had it. It actually worked, after a few false starts. Anyway, enjoy your beer.'

I grimaced. 'It's not very ladylike, is it? For me to sit here knocking back the beer while you're on lemonade?'

'Oh,' said Al. 'I had no idea we were concerned with being ladylike. Don't be so stupid. Drink up.'

I took a sip and made a face. 'I only like white wine,' I told him. 'And that's only by comparison with everything else.'

'Now that is *very* ladylike.'

'Did you have a good time with Boris and his children?'

Al shook his head. 'Yes, and no. Not really. It's complicated.'

I leaned back against the wall. 'Go on then. Tell me about it. I would absolutely love to hear about someone else's complications.'

'Sure?'

'Yep.'

'OK. Prepare for a sorry tale.'

I rearranged myself so I was sitting up straight, brushed my lap, and looked at him.

'Prepared,' I announced.

'Right. I've been – well, I don't want to shock you, but – I've been "seeing" Boris, as it were, for nearly a year now. It's all snatched moments, not as romantic as one might like. We met online, he was married, he still is. I'm his bit on the side.'

He paused, watching me carefully, gauging my reaction.

'You're . . . gay?' I managed to say.

'Yes, Lily. I'm . . . gay. So's Boris. But he's got his little ones and he doesn't want them to hate him, which he seems to think would be inevitable if they knew. They're two and four, just babies, and he can't seem to . . .'

Al straightened his back and pursed his lips, visibly pulling himself together. 'Well, he can't make the break. He says everyone's better off if he carries on living the way he is, staying with his wife, being a dad to his kids, doing all the domestic stuff and meeting me when he can. For months I've been trying to get him to see that this isn't fucking 1897. It's not illegal any more. He's making an idiot of his wife, because she has no idea, as far as I can tell. He could get out, give her a chance to meet someone who's going to make her happy without creeping around the moment her back's turned. It's positively cool to have a gay dad these days, and he's a great dad, so the children would be fine. He's just not brave enough to do it.'

He sighed. 'I thought that yesterday, me meeting his kids – he brought them over to Falmouth to give his wife a bit of a break, that's what he said to her – that might bring things a little closer. But he was so scared. Looking over his shoulder all the time. Couldn't wait to leave.'

'Oh, Al.' I was so far out of my depth that I could not think of a single thing to say. This was impossible to react to. I tried to imagine Grandma's reaction. 'How very modern,' I said, echoing her.

Al roared with laughter. 'Oh, Lily,' he said. 'I do love you. Thank you. Yes, how very modern indeed. Although

I've no doubt it's a problem that's as old as the human race. It makes me want to reach for your beer, that's for sure.'

I pulled it away from his grasp. I seemed to have drunk almost half of it while I listened to his story.

We had chips on the seashore for lunch, shivering as we did so, and walked from one beach to the next. We talked a bit about Boris, and a bit about me. It was easy, and I became fairly certain that I might have an actual friend.

The train slowed down as it drew into Penmere. I stood in a queue for the door, along with about half the people in the carriage. The wind was wild as I stepped onto the platform and huddled into myself. I put my head down and started walking. It would take me ten minutes to get home from here, and by the time I got there I would be warm, if I walked fast enough.

Everyone had their heads down, so it was not surprising when I walked into somebody. Their coat was thick and covered in tiny drops of water.

'Sorry,' I said, barely looking up. I diverted my course to get around him.

'That's quite all right,' said Harry Summer. I stopped in my tracks. 'At least you're well wrapped up in case of collision,' he added.

I turned into a stupid gawping person. My stomach tied itself in knots, my palms tingled, my knees almost gave way. The intensity of the look he was giving me made me wonder if he recognised me, but why would he remember a blushing girl eating a pasty? I hoped he wouldn't.

'You're Harry Summer,' I said quickly, in what I had meant to be a casual voice.

'Guilty as charged.' He smiled an easy smile. His nose was red with cold, but he still exuded charisma.

'I'm Lily. Your cleaner.'

'No!' He stopped, put a hand on each of my shoulders, and turned me around to face him. He took a few steps towards the station light, and I walked where he guided me. Then he pulled the hat off my head, so that my hair fell all over my shoulders and down my back. We were both lit with a queasy yellowish glow. I was horribly aware of my cold red nose which, unlike his red nose, I knew to be shiny and unsightly. 'This,' he said, looking into my eyes, 'is what my cleaner looks like? We thought Fergus was making it up about your gorgeous eyes and amazing hair. You really did walk in on him in the bath?'

I had never felt pretty like this before. My ugly nose had vanished. I had never felt interesting before. I was smiling so hard I thought my face would be permanently rearranged. I had gorgeous eyes. Harry Summer had said so and so had his brother.

'Yes, I did,' I said. 'I didn't mean to. He was very nice about it.' Then I added: 'And it's nice to meet you at last,' because it was clear that I needed to say something else.

'And you, too. Lily, the beautiful cleaner. You do a stunning job, by the way. We adore coming home on a Tuesday. It's our very favourite day of the week. No one else has Tuesday as their favourite day.' He said nothing more, but he kept looking into my eyes. I stared at his face and tried to memorise it. He was different in real life from the way I had imagined him. There was a chemistry about him, something indefinable about the way he made me feel, that made the rest of the world dull and drab.

I walked home elated, and baffled. I was walking on air. He was married and totally unattainable, but I didn't care. I relived our brief encounter, all the way home. That was enough for me.

A few hours later, Julia tapped on my door.

'Hi!' I called.

'Sorry to interrupt,' she said. 'Phone for you.' She handed me the phone and dropped her voice to a loud whisper. 'No idea who it is. A woman!'

I took the receiver. Nobody ever called me.

'Hello?' I asked.

'Is that Lily?'

'Yes?'

'Hi. It's Sarah Summer here.' Her voice was crisp and posh.

'Oh,' I said. My first, wild thought was that she was going to tell me to stop dreaming about her husband. 'Hi,' I added, tense and awkward.

'Hi. Look, Harry said he met you coming off the train. He doesn't often travel that way. He hates it because it's always full of students. But his car's in the garage at the moment, so he had to.'

'Right,' I said.

'Anyway, he says Fergus was absolutely right about you being so young and pretty. Sorry about Fergus, by the way – we thought he was making it all up. And it got us thinking. We're having a Christmas party on the twenty-third – which is madness because we're going to

Barcelona for Christmas the next morning. But could we tempt you to come along and hand out drinks for us? We'll pay you, of course. Only I've been trying to think of someone we could get to help us out, and Harry says you'd be perfect.'

'Um,' I said. Then: 'Yes – yes, of course. That would be absolutely fine. In fact, I'd love to.'

'Fabulous. I'll work out exactly when we'll need you and I'll leave you a note on Tuesday. Does that sound OK?'

'Yes. It sounds great.'

'Brilliant, Lily. Thanks so much.'

Julia was in the kitchen, holding a bottle of wine in one hand and a glass in the other, and contemplating them both, her head on one side.

'If you want some, have it,' I advised, though I could not imagine drinking the stuff for pleasure. She jumped.

'Oh, Lily. Thank God it's you, not Mia. She'd add a drinking problem to her lengthy catalogue of my shortcomings.'

I looked at her. Her forehead was more lined than usual, and she exuded tension. At this point, a good lodger would have asked what the problem was, but I held myself back, because I did not quite know how to do it.

I took the bottle from her instead, unscrewed the top, and poured it.

'Doesn't wine come with a cork?' I wondered, looking at the flimsy metal cap in my hand.

'It used to. Back in the day. I can never remember whether we're meant to think screw tops are better, because they're good for the wine, or worse, because of the poor cork farmers going out of business and having to grow drugs in their fields instead. Or something.'

'You'll like this,' I said. 'Guess who that was on the phone?'

'Oh, I don't know.' She was fetching a glass for me, too. 'The Queen?'

'Nearly. Sarah Summer.'

A smile spread across Julia's face. 'I just spoke to Harry Summer's wife?'

'She asked me to hand round drinks at their Christmas party. It's on the twenty-third.'

We clinked glasses and I steeled myself for a sip. I knew how to pick nettles and make tea from them, how to squeeze a lemon and sugar into a drink that Grandma had enjoyed in Paris after the war, and if I could do that, I could make myself enjoy a glass of wine from time to time.

'To you,' Julia said, 'and your friends in high places. It seems to me, Lily, that you might be about to rise. Meteorically.'

I took an obedient sip. It did not taste as bad as it had last time.

I gathered together things that looked nice, from my cupboard and my shelf of the fridge, and started making them into a pasta sauce, while Julia emptied all the lunchboxes and cleaned them out. I had only just discovered pasta. At the cottage we had always had potatoes for our 'starchy thing', as Grandma always called it. Pasta was a revelation. It was cheap and easy, and it did not go green and start sprouting if you left it in the light.

'You shouldn't actually be able to have a meteoric rise,

should you?' I said, as I put some water on to boil. 'I mean, meteors fall.'

'I guess it depends which way up you are,' said Julia.

'If you were standing under one, you'd probably be fairly sure that it was falling.'

'I guess you would, indeed.'

'To see a meteor rising, you'd need to be up among the stars.'

Julia laughed. I started chopping an onion. This house needed a sharper knife. The one I was using kept slipping down the onion's side.

'How very poetic. Exactly. You know, Lily, I've never in my life met anyone quite like you. You're clearly not going to go on cleaning people's houses in the long term, are you? You're going to get yourself to university or something. Much as I don't think there can be a better place to live than Cornwall, I believe that someone like you needs to get out and about, see a bit of the wider world. Handing round snacks at a party is great, and who knows who you'll meet, but . . .'

She stopped and looked at me – waiting, I thought, for a reaction.

'Coming this far,' I said in the end, 'has taken all I've got. I'll get myself to college soon though, I really will. Look, it seems silly for me to be cooking this pasta just for me. Shall I throw in some more and we can eat together?'

'Oh, do, yes! Can you do enough for John and Mia and me? She's kicking up a fuss about eating with the children, and fair enough really, she's too old for that. It makes my day when I actually see her eating.'

Neither of us returned to the subject of my future. However, as I cooked, and put the food on the table, arranging some dried flowers that I had found on the kitchen windowsill into a centrepiece, I tried to think about it. All I could actually think about, however, was Sarah Summer's party.

chapter nine

The following morning, I was setting out to walk to the beach before work, when Mia came and skulked next to me. When I looked at her, she smiled a shy little smile from behind her hair. I walked over to the door, and she followed. I wanted to ask Mia about her mother, and why she never seemed to see her, but I thought she would probably shout at me if I suggested it.

'Where are you going?' she asked.

'To the beach, then work.'

'I was going to the beach, too.' Her face was expectant.

'Do you want to come along?' I asked.

'Yeah,' she said. 'Cheers.'

The wind was biting, and once we got there, there was nothing to do because we could not afford a drink at the cosy-looking café. The sea stretched away. Our noses were pink, and clouds were gathering quickly, low in the sky. Dogs were running wild along the shore, leaping high in the air, going crazy for sticks.

'Mia,' I said, 'what are your plans?'

She looked blank. 'Plans?'

'I mean, say in five years, ten years, will you still be living here?'

She laughed loudly. 'Are you joking? I'm *so* going to be out of this town. I'm counting down the days, I can bloody tell you that. For sure.' She kicked the sand with her boot, making a little indentation. We both looked down at it. 'I'm starting at sixth form college next September, and the moment I'm done, I'm out of here.'

'Why?'

She looked at me curiously. 'Why not, more like. You know, we're miles and miles from actual anywhere. Why wouldn't you want to live in London, listen to music, go to plays and shops and get a proper job? Cornwall's for old people, boring people.' She looked at me as if I were stupid.

'Right.'

'I mean, I know why you're living with us, because you were looking after your grandparents and they died and you needed somewhere to go for a bit to get your shit together. But when you're sorted with a bit of cash, you'll move away, won't you?'

I didn't want to say that the idea had barely occurred to me.

'At some point.'

'Yeah, of course you will. You actually work and earn money. You can go and live in New York!' She looked at me and grinned wickedly. 'And I can come and stay. For a long visit. And we can go out to all the bars and clubs and stroll around Central Park meeting guys.'

'By all means.'

'There you go. Sorted. And I really like your dress.'

I looked down at it. It was a floral one, a 'tea dress' with a tight, buttoned bodice and a full skirt, like something from a painting.

'Thanks.' I looked at her, in her woollen tights and tiny jumper dress. 'I like yours.'

'Cheers!'

Mia walked beside me to the water's edge. There were two seagulls sitting in the freezing blue water. As we looked out to sea together, snow started to fall, in tiny flakes. We turned and grinned at each other. Mia stuck her tongue out, and I did the same. Standing at the edge of the Atlantic, in the snow, was a magical thing.

'I've got to go to work,' I said, ten minutes later. 'At least they'll have their heating on. Do you want to come?'

She giggled. 'Come cleaning with you? Is it Harry Summer's house? Julia would be mad if I went there. She *lurves* him. Seems pretty boring to me.'

I did not want to talk about him. 'Nope,' I said. 'Sorry. It's some people called Smithson. I've met the mother, and I met the children once, at half-term. They were all pretty normal.'

'Oh. Well, yeah, why not. Poking round people's houses.'

I looked sideways at her as we strode up the hill. This family lived in a chunky Edwardian house with a sea view from almost every window, in a street in which most houses were bed and breakfast establishments. It was another stupidly big house that could easily have accommodated a second family of four.

'What do you do at Christmas, Mia?' I asked as we walked. 'Do you see your mum ever?'

She looked away from me. 'Not ever. No. She can fuck off. Well, she already did fuck off, in fact. Only as far as Plymouth, but she never once bothered to come and see me.'

'My parents did that, too. Both of them. Further than Plymouth, though. That's why I grew up with my grandparents.'

She perked right up at this information. 'Some people really shouldn't have children,' she said. 'I think they should go to prison for doing that. Mums, I mean. Dads leave their kids all the time. That is, like, normal.'

'That's right,' I told her. 'No one thinks twice about it when it's a dad. I've never met anyone else whose mum left them before.'

'Nor have I.'

'We should form a society.' We grinned at each other.

'I hate Mother's Day,' she said.

'Mother's Day! How many times did you have to sit and make a card for yours? I used to do one for my grandma and try to pretend it was the same.'

'That was the best thing about my dad getting together with Julia. Someone to give those stupid cards to.'

My heart felt lighter as we walked up the garden path to the huge house we were going to clean together. The snowflakes were getting bigger, whirling around in front of our faces, but melting as soon as they touched the ground.

I hated cleaning the teenagers' rooms. There were two in this family, a girl called Sasha and a boy called Joe. They went to private school, and they had clothes and shoes that I could see were expensive and fashionable, but they were apparently completely incapable of picking a pair of dirty pants up from their bedroom floor and putting them in the laundry basket. And that was the least of it. I had actually found pornography in Joe's room, including one particular photograph that he had somehow managed to laminate. He kept it stuffed down the side of his bed. When I found it, I had gazed at the vulgar image, horrified and appalled. I had never seen anything like it in my life. I hated it, but I got it out and stared at it every time I went into his room.

I rang the bell, as I always did out of courtesy, and listened to footsteps thudding down the stairs. The door was flung open by Sasha, wearing leggings and a tiny tunic dress that barely skimmed her crotch. Her black hair was fine and silky, and she wore it in a jaw-length bob, which suited her.

'Hiya?' She didn't recognise me, and peered from me to Mia, expectant.

'Hi, Sasha,' I said, walking past her. 'I'm Lily, the cleaner. This is Mia, she's working with me today, so we'll be out of the way quicker than usual.' I was unused to being assertive, and I was rather surprised at how easily it was coming to me at the moment.

'Oh, right,' she said. 'Yeah, hi. Like, don't bother with my room? Because I'm, like, in there?'

'Sure. How about Joe?'

'Yeah,' she said, already heading back up the stairs. 'I think he's in his room too, sleeping, because he's a lazy twat.'

'Is your mum at work, Sasha?' I called after her.

'Er – yeah!' she said, without looking around, as if this were the most stupid question she had ever heard.

I wondered whether I should insist on cleaning their bedrooms and changing their sheets anyway, since Mrs Smithson normally liked me to do it, but quickly decided against it. I set Mia the task of picking up a million pieces of junk from the sitting-room floor and arranging them tidily at the edge of the room. I piled a hundred thousand pieces of paper up on the coffee table, arranged three hundred Christmas cards on the mantelpiece, and put fifty toast plates into the dishwasher and switched it on. Then we got to work on the actual cleaning.

All the cleaning materials were back in their places, and I had left Mrs Smithson a note saying *I brought a helper today, Mia, who I live with. Hope that's OK. We didn't do the kids' rooms as they didn't want us to – hope this is OK too. Merry Christmas! Lily.* I called, 'Bye!' up the stairs without expecting a reply.

Joe opened his door and leaned over the banister. 'Who's that?' he said sleepily.

'It's Lily, the cleaner,' I told him. 'Don't worry. We've been cleaning your house for three hours. Now we're off.'

'Oh. Right. Laters.' He looked at Mia. 'Hey,' he said, in a completely different tone of voice.

I saw them notice each other, smile at each other. Mia chewed on a strand of her blonde hair. Joe straightened up and ran his fingers through his tousled mane.

'Hi, I'm Mia,' she said in a slightly husky voice.

'Joe,' he returned, smiling a sideways smile and, I thought, attempting to raise an eyebrow. 'You on Facebook?' he asked.

She nodded, as I pulled her arm.

Mia smiled a secret smile to herself, and asked me questions about Joe all the way back. I was half-amused by the mating rituals, half-depressed, and completely and utterly baffled.

'So what happens next?' I asked, as we walked up the hill towards home. 'I mean, you see Joe again? How does that happen?'

'Oh, you tell me his name. Joe Smith?'

'Smithson.'

'See, that's better because there won't be so many of those. I find him on Facebook, and I add him.'

There were many things I did not understand about that statement, but I did not like to ask.

'Then?'

'Then,' she told me, 'anything could happen.'

chapter ten

23 December

They lived in a film world. The front path was lit up with starry white lights that hovered just above the ground, as if they were fairies. I was almost sure I saw one of them move, but when I walked up to it, ready to be amazed by whatever powers it had, I saw it was just a light, stuck into the ground, and the glittering must have been a trick of my eyes. I bit my lip, and told myself it was good to have eyes that could transform electric bulbs into fairies.

The biggest tree in the front garden was decorated with baubles and white fairy-lights, and had a star on top like a Christmas tree. This was less magical, because I had already seen the reality. A couple of weeks ago, when I came to clean, a man had shouted, 'All right, there?' from a ladder, as soon as I stepped onto the path. I did my best to react in the way a normal person might, and tried to smile and say, 'All right?' back to him, and, for once, it seemed to work.

I stopped next to him to watch what he was doing, which was ramming decorations onto this tree while yelling friendly, scatological abuse down the phone at a person he called Spike, and I made sure not to stare too much at the fact that he seemed to have total alopecia. There was not a hair on his head, not an eyebrow, and though I did not look closely enough to check, probably no eyelashes or bodily hair of any sort. It was fascinating.

If I had not seen him doing it, I would have imagined Harry and his wife decorating this tree together, laughing in their woollen hats and scarves like people on an advert. As it was, the tree did not seem magical at all.

The snow had lasted a couple of days, then turned to drizzly rain. Everything was soggy and boggy. The scene deserved to be covered in glittering whiteness; yet even with the downpour and the mud, it glittered.

I stood on the doorstep and took a deep breath. Grandma and Granddad had traditionally swapped roles for Christmas, so he would produce the entire lunch (always served at precisely 2.45 p.m.) with a flourish, while she and I would play cards and sip sherry and listen to carols on the radio while we waited. There was no one but the three of us, in the entire world. We would dress up for the day in our smartest clothes, and Grandma would squirt me with her perfume and brush 'rouge' onto my cheeks.

It was easy for me, now, to overlook the fact that the last couple of years had not been like that at all. I liked to remember the good times, when I was young and happy and cherished. With an effort, I turned my mind back.

Last year I had installed the two of them, bickering over a game of Snap, which was all they could manage, while I did my best to recreate the lunch of years gone by. Neither of them was impressed. Grandma barely recognised me, and Granddad could hardly eat. I knew, even at the time, that this would be our last Christmas together, the three of us. I had probably even hoped for it. If I had tried to imagine what it would be like this year, I would probably have pictured myself, in the cottage, cooking a meal for myself, and eating it with the carols on in the background, and a book propped up in front of me. The idea that I might be working as a waitress, in a house like this, would have scared me half to death.

I had dressed as appropriately as I could, given my old-fashioned wardrobe. It was going to be a while, I could tell, before I had the funds for clothes. Sarah had said, 'Wear black and white,' and I had cobbled together a lacy-collared white blouse with puffy sleeves, and a shiny black skirt with swirling black flowers embroidered onto it. It was a bit ridiculous: all I wanted was for no one to laugh at me. I had done my best with my hair, tied it back with an Alice band I borrowed from Mia, and conditioned it ruthlessly into submission.

I stared at the doorbell and tried to pluck up the courage to ring it, because I could not use my own key when I knew they were both there. I was petrified. I stood in the dark, my breath clouding around me, wishing my grandparents back to life. I would have given anything to bring them back to me, even in their squabbling, forgetful, sickly incarnations.

I did it, suddenly, on an impulse before I could stop

myself. I was meant to be here at six: I was five minutes early but I thought that was probably all right. I stepped from foot to foot, irrationally hoping that something had changed, that they were not here, that the party was cancelled and they had gone away early. I did not want to see the man who had such a huge and strange effect on me, with his wife. I did not want to be their servant.

There were lights on inside. I could hear music, the sort of languorous music that might have been called 'easy listening' or might have been jazz. Footsteps approached. The door opened. Sarah Summer stood before me.

'Lily,' she said. She knew it was me. It was not a question. She was indisputably beautiful, with fine bone structure and a wide mouth like Julia Roberts.

I smiled at her. 'Yes,' I said, and then I stopped because I had no idea whether I should call her Sarah or Mrs Summer. It was going to be easier to call her nothing.

She was ushering me in and waiting for me to take my coat off. Her face was friendlier than I had expected. She was wearing tight jeans and a white shirt, with a beady necklace, and her hair was clipped back in a very ordinary-looking way. I was surprised at how casually she had dressed for her party.

'Well,' she said, as I followed her into the hall that I knew well when it was empty. It was strange to see her in it, and to know that she belonged here, and I did not. 'You look fabulous, Lily. That is the classiest version of waitress clothes I've ever seen.'

I opened my mouth to explain but, unsure where to start, closed it again.

'Thanks for coming,' she continued. 'Harry will be pleased.

He said you were just the girl for the job. He says you're wasted as a cleaner.' She laughed and called up the stairs: 'Darling! It's Lily!'

I felt myself blushing. His voice came down from upstairs: 'Thank fuck for that!'

Julia told me, just as I was leaving, that I ought to try to catch the eye of a rich man. 'Not that you even need to try, Lily Button. Your hair will do that for you. If I could have changed one thing about my life, I would have given myself thick hair. Thick curly hair. You have no idea. Anyway, put some lipstick on,' she advised. 'And smile at people. And don't forget us, now that you're on your way up in the world.'

'Julia,' I reminded her, 'I'm not on the guest list. I'm handing out drinks and canapés, for six pounds an hour!'

'*Canapés*!' she echoed. 'See? Meteoric rise. You look lovely.'

I was worried, now, that I had overdone the make-up. All I knew about make-up was the rouge that Grandma had brushed with light spidery strokes onto my cheeks for special occasions, but according to Julia, rouge was now called 'blusher', and was not really necessary for me. Tonight I had put on some very light foundation out of a tube. I was wearing eye-liner, mascara and, on Julia's instruction, lipstick. It was a brownish-red one. I felt like a little girl who was maladroitly trying to be a grown-up. All the same, Sarah Summer seemed not to be sniggering at my painted-on face.

When I stepped into the kitchen, I tried to hide my reaction. Apart from the first time I cleaned it, I had never seen it properly messy. Now every surface was covered, with layer upon layer of things. There were little puff pastry cases, and sheets of paper that looked as if they had been printed from the Internet, and there were supermarket bags everywhere, plonked down on each surface with three on top of the hob. The whole of one worktop was taken up by boxes of glasses, one of which was teetering, on the brink of falling to the floor.

'OK,' I said. I smiled. 'What would you like the end result to be?' I pushed the box of glasses so it was safely anchored and picked up the plastic bags from the hob, finding them a more appropriate place.

She laughed. Her face was so pretty. She was probably in her late thirties, but apart from the little lines around her eyes, she could have been my age.

'Oh Lily,' she said, 'you are an angel sent from heaven. I did broach the idea of buying in some proper catering from one of the many fine eating establishments in this town, but Harry seemed to think there was something charming about us throwing it all together ourselves and being all "oh, just something we whipped up in the kitchen" about it. Needless to say, he's not been planning to spend much time with the apron on himself.'

I took a blue and white striped apron from a hook and put it on. The strings went round my waist three times before they were short enough to tie. I wondered whether it was Harry's.

'So, these are recipes?' I checked, picking up one of the print-outs. I touched one of the plastic bags. 'And these are ingredients?'

'Just do whatever you can. I'm off to change. Can you

believe, Lily, that we're going away tomorrow? Look at the state of this place!'

'It is a little bit mad,' I felt brave enough to say. 'Shouldn't you be packing?'

'Oh absolutely,' she agreed. 'It is. Mad, I mean. We'll do the packing at the very last minute. It all sounded like a good idea at the time. Don't feel obliged to follow any recipe. Just make it up as you go along. Anything you can do that looks pretty on a plate and doesn't poison people will be an unspeakable improvement on anything we might have done. When you come in after the New Year, the place will probably still look like this.'

She breezed out of the room. I picked up the first carrier bag, and started to unpack.

Ten minutes later, I was jigging on the spot to the raucous Christmas music that had been blaring through the house for the past few minutes, the tasteful jazz all gone. I was cutting up logs of goat's cheese and putting it onto slices of baguette, then adding a sliver of red pepper out of a jar. The key was to arrange them on the tray so that they looked good. After this, I was going to do mushroom vol-au-vents.

'Well,' said a familiar voice. 'You are a sight to behold.'

I jumped. He was standing in the doorway. I wondered how long he had been there.

He was wearing an expensive-looking shirt and jeans. Sarah had gone to change, but Harry Summer really was going to wear jeans to his own party. His hair was glossier than ever, and his high cheekbones and friendly, open smile made me want to stroke his face, though I hoped against hope that he could not tell this by looking at me.

'Hello,' I said, feeling the heat rising to my face, hating it.

He walked right over to me, put a hand on my waist and kissed my cheek. I held my breath to make sure I didn't breathe anything nasty on him, and kissed the air.

'Now we've met properly,' he said. 'And we are so grateful that you're here, Lily. Neither Sarah nor I are much cop in the kitchen, I'm afraid. And look, you've nearly sorted us out already.'

His hand was still on my waist.

'It's no problem at all,' I said. He made me feel like the only person in the world who mattered. I knew he must do that to everyone, and that was why he used to be on TV and everyone loved him. My face was sizzling, and I realised that Julia was right: blusher was unnecessary.

'I think,' he said, 'a drink is called for. We can pay you in champagne.' He looked at my face. 'Oh, don't worry,' he added. 'We'll pay you money too.' As he went to the fridge, he carried on talking. 'My brother was extremely taken with you, as you know. A gorgeous young woman walking in on him in the bath is exactly the kind of fantasy he'd come up with, in an idle moment.'

'Mmm.' I did not trust myself to speak. He popped the champagne cork, holding it firmly to stop it flying across the room. I had, of course, never tasted champagne.

'Or, if he wasn't making it up, I presumed he was massively exaggerating. And then Jasmine took him back and we forgot all about the fact that our cleaner was supposedly a nubile young woman with pre-Raphaelite hair, who was funny too. He even badgered me for your phone number, the scurrilous old goat.'

I reminded myself not to let anything I was feeling show on my face, and I tried to look casual. I couldn't think of anything to say, so I said nothing, and started to set out the vol-au-vent cases on the surface, ready for filling. Harry handed me a glass of champagne, then picked up one of my goat's cheese concoctions.

I had never imagined that anyone but my poor dead grandparents would ever think I was special. Now Harry was saying lovely things to me, and his brother had wanted my phone number. I wondered what Fergus would have said, had he rung me up.

'Why can't I throw things together like this?' Harry demanded. 'Or, why can't one of us? You'd think that out of Sarah and me, one person, statistically, would not be a total disaster in the kitchen.'

'It was your wife who got all the ingredients,' I said. 'And she left me all the recipes. I'm just putting different bits on top of each other. So it *is* her doing it, really. She's the statistical winner.'

'Oh Lord. You're a diplomat, Lily. What the hell are you doing cleaning houses?'

I thought it was a rhetorical question, and so I did not answer.

He hung around the kitchen, watching as I cut up mushrooms and searched in the cupboards for a saucepan. I realised that I should have made the filling for the vol-au-vents first of all, before I started the baguettes. Neither of us spoke again, but I was conscious of his eyes upon me all the time. When I moved, he moved, too. He just kept watching. It felt strangely intimate.

'Harry?' said Sarah's voice, and she appeared in the

doorway. She looked at me, and the full champagne glass beside me. 'Are you plying poor Lily with alcohol? Where's mine?'

Her hair was piled up on top of her head, and she was wearing a red dress that draped and clung to her in a way that was just right. She was wearing make-up, but not too much, and she looked as if she had stepped directly from the pages of a magazine. I scrutinised her cheeks to see whether she was wearing any rouge: I thought she was, just a tiny bit.

I was drab and skinny next to her, dressed in jumble-sale rejects.

'You look wonderful,' I told her.

'Thanks, lovely,' she said, and she looked at Harry. 'That was your line, you know?'

He kissed her on the mouth, and stepped back.

'You do look wonderful. You always do. Spectacularly beautiful. I should be used to it by now, ten years on, but I don't think I'll ever stop thanking my lucky stars that a woman like you deigns to spend her life with a man like me.'

I smiled and looked down at the pastry cases I was filling.

He left the room, taking his drink with him. Sarah followed. Soon afterwards, 'Rocking Around the Christmas Tree' was pounding through the house at top volume. Then he reappeared, Sarah behind him. Agitation crackled off him like electricity. He flung the fridge open.

'We haven't got enough bloody champagne,' he said. 'Seriously. I thought we did but I've just had another look down the guest list. Those people would drink a brewery

101

dry. I'm going to nip down to Tesco for another box. Won't be a minute.'

Sarah followed him out of the room. I heard her say: 'But you can't take the car . . .' There were raised voices for a moment, though they were muffled. A minute after that, the front door slammed and she came back, rolling her eyes.

'There's no telling some people,' she said. 'Let's hope he knows what he's doing. Lily, thanks for this. Sorting out this stupid party. I can't tell you . . .' Her voice tailed off. 'Anyway,' she said, with more energy, 'what are you doing for Christmas? Staying here?'

'Yes,' I said. 'I'm staying with the family I live with. They have four children. Going to be busy.'

'Not visiting your own family?'

'I don't really have my own family any more.' I took a sip of champagne. It tasted nothing like I had expected. In my mind, from everything I had read, champagne was a nectar. This was chemical and held no attraction at all, as far as I could see. I put it down. 'So you're off to Barcelona?'

I could see that she wanted to ask about my family.

'Yes,' she said instead. 'In the morning. We were going to visit my sister, but that's difficult at the moment, and then we were going to go to Harry's mother, but in the end we thought, sod it, and booked a break in Barcelona. You know, a little hotel in town, a five-day package. Harry's furious with me for choosing a tiny hotel buried in the little alleyways, because it just looked adorable. Apparently, my crime is to have booked a three- rather than a five-star place. I imagine he'll live. After that, we'll probably go up to London for New Year.'

'Sounds good,' I said. I could not begin to imagine living like that.

'Ever been to Barcelona, Lily?' she asked, and she took another apron from the hook and started taking huge white plates out of a cupboard.

I laughed at that. 'No,' I told her. 'I've never been anywhere. You wouldn't believe the places I haven't been to.'

'You should go sometime,' she said, as if it would be easy and breezy and straightforward. 'There's really nowhere like it. For having a good time.' For a moment, it sounded as if she were being sarcastic. I began putting creamy mushroom mixture into the tiny pastry cases with a teaspoon, while Sarah arranged the other canapés on plates.

Harry came back at half-past seven. I knew it was exactly seven-thirty because we had been watching the clock, waiting for guests. He breezed into the room, bringing a lot of cold air with him, empty-handed.

'Didn't you get any?' I asked him.

He looked down at his hands. 'What? No, apparently not. All the other buggers had got there first. No champagne to be had, for love nor money.' He left the room quickly.

By a quarter to eight, there were only the three of us there, standing together in the sitting room, the music blasting, ready and waiting for people who did not appear to be coming.

'It's not too late to cancel,' Harry said. 'Sarah, just text everyone. Tell them we've got swine flu. We'll drink all the booze and eat Lily's food ourselves. It's too good for our friends anyway.'

'Sure, OK, darling,' she said, but did nothing. The

tension in the room was palpable, and I was not sure it was all due to the missing guests.

The Christmas tree took up the whole of the front window: it was decorated in white and silver and was incredibly tasteful. I thought of the one back at our house, which was a plastic tree covered in brightly coloured tinsel, home-made decorations, and things the children had brought back from school every year. I actually preferred ours, though I could see that this one was much nicer.

There were sprigs of holly on top of all the pictures, and various decorations and streamers, all of them silver, around the place. The double doors that separated the two reception rooms were wide open.

Harry was pacing around.

'What do you think, Lily?' he barked, pretending to be jolly. 'No one's going to show up, are they? They've all had a better offer – do you reckon?'

'I should think they'll be here in a few minutes,' I told him. 'No one wants to be first, do they? At least this way they're not drinking your champagne.'

'Very true, very true. We could learn a lot from young Lily.' He looked at my glass. I had managed to drink only a couple of sips. He looked at Sarah. Her glass was full, though I suspected it might have been her second. His own was empty.

'Come on, girls,' he said in a hearty voice. 'Drink up, drink up! The night is young.'

The doorbell rang. I jumped up, smiled at Harry's mock excitement, and went to answer it. A man and a woman were on the doorstep, both in expensive-looking coats, each holding a bottle of champagne. They were, I thought, in their forties. The man had the eager look of a little boy pretending to be older than he was, while the woman was very skinny and had hair like a helmet. I wanted to reach out and tap it, to see if it was as solid as it looked. They looked at me and then beyond me, as if I were not quite worthy of engagement.

'Good evening,' I said, remembering to smile. 'Please come in. May I take your coats?'

The man laughed. 'Good God,' he said. 'We really are going up in the world.'

The house filled up quickly. These people were Belinda and Michael. Then heavily pregnant Constanza arrived with Seumas (I noticed Harry pointedly not greeting Seumas, and wondered why), followed by Chris and Christina. After that I stopped remembering the names and concentrated on keeping their glasses and their mouths full.

I did not speak to Sarah again for the rest of the evening. Afterwards, I wished I had. I wanted to wind back time and play it out again, to go back to the half-hour we spent in the kitchen together and to talk to her properly. I wanted to see if there was anything I could say to make her feel better about her life; because it was soon horribly clear that everything about her smiling, gracious persona that evening had been fake.

chapter eleven

Queenstown

First of all, he wanted to go and stay with a mate, but it turned out there was not a single one of his mates he trusted. Rachel soon admitted that Mark and Sam were far from being the first and second beneficiaries of what she was now calling 'housewife's boredom control'. Every day that went by, it seemed, something new came to light. It turned out that there was no man in this town that Jack could have sworn, hand on heart, wasn't having it away with his wife. Where were the gay blokes when you needed them?

He went back home instead. His mum had died years before, but his dad was still plodding along, living his life his own way. At Dad's place, the day started on the dot of 5.45 a.m., with a cup of tea and a walk with the dog, and it ended at 8.45 p.m., with a mug of cocoa and a listen to the radio. It was not quite the freedom Jack had imagined: it was like being twelve again, in fact.

'You need to get that wife of yours back,' his dad told him one day, at midday, when they were having lunch.

'Great idea,' Jack said. He was trying to be sardonic. 'After all, the world has nothing else to offer. Adultery and gossip will do me fine.'

His dad frowned over his sandwich. The electric light was shining off his bald head. Jack ran a hand through his own hair, which was, he had always thought, his best feature. It was thick and blondish, and even though he was coming up to thirty, it was not receding, not even a little bit. The other guys were losing their hair all over the place. Not that this seemed to count for much, in Rachel's eyes.

'Well,' said his dad, 'if you were being sarcastic, which I think you were, John, then I haven't wanted to say this, but you do need to tie up the loose ends.'

Jack scowled. His dad was the only one who called him John.

'What loose ends?'

'Those kids.' Dad had something that might have been a triumphant gleam in his eye, though it could have been the light. His house was overlit: there were four lights in this room and they were all on, so there were reflections on everything. None of the overhead lights had lamp-shades on. 'I mean, are they actually yours?'

Jack closed his eyes. 'Of course they're bloody mine.' There had been lampshades, when Mum was alive.

'You done DNA tests?'

'Yes.'

'John?'

'Yes!'

'OK.' His dad nodded. 'That's good then, because other-wise it would have been a tricky situation, wouldn't it?

Glad to hear it. Proves you weren't trusting her though, doesn't it? You don't do a test if you don't have an inkling!'

'Dad. Shut up.'

He went over to the house and put them to bed that night, staring into their little faces as he tucked them in. They weren't as upset about his departure as he'd expected, but that was probably because everyone's parents split up these days. They must have been half-expecting it.

LeEtta was small and blonde, like her mum, with rosy little cheeks. She was 100 per cent Rachel, 0 per cent Jack. Impossible to call. Aidan was small and dark, not much like either of them – and this was suspect. Jack was on safer ground with Sarah-Jane, because she was him to a T. She was Daddy's little girl all right.

As he looked at them, first LeEtta and then Aidan, he forced himself to imagine that they might have no biological connection to him whatsoever. Taking a deep breath, he took his mind to a place in which he had to look on them as strangers; someone else's kids. To his amazement, it turned out that it did not matter even a smidge. Nothing could possibly change the fact that he was their dad. This is what adoptive parents must feel, he mused. How odd that the biological thing counts for nothing at all. He smiled broadly in the half-dark. In this case, he did not care and he never wanted to know.

For a second he thought of the Monsters of Auckland, behind bars for ever. Frank and Jane Smith were their names. The people who had left their baby son in a cot in the corner and ignored him until he died. He wanted to storm the prison they were in and string them up himself, even though he hated the idea of the death penalty and had never been a violent man. As he often did, he put the thought of them from his head. It was too sick to contemplate.

The two girls shared a room. 'Night night, Sarah-J,' he whispered, because LeEtta was already asleep, breathing in a deep, satisfied way that he adored, no matter what.

'Night, Daddy,' Sarah-Jane whispered back. 'Dad, are you staying tonight?'

'I'm at Gramp's for the moment. You know that, sweetie. But I'll always be around. Never far from you.' Even as he said it, he wondered if that was strictly true. He was beginning to get a few ideas.

'Love you, Daddy,' she murmured, and he pushed the thick hair back from her forehead and kissed her.

'Love you always,' he told her, and his heart constricted and he had no idea what he should do for the best.

When he went back in to gaze at Aidan again, the boy had woken up, but he was pretending to be asleep. Jack went along with it, kissed his hair, pulled the sheet up over his little pyjamaed body, closed the door quietly as he went out.

Rachel was at the dining table with a glass of wine and a bottle of beer in front of her. Her lips were pressed together so tightly that they were bloodless, and looked nothing like lips at all.

'What is it?' he asked. 'Don't look so bloody stressed, Rach. I'm giving you an easy time of it, and you know it.'

'Yeah. I do know.'

'So?'

'Jack,' she said, in her high-pitched, slightly nasal voice, 'you know something? I'm not loving this. Everyone in this whole town knowing that I'm the wicked woman doing the dirty on her poor little childhood sweetheart. I know you haven't been any better than me. Your turn to 'fess up. What have you been up to?'

He was surprised. She pushed the beer over to him. He took it and swigged from it deeply.

'What do you mean?'

'You know what I mean. You've certainly not had your needs met by me. You've had no interest at all. What have you been up to? And who've you been up to it with?'

He laughed aloud. 'Nothing. I've been up to *nothing*, darl, with no one. Believe me, you'd know it if I had. I can't keep a secret the way you can.'

She looked him in the eyes, with her piercing blue ones, then shook her head. 'Christ, you're weird,' she said. 'I do believe you're telling the truth.'

'Yep,' he agreed. 'Been looking at some travel magazines.'

She laughed at that. They both did.

'Oh, yeah,' she said. 'That'd be right. Cheat on me with the *National Geographic*. That's my Jack all right.'

After enough beer to loosen his tongue, he decided that he ought to let Rachel know that he didn't care about the ins and outs of the latter two conceptions. He tried to explain it to her, but she jumped straight on the defensive, and did not understand at all.

'Jack,' she said tightly. 'Why don't we just let it be?'

'Yeah, I know,' he explained, raising his voice. 'That's exactly what I'm saying! That is precisely it. I'm saying, whatever happened, I don't care. It doesn't make a difference to me. And above all, I *do not want to know*.'

'You don't care about the children?'

'No, I *do* care! I care about them enough not to care whether or not . . . Jesus,' he muttered. 'This was what I was hoping not to have to spell out.'

Rachel sipped her wine and looked through narrowed eyes. 'You may as well spell it out, matey.'

'Must I? OK. Any idiot can see that Sarah-Jane's mine. Anyway, she was born first. What do they say? A baby born close to the honeymoon is more likely to look like her dad?'

Rachel said nothing.

'The other two: I don't want to know. Please don't ever tell me. I looked at them and imagined the worst, and it didn't change a thing. That's all.'

She was looking at the table, pouring herself another glass of wine. She was the only one who'd been drinking it, but the bottle was almost empty. He looked at her. She was definitely avoiding his eyes.

'You're a good man, Jack.' She stood up. 'End of. I'm going to put on some music.'

'Sure.'

The whole of the living area was open-plan, kitchen in one corner, sofas and stereo in another. It only took her a few steps to get over there, but she fiddled with CD cases for ages before she chose one. He was expecting Madonna or Kylie, someone female who would make her feel strong and empowered, but instead she stuck on Johnny Cash.

111

He thought that might be misery music. He had obviously not explained properly. She should have been pleased.

'Yeah,' she said, sitting down again. 'Look, you're right about Sarah-J without a doubt. And we won't talk about it. That suits me.' Finally, she looked him in the eyes, and he saw the girl he had fallen so dramatically in love with as a teenager. At least, he had thought it was love. More likely it had actually been lust or pheromones or something.

'Cool,' he said, and he reached out and took her hand. She squeezed his back. They sat there, hand-in-hand, while Johnny Cash told them why he liked to wear black. Neither of them had a thing to say.

'When are you going, then?' she said. 'To Spain?'

He laughed. 'Well, not just yet. Next winter. For a bit of a while. I'll need to save a bit and sort things out, but I need to get out of here.'

'You *so* need to do that,' she said, and she was a stranger and his best friend at the same time. 'You said it yourself. All you've ever wanted is to see the world, and instead you've been stuck here in Nowheresville, in a shit marriage. Get out there, Jack.' She was smiling at him. 'Just book it. You've got your mum's money still in the bank, haven't you?'

He nodded. He'd had it stashed away as a travel fund, wanted to take the whole family overseas, but Rachel had always had a reason why they couldn't go just yet.

'So, go! Go to Europe! Finally see bloody Spain at last. God knows, Jack, it's time you were happy.'

'You'd be OK with the kids?'

'Course.'

He took in a deep breath. 'Well,' he said, 'I might start to make a plan. You know, I've got Mum's money – but

112

it won't go far. I'll save. I'll make sure you and the kids are all right. All of them. You know,' he forced himself to continue, 'I meant what I just said. I love them, all of them, exactly the same, no matter what.'

'You're one in a million.'

He grinned. 'Aren't I, though?'

'Get out there. Have a bloody ball.'

He slept on the couch that night. The next morning, he told his dad he was staying for six months, and then he was going abroad on a one-way ticket. His dad laughed and said he would never actually do it, not in a million years. That was typical John, he said. Always with the grand plans, always with the small life.

Jack, however, knew his dad was wrong this time. That knowledge would power him through.

chapter twelve

Christmas Day

My day began, to my surprise, with little Tommy launching himself on to me and yelling, 'Lily! It's Christmas!'

It was pitch black. I struggled to focus. After a bit more wriggling, I pulled him out of the way and looked at my clock radio. It was 5.45. I was completely thrown by the arrival of a little boy in my bed.

'Happy Christmas,' I managed. Uninvited, he got under the duvet with me. His hands and feet were freezing, and I winced as he used me as a radiator, placing his cold fingers on my waist to warm them up, and using my legs for his toes.

'Happy Christmas,' he replied solemnly. 'Can we get up?'

I had no idea. 'Have you been in to your mum and dad?'

'They said I have to go away until half-past six.'

'What about the others?'

'Zac said I had to piss off. Jess said go and see Lily. I didn't dare go to Mia. Can we get up? Please can we? Because it's actually *Christmas Day*!'

I sat up, yawned again, and switched the light on. We both rubbed our eyes, then looked at each other.

'Looks like it's you and me,' I said, and I reached for my thickest woolly jumper and a pair of socks. 'So. Is there stuff in your stocking?'

'Yes. Father Christmas has actually been. Can I go and get it?'

I was unsure. 'Get a couple of things out of the top,' I said, in the end. 'I don't think anyone'll mind that, and we'd better go downstairs and try to be as quiet as we possibly can.'

As we stumbled down the stairs, I thought of Christmases past. I could remember being about Tommy's age. A little older. I did not want to recall the details, but as we reached the downstairs hall, Tommy's hand in mine, trying to keep quiet, it came flooding into my head anyway.

We were in the little terraced house where I lived, in Penzance, with my parents. I must have been eight. I had the television on, and was half-watching *The Snowman*. I was surrounded by presents that I had opened on my own, first thing in the morning. I was attempting to play Connect 4 against myself, and half-heartedly threading beads onto a necklace from a set I had been given, and all the time I was listening to my parents getting drunk and laughing together in the kitchen, away from me.

I remembered plucking up the courage to tiptoe through to the kitchen, still wearing my Hello Kitty nightie, and standing in the doorway, twiddling a strand of hair around my finger. Mummy, who was tall and slender with my wild hair, and whom I idolised completely, looked at me with an expression on her face that showed me that she had entirely forgotten that I existed. She frowned at me as though I were a burglar.

'You don't care about me,' I said quietly. Neither of them denied it.

'Lily, don't be silly,' Dad said, after a while. He was dark-haired and film star-ish. They looked good together and they knew it. They were each other's world. 'All that new stuff – it's child heaven in the living room. What's wrong with you? Go and play with it.'

'Go on,' said Mummy. 'Go and have some fun. And get dressed. Your grandparents are coming to pick you up in a minute.'

That was the end of my life with them. When the grandparents came for me, my parents said they were off for a holiday. It turned out they had known all along that they were never coming back, and I had never seen them since.

I stirred milk and hot chocolate powder in a pan, while Tommy jumped around saying, 'It's actual Christmas!' over and over again. I put on some coffee for myself. It was cold in the house because the heating was only just coming on, but it would soon be warm. I flicked the radio on in the hope of finding some Christmas music, but the local radio presenters were talking about a man who was in a coma after a hit-and-run accident a couple of days ago, so I flicked it off again. Christmas was an awful time to be unhappy.

I had babysat for Tommy, lots of times, but we had never done anything like this. He was a sweet boy, with his shaggy blond hair and his rosy cheeks. I was surprised at how much his affection cheered me up.

I picked Tommy up and hugged him, let him have a

ride on my back to the living room. I deposited him on the sofa, both of us giggling in a muffled sort of way, switched the tree-lights on, and went back to the kitchen to fetch our drinks.

'Merry Christmas, Tommy,' I said, as I put his hot chocolate down on the coffee table.

'Merry Christmas, Lily,' he replied. We had wished each other variations on this theme many times already. He marvelled over a remote-control car and a penguin joke book. We looked at the mountains of presents that had appeared overnight under the heavily-decorated tree. Lit by the coloured tree-lights, they looked enchanted.

A bag of chocolate coins was on the little table, and Tom kept looking at it.

'OK,' I said, in the end. 'You can have three of your chocolate coins as long as you give one to me.' It was strange, being an adult. You could say things in an authoritative voice, and people abided by your rules. He smiled and presented me with one. 'It's not the biggest,' he admitted, 'but it's not the smallest either. It's the most middle-sizedest.'

'Thank you.'

Then we dipped our coins in our drinks until they were just melted enough, and he leaned up against me, and I put an arm around his little shoulders. I looked at the top of his head. This was a new and strangely warming experience. I was responsible for him, for the moment, and he wanted to cuddle up to me. I squeezed, and he responded by turning round and hugging me around the waist. It was the most lovely thing.

* * *

I spent the morning in the kitchen with Julia, eager to be useful. I was cooking the turkey, the potatoes, and a nut roast for the girls. Julia was doing puddings. We flapped around the kitchen together, drinking glasses of the new sherry that I had bought. Julia laughed at it, but I did not care. Sherry was my tipple of choice. I loved it, and the tide of memories it brought with it. As time went by, I seemed better able to pick the good memories and discard the more recent ones.

I ached, day and night, with my secret crush. I was never going to tell anyone how I felt about Harry. It was useless: I had heard the way he spoke to his wife, and I liked her, and they were a perfect couple. Everyone knew that. The way I felt was my secret, and I tried to see it as a temporary thing, and proof that one day I might be able to fall in love with someone I could actually have.

When everything that needed to be in the oven was there, and everything else was prepared, I made coffee for the grown-ups and yet more hot chocolate for the children, and we put the contents of a box of Quality Street out in little bowls, and went to the sitting room to open our presents.

Julia smiled at me as we left the kitchen. I looked away. I was almost overcome, and I did not want to let her see it.

'This is what it's all about,' she said. 'Don't you think? You hear everyone being cynical all over the place about Christmas, but I bloody love it. It's the best day of the year, and I don't care what anyone says.'

'Depends where you are,' I pointed out. I hoped Al was all right. I was seeing him later, but I would have liked to text him and wish him a Happy Christmas. Everyone else had a mobile phone.

Mia came into the room, dressed in a flowing white top and a tiny skirt, with bare legs and thick socks. Her hair was in a ponytail, and her face was white. 'Hey,' she said. 'Happy Christmas.'

'Happy Christmas, Mia,' I said, and Julia went and kissed her.

'Did you have a good night?' she asked.

'Yeah,' Mia said, and she actually smiled properly. 'Met Joe in town. I thought we were going to be hanging out with his friends, but it was actually just the two of us.'

'Like a date?' I checked.

She looked away, a little smile on her lips. 'Yeah. Like that.'

'I'm glad you had fun,' Julia told her, then looked to me. 'He *is* suitable, Lily? I know I've asked you a hundred times.'

'Yes,' I told her, again. 'He's perfectly suitable.' Again, I did not mention the pornography.

When Julia left the room, sorting out the beginning of the grand present opening, I touched Mia's shoulder. A package had arrived for her yesterday, from Plymouth. I had taken it from the post woman, as it was slightly too big for the letterbox. Then I had given it straight to Mia, without anyone else seeing.

'Was that thing yesterday from . . .' I asked, looking round, not wanting to finish the sentence for some reason.

'Yeah,' she said, eyes wide. She took a toffee from a bowl. 'It's from her. Haven't opened it yet. Not sure whether to, really.' She unwrapped the toffee, put it in her mouth and left the room.

Julia was strict about opening the presents in an agonisingly slow manner, and I relished it, recalling exactly how dead I had felt with my parents, being able to rip everything open whenever I wanted with nobody watching. Zac was given the role of Father Christmas, and he solemnly put on a red and white hat and gave parcels out in rotation. John and Julia had bought a new laptop computer for the children, and the air filled with whoops of delight and, shortly afterwards, with arguments about which websites they would visit, and who would have first go. I hoped no one would make me go on it. I would watch what they did first, before I revealed my absolute ignorance of how these things worked.

I had a red handbag from Julia, some sheer red tights from Mia, a bottle of bubble bath from the twins, and Tommy had made me a model Santa out of polystyrene, at school. Its face was painted in an odd grimace, its hat at a drunken angle, and I hoped that I would keep it for ever.

I had carefully bought a present for each member of the family from Trago Mills, the department store in town. My funds were low, but I had managed some floral toiletries for Julia, a scarf for John (because he had lost his old one a couple of weeks ago), a huge box of chocolates for each twin, some make-up for Mia, and a lot of surprisingly cheap craft stuff for Tommy.

As he opened his pots of paint, brushes, and brightly coloured card, Julia raised her eyebrows in my direction.

'Erm, thanks for that, Lily!' she joked.

'Oh,' I said. 'Sorry.'

'No, don't be silly. It's good for him to have wholesome things to do at home. I shouldn't be afraid of a bit of mess. It's too easy to leave all of that to school.'

Tommy's eyes were bright. 'Thank you, Lily,' he said, beaming. 'I've never had my actual own paints at home before.'

He came and hugged me again. I realised that if I ever managed to move on in the world, I would miss Tommy terribly.

I watched Zac and Jess opening the cards that Mia had given them.

'Oh wow!' said Zac, as two twenty-pound notes fluttered out of his.

'Yeah!' Jess gasped, as the same happened to her.

I looked at Mia. She was smiling at them. Julia barely noticed. I wanted to walk over to her and turn her head so that she was looking, to force her to register the fact that Mia, who I knew had an allowance of thirty pounds a month, had given the twins money that could not possibly have been hers. All the same, the very fact that I was here, in the middle of a big happy family, over-whelmed me.

'Oh, I'm going to sneeze,' I said suddenly, covering my face with a hand.

'Hate it when that happens,' said John, with a laugh. 'Here, have a hanky.' He had just opened a box of eight of them, an under-appreciated present from some relative. I took it and pressed it to my face.

'Sneeze has gone,' I announced, surreptitiously wiping my eyes. When I looked up, only Mia was looking at me. She smiled, and took out the package from her mother from behind her back. She turned and opened it, masked from everyone else by the arm of her chair. I was the only one watching. Bizarrely, it seemed to contain a pair of pyjamas that were much too small for her, and which were pink and patterned with teddies and bunnies. She looked at them for a second, visibly calmed herself, and threw them at Jessica.

'Extra present for you, Jess,' she said. 'Got these in the sale. Forgot all about them.'

Jessica caught them, unfolded them and rubbed the soft material against her cheek.

'Wow,' she said. 'Thanks, Mee. They're cute.'

Mia caught my eye. We looked at each other for a few seconds, smiled sadly, then both looked away.

Later in the morning, I opened the present that Sarah had handed me, a couple of days ago, late in the evening, when all their party guests had gone home.

'This is for you, Lily,' she said. I was surprised, and it must have shown on my face.

'I was going to give you some money in a card,' she said, 'but now that I've met you, I – well, I had this upstairs, and I've never worn it, and I know it would suit you beautifully, so I want you to have it.'

'Did you just run upstairs and wrap that up?' I asked, so amazed that I forgot to be shy.

'You'd be surprised how good I am at slipping away.'

It was small and squishy, and it had belonged to Sarah Summer. My fingers trembled as I unwrapped it. Even the paper was special: it was silver and glittery-sparkly like their Christmas decorations.

'Oh, Lily!' Julia gasped, as I took out something soft and silky. It was a grey dress. I stood up and held it against myself. I was sceptical about whether it would suit me, as it looked figure-hugging, but it was the most beautiful object I had ever owned by a million miles.

'You have to go and put that on,' Jessica breathed, and everyone else concurred, so I did.

'I think I want to be a cleaner,' John said, with a chuckle, as I left the room.

'That dress would look crap on you,' said Zac.

'You know, I'm not so sure about that,' said John. 'I actually think I could carry it off.'

Up in my bedroom, away from the warmth of the family, I wriggled into it. Even as I pulled it down over myself, I knew that it was made for me, and I wondered why Sarah had bought it for herself. It reached almost to my knees (it would have been outrageously short on her), and it clung to my waist. The full-length mirror was on the landing, and when I saw my reflection, I could hardly remember to make myself breathe. I was someone completely different. I was someone who lived in a big old house with proper art on the walls. I shook my hair over my shoulders, and smiled at myself. Here, at last, was a girl who looked at the world and saw a future without limits. Here was someone who might, next year, get some proper qualifications. I imagined a future in which I went to university, travelled, had a career.

This person could do all of that. It was a revelation. She was not a scared little girl trying to work out how things were done. She was a woman. I wondered whether one day, I would be able to inhabit her properly. I thought of Harry, and the fact that this dress had come from his house. I ached with longing and hopelessness.

At two forty-five, I presented a turkey that was perfectly cooked. Admittedly it came from Asda and was not remotely free-range or in any way healthy, but it was nice and brown and crispy on the outside, and when I stuck a skewer in, clear juice ran out. The little kitchen was all steamed up, and the whole house smelled like Christmas. The potatoes were perhaps a little bit too crispy on the outside, but they were soft inside, and I did not think anyone would complain about their roast potatoes being too crunchy. I had steamed the carrots and brussels sprouts, but I made up for that by covering them in butter, salt and pepper. I had made bread sauce and gravy. There was a Christmas pudding for afterwards, and a Christmas cake for tea-time, both sourced from Lidl. An outsized apron protected my new dress from splatters. I was exhilarated by every moment.

This was the lunch Granddad used to make, almost exactly. Nobody here knew that. They thought it was Lily's Christmas lunch; and, I supposed, that was what it had become.

The twins had laid the table with crackers, school-crafted decorations, everything they could find. It was so covered in green, red and gold that there was no sign of the white paper tablecloth underneath. I had to shift five trinkets out of the way before I could even put any dishes down.

I watched everyone eating, gratified by the fact that they barely spoke as they concentrated on the food.

'Lily,' said Julia, after a while, 'I cannot tell you how

much this is the best Christmas lunch we've ever had. You have no idea.'

I was pleased. 'Really?'

'Really, Lily,' Zac put in. 'Normally it's like, cold potatoes and bits of turkey you can't eat because they're still bleeding.' He looked at Julia, awaiting her wrath.

'I'm afraid Zacary is right,' she agreed. 'I can cook perfectly OK the rest of the year, but don't ask me to do Christmas lunch. Or any sort of roast, really. That's why we never do Sunday lunch.'

'I'll do Sunday lunch any time anyone wants me to.' I was happy to make this offer. I would have offered anything, right then.

'I'm afraid we might have to take you up on it,' John said, through a mouthful of potatoes.

Straight after lunch, I slipped out of the house and walked down to the beach on my own. I stood on the sand, ignoring the Christmas people with their dogs and their new things, and looked out to sea. The sun was bright, and the water glimmered. A cold wind whipped my hair around my face. I inhaled deeply and told myself to look forward, not back.

I stood on the shingle and stared out to sea. Last year had been a fiasco, with two nearly-dead people squabbling over an infantile card game. This year was surprising. Where, I wondered, was I going to be next time Christmas came around?

I looked at my watch. I was meeting Al, right here, right now, to exchange token presents.

'We'll call it Secret Santa,' he had said. 'Even though it won't be secret at all because there's just the two of us.

125

Here is the sole rule: we buy each other something that costs three pounds maximum. Wrap it up and hand it over.'

I had got him an egg cup with a chicken painted onto it, because he had once said that now that he had a place to live, his greatest pleasure was to start the day with a boiled egg, and a little selection box of chocolates. They had added up to two pounds and ninety-eight pence. I was pleased with myself.

I saw him walking towards me, grinning broadly.

'Merry Christmas!' I shouted. My voice was whipped away by the wind.

'Merry Christmas, Lily!' he shouted back, as he approached. I walked over and hugged him and kissed his cheek. Life felt good. I was so touched when he gave me a Margaret Atwood novel I had mentioned to him that I almost cried.

'This says six pounds ninety-nine,' I said, turning it over.

'Nah, you can pick these things up cheap from Amazon sellers,' he insisted.

'Thank you,' I told him, without having much of a clue who Amazon sellers were. He handed me half a Crunchie bar from his selection box, and we huddled together and looked at the waves.

'How's Boris?' I hazarded.

He laughed. 'Search me. He's with his children.'

On the penultimate day of the year, I was in the middle of a game of bowling on the Wii with the twins when Mia wandered in and handed me the phone.

''S for you,' she said. 'Some guy.'

I took it out of the room.

'Al?' I said.

'No, sorry, Lily,' he said. 'So sorry to disturb you at home. It's Harry.'

I shut the living-room door and leaned into the phone. My heart was pounding. I had been trying not to think about him, about what a perfect break they were having in Barcelona, and now he was on the phone, to me.

'That's better,' I said. 'It's all quiet now, Harry. Are you back from Spain? How was your holiday?'

He said nothing for a few seconds. When he did speak, he was formal and distant. 'Lily,' he said. 'Oh, Lily. This isn't easy. I'm in London. But I'm calling to say – just carry on coming to clean as normal.'

'Why?' I was confused. 'I mean, why wouldn't I?'

'I thought I'd tell you before you hear in another way,' he said. He cleared his throat. 'God, this doesn't get any easier however many times . . . We're keeping it out of the press so I'd appreciate . . . but, anyway, it's Sarah.' He paused for so long that I wanted to prompt him, but I didn't. I dreaded what was coming.

'She died,' he said in the end. 'In Barcelona. Jumped into the sea and drowned. On purpose, I mean. I had no idea.'

And nothing could ever be the same again.

part two

chapter thirteen

Six months later

It was a gorgeous July day. The sea was sparkling, every drop of it separately lit by the sun. Several sailing boats were far out, blown quickly across the bay. Salty air blew into my face. I stood on the cliff path and stared out to sea, and then cast my gaze down at the beach below. I sighed and stretched, looking up at the pale blue sky, then down at the rocks. They were flat and full of little pools, only uncovered at low tide. I would take Tommy onto them sometime, and we could collect seaweed and look at the barnacles and limpets, the sea snails and the tiny crabs. That would be good for both of us, and it would cost nothing.

I stood back on the grass beside the path to let some walkers pass. They had a big black dog. They smiled at me, and I forced a little smile at them, and gave the regulation indulgent look to their dog.

When I got down to the beach, I was almost late. I

heard them before I saw them: Tommy, the twins, Julia, John, and the beginnings of the whole of Tommy's class from school. I had thought that having a party on the beach was a foolish idea, one guaranteed to bring about torrential rain. Julia had vaguely said, 'If it rains, we'll find somewhere to shelter,' and it turned out that she had been right to be so blasé, because the sky was clear and it was not going to rain at all.

Mia was not here, because she had gone to Truro with Joe Smithson, with whom she was completely besotted. I loved to see how happy she was. She seemed to have grown up by about twelve years, since she had been with him. They were officially 'a couple', and I was in awe of the fact that she was suddenly part of a proper relationship. She was able to do something I had never come close to attempting. These days we had serious talks, late at night, about all sorts of things, often ending up on the subject of our mothers. I thought that Mia was now my actual friend, too.

When I reached the sand, I kicked my sandals off, picked them up, and walked across the beach to the spot Julia had chosen. She was spreading out blankets, and a few children were starting to arrive for the party, holding their parents' hands, clutching parcels.

Tommy waved as I got closer.

'Lily!' he shouted. I waved back, and I saw him turn to a flame-haired boy next to him. 'That's Lily,' he informed him. 'She lives in my house. She looks after me.'

I smiled at the pride in his voice. I really did almost feel like part of the family, now.

The entertainer arrived, and almost every child present

tried to throw themselves at him. He stood back, laughed, caught my eye, then took a visible deep breath.

'Right, guys,' he yelled, and by some mysterious children's-entertainer alchemy, he grabbed all their attention, and made them completely quiet, just with these two words. They were generic non-words, too: it was not as if he had said, 'Free chocolate for quiet people.'

'Let's start, shall we? I'll need a DJ.' He looked at me. He did not look like a wacky, clown-like entertainer: he had a shaved head, nice shiny eyes, and an amazing way with children.

'Would you mind?' he asked, in a quieter voice. 'Just press the pause button on this prehistoric thing when I give you the nod? Thanks.'

I played and paused the music for musical statues, and looked at the sea, and it was not long before my thoughts drifted in the direction in which they always ended up drifting . . .

I was pulled back to myself by the game ending, the prize of a little water pistol going to the ginger-haired boy, who had so many freckles across his nose that it was impossible not to smile when you looked at him. Without concentrating, I seemed to have done what was required of me.

I kept looking around, because I had invited Al and Boris to come. Boris moved out of his marital home a couple of months ago, and although he had carefully rented a two-bedroom flat so that he could have his children to stay, he seemed to live with Al most of the time. This weekend, however, his children were with him, and Al was taking a back seat.

Al loved Boris's children furiously, but he was quite clearly jealous of them too. 'Not *of* them,' he had explained recently. 'Only a complete arsehole would compete with little kids. It's more that I wish Boris could be as uncomplicated with me as he is with them. Loving your kids – that's straightforward. Loving a git like me – less so. Which is frustrating because I, personally, have no problem with shouting it from the rooftops.'

'Yeah,' I told him. 'I noticed that.'

At last they arrived, the four of them. Boris, whom I had met many times now, was holding each of his children by the hand. The older one was a boy, Matthew, the younger one a girl, Elinor, and Elinor looked exactly like him, with sandy hair and freckles. The boy must have looked like his mum, so I studied him as they approached. His mother, I surmised, was mousy brown and pale-faced and pretty. Al hated her, on principle, but I felt desperately sorry for the woman. Her world must have been shattered.

Al was walking slightly away from them, and when he saw me, he waved and came running.

'Hey there,' he said. 'Lily. Good to see you, girl.' He looked at the party game, which was Pass the Parcel. 'Room for a couple of little ones?'

'That depends on whether it's the children, or you and Boris.'

'Ha ha.'

'Hello, you two.' I said. 'I'm Lily.'

Elinor, who I knew was only three, looked away from me. Matthew smiled and said, 'Are we invited to this party? We brought a present.'

'I don't see why not,' I told him. 'As long as you don't win *all* the prizes.'

'Hey, Lily,' said Boris. 'You know they're going to want this every time they come here, now? Go to the beach, play Pass the Parcel.'

'How about if we leave them with Lily for a bit then?' Al said. He was trying to be casual. It was strange to see: he was always like this with Boris. All he wanted was to be on his own with him. He hated Boris paying any attention to anyone or anything else. 'We could go for a drink or something.'

Annoyance flickered across Boris's face. Even with my inexperience, I could see that Al needed to back off.

'Mate,' he said, 'they're my kids, and they've just crashed someone's party, and they're little. Think I'll stay with them, if that's all right with you.'

Al shrugged. 'Sure. Hey, Tommy? Happy Birthday! Do you mind these two Passing the Parcel with you a bit?'

Tommy shook his head.

'More the merrier,' said the entertainer.

When I saw him walking across the beach, I thought I was hallucinating. It was the kind of thing I imagined every single day. In my imagination, he would stride across a beach, or track down the house where I lived, and sweep me up into his arms. He would recognise what I knew, which was that I was the one who would make him happy again.

I sighed and looked again at the man who was walking towards us. It still looked like him. He was wearing the polo shirt I had ironed for him, a few days ago.

'Lily!' he called, when I was close enough to hear. He smiled and waved.

I stared at him. I was not the only one. Julia looked, looked again, and started trying to look casual, which meant she shifted her weight from foot to foot, continuously, while shouting, 'That's right, Tommy!' in a shrill voice at her baffled son, who was licking mints and applying them to some other child's face as part of a sticky game. Al and Boris looked up from a muttered conversation, both apparently relieved at having something else to focus on. John seemed genuinely not to notice, and anyway he was too laconic to care. A few of the mothers who had stayed for the party tossed their hair and gazed at Harry, who was famously a widower in need of rescuing.

I walked towards him, feeling their eyes upon me.

'Hello, Harry,' I said.

'Lily.' He came over, put a hand on my waist and kissed my cheek. 'Thought I saw you. I was out for a stroll.'

I looked at him. Being close to him made me feel calm in a way that nothing else had ever done. I knew him, now. Since Sarah's suicide, we had become closer than I would ever have imagined. Through cleaning his house, I had followed the stages of his collapse, and, recently, the beginnings of his rehabilitation.

The first week, I went to their house – to his house – to clean as normal, as he had instructed. It was horrific. I cried all the way round. Sarah was gone, but her things were there, and I found myself clearing away her last coffee cup, and putting her last breakfast plate in the dishwasher. No one had touched anything; this, it transpired, was because Harry was still in London, at his mother's house. His brother, Fergus, had flown out to Barcelona after it happened, and when all the bureaucracy was taken care of, Fergus took him back to London.

I was the first person to enter the house since they left for Barcelona. I had to put some music on the stereo to propel me around, as I cleared away the horribly poignant last mementos. I took the sheets off their bed and washed them. I ironed some of her clothes, and put them away, not sure what else to do with them. I cleaned the shower, the bathrooms, the kitchen, knowing that none of them would bear her traces again.

I heard her voice in my head: *'When you come in after the New Year, the place will probably still look like this.'*

She must have known, then, what she was going to do.

The following Tuesday, Harry was back. I did not see him, but I could see his misery. There was an urn on the sitting-room mantelpiece, where the gerberas had once been. He was sleeping in the back bedroom. The marital bed had its duvet, in its usual white duvet cover, pulled tight across it.

Even now, six months on, Harry still slept in the back bedroom, in a single bed, under a duvet with a Superman cover on it (bought for visiting children, I could only imagine), and the duvet was always twisted and scrunched, with toast crumbs, and food stains, and other, less savoury things, all over it.

Grief was not a tidy thing. It was an ugly, inconsiderate, unpredictable force. I knew that Harry watched pornographic films in the back bedroom, because he often left a laptop on the floor and DVDs scattered around it with

titles like *Star Whores* and *Riding Miss Daisy*. I was careful
not to be shocked by this. I generally put them back into
the right boxes, and stacked them on the windowsill,
resolutely not thinking about it. I changed his duvet
cover and sheet, washed the dirty ones and hung them
out to dry. I cleared away the plates of stale food that
were under his bed, and put all the glasses with little
bits of alcohol in them into the dishwasher. I opened
the window to get rid of the sweaty, boozy, desperate
smell.

On the fourth week, I accidentally locked the front door
twice, trying to get in. When I realised what I had done,
I fumbled to undo it as quickly as I could, and then it
swung open, and Harry was there, looking haggard, but
trying to smile.

He lurched at me and hugged me tightly, which took
me by surprise. I was deeply uncomfortable to see him
like this, all his defences down. He was wearing an old
jumper with holes in it, and pyjama bottoms.

'I'm so sorry,' I said, even though it wasn't my fault.

'Oh, Lily,' he said into my hair. He nuzzled me and
didn't let go for ages: my heart broke for him. 'Thank
you. She liked you, you know.'

'I can't believe it,' I muttered.

'Christmas Day. I was asleep and she went out and . . .'

He loosened his hold and I stepped back. I felt his eyes
on me, and blinked as I looked at the floor. There was
nothing much to say.

'You're not at work,' I said.

'Thought I could throw myself straight back into it.
Been trying. Turns out, not really possible. Ignore me, Lily,

and do what you normally do.' He paused. 'I know you always leave her things.'

'Of course.'

'I'll have to deal with them.'

He had no family there, no friends, no one to support him. I thought that was sad, wondered why nobody had come back from London with him, but I, of all people, knew that families could be strange.

In the months that had passed since then, he had often been at home during my weekly visit. He followed me around the house and talked, sometimes about Sarah, sometimes about other things. After a few weeks, he asked me to help him sort through her clothes. We put them into black bags, and he made me take them away, saying: 'Wear them, give them away, sell them on eBay, I don't care.' I kept some, because they were so beautiful I could not bear to get rid of them, and gave the rest to Mia and her friends, or to the charity shop.

One day in March, the urn was not there any more. He saw me looking at the empty space.

'I scattered her,' he said with a weak smile. 'On the cliffs at Porthleven. It was her favourite place. At least, I think it was. I'm not sure I actually know anything about her any more.'

I tried never to think about the desperation that had led Sarah to walk away from her adoring husband, her perfect house, her exquisite life, and drown herself. Her suicide cut me to the core. I told myself what Harry told me, that it was a chemical thing, an imbalance in her brain, an irrational act that was out of character. All the same, I knew I would never succumb so selfishly, and the resentment I felt towards her had hardened, as the months passed and I watched Harry struggling, on his own, to come to terms with the wicked ending of his fairytale. I had liked her so much, that evening, but now I almost hated her.

This was the first time I had seen him outside my cleaning hours. We stood and smiled at each other, while the sea roared onto the shore, and the children danced around to an old Britney Spears song.

'You're at a party,' he said, grinning and waving at the children.

'Tommy's seven. That's him, in the red shorts.'

He sighed. 'God, they are wholesome and adorable, aren't they? There's something about them, all unformed at that age, unbattered by the world. It's . . . well, this sounds naff, but there's something terribly moving about it.'

I looked at them. I remembered myself at that age, desperately craving love and approval.

'They *look* innocent, but I bet a proportion of those children have had pretty shit lives so far.' I would never have said the word 'shit' a year ago. I rather liked it.

Harry looked at me. I loved the way that, even though I was tall, he had to incline his head downwards to speak to me.

'Really, Lily? That sounds terribly world-weary.'

I nodded. 'Maybe. It's true though.'

He spoke quickly. 'Look, are you needed here? Will you come and have a drink with me? I came out because I could feel myself falling off the edge. Just me and a bottle, you know? Needed to clear my head or I was going to lose the . . . Will you come home?'

I went and told Julia I was off, kissed Tommy, and left with Harry, under the eyes of what felt like hundreds of people. Harry needed me more than they did.

He poured me a glass of red wine, and poured himself a larger one. I followed him to the dining-room table, and sat down around its corner from him.

'Cheers,' he said.

'Cheers,' I echoed, taking a tiny sip. I was not sure my system could handle red wine but I would do my best to keep him company. 'Are you OK, Harry?' I savoured his name on my lips.

He smiled. 'Back from the precipice, thank you. Christ, I'm boring, aren't I? It's all me, me, me, with me.' He was drinking quickly. I sipped mine again. 'There's no bringing her back, is there? Much as I've been dreaming of it. There's not even any bringing her back just to ask "what the hell?" and then send her away again, which happens most nights in my dreams but I wake up before I hear the answer. Her family don't want anything to do with me, you know, because they think I drove her to it.'

'Oh!' I said, disapproving of this.

'I know. So, fuck 'em. Fuck it all. I'm done with moping and agonising. It's time for me to get on with whatever life I can have without her. I loved her, you know.'

'Anyone could see that.'

'And I'll always be fucking angry, but I'm going to have to put that aside or it'll eat me up and I'll wake up one day drunk in the gutter. Now – are you ready for the next part?'

'I am.'

'Promise not to be afraid?'

I was afraid, of course. 'Promise.'

'Right. It's this. My friends have melted away. The neighbours were all concerned and agog for a while, bringing casseroles round and all that, but I'm old news now. It's too soon for them to invite me to dinner and sit me next to their divorced friends, so they're not interested. My brother does his best, in his way, but he's a train wreck. His wife's walked out on him in the more conventional sense – she's always doing that, but she does appear to mean it this time – and he's no use to anyone. My mother and Sarah loathed each other, so all I get from Mum is "she's done you a favour". No, it turns out there's only one person who I have actually felt is here for me through thick and thin.' He finished the last of his wine and went around the corner into the kitchen to fetch the bottle. 'That's you, Lily,' he finished, coming back with it, topping up my glass and refilling his own.

I stared. 'Me?'

'You.' He smiled, and there was no artifice at all to him. 'I know, you're too modest to see it that way. You have no idea of your own charms. You're the only person who's seen the squalor in which I live, and you have never judged me for it. For months, I've been taking Tuesday mornings off just so that I could see you. You're terribly wise for one so young. Which leads me to the next point: weeks ago you mentioned that you'd be twenty-one in July. Have I missed it? Was that actually your party, down on the beach, with the clown and everything?'

'No,' I managed to say. 'Next Tuesday. The fourteenth. But—'

He raised a hand to stop me. 'But nothing. Lily Button, if you don't have other plans, would you allow me to take you out for dinner on your birthday? As a clumsy and inadequate attempt at a "thank you"?'

I was wary. 'Really?'

'Really.'

'But everyone knows you. They'll laugh at you taking your cleaner out.'

He batted 'everyone' away with his hand. 'Let 'em. We don't care about them. Anyway, I'm a washed-up old has-been and no one's that interested, and also, they won't see my cleaner, they'll see a spectacularly beautiful girl twenty years my junior, and my status will go up. It will skyrocket. And all the women in their thirties and forties will roll their eyes and say, "It didn't take him long to pick up a younger model", and I will smile and walk on by with my head held high.'

I tried to think of a reason for not going. I had barely even been to a restaurant in my life. Years ago, I remembered my parents taking me to a pizzeria in Truro from time to time, where I sucked lemonade through a straw and swung my legs and coloured in little sheets that the staff gave me, with rubbish pencil crayons. Grandma and Granddad would sometimes take me to cafés, but Granddad would start reciting obscure speeches from Shakespeare, and Grandma would criticise whatever she was eating, loudly, and after a while I started persuading them to desist. Eating out had never been a pleasure.

He was looking at me, waiting for an answer. I took a deep breath, knowing that I was out of my depth.

'OK,' I said. 'Thank you very much. That would be lovely.'

Half an hour later, when I got up to leave, the atmosphere between us changed. Harry seemed slightly drunk, and I felt very, very drunk. He had put away a huge amount, but a glass and a half seemed to have incapacitated me completely.

I stumbled as I walked to the door. He steadied me with a hand on my shoulder. I felt it there, more significant than it should have been. He did not take it away.

The hall was high-ceilinged and airy, and there was a warm breeze coming in through an open window somewhere. I put my hand on the dado rail, anchoring myself upright.

'Bye then, little Lily,' he said.

'I'm wearing one of Sarah's dresses.' I felt obliged to tell him this, for some reason.

'It looks better on you,' he said. He held my shoulders and drew me towards him. I leaned my cheek on his chest. He kissed the top of my head.

Then I pulled away.

'See you on Tuesday,' I said.

'Tuesday,' he repeated.

I walked down the garden path, smiling to myself. At the gate, I turned and waved. He was standing in the doorway, watching. He lifted a hand, and I set off down the road, imagining the neighbours watching me from behind their curtains.

chapter fourteen

Jack made sure he had a window seat, sat down in it, put his stuff under the seat in front and buckled up. He took the card out of the pocket in front of him and studied it carefully, working out where his nearest exit would be in the event of an emergency. Lucky there was no danger of him wearing high-heeled shoes, and having to take responsibility for popping the inflatable slide.

Jack was missing the kids already, and this troubled him, because he was about to put the maximum possible number of miles between them. He missed his eldest child particularly, because she was funny and he could have a proper conversation with her. He felt bad to be abandoning her when he could have brought her along and shown her Spain. He had always talked about Spain, had tried to speak a few words of Spanish (badly) after his evening class, but any Spanish the kids knew really came from *Dora the Explorer*, the neon-bright cartoon character who taught kids all over the English-speaking world to say: 'Uno, dos, tres'.

Now it was he who was going to be the teacher. In a month, he would be qualified to teach Spanish people to say 'one two three', and 'where is the train station', and heaven knows what else. *Hello*, he said, in his head. *I'm an English teacher.* It was strange and thrilling.

Jack was trying hard to look normal, like a bloke who travelled across the world on a plane all the time. He was, truth be told, beside himself with excitement and, he had to admit, fear. He was holding his knees rigidly together and sitting on his hands to stop them shaking.

When he was a boy, this was the thing he thought he would do. It was what the bright kids did in New Zealand: they got themselves on a plane and headed to Europe for their 'OE', or overseas experience. They worked in bars in London, travelled around Europe on a train, stopping here and there to gather some more money and look at old stuff in museums, and they wrote home to complain about the weather.

He could take himself straight back to Wakatipu High School. That was him. He was the boy who was going to go to Europe, the fresh-faced youngster with a plan in his heart. It was a film that had done it, a film and a girl. The film was called *Live Flesh*, and he had seen it by chance late one night when he was channel-hopping after the parents went to bed. The girl was called Penelope Cruz, and she had been all his, briefly, until she went to Hollywood and got together with a man with the same surname as her, spelled differently. That had been a bit of a betrayal, to be frank. Jack had been disappointed with her. Penelope had belonged to everyone after that, and his obsession evaporated.

For years, though, he had watched the films by that director, Pedro Almodóvar. He had learned to pronounce his name; at least, he was pretty sure he was close. He had dreamed of the Spain of Almodóvar's films: a land filled with transvestites and bright mouthy women in astonishing clothes, and shouting and slammed doors and secrets. That was what he was seeking.

Reality was upon him now, and Jack knew that as soon as he got to real Spain, he would be at a total loss, a stranger far from home. The real Spain would be normal, in some way or another. It would not be a stylised film set.

In his bag there was a *Rough Guide*, and he was planning to read it, again, from cover to cover en route. Including the language section at the back. He was pretty sure that everyone spoke English anyway, but despite all his hard work, listening to tapes over the past six months, he was not sure he was going to manage more than '*hola*' or '*muy bien*', when push came to frightening shove.

A woman came and took the seat next to him. She smiled, and he smiled back, partly in sympathy for the fact that she had the undesirable middle seat of the three. She looked Asian, and was probably in her fifties, and she was well-dressed, like a professional.

This flight was going to Singapore first, and Jack was going to stay there for two nights before flying on to Spain. He was doing this because when he was at the travel agent's in town, Sally had said, 'Of course you'll be wanting to break your journey with a few days' stopover,' and he had agreed because, as a travel agent, Sally knew more than he did. He remembered Sally, with her bright pink lipsticked mouth and her big hair and her ill-hidden glee at booking this ticket for him. The scandal of his and Rachel's sudden break-up would keep the whole town in gossip for a good few months yet, that was for sure. He was glad to be away from it. As he'd left the agency, his ticket completely booked, he had seen Sally glance at him, pick up the phone and hit a redial button. Before he even got five steps down the street.

He would have done this more than ten years ago, if he had not fallen for Rachel; or rather, had she not decided, after years of lust on his part, that she was ready to give him the time of day. It had been the biggest dilemma of his life. He was only seventeen, and on one side there was a beautiful girl who made it very clear that if he went away, she would be out of his reach for ever. On the other, there was the country of his dreams, of the movies that he knew by heart. Rachel was real. Spain was real too, but it was a mystery.

'Don't be an idiot, John,' his dad had laughed at him. 'A girl like Rachel doesn't come along every day of the week.'

'Do what you feel is the right thing,' Mum had said. She was always more diplomatic than his dad. She wanted him to marry Rach, he had known that, because she wanted him nearby and she was after some grandchildren. That was why he had stayed, for his mum. Now he could not even say it was the wrong decision, because once you had the kids, you could never regret it.

''Scuse me, do you know Singapore?' he asked the woman next to him.

She shook her head. 'Not really. I've passed through, but only on my way home. I'm not leaving the airport.'

'Your accent – you're British?'

'My son and his family live in Christchurch, so this is a journey I make once a year. I know we shouldn't, what with the global climate-change catastrophe and everything. But I have to see my granddaughters, and my guilty secret is that I absolutely adore flying.'

He grinned. 'Can I tell you something?' He waited. She nodded. 'I've never been on a plane in my life. Went to the North Island a couple of times, but I always took the ferry. Never trusted that little plane.'

'Well, you can trust this one,' she said, and her English voice and the fact she was grandmother to some little girls was so reassuring that he relaxed back into his seat a bit.

'But how can it stay in the air?' he asked, after a while.

'It's about the thrust,' she explained. 'Thrust and lift need to be greater than drag and weight. It's the engines. The pilot can power them up so much that they can easily cope with the weight of a thing like this. It all works, honestly it does.'

Jack was impressed.

'OK,' he said. 'Thrust and lift. Engines. I'm going to trust you on that one.'

As they taxied along the runway, he watched the safety demonstration closely, repeating details to himself under his breath. Most people were not bothering to watch, even though this was life and death stuff. The woman next to him was engrossed in a magazine, but he let her off because she clearly knew it already. Everyone else, however, ought to be ashamed of themselves. If he was the only one to get out safely, it would serve them all right.

Then he pressed his face to the little window. He literally pressed it, so his nose was against the glass, which did not seem to be glass at all. It was plastic, if anything. And he watched two planes in front speeding up along the tarmac and vanishing from his field of vision. Then his plane idled around a corner, the languid movement of the plane belying the fact that it was about to drive so fast that it would lurch through the sky to a different continent. When they were nose towards the runway, they started going in earnest.

He must have gasped, because the woman next to him put her hand over his, and he gripped it tightly. He craned his neck to see the houses, the tops of the parked cars, the trees and everything disappear. Then there were clouds, and there was deep blue sky all around them, and bits of clouds below.

He let go of her hand which was soft and smooth.

'Well done,' she said. 'I'm Anita, by the way.'

'Thanks for that, Anita,' he said. He still felt jittery. You saw planes in the sky all the time. It was fine. 'I'm . . .' He paused. He could go back to his formal name, John, maybe try a jaunty 'Jonny'. Or he could stick with the name everyone had used for ever. 'I'm Jack,' he told her.

'Excuse me, sir,' called an air hostess. 'Would you like a drink?'

He laughed. 'Jesus, I'll say so. Thanks.'

He tried to imagine meeting Spanish people, and living a Spanish life. Once he had his TEFL certificate, anything might happen. He pictured himself sitting across a table from a Spanish girl, around his age or so, though she could be older or younger, it didn't matter. She had shiny black hair, perfectly straight. It swung like a piece of silk when she looked at her book. She had olive-y skin and huge black eyes. She was thin, like Penelope, but a bit curvier.

He imagined himself asking her out for a drink. '*Quieres algo a beber?*' he would say, and she would smile at his accented Spanish.

'*Gracias*, I would love to,' she would reply, in sexy Spanish-English.

He was gazing at the sea below them. This woman might not exist, yet he felt strongly that, somewhere, she did. He was leaping into the unknown, but a part of him felt that he was making his way to the place he should always have been, and that the rest of it was inevitable.

chapter fifteen

14 July

At seven o'clock, I was ready to go. The family were so excited about my birthday dinner with Harry that I had been tempted to call him and ask him to pick me up from the house after all, just so they could get a good look at him.

'You will be careful,' said Julia, yet again.

'Yes, Julia,' I said. 'I will be careful. I'll be sensible and careful and all those things.'

'Give us a bell if you need picking up,' John added.

'OK, but I won't. I'll be fine.'

'No walking home at all hours,' Julia admonished.

'Excuse me!' said Mia, very pissed off. 'She's twenty-one! I'm sixteen and you don't even *notice* when I go out.'

'They do, Mia,' I assured her. 'They sit up and wait for you, they just don't tell you. They text Joe's mum to make sure you've arrived at their house. It's unusual for me to go anywhere, that's all. In fact, it's completely unheard of. That's why everyone's excited.'

Julia smiled. 'It's not every day our lodger goes on a date with a dashing widower. Ignore our fussing, Lily. We do know you're an adult, really. Have a wonderful time. You look ever so beautiful. Enjoy yourself.'

'Thanks. And thanks for all the presents, and the cake and everything.'

I had never had a birthday like this one. On my previous birthday, the momentous occasion upon which I had left my teens, I had been looking after Granddad on his deathbed, while fending off mad comments from Grandma, cleaning up and secretly packing away our lives upstairs. The fact that it was my birthday flickered through my mind a couple of times, irrelevant.

I was out of my depth with Harry, and I knew it. He was at least forty, and he had been married. Before that, he'd famously had a few girlfriends. He knew how relationships worked. I was carefully telling myself that his inviting me out to dinner did not mean he was in love with me. I knew it was important not to mention the fact that I was so madly in love with him.

He had come to find me on the beach because he was lonely. I knew that. He had talked nonsense about how I was the only one who understood him because he'd had too much to drink. He was taking me out because it filled an evening for him. I did not think badly of him for any of that. I was just glad that I was the person who happened to be there when he needed a distraction. One day, I was sure, he would meet a new girlfriend, a second wife, and when that happened I would move away, because I could not bear the idea of seeing him around town with someone new.

All the same, over the past six months he had occasionally let things slip about their marriage that made me wonder what Sarah had really been like, behind closed doors. He never spoke ill of her. Yet throwaway comments were beginning to make me suspect that the darkness that had made her take her own life had blighted both their existences more than he would ever admit, now she was gone.

As I closed the front door behind me, I pictured a phantom Sarah looking down at me. I knew she was dead and that being dead was what she had chosen, and I did not believe in ghosts, but I could not shake the feeling that I was encroaching on her territory, and that if she had foreseen this happening, she would have been very angry indeed. The fact that I was wearing the dress she gave me at Christmas did not help, but I did not have anything else that came close to that dress. It was like wearing water, in a good way. It slipped and clung and made me look different. It made me look nice. I had dried my hair with styling mousse, and there was no frizz at all. I was wearing a new lipstick that Mia had given me for my birthday and I felt that it was the right colour, a dark red, and made me look older.

The clouds had dispersed, and it was a perfect summer evening. When I caught a glimpse of the sea, I saw that it was still and flat, shining in the light of the setting sun. I reached Harry's road a little bit early, and walked around the residential streets for a while. These were the older streets, the Victorian ones, and the terraces were packed with middle-class families. You could hardly walk a step without hearing someone playing scales on a violin. A woman smiled at me as she put her recycling boxes out, ready for the morning.

Harry threw the door open with an extravagant gesture. As soon as I saw him, my heartbeat sped up. I tried not to let it show.

'Lily!' he cried. 'My God, you look fantastic – a sight for sore eyes. Come on in. Happy Birthday! Hold on a second. Where is it?'

I followed him in, and watched him hunting around. Eventually, he found a small gift-wrapped package, and handed it to me.

'I wasn't sure what to get you,' he said. 'I didn't want to embarrass you. But then I thought I wanted you to have a lovely present to show how much it means to me that you are such an eminently wonderful presence in my life. And that I mean it even when I'm sober. So I got you something that I hoped you might like. Happy Birthday!'

'Harry,' I said. 'Going out tonight is an enormous present.'

'Open it, then.'

He watched intently as I overcame my reluctance and unwrapped a small box. I knew that he was studying my reaction. The smile was fixed to my face. It took me ages to get the box open. It was a hard box, a square one. I wished he hadn't got me anything. Eventually, I managed to prise it open.

I smiled nervously.

'Harry!' I said. 'A necklace. Wow, it's beautiful! But it's too much, it really is, I cannot possibly—'

He put a finger to his lips. 'Shh,' he said. 'Stop talking and let me help you do it up.'

I stood still, feeling the goosebumps on the back of my neck as his fingertips brushed my skin. Then he led me to the hall mirror and stood behind me, holding my hair back then putting it gently down.

It was a beautiful silver necklace. I knew it had not been Sarah's, because I could tell from the box that it was brand new. It was made from silver strands with silver balls at intervals on it. I loved it at once, but I wondered how much it had cost.

'It suits you,' he said quietly, standing behind me. 'Don't feel embarrassed. It wasn't expensive. When I saw it, I thought of you, and I just wanted to give you a token, to say thanks for your friendship.'

I drew in a lungful of air.

'Oh, thank you, Harry. It's beautiful. I will treasure it.'

The town centre was busy with people who were enjoying the sunny evening. Harry led the way up to the High Street, and into a little courtyard with rickety tables and chairs in it.

'Restaurant's booked for nine, down the other end of town. Meanwhile, it's cocktail hour. What's it to be?'

This floored me. I paused, feeling stupid, for too long.

'Can you choose one?' I asked, at last. 'I don't know anything about cocktails. Left to myself, I'd ask for a glass of sherry. Or I'd pluck the name of a cocktail I'd heard of from thin air, and it would be all wrong.'

He smiled, and gestured to a table. 'Take a seat and leave it to me. No tequila sunrise and no piña colada for you, young lady. Though sherry is probably cool again by now.'

I sat on a wobbly chair in the courtyard and wondered if this was really happening. I felt the Sarah of my imagination, watching me from somewhere around. If I concentrated hard, I could feel a chill on the back of my neck, where Harry had touched me.

A couple of students were at the next table, laughing privately at some joke or other.

When Harry came back out and put a glass of clear liquid and green plants in front of me, I tried to dispel the feeling that Sarah was watching me drinking cocktails with her husband.

'What is it?' I asked, instead.

'Mojito.' He raised his, which was the same, and we clinked glasses. 'Many happy returns,' he said.

'Thank you.'

I took a sip. It was minty and limey and strong. I did not ask what was in it. I would find out for myself, later. I would find out how to make it, and one day I would make one for him. I liked it much better than red wine.

'This is lovely,' I said, and we smiled at each other, as the salty breeze blew in my hair.

The tiny seafood restaurant was down a few stairs, cosy with only four tables. We were shown to a corner table, though in fact each of the tables was in a corner, and Harry asked the woman to turn the music up so we could not hear the other people's conversation, and they could not hear ours.

I looked at the couple at one of the other tables. I saw them look at Harry, then look again. I watched them notice me and talk to each other in hushed voices.

'You really don't mind people seeing us out together?' I asked him.

He leaned back in his chair. 'Meaning what?'

'Meaning, do you really want people gossiping about you being out with some woman?'

He laughed, completely relaxed. 'Let them gossip. May they enjoy themselves. Jesus. Should I be hiding away until the public at large reaches a consensus that the right amount of time has passed? No, thank you. Do I care if they judge me for taking a beautiful woman out to a restaurant – no, of course I don't, Lily. I don't care at all. Let them stare.' He smiled across at the people who were looking at us. He even raised his hand and gave them a little wave. The woman waved back, uncertainly.

'Really?'

'I've had a lesson, these past six months, on what matters and what doesn't. That doesn't. I hope you're hungry. There's a seafood platter here that's damn good, but it's for two. How would that grab you?'

I nodded, though before it arrived I would have to make a conscious effort to dispel all of Granddad's mistrust of all things that arrived in a shell. Harry ordered side salads, and asked if I'd like a starter. I said no.

'Good idea,' said Harry. 'Leave some space for pudding. You have to have a pudding, because it's your birthday. Twenty-one today. I can barely remember back that far. Do you know how old I am?'

'No.'

'Do you want to guess?'

'No, I do not!'

'Go on,' he said. 'Guess. Say whatever you like, I won't

be offended. Say I'm sixty-six and I'll be flattered. I feel about a hundred.'

I looked at him. I thought he was about forty-two, so I said, 'Thirty-eight?' He laughed.

'Well done,' he said. 'Forty-four, in fact. More than twice your age. I was older than you are now, when you were born. Now.' He topped up my glass with wine, although we had only been here for fifteen minutes, and I noticed that it was true: I had knocked back most of a glass out of nerves.

'Now,' he said again, when both our glasses were full: 'I want to know everything about Lily Button. I've never asked you a thing, which is dreadfully selfish of me. Where do you come from? Are you a Cornish girl? How is someone so young so wise and self-possessed? And most of all: why is someone as bright and sparky as you are cleaning people's houses for a living? I've asked you that before but you've never answered.'

I closed my eyes, felt the alcohol affecting my reticence, and wondered how much to say. I was a distraction for Harry right now: my feelings for him were frighteningly strong, but I was not afraid of getting hurt. I was grateful for this, whatever happened.

I looked him in the eyes.

'I'll take the easy question first,' I said. 'Yes, I'm Cornish. I was born in Truro. You won't believe this but I've spent my entire life in Cornwall. I've never even been to Devon.'

'Never been to Devon? Or anywhere beyond?'

'That's right.'

'We need to remedy that.'

'I do intend to. So, my parents moved away when I was eight, and I lived with my grandparents after that.'

'Your parents moved away?'

'Yes.' I tried to make light of it. 'You know when people's dads leave? It happens all the time. Well, occasionally you meet someone whose mum left them, though not very often. I just happened to be unlucky enough to have both of them leave at once.'

'They stayed together? And left you with your grandparents?'

'It was the best thing that could have happened,' I said quickly. 'I can see it now. My grandparents adored me and cherished me. I had a sheltered life with them, but it was a happy one. I'd happily have lived like that, in their cottage, for ever. But then they died.'

I wondered whether I really would have been happy in the cottage for ever, if they had been immortal and healthy. There would, I supposed, have come a time when I might have wanted to face the world.

'And you didn't end up with a cottage?'

'It turned out they were rubbish with money. So I answered an ad, and went on benefits, and now I'm financially independent, because I clean five houses a week.'

'Your parents were shits. I hope they died a horrible agonising death, if you don't mind my saying so.'

I laughed. 'I think they're alive, because no one's ever told me they're not, but they're dead as far as I'm concerned, and vice versa, no doubt. So it makes no difference, really, what they've done.'

Harry leaned forward and looked into my eyes.

'You see?' he said. 'I always knew you were interesting. Bloody hell, Lily. They should make a film about you. What are you going to do for a career?'

'Go to college. Get a degree. Actually I need a bit of a kick. It's taken all my strength just to get this far, but I have no intention of actually stopping at this point.'

I crossed my legs under the table. My foot hit his shin by mistake. I moved away, but he pushed his leg forward so we were touching again. Neither of us acknowledged that this was happening.

'Anyway, what about you?' I asked. 'You've got your brother, Fergus. What else?'

We chatted about Harry's feckless brother who, it turned out, had been having affairs for years and had now been thrown out by his wife. I was glad it was Harry I was with tonight, rather than his brother. He also told me about his mother, Nina.

'Sarah hated her, and the feeling was mutual, but Mum's all right really. Can be overbearing but she's a pussycat at heart.' His father had died when Harry was six. As we talked, I copied the way he ate the seafood as, despite the fact that I had just shared my background with him, I was still embarrassed by the fact that I did not know how to tackle a prawn, or things that were bigger than prawns, with claws. I did not give a moment's thought to whether I actually liked them or not, so the slimy things slipped down with no trouble at all.

It was nearly midnight when we stepped out into the darkness, with the harbour at one end of the little street, and the main road at the other. I looked towards the water: the moon was reflected in the still sea, lighting a silvery pathway to the horizon. The stars were all out, even the ones you could hardly see, the ones that came out looking like a white smudge across the sky. The little boats were bobbing around in the harbour, monochrome in the moonlight. The tankers, out at sea, were lit up brightly, in yellow and orange, looking like little havens in the blackness.

Harry put an arm around my shoulder. I had been waiting, hoping, for this. As the evening progressed, we had been leaning towards each other, our legs intertwined, then our hands touching. I was primed, yet petrified; ready for this to happen yet convinced I had read the signals wrong. Certain I was on the brink of making a fool of myself, yet unable to pull back.

I leaned into him, and we walked, together, down to the edge of the harbour, until we were on its brink. One more step would have taken us into the blackness of the Atlantic Ocean. The day when I had wanted to hurl myself into that cold water seemed a million years ago. Sarah had done that, in the end. It had never been going to be me.

'Thanks for this evening,' he said, his voice low.

'No,' I said. 'Thank *you*.'

'Lily,' he said. 'You have no idea. Honestly, you don't.'

I stared at the clear night sky, and said nothing, because I did not want to ruin it.

'See that bright one,' he said, pointing with his free hand, 'just over there – to the right of the moon? That's Venus. At least, I think it is.'

'Is it? Women are from there, then.'

That was a stupid thing to say. It was trite and utterly mood-dispelling. I opened my mouth and tried to suck the words back in. But Harry laughed.

'Some women are from another planet. Not you, Lily.'

He put his other hand on my shoulder and turned me to face him. At that point, I stopped thinking. When he kissed me, I knew that this was the life I had never known I was missing. This was the future. Everything that had happened, had happened for this.

I tingled all over in ways I had never imagined. I had never done anything like this before, but I knew that it was right. My body did odd things, and wanted to do more. The night was warm around us, and there was nothing but us and the water and the starry sky.

When he looked at me, his eyes were more alive than I had ever seen them. He looked properly happy for the first time.

I kissed him, I thought. *He kissed me. I, Lilybella Button, have kissed this amazing man.*

He took my hand, and we walked together along the harbour's edge.

chapter sixteen

A week later

Someone had turned off the old, weak sun, and turned on a stronger one in a different part of the sky. Life was warmer, more exciting, magical. I could not think of anything but Harry. It had only been a week, yet I had no idea what I used to think about. When we were not together, I had to make an effort even to notice other things. I could not believe how much he liked me. It was a strange fairytale, a dream come true.

I tried to be my old self. I called in to see Al at work, to apologise for running away from him and Boris at the party, but he wasn't there. I babysat when Julia needed me to. I ran around, cleaning people's houses, but my mind was never on what I was doing.

I had never come anywhere close to 'having a boyfriend'. I had no idea what it was all about. Mia 'had a boyfriend', Joe; but they were teenagers, practising, messing around. Harry and I were nothing like them. We were serious from day one, and we both knew it.

Al called, a week after my birthday.

'When are you going to get a mobile?' he demanded. 'You're the only person in the world I can't text.'

'Yes,' I agreed. 'I know. I'm fully out of step with the modern world. Harry says I could get a pay-as-you-go one.'

'Ask him to get you one.'

'Al! I'll get my own, thank you very much.' Then I relented. 'Actually, he said the other day that he's got an old handset he'll hook up for me, but I'll be doing my own paying as I go, thanks.'

'Hang on,' Al said. 'Rewind a moment. "Harry says?" So you really did stroll off into the sunset? One day you're bailing on all your mates to walk across the beach with him, and then he takes you out on your birthday, you vanish, and a week later he's giving you a phone? I think I can fill in the blanks there. You having fun?'

I sighed happily. 'So much fun, Al. I had no idea.'

'It'd be nice to see you. Have you got any time for the man who once stopped you flinging yourself into the harbour?'

'Of course I have.'

'How are you handling your alcohol these days?'

'Better and better, thanks.'

'So, let me buy you a birthday sherry.'

The pub was a proper old-style one, with a mixed clientèle incorporating students, fishermen, and everyone in between.

All the outside tables were taken. Al had managed to keep a whole one for us, though I could see some girls nearby looking at him and giggling. He was good-looking enough for that; beautiful enough that even when he was not happy, even when the horrors of his past were visible in his eyes, everyone, male and female, was attracted to him.

Everything around us was lit up by the golden evening sunlight. There were tips of gold on every little wave out there. Across the mouth of the estuary, the grassy hills around St Mawes were bucolic and peaceful.

Al grinned as he saw me approaching. A glint of gold was shining in the sunlight, on his face.

'You got your nose pierced,' I pointed out, staring at it. 'Why?'

He shrugged. 'Why not? On impulse. Showing Boris I've still got a bit of wildness in my old heart.'

I tried to imagine having an impulse like that. 'Wow.'

'Happy Birthday,' he said, handing me a Tesco bag. 'You remember me, right?'

'Thanks,' I said. 'And sorry. But I've only been seeing Harry for a week, and you've been devoted to Boris for *ever*.' I was excited, my heart fluttering around, because I knew that, from now on, I would get to talk about Harry just as much as Al always got to talk about Boris. I opened the bag. It contained a bottle of expensive sherry, a Smarties cake, and a Camembert.

'Thanks,' I said. 'What a fantastic present. You shouldn't have spent that money on me though.'

'I'll get you whatever I want to get you, thanks very much.'

'I appreciate it. If we weren't in a pub, I'd open the

sherry, you know. Actually, it's the most thoughtful present anyone could have got me. And how long has that cheese been in there?'

'It's meant to be smelly,' he explained, 'so it doesn't matter.'

'Thanks, Al.' I leaned forward and kissed his cheek. 'So, what's going on with you? How's Lover Boy?'

'Which Lover Boy would that be? You need to narrow it down a bit.'

I frowned. 'Boris. Are there others?'

'Of course not. It was a joke. Obviously not a very funny one. I don't want to talk about him. Wifey is trying to make him come back and I'm terrified he might actually go. Can't stop myself coming on too strong. I can see in his eyes that I'm scaring him off.'

'She wants him *back*?'

'The stuff with the solicitors has been getting nasty. I didn't mind that. I thought it was good for him to see the vindictive cow for what she is.'

'Al!'

'Sorry. But really. He's been hating it, and then when she called and asked to meet for a drink so they could talk things through, he couldn't wait to go. I knew then that we were in dangerous waters. After threatening seven types of shit, never seeing his kids again, homophobic abuse, all of that going through the lawyers, in real life she was dewy-eyed and "offering chances" left right and centre. "For the children's sake". She got to him.'

I knew Al quite well by now.

'You spied on them, didn't you?'

'Mistake. He spotted me. So now I look like a

possessive wanker, we're barely speaking, and I know, I just *know*, he's going back to her.' He rolled his eyes. 'And that was me *not* talking about Boris. You should hear me when I do talk about him.'

'Al,' I said, 'People can be very strange.'

'Tell me about it. How come you're not, though? You lived with old people. They probably had some old-fashioned attitudes. You ought to think I'm a vile pervert, like that woman does.'

'Well, I don't, and I never did for a moment.' I thought about it. 'My grandparents were old, obviously, but people have always been gay. You don't have to be prejudiced, just because you're old. In fact, it's rather ageist to think so. They were completely liberal in their attitudes, and anyway, their bookcases were full of gay writers. I've read E.M. Forster, Alan Hollinghurst . . .'

'I missed you, Lily. You're really coming out of yourself. It's been fun to watch.'

'Thank you.'

He paused. 'Look, shoot me down over this. I know you will. But . . .'

'But?'

'Well, you need to keep pushing forwards. You're working every hour, you should save as much as you can, get yourself to college. You keep saying you're going to college. It's July. Term starts in September. You should be doing it now. Right now, this instant, before the summer term ends. I know you've only been seeing him for five minutes, and it's sunny and sexy and it's a bit of fun. But – well, take my advice and *don't* settle down with some old guy with a dead wife. He'll want you to be his second wife. You would be a coup for him, and you can't see it. You deserve more than that.'

I laughed. 'Al! I've never been out with anyone before. I'm happy.' I looked hard at him. 'Be glad for me. Let me have some fun before you start telling me off. But you're right about college. I'll do it. I'll sort it out.'

He shook his head, as if dislodging his thoughts. 'Of course. Sorry, darling. I can't help feeling protective of you. From the day you stumbled into the CAB, I've wanted to keep an eye on you. You just seemed so . . . vulnerable.'

'Well,' I said. 'I'm not any more. I'm so happy I don't know what to do with myself.'

chapter seventeen

Madrid

Jack was in Madrid, but as soon as he got there, he located the train station (with considerable aplomb, he felt, getting the Metro straight there with no wrong turns at all), and bought himself a ticket to Barcelona.

Singapore had been an amazing experience. He could say that in retrospect, now that he wasn't there any more. In truth, it had been a little bit full-on, and he had let himself take it at his own pace. Taking it at his own pace turned out to mean breakfast in the hotel, an hour's stroll in the morning, and then back to his room for most of the day with a book or a paper, before an hour's wander again in the early evening, leading up to the big event of the day: dinner.

It would have been all right with someone else to encourage him and chat to him. On his own he was not as intrepid as he had liked to imagine himself, back at home, looking at magazines.

He had looked out for other travellers, but they all seemed to be either in tour groups, stepping on and off their air-conditioned buses, or backpackers, hanging together in gangs. Maybe he should have gone the backpacker route himself, saved some cash, met some buddies. Lots of them were his age and older. He had a vague idea that they were sleeping in flea-infested hovels, sharing bunk beds, eleventy to a room.

As he stood in a queue at Madrid's Atocha station, surrounded by people yelling in Spanish that was so fast that he knew none of his careful memorising of phrases counted for anything, he winced. It was the word 'eleventy' flicking through his mind that did it. His kids used that word. Sarah-Jane thought it was hilarious. Eleventy. It meant lots, and it was a made-up number. That was enough to keep Sarah-J and Aidan in stitches for hours at a time.

'How old are you, Dad? Are you eleventy? Are you eleventy *hundred*?' they would demand.

'Feels that way,' he would usually agree.

And here he was in Spain, as far from his kids as he could possibly have been. He knew no one in this country, no one on this continent. Anita, the nice woman from the plane, was the closest thing he had to a friend, and she was in London, which was apparently hundreds of miles away. She'd given him her number and offered to take him out for a drink if he ever came to London. He might have to buy himself a ticket to Gatwick or Heathrow (he was proud of his new-found knowledge of London's airports), just so he could speak to someone he knew.

Yes, he should have done Singapore like a backpacker. He was twenty-nine, not eleventy-nine. Instead he had shut himself in a bland hotel room and read his Spanish guide yet again. He was glad he was going to be doing his TEFL in Barcelona. It had the best write-up.

He reached the front of the queue.

'*Un boleto para Barcelona, por favor,*' he said slowly, '*a las once, por favor,*' not really able to believe that this would get him the piece of paper he needed. A ticket was passed his way. He handed over some cash and waited to be elated by his success. And waited some more. The travelling lark was not quite the joyous experience he had expected it to be. Perhaps Barcelona would grab him by the scruff of his neck and force him to enjoy himself.

The train was clean, and his reserved seat was next to the window. He settled down with the crisps and chocolate he had bought at the station, put his *Rough Guide* and one of the novels he'd picked up at Christchurch airport, a place he was already thinking of with fond regret, into the pocket of the seat in front of him. He waited. People strode purposefully up and down the train, talking loudly and incomprehensibly. He would just stay here, get through the journey. At some point, he would probably have to get up and locate the toilet facilities, but apart from that, he would sit it out until he got there. Then he would be able to send an email home saying: *I spent a couple of days in Singapore, flew to Madrid and took a train to Barcelona.* It would sound damn good to the folks at home. They would be impressed by him. His mean old dad. Rachel. The kids. All of them would be surprised at how cool and capable he was. None of them ever needed to know that he was cowering away from actually experiencing any of it, surrounding himself with an invisible force field, avoiding eye-contact with anybody. They thought he was brave, and he was the only one in the world who knew how scared he was.

The language school had arranged somewhere for him to stay. That was, he knew, the best bit of luck he'd had yet. As he stepped off the train and fought his way through the station, he held a piece of paper in his hand, and that piece of paper had his new address on it.

He headed for the exit of the station, Barcelona Sants, so he could have a little look around. It was unlikely, really, that he was going to find the apartment, with its strange forward slashes and rows of numbers, right here. Not bang outside the main train station. That would be too much to ask. Still, it was worth checking, just in case.

Five short days ago he was squeezing goodbye to Sarah-Jane, Aidan and little LeEtta, giving Rachel a peck on the cheek and a manly handshake to his bitter old dad. Now he was very tired indeed and all he could think about, in this strange new continent, was sleeping.

There was a girl walking past him, coming into the station as he walked out. He stared at her hard. She was not quite the woman of his imagination: her face was wrong and her hair was too short. All the same, she was closer than a Kiwi girl. She looked casually into his eyes as they passed each other. He smiled and felt a little braver.

Outside the station, it was not at all as he had expected. In the book it was all little alleys with *pintxo* bars (he had been sure to learn the right terminology: it was not called *tapas* here) and old churches. Instead, there were cars everywhere and it was busier and more choked than Christchurch. Lucky he'd been to Singapore on the way, or the crowds might have freaked him out. He stood in the unforgiving sun, on the wide pavement, along with groups of people all waiting for different things, and watched a couple of buses come and go. The cars were nipping all over the place, on the big roads, pretty fast. He hoped his apartment was not around here.

Across a couple of scary roads, he could see a little café. Hitching his backpack onto his shoulders, and reminding himself to look the other way before he crossed, he set off. His mission: to get there without ending up under the wheels of some Spanish Renault or something.

He successfully ordered a *cafe con leche*, and found a table on the pavement away from the shade. He wanted one in the shade, but they were all taken. There were little groups of people all over the place, and lots of them had backpacks like his. He'd been pleased to leave the New Zealand winter and head to the European summer, but now he was thinking a little bit of chilly weather might not go amiss.

With sticky, sweaty fingers, he opened the guide book to the page with the biggest city map he could find, straightened out the piece of paper with his address on it, and looked around for the waiter.

The guy was straight out of *Fawlty Towers*. He was short and a bit bald, with a moustache and a jaded manner.

'Er,' said Jack, with his best smile. '*Desculpe. Donde esta . . .*'

He handed the man the piece of paper and gestured at the map. The man took it with a swift gesture, nodded, then grabbed the book. He looked at the page for a while, then turned to another one. With his ordering pen, he marked a little cross, and handed it back.

'Metro Arc de Triomf,' he said, circling the little M on the map. Although he did not smile, Jack was phenomenally grateful. He paid for his coffee, and left the same amount again as a tip. That was why he had saved for six extra months: so he wouldn't have to scrape by on the money his mother had left him. So he could do friendly things like that for people who helped him out.

The Metro freaked him out all over again, but when he found the right line, the green one, and got on a train, he felt a bit better. He stood next to his backpack, swaying along with the motion of the carriage, feeling like a real traveller. Just another guy on the Barcelona Metro. When he realised he was travelling in the wrong direction, when the first station he reached was Plaça del Centre when it ought to have been Tarragona, he even managed to grab his bag, leap off, and change direction before any harm was done. He had to change Metro lines at Espanya, which he accomplished, he felt, with a certain nonchalance. Before he knew it, he was walking up the steps at Arc de Triomf, past a load of roadworks and standing, map in hand, wondering which way to go from here.

He found it in the end, with help from three separate passers-by. His apartment was in one of the real European apartment blocks, on the fourth floor with no lift. He pressed the buzzer for flat six, and when a woman said something, he said, '*Hola, soy Jack*.' A hoarse buzzer sounded, and he pushed the front door.

The hallway was dark and dusty and beautifully cool.

The floor was covered in cracked grey tiles, and a stone staircase led upwards. Ignoring the closed doors on either side of him, he set off upwards, in search of flat six.

He was in.

chapter eighteen

Saturday

I was sitting in the beach café, wearing a pretty flowery dress and ballet shoes, and my hair was clipped up with hairpins, exactly as Grandma's used to be, though with more strands escaping than she would ever have allowed.

I stared out of the window, at the tiny waves lapping lazily at the shore. Harry was opposite me, preoccupied. This happened from time to time. He was still affected by what had happened to Sarah, and every now and then he would tune out from real life for a few minutes. He had explained to me that he needed head space, sometimes, and I was happy to give it to him.

'Nothing to do with you,' he reassured me. 'At least, only in a good way. It takes me by surprise, occasionally, the way everything has changed this year.'

I watched him thinking. He was cupping his coffee cup in both hands, and it was a touching, childish gesture.

I was scared of my own happiness. If and when this

ended, I had no idea what I would do with myself. The very idea made my breath come in panicky gasps which I quelled with an effort.

'Lily,' he suddenly said, and I saw that he was looking at me, while I had still been staring at his hands.

'Yes?' I said, with a smile. I was always nice with him, always eager to do what he wanted, because he made me so happy.

'You know something? I've got a car in the garage out the back, and I never drive it. Let's trade it in for something fun.' He was grinning like Tommy, a little boy thinking about his toys.

'OK,' I agreed. 'Today, you mean?'

'Today, I do mean. We can drive it into Truro and see what we can do. The sun is shining, the sea is sparkling, and the most beautiful girl in the world is sitting opposite me. I think we need something small and sporty. What do you reckon?'

'Um, I know nothing about cars. That sounds lovely, but you know, I'd be happy with anything.'

'I know you would, my darling. But I'm in the mood for some fun.'

We drove into Truro in his old car, which still looked new to me, and he was soon deep in conversation about 'part ex-ing it' with a man at a garage. I could tell that his enthusiasm was unusual, from the man's reaction. The man, dark-haired with a thick moustache, looked very much like someone who could not believe his luck.

'What's grabbed your fancy?' he said. He looked at me and smirked a little.

Harry followed his gaze. 'Something fun,' he repeated firmly. 'Two-seater. Can we test drive that MR2?'

We test drove the MR2, but Harry declared that he needed more luggage space, and we moved on to another dealership, and then another. By the middle of the afternoon, we were on the road back to Falmouth in a nearly-new red BMW. The old car was left behind, and Harry had paid an eye-watering amount of money on his credit card for the balance.

We drove home with the roof off, my hair streaming back in the wind. It was too noisy for conversation, but we held hands whenever Harry's left hand was not needed for the gears. I cringed at the way everyone looked at us as we passed them, because I had never imagined that I would be a person in a show-off car, and it was hard to sit there and try not to imagine what they were saying about us. I tried not to mind. I tried to say, 'Let them stare.'

Harry grinned all the way home, and squeezed my hand whenever he could. I could see that he loved the attention the new car got us. The interior was walnut-effect wood, and the seats were white leather. It was a car from Hollywood.

He reversed it quickly into a space outside the house, and turned to kiss me.

'I'll keep it in the garage really,' he said, 'but for today, I want to leave it where I can see it through the window.'

'And where the neighbours can see it,' I suggested.

'They all think I'm having a midlife crisis anyway. Might as well provide the wheels to confirm it.'

We worked together to secure the top of the car, fastening it down.

'I should probably be going,' I said. I had told Mia I

would be home tonight, and I thought I would offer to cook dinner.

Harry took me by the shoulders and turned me around to face him. I loved it when he did that. We were standing on the pavement, in the shade of the tree in his front garden. Dappled light fell on us.

'Lily,' he said, his voice so low and gentle that I had to concentrate even to hear him properly. 'Lily. Will you stay here? Stay with me tonight?'

I took a little step back. 'Stay with you?'

He knew about my absolute lack of experience. I wanted to stay with him, to sleep with him; but the idea of sex felt like a horrible and embarrassing hurdle. 'I don't know if I'm . . .' My voice tailed off. *Ready* was what I had been going to say. But I was ready – I was just terrified. 'I would have no idea what to do,' I said quickly. 'I'd be terrible.'

He laughed. 'Believe me, you would not. If you don't feel ready, that's fine. The last thing I want to do is to pressure you. But I just . . .' He took my hand and played with my fingers, pushing each one up and down in turn. 'I just have a feeling that you're letting it be a huge barrier in your mind, and it doesn't need to be. I promise you, you'll enjoy it, and once you've discovered that you enjoy it, there'll be a whole new horizon open to you. But like I said, the last thing I want to do is to make things difficult for you. If you want to go more slowly, come and spend the night with me with no funny business whatsoever.'

I smiled at him.

'Oh, Harry,' I said. 'Thank you. Could we sleep in the attic room? I'd feel a bit weird . . .'

'Of course we can,' he said.

'I'll need to call Mia and rearrange things.'

'She sounds like a girl who'd understand.'

When I woke the next morning, it was half-past ten. Birds were singing outside the window and the room was bathed in sunlight, because the curtains were white and flimsy. I was alone in the attic room.

I closed my eyes again. That had been a momentous night for me. We had started off taking it slowly. We had ended up not taking it slowly at all. I grinned. I was no longer a virgin. I loved Harry completely. It had all been far better than I had hoped for.

I heard his footsteps coming up the little flight of stairs. There was a muttered 'Bugger!' as he hit his head on the low beam. Then he was in the doorway.

I sat up in bed, holding the duvet close, newly shy. He was carrying a tray which had a bunch of red roses on it, a full cafetière of coffee, two mugs, a plate of toast and a newspaper.

'Good morning, my darling,' he said, smiling broadly. He had been out, and he was dressed in a pair of blue sailing shorts and a blue and white striped T-shirt.

'Hello,' I said, and our eyes met and I tingled all over. 'You look like a sailor.'

'You look like a mermaid. I'm glad you're not.'

'Me too.'

He sat on the bed. 'How are you doing this morning?'

'I'm doing great.'

'You're sure?'

'Completely sure. Harry? Thank you.'

'Thank *you*. You have no idea how honoured I am.'

I smiled at him. I would smile at everything today. I felt I had conquered Everest. If my parents were here, I would smile at them and thank them for leaving me, because by doing that they put in motion the chain of events that had led me here. I loved everyone and everything.

'What would you like to do today?' he asked. 'Take the new motor for a run? Or stay at home?'

'I wouldn't actually mind,' I said, 'staying right here, all day long.'

chapter nineteen

The following weekend, Al and I got off a bus at a stop on the dual carriageway that led to Truro, and walked down small roads until we reached the King Harry Ferry. It was an old-fashioned chain ferry, and I loved it at first sight. I loved it that the cars were queueing all down the road, while we walked past them straight to the front of the queue. I loved the bench with a realistic sculpture of a man sitting on it.

'Look,' I said, pointing.

Al, who seemed preoccupied and looked haggard, nodded.

'Mmm,' he said. 'He's cool.'

'What's wrong? Is it Boris?'

He sighed. 'Can we not say that word, please?'

'Oh. Did he—'

Al turned on me. 'I said, let's not talk about it! Of course he did. Now let's talk about something else. I cannot go there.'

We walked onto the ferry before the cars were allowed on. It was completely open, like a bit of road that clanked across the wide river. The sky was filling with clouds. We climbed up a set of metal steps and stood on the cast-iron balcony. There was a sculpted sea captain up there, lifesize and lifelike. We leaned on the railing and looked at the huge ships. They were moored here, incongruous in the picturesque scenery. There were three of them, chained together, higher than a tall building, looking sad and forlorn as they overshadowed the trees and the tiny boats around them. They were massive ocean-going liners, in a completely bucolic setting.

'Wow,' Al said, perking up briefly. 'They are something. Wonder where they're from?'

I gazed at them as we clanked across the river. Wherever they had come from, it was thousands of miles away. I had never been anywhere and suddenly, unexpectedly, I felt a pang of longing. I wanted an adventure. I had never wanted anything like that before.

I looked at Al. I thought I saw the same thing on his face: some sort of longing.

'You want to get away, don't you?' I said.

He carried on staring straight ahead. 'If I don't get away from here, I'm going to lose it. I keep going to Truro, and hanging around outside the lovely family home where Boris lives with his darling wife and their perfect nuclear family. I just watch them. It feels like the only thing in the world I can do. She called the police on me the other day. I have to get out.'

'What did the police say?'

'Nothing, because Boris came out and told me to scarper before they got here. And I came home feeling like I'd won, somehow, because he'd spoken to me.' He sighed. 'I used to love living here. Never imagined I'd go anywhere else. I ended up in Cornwall because it was the end of the line. That's what all the crazies do. We get on a train because Cornwall sounds like a cool place to go, and then we get off in Penzance and see where we end up. I made it to Falmouth because I wasn't like the rest of the nutters. I was doing all right. Then this shit happens with Boris and . . . Lily, it scares me. I can look at it when I'm with you and see my behaviour is irrational. But I can't stop doing it.'

Neither of us said anything.

'There's a wide world out there,' he added, after a few minutes, 'and it's not all about me. I could go to Africa or something, you know. Do some good in the world.'

I took a deep breath of salty air. 'I'd miss you.'

'Oh, you're fine. You've got Lover Boy now. Marry him, have a kid, divorce him and get rich.'

'Al!' I stared at him.

'Sorry. It's what I'd do if I were you.'

'No, it's not. It's not at all. I know how you feel about Boris, Al. I do, because I feel the same about Harry. So don't say rubbish like that to me. Please?'

He shook his head and looked at me properly.

'No. Sorry, Lily. I'm talking crap because – well, because it's hard not to be cynical about marriage, right now.' The ferry clattered to a halt. 'Ignore me.'

'Well, I'm not marrying for money,' I said forcefully. 'I'm going to have a career, you know. I followed your advice. Got myself on a one-year access course. Starting in September, at Truro College.'

He smiled at that. 'Good girl.'

Although there were a few drops of rain in the air, we

sat at a table outside. I had scraped some cash together, and the fact that Al didn't drink alcohol made a trip to the pub a much cheaper prospect.

'Lemonade?' I stood up, ready to go into the bar.

Al twitched. 'Mmm. Actually . . .' He bit his lip. 'Yeah, OK, lemonade. Oh, sod it. Let me buy them.'

Despite my protests, he made me sit down. While he was at the bar, I picked up a local paper that had been abandoned on the next table, and started to flick through it. It seemed to be mainly about council meetings and the possible resiting of the Post Office, with an update about the man who had been knocked down at Christmas and was still in a coma. He had come back into the news lately because of a potential new witness, but he did not seem to be getting any better.

I turned the page and saw a huge photograph of Tommy, wearing a wetsuit, standing on the beach with a group of other children. The smile spread across my face as I read the headline: *Falmouth Children Win Council Award*. I tried to imagine how chuffed Tommy must be with his appearance in the media. He and his surf club friends had won a prize, I read, for collecting litter from the streets. I vowed to go there later in the afternoon and congratulate him.

Al came back, with two glasses of lemonade and a bag of crisps. He handed me the one with a slice of lemon in it.

'Cheers,' he said. He took a huge gulp of his drink and smiled. 'Ah,' he said. 'That's better.'

I smiled back at him. Then I reached for the paper and tore out the piece about Tommy. I wanted to hang onto that for ever.

chapter twenty

August

My new job was both easier and more boring than the old one. I had given up all my cleaning jobs, and Harry had found me four weeks' work at a solicitor's office in Truro, covering various of their admin people's holidays.

'There are prospects with this sort of work,' he had explained, stroking my face. 'It gives you an insight into working life, and it looks good on your CV, your university application, whatever. No one ever offered anyone anything on the basis that they were a good cleaner. Harsh but true. Apart from cleaning work, maybe.'

And so I was here, tackling piles of routine, easy work, and even though I had never done anything like it before, had never even been inside an office, I found it completely straightforward, and I did a lot of daydreaming. But I found I missed my insights into other people's houses, and try as I might I could not get my head around the minutiae of office politics. Banter, while less terrifying an idea than it had been a year ago, would never be my forte, and I got on with my tasks quietly, only speaking when it was utterly essential.

This afternoon, I put the last document into its file and felt a disproportionate sense of satisfaction. That pile had been 43 centimetres high when I arrived: I had secretly measured it. Now it had gone.

I tidied the last things on the desk, picked up three coffee mugs from around the room and took them into the kitchen. Margaret was in there, spooning instant coffee into four cups. The fact that actual lawyers could drink instant coffee astonished me.

'I'm off,' I told her. 'The filing's all done.'

She took the milk out of the fridge. I liked Margaret. She had staring eyes and windswept hair, and she noticed everything.

'*All* the filing?' she said. 'You tackled that pile and got to the bottom of it?'

'I did. I'll see you in the morning.'

'Lily, that paperwork has been sitting there for months – if not years. And look at you – you're only supposed to stay until four.'

I looked at the clock on the wall. It was twenty past five.

'I wanted to get it done,' I admitted. 'There's something satisfying about imposing order on chaos, don't you think? It's like Rumpelstiltskin, spinning straw into lovely tidy gold. I couldn't walk out of here leaving even a bit of a pile, because people would have started to put things on it again. Now it doesn't exist, so they can't.'

She laughed. 'What can I say? Harry was right. We all

wondered at his motivation, but you're good. Thank you, my dear.'

I walked quickly to the station. As I walked, I ran a commentary in my head, savouring every moment.

'I'm leaving work,' I said to myself. 'Walking out of the office. Saying goodbye to the people who are still here. I've done the filing. I'm only paid to stay till four but I stayed late. I'm out of the office, walking down the street. Just another admin worker on her way to the station.' I loved it, relished every moment of my working life. I was four days into my job, with a firm of solicitors called Harris & Riddick, and I never wanted it to end. I was earning reasonable money, and I was learning lots about the law, which meant I had plenty to ask Harry, in the evenings. I skimmed over the documents that I was filing, and I knew that there was a world in there, a dense and complicated world, and that it was fascinating. If I ever became a lawyer (as I sometimes did, in my daydreams), I would thoroughly enjoy spending my working life disentangling problems for people.

I was starting my course in three weeks. That was the first step towards my future. I was scared at the idea of going back into a classroom, but it was exciting too. Options were opening up for me.

On Tuesdays I had to leave the office exactly on time, because I collected Tommy from holiday club for Julia, but on other days I was free to work late, to meander around Truro and then tackle the hill to the station when I wanted to.

There was a crowd on platform one. This was a

rush-hour train, in holiday season, and there was only one carriage. It arrived, and people spilled off it, expanding to cover the whole platform, and walked away.

I was squashed against all sorts of people, in the middle of the carriage, looking down at the people who had managed to bag seats.

'The thing with living in Cornwall, in the summer,' said a man, and I thought he was speaking to me until I noticed a very short woman under his arm, 'is that it turns into, I don't know, London or something. The tube doesn't get much worse than this, does it?'

I looked around. It was easy to tell the holiday people from the working people. I was a working person.

'The tube?' squeaked the woman. 'It's way worse. You have to stand for forty-five minutes with your face pressed into some bloke's armpit. I mean, I'm pressed into *your* armpit, not a stranger's, and that's luxury. Almost a pleasure.'

They laughed. Harry had said he would take me to stay with his mum and Fergus one of these days. I was nervous about it, but excited too. I wanted to go to London, to try out the tube for myself, to ride on the London Eye and take a boat down the Thames, and go to the Globe Theatre and the National Gallery and the British Library. There were, it was beginning to seem, thousands of things I wanted to do.

I got off the train at Falmouth Town, along with a lot of other people. I heard my new phone beep with a text as we were walking, en masse, down the slope, but I could not look at it until we were out of the crowds. I hung back and took it out of my bag.

It was from Al. I tried not to feel disappointed. *can I cu2nite?* he wrote. I had been amazed, when I started using the mobile phone, at the way people actually used the phenomenon of 'textspeak'. It grated on me so much that I could hardly look at it. I imagined Grandma's reaction to such a travesty.

'But Lily, those are not words!' she would have said.

'The language of Shakespeare and Chaucer,' Granddad added, in my head. 'Massacred! Yes, language evolves, but this is beyond the pale!'

Busy tonight, I wrote, carefully spelling out each word. *How about tomorrow?*

Am off tomoz he replied, as I turned left onto the wide avenue. *need to CU 2nite. just 2say by?*

You're actually leaving? I wrote. *Of course you must say bye and tell me your plans. Going to Gylly cafe with Harry at 8.30. Come and say hello, and bye.*

Gr8!

I walked back to Harry's house, quickly. I had not slept in my little Barbie bed for longer than I would admit, even to myself. We had pretty much moved into the attic bedroom. I remembered so clearly how I had play-acted being the lady of the house, when I used to clean it. Now it was real.

Harry wanted to use the main bedroom: he said he was camping out, that it was ridiculous to move around the spare rooms as he had done. However, I could not bear the idea of sleeping in their bed. It felt too weird: I still sensed Sarah's presence, and I knew that if I tried to sleep with her husband in her bed, I would lie awake imagining her whispering malevolent things into my ears. The more details Harry let slip, the more I realised that Sarah had been completely different from the lovely woman I had met. Even though she was dead, I was rather scared of her.

The set of keys I had as a cleaner had now become the set of keys of someone who almost lived here. I cleaned and tidied, whiling away the time until I was due to call at Harry's office and pick him up. Although I was no longer the cleaner, no one else was either, so I tried to keep the house the way it used to look. It was not difficult because we went out so much.

As I was leaving the house at half-past seven, I met a woman standing on the pavement with a baby in a sling. She was jiggling around, patting the baby's head and saying, 'Shhh.' I recognised her and, feeling brave, I smiled. She had long black hair and she looked nice.

'Oh,' she said. 'Hello. You're Harry's friend.'

'Yes,' I said. She had been at the drinks party, heavily pregnant. I had forgotten her name. 'I'm Lily,' I said, deciding not to remind her that I had served her champagne and canapés. I knew she had been one of Sarah's friends: that would have been the last time she saw her.

'Constanza. And this is baby Daniel.'

I went over and peered at him. His face was screwed up, and he was making little dissatisfied noises.

'He's gorgeous,' I said, and I touched his black hair. 'How old is he?'

'Coming up for seven months. Quite the big boy now.'

'Hello, Daniel.'

We stood around for a few seconds, not quite knowing what to say.

'Well, I'd better go,' I said, just as she opened her mouth to say something. 'Oh, sorry, what were you going to say?'

'Nothing,' she said. 'Nice to see you again, Lily. I'm sure I'll see you around.'

The sun was shining brightly, the shadows lengthening. The town was painted with gold. I walked slowly, because I did not want to arrive at Harry's office covered in sweat. The sea was in the air, and leaves were swaying resentfully in the most sluggish of breezes. I passed a family looking up the hill, out of town. 'If it wasn't so bloody hot . . .' said the woman.

As we walked towards Gylly Beach together, he did not quite take my hand, but he kept brushing against me. Our fingers would meet, as if accidentally, then fall apart.

'I met Constanza just now,' I said, as we strolled. I looked at him. He was wearing a white shirt with his sleeves rolled up, and he had taken off his tie. I loved his muscular arms under rolled-up sleeves.

'Oh, did you?' he said, half-smiling down at me. 'And what did she say?'

'"Hello". We talked about her baby. She was sizing me up, in a bit of a knowing way, I thought.'

'Oh, let her. She's all right, Constanza. She was a good friend of Sarah's, but I'm sure she'll be all right with you. Watch out for her husband, Seumas. He's a shit.'

'Why?'

'Just trust me on this one.'

It was so hot that the blobs of tarmac on the road were melting into sticky black pools. A few seagulls flew low overhead, made cocky by the abundance of outdoor eating in town, made energetic by the amount of scavenging they had managed to do.

Harry took my hand and pulled me so I was walking closer to him. The sun was bright and his complexion was golden.

'Are you sure?' I asked, nodding down at our linked fingers.

'Yes,' he said. 'I am bloody sure. You know, Lily, I am not seeing us – you and me – as a short-term fling. Not a rebound thing. Does that sound all right?'

'Yes,' I said, fighting myself to stay level-headed. 'It sounds just fine.'

He smiled and brought my hand up to his lips. 'I can't believe a sexy young thing like you would give a miserable old widower the time of day.'

'Well yes, that's true, it is a bit of an effort for me. You are pretty boring.'

His fingers squeezed mine, and when I followed his gaze, I understood why. Belinda, the woman I had met at his party, the skinny one with the helmet hair, was walking towards us on the other side of the road. I tried to pull my hand away, but he held it too tightly.

Her hair was styled into a solid mass again. Her face was matte with make-up, layer upon layer of it. Her body was unnaturally thin, and she was dressed in a knee-length cotton dress and a tiny cardigan. I immediately felt gauche.

'Oh, Harry!' she called across the road, and Harry stopped walking, so I did, too. He did not release his hold on my fingers at all, but waved to her with his other hand. She crossed over to us, her eyes glittering.

'Well, hello Harry,' she said, raising her eyebrows in my direction.

'Hello, Bel,' he said lightly, and kissed her cheek. 'This is Lily, a very good friend of mine.'

I stood there as she coolly looked me up and down.

'Hello, Lily,' she said, extending the tips of her fingers. I shook her hand, feeling stupid. Her handshake was insubstantial: it was like shaking a butterfly.

'Hello,' I said back. Harry put his arm around my shoulders.

'Well, you look happy,' she said to him.

'Yes,' he said, with a wide smile. 'You know what they say: just when you're not looking, along it comes.'

'Mmm.' She examined me again, and frowned slightly. 'Going somewhere nice?'

'To the beach,' Harry told her. 'For some food. There's a band on at the café. You remember, Bel – the kind of thing young people do on a summer's evening?'

'Oh, you're a young person again now, are you? Super. Well, good luck to you. Both of you.'

I smiled at her, mainly with relief, and we carried on walking.

'Wow,' I said, as soon as she had gone. 'She didn't like *that*. Constanza was much nicer.'

Harry was delighted. 'That's because Constanza *is* much nicer. Now the grapevine will go into overdrive. She didn't recognise you – that's good. You'll just be some young lovely in her eyes. It's better than her going round saying I'm shagging the cleaner.'

'I'd much rather be a young lovely.'

'You could see it in her eyes, couldn't you? It was "I

own a piece of information! And I'm *telling*!" Stupid old bat. Ridiculous bitch.'

I took his arm again. I knew how hard this was for him.

'Thanks for doing that,' I told him, and he looked into my eyes, and nodded.

The café was busy. I had never even been in there before this summer, but now we went often, because Harry liked how happy it made me, the first time. It had become our place.

I was regretting having told Al he could come along. All the same, I could not just let him vanish. I needed to make sure he was all right. He had done the same for me.

There was a long queue at the bar.

'Shall I grab that table?' I nodded to where two people were getting up and leaving a little table beside the open glass doors. He nodded, and I pushed my way past a few other people with the same idea, and put my bag on it. I caught the eye of the student-looking man who was just behind me, and smiled triumphantly. He narrowed his eyes and swore at me under his breath.

When Harry arrived, with a bottle of wine in a metal cooler gripped between his left arm and his body, and two glasses and a menu in his right hand, I looked up and vowed that I would do whatever it took to hang on to him.

'What was your school like?' I asked, as he poured the wine.

He looked up, surprised. 'My school? Why?'

'Because I want to know all about you.'

He smiled and poured the wine. 'OK. School. It wasn't

fun. I went away at eleven. I hated it, to be honest. I'm two years older than Fergus, so I was shipped away while he got to stay at home with Mother. That was how I saw it, at that age. She wanted *me* out of the house but she let *him* stay. Of course, I settled in, and during the holidays I lorded it over him, and when he came to school two years later, I was delighted to see him snivelling around the place.'

'You went to boarding school?'

'Oh, yes. Didn't I say?'

'Seriously? That still happens?'

'Well, we're going back more years than I'd like to remember, but yes, of course it does. Still supposed to be character-forming. Only in a certain sector of society, of course. The monied classes get to neglect their children. And the schools today, apparently, are a million miles away from what they used to be, depending on where you go. Eton, for instance, gives a fantastic all-round education. Lily?'

I frowned. 'What?'

'Please would you stop looking at me like that?'

'Like what?'

'Like a gun-toting revolutionary Communist confronted with a member of the bourgeoisie?'

I shook myself and rearranged my features. 'Sorry,' I told him. 'It's just – Eton? I thought you'd say you'd been to private school, but . . .'

He made a sad face. 'Am I too posh?'

'Don't be silly. I'm just, I suppose, very aware that although my family were as middle-class as anything, I've only got a clutch of GCSEs to my name, and no A levels at all. I'm feeling excited about starting a pathetic little access course. Talk of Eton makes me feel a bit inadequate.'

'Don't be ridiculous. You nursed two old people until they died.'

'Which doesn't make me sound like much of a nurse.'

'Admittedly not, but you know what I mean. You're stronger than anyone I've ever met. And I was handed an education on a plate, I realise that. You couldn't go to my school and not come out with good grades. But I suppose boarding school brings an entirely different set of problems, all of its own.'

'Oh, I'm sure it does. No child of mine would ever be packed away to school.'

'I'll tell you what,' he said, in the calmest of voices. 'I propose a compromise. Let's pick the happy medium, between expensive neglect and lack of opportunity. We'll take the middle option and send our children to private day school.'

I tried to keep my demeanour as casual as his.

'They'll have to go to Truro then,' I said. 'That's where the posh schools are, isn't it?'

'We'll get you a little car. You can drop them off.'

'Unfortunately,' I said, breathing deeply, staying determinedly unruffled, 'I can't drive.'

He laughed. 'You can't drive?'

'We had an old Mini but I never learned to drive it. By the time I was old enough I was a full-time nursemaid.'

'Of course you were. Everyone needs to be able to drive. We'll get you some lessons. I'll ask around. I think there's a woman with a driving school somewhere about. You'd probably be more comfortable with that?'

'Sure.' I tried to imagine myself, driving. Changing gears, steering round corners.

'While we're on that subject,' Harry said, 'you know what I hate?'

'No, I don't. What do you hate?'

'I hate men who can't drive.' He looked suddenly animated. 'I hate a man who declares: "Oh, I don't drive," because they all say "don't" instead of "can't", as if it's a choice and not a failing. In the modern world, driving is a vital skill, especially for a man. Those men who pretend to be all lofty and "not drive" are pathetic, effeminate nancies.'

'Wow,' I said. 'You really *do* hate them.'

He looked rueful. 'Sorry. It's one of my bugbears.'

'Clearly.'

'Now you think I'm homophobic too. And you have a gay best friend.'

'I don't think you're homophobic. "Pathetic, effeminate nancies" is a fine turn of phrase.'

'Like this guy, for instance,' Harry whispered.

I looked up, and there was Al, heading towards the table. Many pairs of eyes were following him, and he did look more striking than usual. He was wearing a pair of tight shorts and a vest. This was the first time I had seen him in anything other than sober, ordinary clothes. His eye was twitching visibly.

I looked quickly at Harry.

'Al!' I said. 'Harry, this is the very friend we were just talking about. Al, this is Harry. Al, you look different.'

Harry laughed and stood up, and I wondered whether I ought to leap to my feet as well, but decided that I would just look stupid if I did. I watched as he shook Al's hand. I watched Al checking him out.

'Nice to meet you, Al,' Harry said, in his formal voice. I looked at both of them. Al was so different from the sensible man I had met last year. He was like a different person. 'Would you care to join us for a drink?' he continued. 'I'll go and fetch another glass.'

'Al doesn't drink alcohol,' I said quickly.

'Oh, one glass will be fine,' Al said, just as hastily. He took a chair from a neighbouring table without asking, and sat down. The moment Harry was out of earshot, he leaned across to me and said: 'He's better-looking in real life.'

'He's lovely, isn't he?'

'If you hadn't got in there first, I'd have had him myself. A touch of the Nigel Havers. I love a posh bloke.'

'Al,' I said quickly, 'what's going on? Where are you going? And what are you dressed like that for?'

'Like I said before. Time to move on. Reinvent myself. Boris is busy playing the happy hetero, so I thought I'd go to the other extreme. That way, things get balanced out.' He leaned back in his seat and looked at the ceiling. 'Boris and his wife got an injunction against me,' he said quietly. 'So it's time to get the fuck out of here.'

'What did you do?'

He shrugged. 'I may have turned up at their house a few times too many. You know that. But so what? They're the ones living a bloody lie, not me.'

'Oh, Al.'

He smiled, which was clearly an effort. 'So,' he said. 'I've met someone online. He lives in Scotland. I'm heading up there. Trying my luck. Got to be worth a go, and tearing myself away from Truro can only be a good thing. Putting hundreds of miles between us, before I do something properly crazy.'

'Are you sure? Is it safe, meeting people online?'

'Lily Bellybutton. I can look after myself, believe me.'

'You shouldn't be drinking.'

'I'm fine. New start, clean slate. The odd drink is OK. Can't go to Scotland, of all places, without being able to put away the odd drink. I've given up work. Taken my own advice about benefits.'

'Will you be all right? Stay in touch.'

'I've got my phone. Only a text away. Or a call. Any time you like.'

Harry poured Al a glass of wine and handed it to him. Al thanked him politely. We all took a sip, and a difficult silence descended.

'Harry,' I said, in a false voice that I did not like at all, 'Al's going away tonight. To live in Scotland.'

'Ah. Scotland. Always liked it. Edinburgh or Glasgow? Though I gather there are other parts to that fine country too.'

'Glasgow,' Al said. He knocked back the contents of his glass and stood up. 'In fact, I'm off now. Don't want to screw up your nice evening. Bye then, lovebirds. Lily, don't forget me, will you? I might be back. You never know. Might not be able to keep away.'

His sudden exit took me by surprise. I stood up and kissed his cheek, and he was gone.

* * *

When we got back to Harry's house, much later, we were both a bit drunk. We were almost always a bit drunk. Harry opened the door and blinked hard, focusing his mind so that he would be able to turn off the alarm successfully.

'Do those numbers mean anything?' I asked him. '81181825?'

He laughed. 'Do you know what? You'll think I'm an egotistical freak. It's my name, translated into numbers. H is the eighth letter of the alphabet. A the first. Two Rs: eighteen, eighteen. Then a Y. Does that make you hate me?'

When the beeping stopped, I crossed the threshold too.

I laughed. 'I wish you'd told me that before. I'd have found it much easier to remember.'

'Gorgeous girl!' he exclaimed, and he pulled me inside. He kicked the door, and it closed with a bang. 'You are adorable, you know. You'll be all right without your friend Al in town.'

I stepped back.

'I know I will. It's him I'm worried about.' I took the key from Harry's hand, and double-locked us into the house. 'Really worried. I think I should go after him, before he gets on the train, and check on him. He should not have been drinking.'

'Well,' said Harry, and he was smiling at me so tenderly that I hardly listened to what he was saying. 'He's an adult. Honestly, I've been around a lot of years, and I can see that he's someone who can look after himself. You're not his mum and he wouldn't thank you for running after him.

Keep in touch, be at the end of a phone, but don't tie yourself up in knots.'

I was about to point out that I owed Al a huge amount, but then Harry leaned down and kissed me.

'How about a nightcap?' he asked.

'OK.'

'A glass of your special sherry?'

'Thank you.'

I was shocked at how quickly I had got used to Harry's lifestyle. I accepted expensive drinks without a second thought. My wide-eyed excitement at going to restaurants and bars was already beginning to fade. I had always assumed that if I were able to afford that sort of lifestyle, I would be constantly entirely happy, but I was beginning to realise just how quickly luxury became normal.

I followed him into the kitchen, and while he fixed the drinks, I pulled myself up onto the worktop, swinging my legs, watching.

He frowned with concentration as he poured the drinks, and I thought how much I liked the small wrinkles and lines on his face. They showed that he had lived – that, unlike me, he had experienced life, and this was reassuring.

He noticed me sitting there and, as I had known he would, he immediately put down the bottle and walked over to me. He pulled my hips to the edge of the worktop and kissed me again. I put my arms around his shoulders.

This was the strangest thing: the physical compatibility. I had never imagined I could feel like this about anyone, but with Harry it was perfect.

'I used to have such a crush on you,' I told him, nuzzling his neck.

'Used to?' he echoed, pretending to be hurt.

'Well, it's not a "crush" any more, is it?' I murmured. 'A crush is something that happens from a distance, that's unreciprocated. When I spoke to you I'd get all jittery and scared and I went bright red, I know I did.'

He laughed and stepped away, looking extremely pleased.

'Well, I must admit,' he said, handing me a glass of sherry, 'I thought beetroot was your natural colour.'

'But you were married, and you were happy, and I knew . . .'

Harry took me by the shoulders, suddenly serious.

'Lily,' he said quietly, in a tone I had never heard him use before, 'there is so much you don't know about my marriage. We made an effort to show the world that we were perfect and happy. That was our "thing". The shared goal that probably kept us together. But the things that went on behind closed doors . . . It's easy, with hindsight, to see that Sarah was unbalanced. Obviously she was. And, looking back on it, it got worse year by year. I would tiptoe around. You must have noticed how much crockery we got through, when you were cleaning the house. Plates and cups smashed all the time. It's – it's hard to get over how different life is, now.'

'It didn't look that way.'

'Of course it didn't. She was a spectacular actress. Another thing: I always wanted children. She didn't. I used to hope she'd leave me. I tried to leave, myself, more than once. But she threatened to . . . well, to do the very thing that she did, in the end, do. It was no idle threat and I knew that. But Lily: something happened in Barcelona that

I never thought I was going to tell anybody. The missing part of the jigsaw. In Barcelona, I told her I was leaving her. And I actually meant it, and she knew that I did.'

He picked up his glass of sherry, knocked it back, and winced.

'That Christmas party was the last straw,' he continued, one hand on my waist. 'Things had been bad for years, but when we were there, acting the gracious hosts, I looked at you, so sweet, so genuine, and then at her, and I thought, What the hell am I doing here? And I knew it was time to get out.'

'You were leaving her . . . ?'

'I wasn't leaving her *for you*. But I was leaving her because you made me realise that there were other women out there. You made me suspect that I could have a different life. And I started thinking about what it would be like not to be tiptoeing around, second guessing someone . . .'

'She actually killed herself. Because of me.'

'No. She killed herself because of me. Because of herself. That's the only reason there is, isn't it?'

Nothing was quite the way it seemed. I had played a role in Sarah's death. The knowledge made me shiver violently. No wonder I felt her angry presence all over the house. I looked at the glasses on the side, expecting them to be dashed to the floor there and then.

'Move in with me, Lily,' he said suddenly. 'It's been messy, but we're left with the best thing that's ever happened to either of us. Please, darling, don't dwell on what I just told you. I only told you because I didn't want there to be secrets. It's stupid that you pay for your room in that house and you never go there. Give them notice. We'll go over this weekend and pack all your stuff into the car. We may not have a lot of boot space, but I'm ready to hazard a guess that there's not much to go in there anyway. I love you, Lily Button. Move in with me. Grow old with me. Have my children.'

I started to cry. As I looked at him, my vision blurry, I realised that there were tears in his eyes too. We held tightly to each other and sobbed.

'Of course I'll move in,' I told him. 'Of course I'll do all those other things. Of course. Of course.'

chapter twenty-one

Barcelona

Jack was being observed giving a private lesson this morning. There were going to be three of them in the room: Patrick, his tutor, and this woman, whose name was Camila. She had been assessed as at 'lower intermediate' level, which meant she should already be able to chat a bit and use past and future tense as well as present.

His stomach was in knots as he waited for her. Perhaps this woman was going to be The One. One of these days she was going to walk into his classroom. He had a feeling it was going to be today.

He sat on the edge of a Formica desk, because he thought he might look good that way, if he was being informal. He ran his fingers through his thick blond hair, then patted it down again, because he seemed to have stood it up on end as though electrocuted.

He had been amazed to find that, as soon as he had opened up a bit and stopped being scared of his shadow, he was fending women off with a stick. He got a weird amount of attention and he could only assume he stood out for not being dark like the Spanish men. It was a bit embarrassing sometimes. One thing was for sure, though: he was a married man, and although his marriage vows were not worth the paper they were written on, or the air they had been spoken into, he was not going to break them until he met The One.

Sometimes they were nearly The One. He would think he spotted her on the street, and he would walk fast, dodge through crowds to catch up with her, ready for a 'how I met the love of my life' moment, but it was never quite right. He would get there, and catch her profile, and her nose would be wrong, or her mouth, or there would be something about her that was nearly right, but not quite.

Maybe today was the day. He bit his lip as the door creaked open.

Patrick and Camila came in together. Patrick was a laid-back bilingual expat, dressed today for the beach. Camila was small, with short grey hair, and although he could see she was a fine-looking woman, she had to be a quarter of a century older than he was. He grinned at her anyway.

'Good morning,' he said clearly. 'How are you?'

'Very fine,' she said. 'How are you?'

Jack shared the apartment with three other TEFL students. There were Alex and Kayla, the American girls, and Peter, the English guy. They all rubbed along together pretty well, now that Jack had settled in and let his guard down.

Mostly, he was having the time of his life. Sometimes, he wasn't. That was when he borrowed Alex's laptop and called the kids on Skype. He would tell them about Spain ('there are so many people, guys, all crammed in. Every single building I've seen has stairs!'). But they were not particularly interested in Spain. They wanted their dad back, and that was all they wanted. Only the other day, little LeEtta, her blonde hair noticeably longer now than when he left, tried to climb into the computer to fetch him, and he had to end the conversation before they noticed his tears.

The rest of the time, however, he was in his element. Apart from his constant quest for the woman of his dreams, everything was exactly the way he had longed for it to be. He chatted to his fellow students and joined in their Friday nights out with gusto. The bars in this place! The clubs you could go to! It was like nothing he had ever dreamed of.

No one went out until after ten, apart from the English speakers and tourists. When you did go out, you could be whoever you wanted, and do whatever you wanted, and no one cared. The more wacky you were, the better.

Because all four of them had been allocated this apartment by the TEFL school, they were automatically all native English speakers, and at first Jack was grateful for that. By the time he had settled in, however, he was slightly sorry. It would have been interesting to meet some local people, or people from cultures that were stranger to him. Though when you started talking to the others, it turned out that they were, in fact, pretty strange. The two girls were younger than him, twenty-two or so, and they went out most nights, bringing guys back to the apartment so often that Jack was never sure if he had met them before or not, when he ran into them coming out of the tiny bathroom. He practised a cheerful, 'Morning, mate – *hola*' that could have worked whether he was supposed to remember them from last time or not.

He even went out for beers with Peter, to gay bars, and he did not feel that anyone was trying to cop off with him, because clearly, they were not. Peter got attention all the time, but Jack got none.

'How do you do it?' Peter asked him one night, as they sat together in a bar. There was dance music playing, with an insistent beat that was faster than Jack's heartbeat, and he felt his own pulse speeding to keep up. The ceiling was high, and the decor was cream and clean, with painted walls, and wood everywhere.

'Oh, you know,' Jack shouted, to be heard above the music. 'It just comes naturally. How do I do what, you idiot?'

'I was watching you today. Teaching. You just stand in front of a roomful of kids, and they all look at you, and you clown around enough to make them like you, and then you've got all of them in the palm of your hand.'

Jack shrugged. 'That's just how you teach, isn't it?'

'Yeah, it's how *you* teach. Clearly. I can't pull it off.'

'But you know your tenses and all that.' There were tenses in English, it turned out, that Jack had never known even existed. He liked the philosophical names they had. Past imperfect: you could say that again. Future perfect: let's hope so. And so on. He was putting in his hours, cramming in all the grammatical detail, and he hoped he would get there one day.

'Yes, but that's the boring part. There's no point knowing the arcane points of grammar if you can't make it interesting enough for your students to pick it up.'

'What are you talking about, Pete? You're good. I've seen you, too. You have no problem.'

Pete shook his head. 'Nah. You're better. You're one of life's born teachers. You'll be doing it for ever, I reckon. Travelling the world, teaching every woman you meet to say "I love you", until you come across Ms Future Perfect.'

Jack laughed. 'I know. I should give up – compromise. That's what you think, isn't it?'

Pete shook his head. 'Actually, I don't. I think you've been burned by the crap that went on in your marriage more than you're letting on. Your wife treated you like shit, and coming to the end of the earth and licking your wounds for a while seems like an eminently sensible course of action to me.'

Jack did not want that to be the case. He did not care what Rachel had done. This was about him, not her.

'Maybe you're right,' he conceded. 'Up to a point. But you know what? When I was still in my teens, I wanted to travel but I settled down with Rach instead because she was gorgeous and she was actually there, sitting next to me on the bus. Reality won me over. Everyone said we were so great together. This time I want to follow the romance. If it ever happens.'

'It's like you're having a mid-life crisis,' Pete said, 'but you're not even thirty yet. You know, no one I know of our age has been married. You kind of fast-forwarded it all, didn't you? Wife, house, kids, infidelity, divorce, escape – all in your twenties. It's impressive. What are your thirties going to bring you, Jack?'

Jack grinned and sipped his mojito.

'You know what?' he said. 'I have no idea. And I love that.'

chapter twenty-two

September

I had not been in the house for weeks. Even using my key felt strange.

'Hello?' I called, as I stood in the hall. After a few seconds, a door opened upstairs and Mia hung over the banisters. She squinted at me from behind red swollen eyes and sniffed noisily. 'Mia! What's happened? Are you OK?'

She sniffed again and wiped her face with the back of her hand.

'Hey, Lily,' she said in a sad little voice. 'Haven't seen you for ages.'

She wasn't coming down, so I took my boots off and went up the stairs. She looked as if she had been crying for hours. She was wearing baggy pyjamas – washed-out pale blue ones. I put my arms around her, and she leaned on me, though she was tense.

'What's happened?' I asked again. 'Is it Joe?' I checked.

At the mention of his name, she wailed. Romeo and Juliet, I supposed, had been teenagers too.

'He . . .' She wiped her face and visibly pulled herself together. She moved away from me, so my hand was no longer on her back, and turned her face towards the wall. 'Nothing,' she said in a tight voice. 'It's all right. It's really nothing.'

'Hey,' I said. 'Mia, tell me. Please. You might feel better if you did.'

'No,' she said. 'Honestly.' With a lurching gasp that made her whole body shudder, she gathered herself. 'Have you come to get some stuff?' she asked.

I looked around the landing. There was a heap of Match Attax cards that someone had shoved out of the way into a corner. Both Tommy and Zac had collected them. The boys' door was open and the sight of their duvets flung back on their beds, exactly the way they had left them when they got up, made me oddly sad.

'Shall I make a cup of tea?' I twiddled my hair around my finger and looked into her face. The only way I could think of to look after someone was Grandma's way, the old people's way. I wanted to sit her down, give her a hot drink and something to eat, and tell her everything would work out in the end.

'No, thanks, I'm fine.'

'Look, do you want to meet during the week? You can come over, if you like.'

She flashed a glance at me, then looked away.

'What do you mean?' Her voice was still shaky.

'I mean, come to Harry's house, have a cup of tea with me there, get a change of scene for a bit.'

She looked at me properly with her pale blue eyes.

'Why did you come back? Today?'

'Oh, I needed to see your parents. John and Julia, I mean.'

'Yeah, I knew who you meant.'

'Sorry.' I wanted to ask if she had heard from her mother.

'They'll be back in a minute. They went off to Truro to go and see a baby. Remember Fiona? She lives at number nineteen. She had her baby, but it came early so it's still in hospital.'

'Oh no! Is the baby OK?'

'Yeah, going to be. It wasn't *that* early, I don't think. They took Tommy with them. Twins are at a party. But Dad and Julia and Tom went out ages ago, so they'll be back soon. And no, I'm not OK really. It's just weird you turn up today, because I loved having you here and you're never around any more, and I look for you at college but you're never there, and my mum wants to see me, and Joe . . .'

I put my arm around her fragile little shoulders.

'Mia,' I said, 'do you want to see your mum?'

'Yes! I do – and I don't. I'm sick of keeping it all secret. And you're leaving, aren't you? You're not going to live here any more.'

I struggled to reply. She turned and ran back into her room.

I took the sheets off my bed and carried them downstairs to the washing machine in the kitchen. There were toast plates in the sink, pieces of cereal trodden to dust on the floor, drips of milk making a trail across the worktop. I was pleased to see my cafetière out, with an inch of coffee at the bottom of it.

There was still space in the machine, so I went back upstairs to the laundry basket. As I was coming downstairs with my arms full of dirty clothes, the key turned in the lock and Julia, John and Tommy came in, mid-conversation.

'It just sends a chill through you,' Julia was saying. 'There but for the grace—' She noticed me and beamed. 'Lily! What a lovely surprise!'

'Hello, stranger,' said John. 'Good to see you. Even if your arms are full of our dirty pants.'

'Lily!' Tommy shouted, and he flung himself at me, headlong. I was pushed back into the staircase as he bumped into me with a soft *whumph*. He hung onto my legs, and I carefully turned around and pushed the washing through the banisters to free my hands so I could pick him up.

He was surprisingly heavy, and he seemed to have grown while my back was turned. He encircled me with his legs like a baby monkey. I kissed the top of his head.

'You've got bigger,' I said. 'Sorry. That's a horrible grown-up thing to say. But you have. How are you?'

He wriggled down. 'I'm going to start football. On Saturday mornings.' He began demonstrating kicks, running up and down the little hallway.

'Oh, Tommy,' said Julia. 'Shoes off, for a start. And go and do your kicking in the garden or something. Leave your shoes on, in fact, and go straight back outside.'

'Lily, will you come and watch me?'

'I will in a minute,' I told him, picking up the washing

again, piece by piece and taking it through to the kitchen. I was awkward about the thing I was going to tell them.

Julia followed me into the kitchen.

'Harry's not with you?' she asked. She put the kettle on. I remembered how I had enjoyed cooking for her, sitting at the little table drinking coffee with her, talking to her. They had been good to me.

'He's going to pop along in half an hour or so, if that's OK. You've been to see a baby? Sounded like it was a traumatic experience.'

She screwed up her face, before recognition dawned.

'Oh, right,' she said. 'What I was saying as we came in? No, the baby's fine. He was only three weeks early, and they're just keeping them in for a few more days as a precaution. Little darling. Finlay George, they've called him. Full head of black hair. I could have stayed and stared at him all day.'

'Do congratulate Fiona from me,' I said, feeling very adult.

'Thanks, I will. No, the chilling thing was that while we were up there, we ran into the Manns. We vaguely know them – they live out in Budock.'

'The Manns?' I echoed.

'Darren Mann's parents. He was in that hit and run in town at the end of last year? Horrific business. And seeing May and Terry like that – absolutely devastated.'

'Oh,' I remembered. 'That. Yes, that was dreadful, wasn't it? How's he doing?'

'Oh, Lily, he's doing dreadfully. We went over to talk to them, because there's nothing worse than people cold-shouldering you if you've been through a tragedy because

216

they don't know what to say. And they'd just been asked to think about switching off his life-support.'

Silence hung in the air.

'That's horrific,' I said eventually, knowing it was inadequate.

'Isn't it just? One of those random things. Darren wasn't even drunk. Not that it would have made any difference. He was just picking up some fish and chips, and this car drives up on the pavement, knocks him down, and speeds away. It had its lights off, May said, which is why no one got a proper look at the number-plate. A silver car. There are millions of the bloody things. I hope they get him though. Or her. Probably him. It makes you want to bring back the death penalty, and that's not something I'd say lightly.'

'No, you're right. They will get him – I'm sure they will. Something like that can't stay hidden for ever.'

'Well, let's hope so. Now, what is there to do but carry on? After all that I could do with a drink, but we'd better stick to coffee. Will you have one?'

I nodded. 'Please.'

Julia looked at me.

'You know, Lily? I always knew you'd go far, but we never imagined this would happen. Do you realise how different you look? You are positively glowing.'

I grinned back and tried to put Darren from my mind for the moment. 'I feel it, actually. I'm so glad you're pleased for me. I know people think it's ridiculous. I do sense some hostility from people Harry knows. They see him taking up with a younger woman soon after his wife's death, and they get their disapproving faces on.'

Julia laughed. 'Should we wait for Harry before we have the coffee?'

I shook my head. 'He won't be able to stop. He's just bringing the car so I can pack some stuff into it.' I inhaled, ready to impart my news, but Julia filled the silence too quickly.

'Well, of course they disapprove. People love to. "Cat's bum mouth", that's what we call it at work. Healthcare professionals can be guilty of it, that's for sure.' She turned and pulled the face in question at me.

'That's exactly it!' I giggled. 'So, to the outside world we seem to be fulfilling every cliché in the book, and I can't walk down the road without seeing cat's bum mouths everywhere I look, but from the inside it doesn't feel a bit that way. It feels like . . .' I grasped for any words that could possibly explain it. 'It feels as if the flowers spring out of the ground just for us. As if the stars shine for us. It's impossible to describe without churning out the clichés: in fact, I keep going back to Shakespeare's sonnets, but even those seem a bit too cynical. You know, all preoccupied with how immortal his writing's going to be.'

'Everything seems to have gone elemental, all of a sudden,' Julia mused. The kettle boiled, and she started carefully spooning coffee into the cafetière. 'Birth, love and death. None of the ordinary in-between business.'

'I only wanted to be ordinary,' I said, thinking aloud. 'That was my one goal in life. To learn how to live an ordinary life. Anyway, he asked me to live with him, so I'm going to move out of here. I'm sorry. I hope you find a nice new lodger. I'll keep paying the rent until you get someone.'

She got two cups out. 'We were expecting it, to be honest,' she said. 'Which doesn't mean we won't miss you.' She turned to me. 'This is a bit of a ridiculous thing to ask, because I know what you're going to say, but you are sure, aren't you? This *is* what you want? It's only been a matter of weeks.' She looked at my face and hurried on, 'I'm only saying this to you because someone has to, Lily, and you don't have any family around to do it. If you want to take things more slowly, don't be afraid to tell him that. And if you ever need a bolthole, you can come back here.'

'Thanks,' I said. 'But I won't. I've never been happier.'

'I know – I can see that. You're radiant. How's college going?'

I avoided her eyes. 'I haven't been much. Harry says it'll be too easy for me and I don't need to take it seriously until next year.'

'Lily, you have to keep on top of it.'

'I know.'

She handed me a mug of coffee and a chocolate Hobnob.

'Thanks,' I said. 'I'll always stay in touch, you know.'

'Too right you will,' said John, coming into the kitchen and apparently sizing up the situation in an instant. 'We want to be invited to the wedding.'

Harry knocked on the door at the appointed time. Julia had changed her clothes and put some lipstick on. John smiled and blustered at him in a male manner. Even Tommy came in from the garden where he was playing football and Mia edged down the stairs, hiding her blotchy face behind her hair.

'You know,' said Harry, looking around at them all, 'it occurred to me that you're Lily's surrogate family, and I've never actually met any of you properly. It's high time we rectified that.'

'We're just delighted to see Lily so happy,' said Julia. 'Would you like a coffee or something?'

'I'll tell you what,' Harry said. There was something about him. It was, I thought, charisma. He was the centre of any room he stepped into, and everyone warmed to him instantly. 'Why don't I get Lily's worldly goods into the car, and then, yes, I'd love to join you all for a coffee.'

'I'll give you a hand,' said John, and the two of them transported my boxes of books, my few bags of clothes, and the small amount of other bits and pieces I owned, into the small boot and the tiny back-seat space of the BMW. Mia hung back watching them. She had cleaned up her tear-stained face, but it was still obvious.

'He's really nice,' she whispered to me. 'I can see why you want to live with him.' I smiled at her. 'It's just Joe,' she added, picking up our previous conversation. 'His dad lost his job. He's got a new one, but it's in Newcastle. They're moving in a couple of months.'

'Oh,' I said. 'I'm really sorry.'

'Yeah, I know. It sucks. Nothing anyone can do about it. Can I come round to your house one day, then?'

'Of course you can. Any time you like.'

Harry and John were coming back in, satisfied with a job quickly and easily done.

'Nice car,' John was saying. 'New?'

'Yeah. You know how it is. One of those life moments.

Everything else has changed – better change the car while I'm at it. Now, Mia, I've heard all about *you*.'

She blushed furiously and looked at her feet, which were clad in huge woollen socks that made her legs look like matchsticks.

'And it's lovely to meet you at last.' She grinned at him and he gave her one of his warm looks. 'Tommy?' he said, shaking Tommy's hand. 'I'd recognise you anywhere – you're famous, aren't you? I'm sure I saw you in the paper.'

Tommy beamed at him and I looked at Harry with pride. Every member of the family loved him, instantly. I was inordinately proud.

On the news that night, we heard that Darren Mann's life-support had been switched off.

chapter twenty-three

October

There was an end-of-day feeling when we reached the beach. I couldn't stop looking at Harry. I was starving: we had stayed in bed all day, only getting up an hour ago. I thought, however, that Harry had left me sleeping at various points, and that this had to be how he had magicked up the heavy picnic basket that we were now carrying between us. It was so heavy that Harry had insisted we take a taxi, and he had got the driver to bring us here, to Maenporth, the next beach along the coast path, a few miles from town.

The sun was setting, and the car park was emptying. There was a slight chill of the beginning of autumn in the air. A few children had been out in kayaks, and they were now coming in, walking up the beach, shivering in their wetsuits. A man barked orders at them as they took their canoes to a waiting van and helped him strap them onto the sides and the roof. The café was still open, although it looked as if it were about to shut. A couple of serious walkers came onto the beach from the coast path, walked across it, and set off up the other side, in the direction of town. They smiled as they strode past us.

Harry chose a spot in the very middle of the coarse sand, and we put the basket down. I stood and looked at the ocean, which was glowing in the golden evening light, pulsating, alive. There were a couple of yachts out at sea, their sails harnessing the breeze. The tankers, as ever, lurked close to the horizon. When I looked around, there was a red and white checked picnic blanket on the sand, with two champagne flutes and a bottle of Moët on top of it. Harry was hovering with a match, next to a little barbecue, a small one in a foil tray.

I sat down next to him.

'Want me to have a go?' I asked, and he reached out and took a strand of my hair, tucking it behind my ear. I felt myself trembling, although it was a warm night.

'Go on then. You'll do it first time, won't you?'

I took the matches from him, lit one, and dropped it straight into the tray. The coals began to glow at once. Harry placed two burgers on top of it, and put a Marks & Spencer's salad down in front of us. He passed me a china plate and picked up the champagne.

'Cold?' he asked, as he eased the cork out of the neck of the bottle. I was still shivering slightly.

'Not really,' I said. 'Happy.'

I thought he was going to give me his jumper, and I was looking forward to feeling small and snug inside it. Instead, he whipped out a wrap from a side pocket inside the hamper.

'*Voilà, Madame*,' he said. 'One pashmina.'

It was soft, dusky pink, probably cashmere. I knew that it had been Sarah's, because I had seen it hanging up when I cleaned the house. I bit my lip and reached for it, but Harry opened it out and wrapped it around my shoulders, enveloping me. I smiled. It was warm and gorgeous. It didn't matter that it had been hers, because she was gone and now it was mine.

We sipped champagne as the sun set. There were other people on the beach, a couple of other barbecues. A wedding party crossed the road from the hotel opposite, and forty or so people had their photos taken in the fading light. All of them looked at us, at Harry and me, leaning on each other, enjoying our barbecue, drinking our expensive champagne. I had no one in the world apart from Harry, and I was happy with that. I only wanted him.

'I'm glad it's me,' I said, when it was almost completely dark, when Harry produced a thick candle, pushed it into the sand and lit it.

'You're glad it's you?'

'You. Getting over Sarah like this. Finding someone else. I'm glad it's me.'

'Oh, of course it's you. It could never have been anyone else . . . Lily?' he said.

'Yes?'

'This is going to sound premature and impulsive, but I can promise you it's not impulsive. I've given it a huge amount of thought. I think we should get married.'

I could not say anything. My head was spinning.

'Married?' I managed to stutter.

'Yes. It's simple enough, the way I see it. I love you. I believe that you feel a similar way about me?'

'Oh, yes,' I managed to say.

'Well then. I know what I want for the future, Lily. I want you. I want you to be my wife, and I would love it if we could have a family together. Some little Lilies and little Harries. I know you're young, and of course I'll support you in your education, but I can see you might not want to be tied down to some sad old codger . . .'

'No, no, no!' I exclaimed. 'I do want to! I'd love to marry you, Harry. I'm just amazed. I thought people lived together for years before they got to this part. It's the most incredible thing that's ever happened to me.'

He was beginning to smile. '*People* live together for years, sure. But we're not people. We can do it our way.'

There was a crisp wind blowing my hair around. The sun was half-sunk into the sea. The waves splashed gently onto the shore and the pebbles made a tearing sound as the water pulled back through them.

'Yes,' I said, aware that I was sounding prim and formal, that this was a situation in which it was impossible not to follow a script. 'Yes, please, Harry. I'd absolutely love to marry you.' Suddenly I thought of Tommy. I could probably manage a couple of children, too, I decided, at some point.

He smiled at me in the dusky light.

'Thank you,' he said. He raised his champagne glass. 'To the future, Lily Button.'

I clinked glasses with him. 'Lily Summer,' I said. 'That has a better ring to it, don't you think?'

'Now, is that why you're doing it?' he asked seriously.

'Yep. The only reason. Actually, I think I've been in love with you since the very first moment I ever set eyes on you. I walked past you on that lane that the Trago's trucks use, and you said hello to me – and that was that, as far as I was concerned. You won't even remember.'

'I'll tell you something,' he said, 'I do remember. You're more striking than you think, with that hair of yours. I felt flattered that a beautiful young girl with a pasty was blushing at the sight of me, and believe me, a man doesn't forget a thing like that.'

'Really?'

'Really.'

'I'm going to tell you every day. I love you, Harry.'

He was beaming. 'Thank you, my darling. I love you, too, but I may have mentioned that already.' He cleared his throat. 'So, I have a piece of jewellery that I hope you might like.'

It came out of his pocket, a hard little box. Inside it, there was a ring. It had a small square jewel in it which caught the last of the evening light and, for a second, dazzled me. I blinked, and Harry took it and gently put it onto the fourth finger of my left hand.

I looked out to sea, then back again. It was still there. *I am engaged*, I told myself. We would have a wedding. I would have to meet his family properly, and hope they liked me. Mia and Jessica could be my bridesmaids. Al could come, if I could get his attention. If he was still all right. Al was a constant nagging worry that underscored all my happiness. He had not responded to my texts for over a week, and I was not sure how else I could check up on him. Catching a train to Glasgow and wandering around in the hope that I stumbled across him did not seem like a practical plan.

There were not many other potential guests on my side, unless I went back out to the cottage and cycled around inviting old ladies, just to make up the numbers. I would write to my parents again, just to give them the chance of coming over to see that I really was all right without them.

I looked at Harry, strong and loving and kind, sitting beside me with his arm around my shoulders. We had hardly touched the picnic. Against all the odds, I had found a wonderful man who wanted to spend the rest of his life with me. This, I decided, was my Happy Ever After.

Harry was working harder than ever, during the week: as a partner in the practice, the money he took home depended on how much work they had. 'I want us to have a stunning wedding,' he said. 'Because there's one thing I'm not compromising on. Nobody is going to say it's "only" a second wedding. This is going to be in a different league from my first one. If you want a religious service, we'll fly in the Pope. If you want a secular one, we'll send a limo for Richard Dawkins. You want to be married by piskies, we'll send someone into the woods to round a few up. Whatever you like.'

'Well,' I said, 'we can't have a religious wedding because we don't go to church, or believe in God.'

He had roared with laughter at that. 'Lily,' he said, 'you cannot help it: every time you open your mouth you remind me why I adore you. Of course we can't have a religious ceremony. Tell that to the world at large. You're quite right.'

'I don't have many people to invite.'

'So we won't have a "bride's side" and a "groom's side". Let's see if we can find a suitably fabulous venue, and take it from there.' He hesitated, then said: 'First time round, it was all done by the book. I let my mother take the reins rather. But it's only now that I can look back and see that I let her do that because, although I told myself that it was what we both wanted, my heart was not fully engaged. That marriage was not the right thing for either of us, in retrospect. This one is – it's the most right thing that has ever happened to me – and so I want to make it perfect. And quite apart from that, all those cat's bum people are going to have to eat their words.'

'Through their cat's bum mouths,' I said. I had reported Julia's use of the phrase, and he had instantly adopted it.

As Harry was going to be late home, I decided to do something brave. Getting married – standing in front of Harry's family and friends, all of whom had known Sarah, and being the much-younger second wife – that would take courage. I was going to have to get used to it.

Harry had said I should make friends with Constanza and tell her about the wedding. At the same time, I had to keep well away from her husband for reasons that were still unspecified.

I walked down our front path, feeling nervous that Seumas might be going to open the door and glare at me like a pantomime 'bad sort'. A few metres of pavement, and I walked back up their path, marvelling at the way their garden was so different from ours, with a baby swing hanging down from an apple tree, and a path that was made from paving slabs, rather than crunchy little stones.

I pressed the bell. It was an old-fashioned brass one, a round button with concentric circles around it, and it rang loudly inside the house. I stood, shifting my weight from foot to foot, wondering whether I could run home before anyone answered. However, the risk of them catching me halfway out of their garden was too high.

Constanza opened the door, looked at me blankly for a moment, then smiled, but I didn't think she meant it. Her glossy hair was tied back.

'Hello,' she said. 'How are you, Lily?'

'Fine,' I said, and my prepared speech left me completely. 'Um,' I said, 'I just kind of thought I should say hello. Um . . . So, hello.' I started to turn to leave.

'Hello to you too,' she said. 'Look, come in. Daniel's sleeping, but he's going to wake up in ten minutes or so.'

'Sorry about ringing the bell.'

'No,' she said, 'that's fine. He's always slept through bells and phones and stuff.' I examined her, trying to work out whether I was welcome here or not. She was wearing a skinny pair of jeans and a black top.

'You don't look like someone who had a baby recently,' I blurted out. 'Sorry, is that rude?'

She smiled. 'I had him nine months ago. You know what, I waddled around like a whale, except that they don't waddle – like a fat penguin or something – for the first six months, and then he started sleeping at night, so I stopped eating chocolate all day every day just to get me through the next hour. And hey presto. It's a bit of a relief because I was afraid I was going to be a heffalump for ever and that I'd never sleep or go for a run or a swim ever again.'

We had emerged in their kitchen, which was painted blue, and arranged completely differently from ours, even though the house had the same layout.

'However,' she continued, 'I cannot shake the coffee habit. I'm on at least eight every morning, then I drink herbal tea and water all afternoon. It's still morning, isn't it?'

There was a huge clock, the sort I had seen in old films set on stations, taking up most of a wall. It confirmed that it was quarter past eleven.

'I'd love a coffee,' I told her.

'Great. So, Lily . . . are you, um, officially living next door now?' She seemed to feel awkward with the whole idea.

'I am,' I told her. 'Yes. I know it must seem a bit weird to you. Soon, I mean.'

'It only seems like yesterday,' she admitted. 'It was such an awful thing to happen. You and Harry got together fairly recently, did you?' Her back was turned as she fiddled with a very complicated coffee machine that seemed to take up most of the worktop.

'In July,' I said.

'Quite a whirlwind.'

'I suppose so. Yes. It's hard to explain but it doesn't feel as if we've rushed anything. I'm very happy.'

Constanza pressed a button, and the machine started making steamy gurgling noises. She turned to me.

'Well, as long as you're not rushing—' She suddenly stopped, mid-sentence. 'Oh my God! Tell me that is *not* an engagement ring!'

I held it out, as women were, I thought, supposed to do. I smiled until I thought my face would crack, because this was the first time I had told anyone and I didn't care what she thought.

'Yes,' I said. 'I mean no. No I can't tell you it's not one, because it *is* one.'

'Wow.' She stared at the ring. 'Um, is this an abstract sort of engagement, or do you have an actual date?'

'Not a date yet, but it'll be sometime next year. We're just trying to find a venue.'

'Bloody hell.' She looked at me, and her forehead was furrowed. 'Look,' she said. The room was suddenly filled with the smell of coffee. Coffee, and disapproval. A stream of black liquid dripped into the two cups she had left out to catch it. 'Oh, Lily. I don't know you and it's none of my business, but – the walls in these houses are not as thick as you might imagine them to be. We hear things. It's all been quiet since you moved in, granted, but when Sarah was alive they used to have the most tremendously noisy fights. There'd be screaming and shouting. Things would be thrown. I had the sense there was a lot of volatility there.' She tailed off, and looked at me with huge brown eyes.

'But not any more,' I reminded her. 'You just said that.'

'Milk?'

'Yes, please. No sugar.'

She passed me the cup. I put it down.

'Can I just use your loo?' I asked.

'Of course. In the same place as yours, tucked away under the stairs.'

I put the wooden toilet lid down, sat on it and tried to pull myself together. This was exactly the way everyone was going to react. I was going to have to get used to it. I needed to brazen it out. I tore off a single piece of loo paper and wiped my eyes. I splashed some water over my face and studied myself in the mirror. My face was pale, my hair bushy. The mirror had an ornate gold-painted frame and it made me look like a rather dishevelled portrait. I did not care what Constanza thought, I told myself. In fact, I cared enormously. I wanted the world to be as happy as I was. I supposed they would get used to the new state of affairs, sooner or later.

When I got back into the kitchen, Constanza had gone. I could hear, far away upstairs, the distant sound of a baby crying. I picked up my coffee and went to read the pieces of paper that were stuck to their fridge. There was a letter from the baby clinic about a vaccination appointment. A print-out from the library of books borrowed: *Spot at the Park*, *Clara's Counting Tea Party*, *I Won't Bite*.

There was a double-beeping sound from the direction of the coffee machine, but when I looked at it, I saw that it had actually come from Constanza's phone, lying beside it. I wondered whether to go and pick it up. Was it paranoid to assume that she had texted someone about our engagement? I was desperate to know, but I could not do it. I did not appear to be brazen enough to pick up a stranger's phone and read her messages.

Just as I was edging towards it, I heard Constanza returning, talking baby talk.

'Sorry about that,' she said, coming back into the kitchen and handing me the baby while she poured milk into the coffee. I was taken aback, and his face immediately crumpled and he reached out both arms for his mother. 'I only ran upstairs to grab him but he'd done the most massive poo, hadn't you, sweetie? He's nice to know again now though. It's all right, Dan. You can spend a few seconds without being surgically attached to Mummy, from time to time, you know.'

I looked at the baby. He looked better today than last time. He had round rosy cheeks, enormous black eyes, and a head of black hair. He looked back at me, and his face straightened as he scanned my face solemnly.

'He's gorgeous,' I said, pretending not to notice Constanza picking up her phone and quickly reading the text. He grabbed a handful of my hair and pulled it hard.

'Ow,' I said, but I laughed because it didn't really hurt.

'Daniel!' Constanza reproached him. 'Go through to the sitting room, Lily. You can put him on the floor if you like. He's got some toys in there.'

It was a while before she followed with the drinks. I could hear the tiny sounds of keys on her phone as she replied to that text.

chapter twenty-four

I knew where Boris lived because Al had recited his address many times, his voice sharp with jealousy. He would say 'thirty-five Ashby Street' in tones dripping with hatred of all the domesticity that such an address implied.

I found it easily. It was about twenty minutes' walk from the station, and as I trudged under skies that were threatening rain, I ran through what I had planned to say in my head. By the time I got there, I had my speech ready, but as I stood in front of the door and searched myself for the courage to ring the bell, every word of it flew out of my head and away.

Weak Boris, his vindictive wife and their gorgeous children lived in a standard terraced house on a road of terraced houses, just up the hill from the city centre. The front of their house was brick, the door blue. It was completely ordinary.

I looked over the road, trying to work out where Al would have hidden, when he was spying. There were cars parked all the way down both sides of the road, so I supposed it would be fairly easy to skulk, though he must have been very conspicuous to the people in the houses opposite.

I rang the bell suddenly, and regretted it at once. After a few seconds, there were footsteps indoors. I clenched my fists tight and willed it to be Boris.

She was small and pretty, with light brown hair and a slightly harassed air. She looked wary of me, a stranger on her doorstep.

'Hello?' she said. 'Can I help you?'

As I launched into my prepared story, about looking at houses in the area and wondering if I could ask her about a couple of things, parking for instance, her daughter, Elinor, appeared beside her, clinging onto her mother's legs.

She grinned as she saw me.

'Lily!' she shouted. 'It's Lily!'

I stopped, mid-word. 'Oh,' I said. 'Hello.'

The wife, whose name Al would never say (so I had no idea what it was), looked confused.

'You've met my daughter?' she said.

'Um.' I sighed. 'Oh God. Look, I'm really sorry to turn up like this. There's no point trying to pretend it's anything other than the truth and you're probably going to slam the door in my face. But my name's Lily, and I met your husband – um, Stan – because I'm a friend of Al's.'

I watched her face close off.

'I don't think, in that case,' she said, 'that I have anything to say.'

'No, I know. I'm not here to harass you or anything. Al's gone to live in Scotland and I haven't heard from him

235

for ages. I'm sorry to do this but there's no one else I know who might have heard from him. I'm terribly worried that – well, that he's done something stupid.'

She glared at me. 'Well, frankly, for all the trouble he's caused us, that would be the first considerate thing he'd ever done in his life.'

'I can see why you feel that way.'

'Oh, look. Come in. God knows why, but he put us through hell and there aren't many people I can talk to about it. Stan has probably heard from him. I told him I simply don't want to know any more.'

'Are you sure? You want to invite me in, I mean?'

'If he really has vanished in Scotland, then I'd be interested to hear your take on him. As far as I'm concerned, he's a . . .' She looked down at Elinor. 'Why don't you go and play, Ellie? Where's Matthew?'

'Don't want to.'

'Go and tell Matthew to put *CBeebies* on, then.'

Elinor grinned, and ran up the stairs.

'Look, Lily,' she said. 'You look like a nice girl. Please don't turn out to be mad, or to be shagging my husband, or anything like that, OK? Because I would not hesitate to call the police, that is for certain.'

'I promise.' I followed her into the kitchen at the back of the house. She put the kettle on and fiddled around with mugs and tea bags, clearly nervous. She was not at all the way I had pictured her. Al had described a vicious deluded woman, determined to hang onto her marriage for convention's and appearance's sakes. The woman in front of me was sad, even desperate, and she was nicely dressed, unpretentious, normal. Nobody's life, I was beginning to see, was properly normal.

'Al helped me out,' I volunteered, as she made two cups of tea. 'I was in a bad place, and he literally saved me – a year or so ago. I owe him. I know how he behaved towards you and your family and I'm sorry.' I decided to steer well clear of any mention of Boris. 'All I want to know is whether you have any clues that he's all right. Or that he's still alive.'

She handed me a cup of tea. 'There's sugar if you want?' I shook my head.

'Well, I have to thank him, in a sick sort of way, you know.' She laughed, but not happily. 'He was so possessive, so obsessive, with Stan that he sent him straight back here, begging for a second chance. I didn't want to take him, because it seemed like masochism of the worst kind, but he was so sorry, so desperate, that I agreed, under some very definite non-negotiable rules. We were tentatively doing all right, and then the stalking began.'

'You got an injunction?' I tried to hide my reaction to the difference between her account and Al's. I twiddled my engagement ring, unthinkingly.

'We did. It didn't put him off. It was being arrested that put him off, thank God.'

'He was arrested?'

'He didn't tell you? Spent a night in the cells. Then vanished. To Scotland, you say? Best place for him. Land's End to John O'Groats. That suits me.'

There was the sound of a key in the door.

'That'll be Stan,' she said quietly as the front door banged shut.

He froze in the kitchen doorway, looking with some panic from his wife to me, and back again.

'Hi, Stan,' I managed to say, though I had always called him Boris before.

'Lily,' he said.

'It's all right,' his wife said. 'Lily's just come to ask if we've heard from your friend. He's gone missing, apparently. I'm trying to find it in my heart to be concerned, but I'm afraid I can't.'

She left the room, and Boris sat down heavily.

'Bloody hell,' he said. 'Emma let you in? She's quite something.'

'I really like her. She's not like Al said.'

'I know. Is that an engagement ring?' I nodded. 'Congratulations.'

'Thanks.'

'Look, he's been emailing sometimes. Erratically. Last one about a week ago. I think he's down and out.'

'Boris,' I said, 'would you reply? Just to tell him to contact me? I think he needs someone. It's not you – it's me. He saved me once. I need to save him back. If you do that, I promise I will do everything in my power to stop him contacting you ever, ever again.'

He sighed and walked to the fridge. As he opened it and perused the contents, he said, in a falsely-casual tone, 'OK. I'll give it one shot. That's it.'

'Thank you,' I said. 'Thank you so much.'

chapter twenty-five

I stood at my upstairs window. A sunny winter's day was a magical thing. Everything glistened. There were no sailing boats to be seen: the air was still. The few people I could see hurried by with their dogs or their pushchairs, wrapped against the weather. I suddenly wanted to be there, to be down by the sea, filling my lungs with cold air. I loved this room, but I wanted to be out in the world, right now. I wanted to be accepted.

Everyone hated my engagement. News had travelled fast, and apparently Harry and I were now both public property, and funny. When we went out, people would look at us on the street and smile at each other. I tried not to care, but it was disconcerting and horrible. When we were married, people would get used to us. Harry said we would soon be old news, and I hoped he was right.

I finished the floor, and picked up my coffee cup from the desk. As I lifted it, I discovered that there was more coffee in it than I had thought, as it spilled over the side and dripped down the front of the desk. I yanked the desk out from the wall, hoping that there were no stains on the carpet or the paint behind it.

I wiped the drops off the wall quickly, pleased that the spill was not worse. There were a couple of things stuck behind the desk, things that had obviously fallen down the back of it. Without thinking about it, I picked them up. It was nothing. Just a book, and a map. The book, however, was called *Teach Yourself Catalan*, and there was something spooky about that. I wondered whether Sarah had left it there on purpose, so that he would discover it one day; so that his heart would jolt and start racing as mine was now doing.

My hands shook slightly as I picked up the map and turned it over. It showed Barcelona. When I opened it up, I saw that it had been drawn on. A few spots, scattered over it, had been marked in red pen.

I opened the Catalan book, and flicked through the pages. On the inside of the back cover, in red again, there were three words. They read: 'find teaching work.'

'Harry,' I said, as we lay in bed on Sunday morning.

'Hmm?'

'Can I ask you something?'

'You know you can. Fire away.'

I moved away slightly.

'You know when you went to Barcelona? When Sarah died?'

'What? Yes, of course I do. Why?'

'Well – what happened?' When he did not answer at once, I carried on speaking. 'It's just that it was so recently, and everywhere I go people are looking at me with contempt.

I feel I've stepped straight into Sarah's shoes and I'm living her life, and it seems odd that I can't imagine . . .' I tailed off, unsure of what I wanted to say.

'Oh, Lily,' he said easily. 'I should have known this would come up at some point. OK. You want a blow-by-blow account?'

'Is that weird?'

'No, no. By all means, but let's only talk about it once. It's not something either of us should be dwelling on. Well, we were staying in a five-star hotel, the grandest one in the city. My timing was admittedly bad, but on Christmas Day I told her that we needed to go our separate ways, as I mentioned. She did not take it well.' He raised his eyebrows. 'That's an understatement, of course. I believe she put some sort of sleeping draught in my coffee that night, because when I woke up in the morning, she was gone. There was a note, but it didn't make much sense. *Can't do this any more. Sorry but everyone will be better off this way.* Then a load of rambling about how miserable she'd been for all this time and how she wasn't going to be humiliated by me any more.'

He paused and inhaled deeply, visibly collecting himself. 'I suppose she decided she would rather die than be divorced. Not of sound mind. The police fished her out of the water later that morning. There was quite a crowd, by all accounts. That's just about it. What more do you want to know? Ask me anything. This is the only time we'll talk about it.'

'It's funny,' I said, 'because I remember, before you went, Sarah said you were staying at a little place in the back streets. She said you were cross because she chose it, and it only had three stars instead of five, and that you would prefer to be in a posh hotel.'

He laughed. 'She did try to inflict some grotty little place on me, yes. We had words about it. I changed it to a proper hotel. Not that it made the slightest bit of difference, in the end.'

'Were you there when her body was pulled out of the water?'

'I wasn't,' he said. 'No. There are some things in life one doesn't want to witness, and believe me, that was one of them. I was groggy from the pills for days. Fergus flew out and took care of the grim realities of it all for me.'

'You . . . you actually saw her body, then?'

He shook his head. 'I just couldn't bear it. Fergus identified her and sorted out all the details. He took care of everything. Anything else?'

I held him. 'No. Sorry for asking all that.'

It was easy to find the Expedia booking for their holiday in Barcelona, by digging around on the computer in the living room. It was in front of me in black and white: they had flown British Airways business class, and they stayed at the three-star hotel. Harry had lied.

I did not hold it against him. He was impressing me, and he did not want to admit that they had stayed at somewhere modest and characterful. In fact, his lie made me fond of him: I told myself that the fact that he thought I would think more of him if he pretended they had stayed at a posher hotel was adorable.

chapter twenty-six

November

I stood on the platform at Truro station and kicked my heels while I waited for him.

I wanted to be happy, but there were too many things crowding in. The main one, my secret biggest fear, was about my parents. I was terrified that they would ignore me again; and I was equally stricken by the opposite fear, that they might turn up. I had written to their last address, and this time I had sent a proper letter.

I wrote it as simply as I could, and then rewrote it to take out any traces of resentment. I told them I was fine, that I was asking nothing of them at all. I said I was perfectly happy, that Grandma and Granddad had brought me up well and that I hoped they were living happily in New Zealand. I said I had met a wonderful man and was getting married next spring, and that I would love it if they were able to come. I even added that we would probably be able to help them out with their air fares. *All*

243

I want is to see you again, and for you to have the chance to know that, whatever has happened in the past, all has worked out for the best, I finished. I hesitated about using the word 'love', but in the end I put it in: *Love from Lilybella*. At least the emphasis was on my name in that phrase, and not on the word 'love'.

Lilybella. I was not looking forward to having to enunciate my full name during our wedding ceremony. When we found a registrar, I was going to ask whether I could just call myself 'Lily'.

My parents wanted a fairy or a pixie child, not a baby. The reality was a crushing disappointment to them. They gave me a silly fey name: Lilybella Tatiana Blossom. Despite this, I had come out as a normal, crying, pooing baby, and in the end they had travelled to the ends of the earth to escape the fact that I was human, and annoying.

Lilybella Tatiana Blossom Button: it was a ridiculous name, and I could not wait to become Lily Summer.

I had posted that letter, in a purple envelope because I thought they might like that, to their address in 'Mount Eden', just over an hour ago. I gave my new email address in case they found it easier to communicate that way.

It was four o'clock, but the shadows were already lengthening. My breath puffed out in a cloud, and everyone was wrapped in thick coats, scarves and hats. In the shadows, the ground was icy, slick and white.

I sat in the ticket hall, jiggled my legs, and waited.

I was about to meet my future mother-in-law. This was a pivotal moment. Nobody was happy about our engagement. Everyone had an opinion, and it was transparently the same one every time: I was after money and status, and Harry had had his head turned by his young cleaner. He was being taken for a ride and I was a flinty-hearted gold-digger.

Julia, John and the family were the only people who were genuinely happy for me. Mia and Jessica were wildly excited about their duties as bridesmaids, and Tommy had happily agreed to be a pageboy. Zac had laughed in my face when I offered him the same role.

'Er, thanks,' he said, when he managed to draw breath. 'A pageboy? Right. I don't think so. Thanks, though.'

I looked at my phone as I waited. Boris had texted me to say that he had emailed Al three times now, with no response. I was waiting, monitoring the phone, all the time. A week ago, I had left a message on Al's answer-phone, telling him about the wedding, but he had not responded to that, either.

Harry came into the waiting room and looked around. He did not see me at first, and I sat and looked at him. I relaxed, smiled and felt my worries departing. I saw the other half of myself. We knew it was right, and nothing else mattered.

His face lit up as he saw me.

'Hello, darling,' he said. I stood up and he kissed me. I loved it that he was just the right amount taller than I was. I felt protected by him; but I hoped that he now felt protected by me, too. I would show him what a partner-ship could be.

I had dressed carefully for today in a thick maroon dress that almost reached my knees, my Victorian riding boots, and a duffel coat. All of it was Grandma's choice: she had been gone for well over a year now, but I had not had a spare penny, in that time, to buy myself anything else.

I had dried my hair carefully so that it looked thick and curly rather than frizzy and bushy, and put on a small amount of make-up. I was getting a little bit better at that, I thought.

'You look great,' Harry said as we walked out to the platform. 'Just right.'

'Thanks,' I said. 'Grandma knew her stuff.'

'You're not still wearing your Grandma clothes?'

I laughed and squeezed his hand. 'All my clothes are Grandma clothes.'

'Hmm.'

I waited, but he said nothing else.

We crossed the rail bridge together, our feet tapping the steps in unison as we went up, across, and down. There were quite a few people waiting for the train, and Harry tucked his arm through mine and led me down the platform.

'Excuse me,' he said, to a passing station worker. 'Which end is first class going to be?'

'Far end, mate,' the man said, pointing down the platform towards the level crossing. Mist was rolling in, and I could hardly see the end of the platform. When I looked to the left, towards the car park, the cars vanished into the fog.

'I always do this journey first class,' Harry said. 'It's unbearable if you don't.' His phone beeped, and he looked at it and grimaced and switched it off. 'My brother. I hope he's not going to annoy you too much this weekend. Tell me if he does.'

The seats were huge. Ours were opposite each other, with a table between us and no one else nearby. I laughed at the luxury.

'I've never been on a train before,' I said, sitting in the seat he indicated for me. 'Not a big one. Only the little local ones that only have one carriage. This is in a different league, isn't it?'

'Your first proper train. Your first trip out of Cornwall.'

I smiled to mask my fear. 'My first meeting with your mother.'

'Oh, for God's sake, Lilybelle. Don't worry about her for a moment. Promise me you won't?'

I looked outside. The train started to move, and Truro began to slide past the window.

'Everyone thinks we're some awful old cliché,' I said without looking at him. 'And your mum will surely think that more than anyone, because she won't want her son to be grabbed by some gold-digger.'

Harry reached across the table for my hand. Then he leaned right across it, and gently turned my chin so I was looking at him.

'Look,' he said. 'I had not quite anticipated the reaction. It's harder for you than it is for me. I'm sorry. We're kind of feeling our way here, aren't we? It's an odd situation for both of us. But I promise you, you'll like Nina. She will adore you. She and Sarah never . . . Well, let's not speak ill of the dead. Let's just say Nina has always wanted more grandchildren. And she hated me being widowed and miserable. She'll love you. Plus, she's under very strict instructions from me not to say a single word that might upset you.'

I smiled at him. 'Really?'

'Oh God, yes. And she does listen to me. She's not one of those scary mothers-in-law. Don't worry.'

'Promise?'

'I promise.'

We sat back and read in happy silence. I was reading Nabokov's *Laughter in the Dark*, while Harry had spread a lot of work papers over the table. We chugged along for a while. I kept looking up from my book, and gazing around. The novelty of this mode of transport was not likely to wear off, I felt, for some time; though I had thought that about every aspect of my new life, and I had got used to the rest of it quickly enough.

At Lostwithiel, a couple got on and sat at the table across the aisle from us. We all smiled at each other, members of the exclusive First Class Club. The man, sitting at the seat closest to me, got out the paper. I glanced over at it, unable to concentrate on my own reading matter.

Then a headline caught my eye. *New Lead in Stein Hit and Run*, it said. I knew it would be about Darren Mann, because it had happened outside Rick Stein's chip shop. I tried to read the report, but could not make it out without the man seeing what I was doing. I decided that when he put his paper down, I would ask if I could borrow it.

Harry looked up. 'Hey,' he said. 'A momentous event, my darling. This is the Tamar, Lily. You are about to leave Cornwall for the very first time.'

As we chugged into Devon, and stopped at Plymouth, I was surprised at my own excitement. I was venturing east, and I had never been here before. The train track gave a good view of the city, and it was much bigger than Truro. I gazed at the rows and rows of houses, stretching out as far as I could see. Mia's mother might live in one of those houses.

'It's a shithole, isn't it?' said Harry.

I laughed. 'I wasn't thinking that at all. It's just that there are so many houses.'

'Ha. Wait till we get close to London.'

By the time we were standing on Mrs Summer's doorstep, it was raining hard. I was starving, and freezing, and back to being terrified.

London was strangely the way I had imagined it to be. Paddington station was busy, but it felt safe, because everyone was wrapped up in themselves, and everyone was moving all the time. Even the ones who were standing still were on the move, between places. I loved the orange lettering of all the destinations on the boards. I loved the condensation in the air. I was enchanted by it.

'Come on, gorgeous,' said Harry, with a laugh, pulling at my hand. 'This is not my mother's house. This way.'

I had assumed that we would get on the tube, because this was how Londoners got around, but Harry swept me towards the taxi rank, settled me into the back seat of a black cab, got in next to me, and gave the driver an address which was, he said, in Belsize Park, North London.

The journey seemed to take for ever, and I sat in silence, gazing out of the window, taking it all in. I had never been here before, but London felt familiar. I liked it at once.

As we stood outside the heavy black door, on the

threshold of a forbidding stone house that was screened from the road by high trees, I realised I was properly frightened. I gripped Harry's hand. He squeezed mine back.

When the door creaked open, I tried to put a smile on my face. I looked sideways at Harry. He winked.

The woman stood in the doorway for a moment, looking out at the two of us. She had long black hair that was clipped away from her face by two sparkly slides, and she was wearing a pair of expensive-looking black trousers and a blue and white striped top. I knew, because Harry had told me, that she was sixty-seven, but she could easily have been ten years younger. Twenty, even.

'There you are!' She looked at Harry, and then at me, and then she smiled. I stood to the side as she ushered us in, but Harry put a hand on my back, and made me go first.

'Hey, Mumski,' he said, and he kissed her on both cheeks. 'Good to be here. It's been ages. I'd like you to meet my very darling fiancée, Lily. She's nervous so be nice.'

'Lily,' she said, in a warm and husky voice. 'Lovely to meet you, darling. Look at you! Did you just walk out of a painting? Rosetti and Millais would have killed for the chance to paint you.'

The house smelled like a place with money. It smelled of food, and then polish, a smell I knew well from my cleaning days. There were other things in it too: toiletries, perhaps, and definitely red wine, but all of it smelled exclusive. The carpet was soft underfoot, even through my boots.

I took a few more steps inside, then turned and looked

around. I was in a big hall, with a wide wooden staircase going up on one side. Jane Austen's characters had lived in houses like this. The walls were partly wooden, with a wooden rail at about waist height, and above that they were painted dark blue. There were doors everywhere and I knew that I would be lost in this house if they left me alone for half a minute.

Harry came and stood right next to me. As soon as his hand was on my shoulder, I felt better.

'You must call me Nina,' said his mother. 'The boys do, half the time, even though I'm forever telling them not to.'

She put both her hands on my shoulders (Harry quickly withdrew his), and kissed me on each cheek. She smelled of perfume and hairspray and cigarettes.

'Hello,' I said, sounding like a little girl. I shrank back towards Harry a bit, without meaning to. 'It's nice to meet you.'

'We've been *dying* to meet you. Oh, Harry! Like you said, she's adorable. Come through and have a drink. Not that you really look old enough for a drink. How old *are* you, darling?'

'Twenty-one,' I said, following her into a sitting room that was furnished with three floral sofas and two huge armchairs, a threadbare rug, two dark wooden coffee tables, and a side table. There was a tiny television up on a shelf, its screen dusty. Classical music was playing somewhere. Delius, I thought. I kept quiet until I was handed a glass of red wine.

'Thank you,' I squeaked. She looked at me, as if amused, and sat down in the biggest armchair.

'Don't worry, darling,' she said. 'I don't bite.'

I giggled. 'Thank you for inviting me to stay,' I said.

'Oh, not at all. Harry didn't want me to frighten you away so he hasn't allowed me to meet you until he had the ring safely on your finger. Harry, there's a tray of snacks in the kitchen. Bring it through.'

'Oh no, I will,' I said immediately, and started to stand up, but she motioned me to sit back down.

'No, you won't. Harry will,' she said. 'Let the men wait on the girls for once. Fergus'll be here in a minute and we can put him to work, too. May I see the ring?'

I walked over to her, and she patted the sofa beside her, so I sat down and held out my left hand. She took it and held it up, scrutinising it.

'Yes,' she said. 'Excellent. I'm glad he has taste, that boy. Fergus doesn't. He bought Jasmine a monstrous thing, back in the day. Set the tone for the union.' She lowered her voice. 'Harry is like a new man, darling. I know how much he wants my blessing, and to be honest, he had it the moment you walked through the door. But he's twice your age. What on earth do you see in him?'

Her eyes twinkled, and I felt my heart pumping.

'It's funny,' I said, 'because I would never have expected this to happen, but we just seem to be able to talk to each other. Everyone else seems quite cynical, but I promise you, there's nothing to be cynical about.'

'Oh, they're jealous,' she said, dismissing them with a wave of her hand. 'And when you can talk to each other, everything else follows. Yes, I remember that, dimly. You knew the first wife, didn't you?'

'Sarah?' I said. 'Well, I didn't exactly know her. I only met her once but I liked her.'

She laughed a barking little laugh, kicked her pumps off and tucked her feet under herself. She was supple, and looked like someone who might once have been a ballerina.

'Yes,' she said. 'You would have done. She was very good at being Little Miss Adorable. Couldn't stand me, of course, because she knew I could see right through the act. Between you and me, she was not well, and she made Harry's life hell.' She looked up, and so did I, as Harry came back into the room, bearing a tray of food which he set down on the coffee table in front of us. I had expected crisps in bowls, or something equally snack-like, but in fact there were proper canapés, much posher than the ones I had handed around at that party that seemed to have taken place a million years ago. There were mini-samosas, and cheese pastries, and little vegetable tarts, and it all looked home-made.

'These look amazing,' I said, wishing I were able to choose the right words, knowing that 'amazing' was far too childlike a term to use in this house. 'Did you make them?'

Nina and Harry both laughed.

'Now, that *would* have been amazing,' she said. 'No, my lovely Rosita made them for us. She's done a damn sight better than I would have done, that's for sure. Never been much of a cook, Harry, have I?'

He smiled, sitting down and crossing his legs. '*Au contraire*, Mother,' he said. 'So, you like Lily's ring?'

'I like everything about Lily. Remind me how you two met?'

She was addressing me, but I turned to him to answer because, although I had never been ashamed of being a cleaner before, I was now.

'Falmouth is a small place,' he said, and he smiled at me. I looked into his eyes and knew that it was all right. Harry and me were what mattered; and anyway, his mother had just said that she liked me. 'Sarah used to give Lily bits of work here and there, you know. And when suddenly there was no more Sarah – well, Lily was one of the very few people who stuck around. You know, everyone says "Is there anything I can do?" and I knew full well that if I'd said: "Yes, there is, actually – could you come and put the rubbish out and while you're here, could you clean up the kitchen and change my sheets because I don't seem capable of anything very much" – well, they would have run a mile. Not Lily.'

I put a samosa in my mouth and immediately slurped down half my glass of wine, because it was so spicy that it made my eyes water. I tried to pretend that had not happened.

'Do you know London at all, Lily?' Nina asked politely.

I shook my head, my eyes still smarting from the spices. 'No,' I managed to say. 'Never been here before.'

She smiled a broad and warm smile. 'Then we'll have to make sure you see some sights.'

Fergus turned up at the last moment before dinner.

'Lily,' he said, and he hugged me tight, then held me at arm's length. 'How great to see you again. Different circumstances, hey? Congratulations are in order.'

'Thank you,' I said, and he told Nina the story of me

walking in on him in the bath, and so she found out that I was the cleaner, after all, and it turned out that she had known it all along anyway and never held it against me.

Dinner was chicken and little sautéed potatoes with bowls of steamed vegetables. Conversation centred around our wedding, and was mainly between Nina and Harry. I tuned out after a while and looked at Fergus. When our eyes met over the varnished table, he winked.

'So how are things?' he asked quietly. The other two were discussing whether it was all right to invite some third cousins if we weren't inviting all the second ones.

'Lovely, thank you,' I said. 'Very different from when we first met.'

'I'll say. Look, the engagement took us all by surprise. It's a brave thing to do. Are you sure?'

'Oh, don't you start,' I said.

'Well, I know it's not my place to sound a note of caution . . .'

'How are you? Are you back with Jasmine?'

He pulled a face. 'Not really. Sometimes. God knows. Trouble is, you'll have got me in trouble with Mum now. She'll be on my case about finding a nice second wife, I know she will. Easier when you don't have kids though, that sort of thing. Here, have some more wine.'

It was after midnight when I excused myself from the table, because I was tired and drunk and full, and I had a distinct feeling that they wanted me to leave so they could talk about me. Fergus had just left in a taxi to his marital home. 'See if she's changed the locks today,' he muttered as he left.

'If she has,' Nina said sharply, 'you come straight back here.'

Harry led me upstairs to the bedroom and kissed me. He put my bag in the middle of the floor. His was still downstairs, and I supposed he would bring it up when he came. I could hardly stop yawning.

'All OK, then?' he asked. 'Not as bad as you feared?'

'Nothing like it,' I told him. 'Thank you.'

'See?' he said. 'You look knackered. Go to bed at once. Bathroom's through there.'

I wanted him to stay with me for a little bit. I wanted to press myself against his chest, but before I could try, he headed back down the grand staircase.

I stood in the middle of the room and looked around. There were shutters at the window, which were closed, but it was a huge window and I knew the room would be full of light, in daytime. The bed was bigger than a normal double, like our bed at home, and the walls were painted pale blue. The carpet was dark blue, and the bedspread was blue and with a floral pattern on it. I frowned as I tried to picture a teenage Harry living in there, with posters on the walls and rubbish on the floor, but failed. This was a serious room, an adult room.

The bathroom was en suite. This was excellent, as it saved me padding around and getting lost in the house. I was self-conscious with everything I did, and was nervous about sitting on the loo in case I somehow made such a noise that they heard me downstairs. I made sure I locked the bathroom door. I brushed my teeth, changed into the pyjamas that I had remembered to pack, and climbed into bed.

I lay in the darkness, waiting to sleep, staring at the ceiling. I drifted off, but dreamed so vividly of Sarah that I jolted awake, again and again. When half-past two came, I got out of bed. Harry was still not here, and he never stayed up late. I imagined him asleep on the sofa, uncomfortable and getting cold, because the house was freezing now that the heating had gone off. Nina would have gone to sleep long ago, I was sure. It took me twenty minutes to convince myself that I could be brave enough to tiptoe down the stairs, find my fiancé, and bring him back with me. Nobody could object to that.

As soon as I was on the stairs, I knew I was right. There was no sound of conversation. All the lights were off. The stair carpet was thick and soft beneath my bare feet. The whole place was hushed, like a museum. There was the sound of a clock ticking, and that was all.

The hall was very dimly lit by a pale light outside the front door, coming in through the little window above it. There was just enough light for me to see the three closed doors leading off it. I stood on the stairs and tried to work out which one I would need to open. I assumed that Nina's room was upstairs, but it might have been on the ground floor, anything was possible, and it would be beyond awful to barge in on her.

I picked my door, and walked down the last few stairs.

It all happened at once. There was a red light on the wall opposite me, which I only noticed when it started flashing furiously. After a few flashes, all hell was unleashed.

The wailing was so loud in my ears, and so inexplicable, that I thought it must all be a dream. I could not move, as my feet were nailed to the ground, and I waited to see what would happen next.

It was like a siren, but it was so loud that it inhabited every single part of me. It did not stop. It seemed to go on and on and on. The whole house was screaming at me.

Someone pushed my shoulder, shoving me out of the way. Someone else came thundering past. I was too dazed. I sat down on the bottom step. Then, suddenly, it stopped. The absence of the shrieking was almost louder than the noise itself had been. The last bit of it echoed around the room, bouncing off the walls, getting into everything. I looked around. The hall light was on. Nina, wearing a silky nightdress, was standing in front of a box of switches, which she had opened up on the hall wall. She pressed a few more, then, without looking at me, picked up the phone from a varnished table, and made a call.

While she was cancelling something, in a voice that was both sharp and sleepy, Harry came and sat down next to me. He, I noticed with some confusion, was wearing his pyjamas, too. He never wore them at home, but he had taken them out of his drawer especially for this trip.

'Lily,' he said. 'Oh Christ, I should have said – there's an alarm at night. What were you doing? Getting a glass of water?'

I looked at my lap. I wanted to say that I had been looking for him, but I knew I had got something wrong. 'Yes,' I said instead, seizing on the excuse. 'I woke up thirsty. You know I'm not good with red wine. I had no idea. Sorry.'

Nina put the receiver down and turned to us. I did not look her in the eye, because I couldn't bear to.

'Sorry, Mrs Summer,' I said in my meekest voice.

'Mum, we completely forgot to tell Lily about the alarm,' said Harry. 'She wasn't to know. She was only after a water glass.'

'Oh, Lily,' said Nina. She yawned again, seemed about to say something else, shook her head and walked past us up the stairs and back into one of the rooms up there without another word.

Harry stood up. 'Now, let's get you back to bed, shall we?'

'Harry?' I said in a quiet voice. 'Would you sleep with me? Your mother wouldn't have to know. You could creep back to your room early in the morning.'

He looked at me and laughed. 'I wish I could, gorgeous girl,' he said. 'But it's her house, her rules. Best we don't.'

He led me back to bed. I was mortified, but somehow, I went straight to sleep.

chapter twenty-seven

Nina laughed about the alarm in the morning.

'It's linked directly to the police station,' she said, as she passed me a cup of black coffee. I wanted milk in it, but I didn't dare ask. 'When I called, they were already sending a car out. Good to know they're there, actually. I should do that once a year to make sure they're not ignoring me. Once every two years, perhaps, to avoid crying wolf.'

'Sorry,' I said yet again. I had no idea that people who lived together and were engaged might not be allowed to share a bed. It seemed ridiculously old-fashioned. I was intensely grateful that Nina did not know the real reason for my disastrous venture downstairs.

She smiled warmly at me. 'Tonight I'll only set it for the front door. We should have warned you. It's not like Cornwall, here. You have to protect yourself.'

Straight after breakfast, we walked to a place she called 'Hampstead Village', although it was not a village at all. It was a few streets with some very posh shops on them.

It was a freezing morning with a bright blue sky. People bustled past us. Women with make-up that was just right, and with clothes that made me realise how shabby and worn mine were, walked purposefully with glints in their eyes that showed they knew they were better than everyone else. Nina fitted in with them perfectly. Nina: my mother-in-law. Fergus, my brother-in-law. It was hard to take in the fact that I was actually marrying into this family and that they were happy about it, even if no one else was.

Lots of women pushed children in complex buggy-machines. I could have stood on the side of the pavement and watched them all for hours, but I kept up with Harry and Nina.

'My grandma would have loved it here,' I said. 'This is exactly her spiritual home.'

Nina rubbed my arm. 'Ah, Lily. Well, she lives on in you and so you'll have to experience it for her.'

'Yes, I suppose I will.'

'Talking of your family, do we know whether your parents will be coming over from New Zealand for the wedding?'

I sighed. 'No,' I told her. 'We don't know. But I do know really. They won't. They couldn't have made it much clearer that they're not interested.'

'But for their daughter's wedding?'

I smiled. 'They didn't bother to come for my grandparents' funerals, so please, don't hold your breath.'

Harry interrupted. 'Lily's parents are worthless bastards who don't deserve a hair on her head. If they did show up, they'd have some explaining to do. Let them fucking try.'

I was surprised at this outburst. I had never seen Harry furious before.

'Harry, please don't use that language,' Nina said mildly. 'Well, Lily. We're your family now. And before you know it, you'll have a little family of your own.'

She steered us into a shop.

'Right,' she said to Harry. 'I'll leave you to it. Don't want to be an overbearing mother-in-law. God knows, not this time round. I'm off to the deli. Lily, do you like olives?'

'I love them.'

'Good. Let's meet up in, say forty minutes or so, at Ginger and White.'

Harry smiled at me, and gestured around the shop. It was a clothes shop, and I did not need to look at the price tags to know that it was not a cheap one. The clothes were flowery and frilly, 'vintage' style.

'Right,' he said. 'You can't carry on going round in clothes your granny bought. We need to kit you out a bit. I know nothing about this sort of thing but Mum said this would be the place. What do you like?'

I looked around. 'All of it,' I said. 'But you don't need to buy me clothes.'

'Of course I do. I stopped you working. You need clothes to wear.' He took my hand. 'We're getting married, Lily. What's mine is yours.'

As a shop assistant approached, he gently pushed me forward. I was uncomfortable. I felt she could see straight through me, to my clueless rural heart.

'Um,' I said. 'Can I try on a few things?'

'We're looking for a whole wardrobe for my fiancée,' Harry told her. 'A bit of everything. I'll grab a seat, if I may, and leave you ladies to it.' He sat down on a wooden chair and opened the paper.

The woman looked me up and down as if I were a slave at a Roman market.

'Absolutely,' she said. 'You have gorgeous hair. You're going to be *very* easy to dress. Size eight?'

Half an hour later, Harry paid for two dresses, a pair of beaded jeans, some black trousers, three tops, a 'mid-season coat', two cardigans and a jumper, while I stood around feeling guilty. He handed me a bag, and carried the other two himself.

'Thank you,' I managed to say.

'That's just the start of it,' he said with a chuckle. 'You're very welcome. Now, let's go and show this to Mother.'

Nina approved and sent me to the loos to change into my new jeans and jumper because we were meeting Fergus at an Italian restaurant, and then going for a walk on the Heath.

Fergus kept staring at me during lunch. He and Harry each shovelled away a steak, and they drank a bottle of red wine between them, but all the time, Fergus's eyes were upon me. I was self-conscious as I picked at my risotto and sipped at the drink I had ordered because it was the same as Nina's: it was called a 'spritzer' and it seemed to be watered-down wine, which suited me well. Nina ate a small salad with no dressing, and I realised how she managed to be as skinny as an eleven-year-old child.

I kept looking at Fergus, and our eyes kept meeting. His looked troubled, but he said almost nothing to me at all. Anyone watching our table would have thought Fergus was the one I was going to be marrying. We seemed to be making eyes at each other; but we were not. I was not quite sure what we were doing.

I felt good in my new clothes. I almost felt as though I would be able to belong with these people, one day, when I got used to it.

I put my fork down with half the risotto left on the plate: I seemed to have no appetite. Nina smiled her approval and leaned across to me.

'Quite right to leave food on your plate. A lady always does. It shows self-restraint and it keeps you from bursting out of your clothes.'

I tried to look as if this was my reasoning, too.

'We need to regulate our own food intake,' she continued. 'Rather than delegating the job to some smelly sous-chef back there, and eating the exact amount *he* allocates us. People are so unthinking. It's one of my bugbears.'

Harry looked across. 'You passed that test, Lily,' he said, 'and you didn't even know you were sitting an exam, did you?'

'Oh,' said Nina. 'Lily passes every test. She's one of us already.'

From the restaurant, we walked to the Heath. I could see that I was supposed to be overwhelmed by its splendour. However, I found it hard. I kept turning and staring at the black taxis, and even the ordinary cars, passing on the roads at the edge. We had grass and trees and ponds in Cornwall, but in Cornwall it was better than this. This was London: I was here for the first time and I wanted a bit of bustle. I walked briskly like the rest of them, following them up hills and through copses, on what was obviously, for the Summer family, a well-worn trail. The sun shone, our breath hung in the air around us, and I wished we were in the West End. I wanted to see the Thames, the Houses of Parliament, the London Eye. I wanted to walk down the Strand and up Oxford Street. I wanted to see the seedy dives of Soho and the traders of Covent Garden. I was so frustrated to be tramping along a downbeat urban version of the coast path that I had to bite my tongue to stop myself asking if we could do something more interesting.

Fergus stopped to tie his shoelace. The others walked on.

'Lily?' he called softly, and so I waited for him.

'Yes?' I said.

He hung back for a few more seconds. 'Walk with me a minute?'

'Of course.'

'You like the Heath then?'

'Yes, it's lovely.'

'Yeah, pretty boring when you live in Falmouth.'

'No, it's lovely.'

'Lily, you have to say that for Mum, yes. But not for me. You'd rather be seeing London.'

I smiled. 'You said it, not me. I'm sure I'll have plenty of opportunities to see the sights.'

Fergus was slightly taller than Harry, and he was broader, but they were so alike in their faces that they could have been twins. Despite this, their whole manner was completely different. Fergus seemed anxious now.

'You're very diplomatic,' he said, in a low voice. 'Look,

Lily, I know we hardly know each other, but I'm very fond of you. And I need to look out for my big brother, too. I just want to check that you're both sure that this marriage is really the thing for both of you?'

I rolled my eyes. I was strangely comfortable with Fergus. 'Not again?'

'Harry and Sarah weren't happy. I don't want you to end up miserable too. Either of you.'

I looked him straight in the eye.

'I'm only worried about two things,' I told him. 'Number one, I'm terrified at the prospect of standing up in front of all your family and Harry's friends and people who miss Sarah, and marrying him when half of them will be sniggering about me. Number two, I have no idea whether it would be worse for my parents to stay away, or for them to come.'

'Well, don't worry about either of *those* things,' he said. 'If your parents come and give you a hard time, they'll have to get past me, among many others. We'll all look out for you. It must be difficult though. That's why I'm so concerned about you. You are young, Lily. It's easy to forget just how young you actually are. I don't want you to make a horrible mistake.'

I bestowed my most serene smile upon him.

'I don't know why we work together,' I said, 'but we do. We make each other happy. The next-door neighbour said so. She said it used to be noisy and now it's peaceful.'

He almost snorted. 'I don't think that's quite what Constanza meant. Look, you make him happy because you are pretty, young and adorable. He makes you happy because he's wild about you, and he's older and he makes you feel safe. Why don't you just live with him a while longer and see what happens? Don't look at me like that, Lily. I'm just trying to help.'

I tried to smile. 'I know. But being with Harry is the one thing that I feel certain of. It really is. I'm not like Sarah.'

He lowered his voice. 'The first time I met you – the only time I've met you before – you were so lovely, and you exuded this sense that things were going to happen for you. It was enchanting. Don't look so surprised. One of the enchanting things was the fact that you had no idea. And, well, I would never have guessed that now, only a year or so later, you'd be getting ready to marry my brother.'

We walked on for a while, passing some people with a big brown dog.

'I want you to go places.'

'Is that what you wanted to say?' I asked.

'Pretty much.'

'I appreciate that you're looking out for me. Now can we talk about something else? Tell me about your children.'

He sighed. 'OK. You'll have to meet them. I'll bring them to Cornwall next time Jasmine lets me take them anywhere. They'll be at your wedding of course, assuming . . . but it would be nice for you to get to know them sooner.'

'Would your daughter like to be a bridesmaid? I don't even know her name.'

He laughed. 'Of course she bloody would. She's a little

girl. That's all they ever think of, apparently. Her name's Arabella. It was her mother's idea.' He paused, then said in a different tone, 'Look – what happened with Sarah: what has he told you?'

'Well, that he'd just told her he was leaving. And that's why she did it.'

'Ah,' said Fergus. 'Right. Well, I wasn't there.'

'But you came out afterwards. You were there when they pulled her out of the water. You identified the body.'

'Yes,' he said. 'Yes. And then I had the body cremated.'

'You liked her,' I said. 'Didn't you?'

'She was a brilliant woman. My brother has excellent taste in wives.'

I tried to work out how much I could say to Fergus. I was not sure whether I could trust him, or what it was that he wasn't telling me.

'Did you have an affair with Sarah?'

He laughed at that, and the tension lifted for a moment.

'No,' he said. 'Of course I didn't. My brother's wife? She was a good friend though. I'd do anything for her. I would have done anything for her.'

He walked fast, away from me, taking long strides until he caught up with Harry and Nina. I saw Harry look back at me, and then slow his pace until I caught him up. I blinked hard.

'Hey,' he said. 'Are you all right, Lily? What's Fergus been saying?'

I made an effort. 'Nothing,' I said. 'Honestly, nothing. I'm fine.'

'If he's upset you . . .'

'He hasn't.' I thought quickly. 'I'm just not used to being happy.'

He squeezed my hand. 'Good. Because anyone who upsets my Lily, even if they don't mean to, will have me to deal with.'

chapter twenty-eight

They did not look as though they had been there long. They were looking at the door as if expecting someone to answer it. There were two of them: a man and a woman. I knew who they were, what they were, at once. They were in black, in uniform black. I wanted to turn and run, but as I stood, rooted to the spot, the man turned around and saw me. There was no escape. I walked slowly up the path towards them.

It was Harry. Something had happened to Harry: I knew it. This was how it worked. The police turned up, and your life was torn apart by the information they imparted.

I looked up and thought I caught a glimpse of Constanza watching from the upstairs window, next door.

'Hello,' called the policeman as I approached. 'You're Miss Button?'

'Yes,' I said. This man should not be smiling and looking so reassuring.

'No need to worry,' said the woman, who had an open face and a happy air. 'Could we come in for a moment?'

I cast my mind around wildly. I could not think of a valid reason for saying no. 'All right,' I said, and I unlocked the door and led them to the kitchen.

'Gosh, these houses are something, aren't they?' the woman said with a sigh.

'They are,' I agreed, seeing my surroundings through strangers' eyes and being bowled over all over again.

They introduced themselves, but I forgot their names at once.

'Coffee?' I asked, biting my lip. 'Tea?'

'Oh, yes,' the man said. 'I'd murder a cup of tea. Thanks.'

As I boiled the kettle and got cups out, I tried to anticipate what might be coming. They had said there was nothing to worry about. It suddenly occurred to me that it might be Al.

'Here you go.' I put the cups down. We all looked as they trembled like butterflies in my hands.

'Right,' said the woman. 'You have no idea why we're here and we're making you nervous.'

'Is it Al?'

'No. Nothing to do with anybody of that name. This is just a routine check and you are not in any trouble at all. This is going back a bit, I know,' she said, 'but Lily, can you remember what you were doing on the evening of December the twenty-third last year? The day before Christmas Eve?'

'I . . . December?'

'Yes.'

'December the twenty-third?'

'Yes.'

The clock on the wall ticked the seconds away, and my

mind was entirely blank. It took me a long time to take myself back to last December, nearly a year earlier.

It came to me in the end: 23 December had been the night of Harry and Sarah's drinks party. That was the last time anyone in this town had seen Sarah.

'I was here,' I said. 'Harry's wife, Sarah, was still alive, and they had a party. I handed out drinks and things. I was here from about six o'clock, working for her. She paid me.'

'You were here? And Mr and Mrs Summer were here too?'

'Yes.'

'For the entire evening?'

'Yes.'

The man cleared his throat. 'Could either of them have left the house for a while at some point? Early in the evening, perhaps?'

'No.'

They had, of course. Harry went out for champagne. He came back empty-handed. I tried not to think about the direction in which this might be going. I could not say anything that might get him in any sort of trouble.

'No,' I said again. 'I was here. I was in the kitchen a lot of the time, but I know they were both in the house. The guests began to arrive at about a quarter to eight. Lots of the neighbours came. I'm sure they'd all help you if they could.'

The woman was looking at me hard.

'You're absolutely certain that neither Mr nor Mrs Summer could possibly have left the house, at around seven o'clock?'

'I'd say I'm ninety-five per cent certain,' I said. 'Like I say, I wasn't in the same room as them for a lot of the time.'

'Lily, can you drive?'

'No. I've never learned.'

'OK, that's all. Thank you. Can we take your contact details in case we need to speak to you again?'

'Of course. I'll write my numbers down for you.'

'And don't worry,' she said again. 'This is nothing that you need to be anxious about.'

As soon as they left, I called Harry. His mobile rang and rang, then diverted to voicemail. His work line went to his voicemail straight away. I tried to make my voice casual as I left him a message. 'The police just called by,' I said. 'That was weird. They wanted to know about that Christmas party last year. I didn't say anything much because there wasn't anything to say. Anyway, see you later. Love you.'

I paced the house for a while. Harry had gone out, and I was the only one who could possibly know. My internal compass seemed to be spinning wildly. I had no idea what I ought to do.

My mobile rang, and I snatched it up, but it was not him.

'Hello,' said a nervous female voice. 'Is that Lily?'

I wanted her off the phone, whoever she was. 'Yes?'

'It's Emma Finnigan.'

It took me a moment to place her. 'Oh, Emma. Are you all right?'

'Yes. Look, I know Stan has sent a message to your

friend. But I just wanted to let you know that I've asked him to move out again, for a while. It was all too much. We both needed a break from each other. So if you hear from him . . . well, I just wanted to let you know.' She paused. 'And if . . . well, if you do hear from your friend,' she could not bear to say Al's name, 'and if he turns out to be with Stanley, would you let me know? I'm sorry to involve you.'

'Yes,' I said. 'Yes, of course. Emma, are you all right?'

'You know, when he left before, I was so certain that if I could get him to come back, everything would be all right. Now that he's gone, I can breathe again.' And she hung up.

I tried Al's phone again, but it went straight to voicemail. Then I put my phone where I would definitely hear it, and decided to get on with the ironing.

I spent a peaceful hour straightening out a week's worth of Harry's work clothes and a few of my things, while listening to an afternoon play about time travellers. I forgot about Al and Boris and Emma. I forgot the police. I forgot everything apart from the fact that I was, here at least, capable of taking something messy and restoring order. I had found a spray called 'ironing water' at the back of a shelf, and I used it now, spraying each item before I ironed it. It had a gentle smell of lavender about it, and even though it had clearly belonged to Sarah, I liked it.

When the play ended, I hung everything up in the right place and, almost in a trance, poured a glass of water and went upstairs to sit at the desk and think. I had been trying to block it out, but I was afraid.

I had been uneasy when Harry went out in the car after drinking. Sarah had been, too; but he had gone anyway. Then he came back and poured himself a massive drink.

There was no place in my head for so treacherous a thought. I banished it, and turned to the more pressing problem of Sarah, instead.

She had bought a book about learning Catalan. She had marked places on a map that was now hidden at the bottom of my underwear drawer. She had written a note about teaching. From this, I drew the only possible conclusion: Sarah had deceived my beloved Harry. She had secretly learned Catalan, and slipped away from her old life. I had no idea why, nor where she could be now, but if she was not dead, I could not marry Harry; because he was still unwittingly married to her.

I took out the map from its new place, spread it before me and looked at the points she had marked on it. I did not have a clue what was at any of them. It made no sense to me at all.

I had loved being in London. I wanted to see it all, to see more. I had money, now, because Harry had set up a bank account for me and filled it with funds. I could think of no better use for it than this: to save him from bigamy. If she was dead, I would feel silly and delighted, and I would be able to marry him with my head held high, and live happily ever after.

I went downstairs and sat at the computer. Then I stood up. My computer skills were not good enough, yet, for me to do something like this and erase the traces. I would go somewhere else to do it. I would protect him from all of it, until I discovered something that he had to know.

The police's visit played on my mind more than I wanted. I called him again. There was still no answer. This time I did not leave a message.

chapter twenty-nine

Barcelona

Jack was 'personable', apparently. That was what they said, and that was why the very language school at which he had done his TEFL course offered him an actual teaching job the moment he was qualified. He was still not completely sure about his past conditional, but he was not going to point that out to anyone.

'More people are wanting to learn English than ever before,' said Hugh, one of the bosses. 'We can take you on for, say, forty-two hours a week. How does that sound?'

Jack totted up the money. It sounded good. Although there was no payslip or health insurance or anything, he was soon earning more than enough to support himself, so he sent home a chunk of his savings for Rachel and the kids.

He had to move to a different apartment, because the first one was kept for people doing the TEFL course. He moved by cramming everything into his backpack, going across town on the Metro, unpacking it in his new room, then repeating the manoeuvre, twice.

Peter moved with him. Their new flat was big but, somehow, also poky. They shared with a Serbian woman, a Polish girl and a man from Mali. They were all on top of each other, and it was not exactly luxury, but it was home. Soon there was nothing Jack liked more than kicking back with a beer after work, hanging out in their little kitchen and chatting to whoever happened to be there. Sometimes they chatted in bad Spanish, sometimes in bad Catalan, sometimes in English. The other thing he liked to do was to cook. This was a revelation to him, because when he was married, Rachel had done all the cooking, and it had never occurred to either of them that it could be any other way. She was a terrible chef, but he never minded. Often he would come home from ten straight hours of fixing people's plumbing, to find a plate of clammy pasta, with soup made from a packet, poured all over the top of it. He would wash it down with beer and thank her anyway.

Now, however, things were different. Peter showed him that he could order books from British websites, and have them shipped out here, and when he realised how easy it was, he had started shopping. One of his books was a thick cookbook called *Appetite*, and from the moment he made himself a shopping list for the ingredients he was going to need for haddock fishcakes, he knew he had found his new love. He loved nothing better than cooking. He knew the shops now, knew which day to go to the best market for vegetables, knew where to get meat and fish, and who had the best cheeses. He would swerve out of his way after work, and come back to the flat with bags full of red peppers and filleted fish, herbs and spices and the vegetables that had looked good. Then he would get to work. He fed his flatmates most days, and they happily gave him money towards ingredients and did the washing up.

This particular wintry morning, he headed into work, a bag full of books and a head full of food. It was getting cold, and he almost welcomed it after the city in the summer. Everyone thought that, because he was a Kiwi, he had never been cold in his life before. He spent a lot of time telling them that there were snowy mountains near where he lived, that there were ski-lifts and a huge snowboarding scene. They never believed him. 'Yes,' they would say, 'up the mountains. Sure. That's different. It's not really *cold* though, is it?'

He liked this city a lot more once the summer was over. It was less busy, and the people who were there were all interesting. Not that tourists were not interesting (he still felt like a tourist himself), but when they were on holiday, with their maps and everything, they seemed a bit samey, taking up all the space on the pavements and queueing for museums all over the place.

He arrived at work, found the room he was using first, and started unpacking. He was nearly ready, when a woman knocked on the door.

He looked at her, and for the first time in a very long time indeed, he felt a stirring of interest. She was not exactly the woman of his teenage dreams, but he felt that he liked her at once. She had short black hair, a nervous smile. She was not skinny like so many of the girls around here. She looked soft, and he liked that.

'Hi there,' he said. They were only meant to speak English, but he made a point of always talking slowly until he knew where someone was from.

'Hello,' she said. English was her first language. 'Sorry to barge in. I'm looking for someone called Hugh. Is he about?'

'Yeah. Down at the end of the corridor, the door that's straight in front of you.'

'Thanks.' She stepped into the room, eyes wide. There was something tucked into the front of her jacket. 'What's he like?' she asked. 'Anything I should know? I'm looking for bits of work.'

'Yeah, he's fine.' He took a step closer. 'Hey, what's that in there?'

She laughed. 'It's a baby. Hence my nerves. A new little baby, but I need work.'

Jack sighed. The first time he'd been attracted to a woman at first sight, and she had a brand new baby stuck to her. He would have to become more observant.

'Good luck,' he told her. 'Hope you get what you want.' Then he shook his head. He had five students coming this morning for a group session in business English. Business English was his least favourite because half the time he did not know the right word for something any more than they did. It was a constant game of bluffing and trying to stay one step ahead.

He sat down at his desk. He was a teacher. He was the boss. He loved it. He took out a postcard from the front of his bag, and started to write a quick note home to the children. He sent them postcards at least twice a week. That way, they might remember who the hell he was.

In fact, he wanted to chase that woman and ask for a hold of the baby, but she would only think he was mad and weird.

Dear Sarah-Jane, Aidan and LeEtta, he wrote. *Well, your dad is properly a teacher, and today I'm teaching business people to speak English! How posh does that sound? So what's the news in Queenstown? Is your mum OK? Here in Spain it is winter. Pretty, pretty cold, I can tell you.* He put his pen down, and stared out of the window at the rooftops. He wanted to smell that baby's hair. He wanted to hug his children. Business English had never seemed less appealing.

chapter thirty

Mia was suddenly taller than me. I stood still on the familiar doorstep, surprised.

'How did you do that?' I asked her, looking up slightly.

'I didn't do anything,' she said. 'Just happened.'

'Is it nice up there?'

'Lily! I'm not that much taller. I think we have the same view. You're making me feel like the . . . like the Empire Estate Building.'

'Empire State,' I corrected absently, following her into the house.

'No, I'm sure it's Empire Estate.'

'I'm pretty sure it's not.'

Mia sighed. 'Yeah, and you're going to be right. Let's look it up. Nice to see you, by the way.'

I followed her into the living room and she switched on the laptop.

'Guess who I spoke to yesterday?' she said quietly, as the computer powered itself up.

'Who?'

'You're not going to guess? You're the only one who should, like, appreciate this.'

'Not your mum?' She turned around and grinned at me. '*No*! How come?'

Mia shrugged. 'She added me on Facebook. Then asked for my number.'

'And?'

She looked quickly at the door. 'I haven't told Dad or Julia. I gave her my mobile number. She sent a few texts. It was almost like she was too nervous to call me. So I called her. She sounded a bit of a mess, to be honest. Not like a mum at all.'

I sighed, trying not to be jealous. 'Is she still in Plymouth?'

'Yep. She wants us to meet. I'm not sure.'

'So you didn't tell her to fuck off, like you once said? No,' I agreed. 'I wouldn't either.'

'Well, I know *you* wouldn't. You write to yours all the time, don't you?'

'Not all the time! Twice: once because of a funeral and once for a wedding. But yeah, I'd be over the moon if they replied. If they actually wanted to see me. No matter how weird and awful it actually was to see them, I'd take that any day.'

Mia nodded and turned back to the screen. 'You see? I knew you'd be the only one to get it. Hey, what did anyone do before Google? I mean, how did you find anything out? Look it up in a book or what?'

I watched her typing the words *Empire Estate Building*, dressed in a cobwebby knitted dress and a huge necklace. She looked completely grown up.

'Are you sure you want to be a bridesmaid?' I asked.

Mia looked round and gaped at me. 'Are you joking? Don't you want me? Do I have to be shorter than the bride?'

'No, no. You'll look amazing. Look at your long legs. Your hair. Everything about you is long. I just thought – you seem like an adult. Isn't it a bit babyish?'

'I can't wait. It's not like I'm, like, thirty.'

'How are things with Joe?'

'Yeah. He's moving in January. We've knocked it on the head.' She carried on talking quickly. 'It's cool! It was fun, but moving on is cool too. Hey, you were right. Empire State. I never knew that, *never*. And now I do.'

I looked at the little laptop. 'Before we head out,' I said, 'could I use that for twenty minutes or so? Would that be OK?'

'Yeah, sure. I'll leave you to it. D'you want a cup of tea?'

I did what I needed to do, and it was surprisingly straight-forward. Then I called a mini-cab, and took Julia, Jessica and Mia into town for lunch. As I sat between the two girls, looking at the back of Julia's head, I fought down an urge to tell them how wrong everything seemed. There had been a heavy frost overnight and the world was tinged with white. The car drove slowly up the hill. Life seemed to be running away from me. I did not have any control over it, and I was forever shutting down the part of me that wanted to slam on the brakes. If I told Julia, she would help me. She would help me postpone the wedding, face up to the things that were lurking.

Yet I would not tell her, because I was afraid. I was

afraid that she would delight in my unease (though I knew, really, that she would not), and I was afraid that if I asked Harry whether we could keep the engagement but put off the wedding, he would walk away from me completely, and I would have to return to my little bedroom and go back to being alone. I could not throw away Harry, the love of my life.

I decided not to say anything. We would have pizzas for lunch and look out at the boats on the water, and talk about bridesmaids' dresses; and if I acted as though everything was fine, perhaps it would be, in the end.

When I heard his key in the lock, I bit my lip, screwed my eyes closed, and told myself I had to do this.

'Lily!' he said, with a smile. 'My God. However vile a mood I might be in, when I see your face I'm like a teenager again. How was your lunch?'

'It was fine, thanks. We were thinking about dark red for the bridesmaids' dresses. It would suit both of them. And could we have gerberas for the flowers? They've always been my favourite.'

'Bloody gerberas!' He hung up his overcoat, carefully, on its hanger, and turned to me. He was smiling and frowning at the same time. His hair was thick and wavy and I was glad he was not losing it yet. That stopped him from seeming middle-aged. 'Does it have to be? My first wife used to fill the bloody place with the things. What about lilies, in honour of you, darling?'

'Aren't lilies flowers of death?'

'Are they? First I've heard. If they are, better not, I suppose. Roses then. But the dark red sounds good.'

'Harry?' I said. I had not managed to talk to him about this yet, because he came home late last night and left early this morning. 'Harry, did you get my message on your phone yesterday? That the police came over wanting to know about the party last Christmas?'

'Oh, yes – that.' He hung his tie over the banisters and strode to the kitchen to get a drink, with me following him. 'Load of nonsense. They came to me, too. It's nothing, forget about it. You won't be hearing from them again. I'm just heading up to change.'

Five minutes later, he called my name. I ran upstairs to our bedroom. Harry was standing in front of his wardrobe. Mine was on the other side of the mantelpiece, both of them built into alcoves. I struggled to stop myself thinking of mine as *Sarah's*.

'Sorry, darling,' he said, kissing the top of my head. 'It's just, I don't seem to have a shirt for tomorrow. Not that I expect you to skivvy for me. I know you've got lots of planning to do. Shall I iron one myself?'

I looked at his wardrobe. I had hung a row of them up, in there, yesterday. Now all those hangers were empty. I took the lid off the wicker ironing basket. They were all in there, crumpled and messy, unwearable. I took the top one out. Green and white stripes. I had ironed up and down those stripes. Now it was in desperate need of doing again. So was the next, and the next.

Yesterday afternoon, I knew I had been in a bit of a trance. But I was so certain I had done it. I thought I had spent an hour ironing. Yet it seemed that I had not actually done it. I took two hands full of my hair, and gripped it tightly. This was madness. Proper madness. It had to be.

'Sorry,' I said to Harry, my voice faint.

'Oh, don't be ridiculous,' he said. 'For God's sake, you're not a maid. I'll do one myself.'

'No you won't. I'll do them.' I picked up an armful of them and set off downstairs. As I went, I buried my face in them.

They smelled distinctly of lavender ironing water. I had no idea what was going on.

chapter thirty-one

Harry parked in what looked like a random car park on a small cliff. His little sports car gazed out to sea, while two much more ordinary cars were parked together in the corner.

'I think it's this way,' he said. 'I must say, it's not winning me over so far.'

I shivered. A fierce wind was coming off the sea, and there was a heavy Cornish light lying across the landscape, almost tangible.

We were inspecting a wedding venue. Harry had already booked it, so we were hoping to like it. It was supposed to be a fort.

The stone stairs twisted down in a spiral, and suddenly we were in a huge room, with stone walls and floor, columns like a church. It was enormous and grand, and its unexpectedness took my breath away. It was built into the cliff on one side, with windows at the other that looked out on the lawns and the sea.

I took his hand and tried to sound enthusiastic. I had

spent the whole of the previous morning searching through his paperwork in search of Sarah's death certificate. The fact that I had found nothing did not, I was reminding myself, mean anything at all.

'Like it?' Harry said to me, as a woman in black and white clothes approached us. I nodded, but he wasn't looking. 'Hello,' he said to the woman, extending a hand. 'Harry Summer. This is my fiancée, Lily.'

'Hello, I'm Gloria,' said the woman. 'Thank you for coming to visit. Now, shall we start with a little tour?'

I wandered along with them, half-engaged, admiring the beautiful venue, tuning out from the details about numbers of guests, caterers and string quartets. Harry radiated contentment: this was exactly the spot in which he wanted to get married. It was grand and beautiful, and the local registrar was happy to come out and marry us in whatever sort of ceremony we wanted.

If the unthinkable was true – if Sarah was *not* dead – then we would never have this wedding. I tried to relax: I could see that Harry recognised that I was tense. I had that matter in hand. There was nothing more that I could do, for the moment.

'Now,' Gloria said, at the end, as I perched on the edge of an enormous sofa and stared out of the window, while she and Harry sat in armchairs and talked business. She had a sheaf of papers in front of her. 'I know you've paid a deposit and made a booking for . . . when was it? May, wasn't it?'

'Yes, May the fourteenth,' Harry told her. May the fourteenth. Months and months away.

'Yes. Well, you were frankly lucky to get that date:

June, July and August are booked solid for three years at the moment. But we have just had a cancellation for January. I know it's not exactly wedding season – it wasn't a wedding that was cancelled, it was a birthday party, so there's no bad karma, I know people worry about that – but I do remember you saying on the phone that the two of you were keen to tie the knot as soon as possible. And so if you did want a winter wedding, there is that possibility. We make it very cosy in here, actually. A roaring fire.'

We all turned to look at the enormous hearth. It would be spectacular with a fire in it.

Harry smiled at me. 'January? What do you say, Lily? I think that sounds rather wonderful.'

'January?' was all I was able to reply. That was just weeks away.

'Yes,' said Gloria. Her hair was tied back in a tight little bun, and she had lipstick on her teeth. 'The weekend of January the twenty-second.'

'I think I'd prefer May,' I said.

Harry laughed. 'I know. January's rather soon – it would make Christmas rather hectic. But you know, darling, the weather is just as likely to be crappy in May, and imagine us all in here, huddling away from the cold. It would be fearsomely romantic.'

'Well . . .' I said.

'Yes,' he decided.

We stood in the car park above the fort, and he leaned into the phone as he called his mother.

'She was delighted,' he said. The wind blew my hair

around my face. 'Beside herself. She's sorting out the caterers. Apparently we have to use an outfit she knows in Hampstead. Best just to let her get on with those kinds of things herself. Gloria's getting her florist to call us. I know Constanza has a friend with a string quartet in Falmouth so I'll see if I can book them. What else?'

'Harry,' I said. He looked down at me, and seemed to focus on me properly for the first time.

'Hey, Lily!' he said, and he kissed the top of my head and pulled me close to him. 'Don't look so scared. It's just a piece of paper. Don't let the arrangements over-whelm you. It's better this way: one big flurry and it's done. There's nothing you have to do but get fitted for a dress and turn up on the day. That's it. It's not about the wedding – that's for Nina more than anyone else – for Nina and to put two fingers up to the world. It's about the marriage.'

'I know. It's just . . .'

'What is it?'

I took a deep breath. 'I need to do something. Can I take Mia away for a weekend? Kind of like a hen weekend, but just her and me? I've only left Cornwall once and I haven't really got anyone to do anything exciting with. But I'd like to do something, like other people do.'

He looked surprised. 'Of course you can. Go away with Mia, go to a spa or something. It's a great idea. We'll make sure you have a wonderful time. We'll need to find a weekend between now and January.'

'What about the first weekend in December?' I said, trying to sound casual. 'In a couple of weekends' time?'

'Absolutely. Avoid the Christmas rush.'

I smiled. 'Thank you.'

Harry was at work, and I was giving the house a proper clean like I used to do, when a bang on the front door startled me so much that my heart started pounding. The post woman knocked gently. No one else ever came to the house.

There it was again. I looked out of the window, but could not see who it was. I could see the sea and lots of trees and houses, but not my own visitor. I took the stairs two at a time and opened the door nervously.

'Al!' I screamed. I threw my arms around his neck. 'Al, you're back!'

I hugged him and, tentatively, his arms were around me, rubbing my back, a bit trembly. When I stepped back and looked at him properly, I was shocked. His face was bloated, his eyes unfocused, and he had lost a lot of weight. He did not smell good, either.

'You look terrible,' I said gently. 'Come in. Have a cup of tea.'

He followed me into the house, closing the door carefully behind him, stopping to take his shoes off.

'Um,' he said. 'Congratulations. When's the wedding?'

'Probably in January,' I told him. 'I could show you seating plans and colour schemes, but I won't.'

'Let's have a look at the ring.'

He took my left hand and looked at it. I felt like a girl from a film, holding my hand out. I was getting married, to my darling Harry. And now Al was back.

'So,' I told him. 'I was worried about you, Al. What's been happening?'

He sat down at the kitchen table. 'Nice pad.'

'Thanks.'

'You've done better than me. Christ. Never meet people online – not that you're going to need to meet anyone for the moment. It doesn't work. You know what people do online? They lie.'

'I'm sure they do. How bad?'

'Bad. But then Boris emailed. He emailed me three times and said I should get in touch with you. And you left me all those messages. So I'm back.'

I got to work making tea, reminding myself of Boris's wife, Emma. If in doubt, make a cup of tea. Grandma would have approved of that.

'No chance of anything stronger?' he asked, but in so defeated a voice that I knew he did not expect it.

'No. Sorry. Al, do you need to get some more of those pills that make you sick when you drink?'

He waved a bony hand, dismissing the idea. 'Yeah, I will. One of these days.'

'What are you doing?' I put a cup of tea in front of him, and a plate of cupcakes that I had made for Harry to take to work. He took one immediately.

'Oh Christ, Lily, I've missed you. What is it about you that makes me feel I'm letting you down if I don't face up to things? I'm an alcoholic, I know that. We all know it. I lost it, lost the plot, all my hard-earned sobriety and sanity, over Boris. It's scary, and suddenly, there was drink, my best friend, willing to welcome me back into its smelly arms.'

I touched his hand. 'But you know what, Al? I can imagine how it happened. If Harry – well, if he suddenly

293

left me to go back to Sarah, if she wasn't dead – I can see exactly how I'd go crazy too. When you love someone like that, you can lose sight of reason.'

'Maybe one day I'll see it as a proper adventure. Glasgow – now that's a city. You'd like it actually. I thought it would be a hard-drinking hellhole, but it wasn't – parts of it were very posh. I sat on the train heading north, and for a while putting all that distance between me and Boris felt good. Really, really good, you know? But that was partly because I had this guy, Jonathan, built up in my mind as the new love of my life. And he wasn't. He was an idiot, a scary idiot, and he was into some very weird stuff – trust me, you don't want to know. Then it turned out he was obsessed with Maggie Thatcher. Had a room in his flat devoted to her. It was worse than Boris and his fucking wife, I can tell you.'

'Oh, my goodness.'

'Yes, your goodness. It was all a bit freaky, but he liked the look of me, and it became quite hard to get away. But I made it out in the end, down the fire escape.

'Anyway . . . Then I wandered around Glasgow having adventures. But it was still about Boris. All of it. When I found his emails telling me to come and see you, I couldn't get back here fast enough. I have no idea what I'm going to do. I fare-dodged all the way down here on the train because I've got nothing. No cash. No place to go. No job. No prospects. I don't feel the urge to go to Boris's house, though. That's good, isn't it?'

'But you sorted yourself out with benefits?'

'And spent it all on booze and men I didn't like.'

'You can do it. I'll help you. We'll get you together.'

Al drank all his tea in one gulp.

'Lily,' he said. 'You're getting married. You live in a huge house. You go to college. What would your fiancé say if you said I was moving into one of what must be your many spare rooms? He'd hit the fucking roof.'

I tried to imagine myself broaching the topic with Harry.

'I don't think I'd be able to ask him, Al,' I said. 'Because it's not my house. It's not up to me.'

'I wouldn't do it to you, Lils. I'd ruin your marriage.'

I went and found my purse. There were three ten-pound notes in there. I gave them all to Al.

'You mustn't spend it on alcohol,' I said bossily.

'OK, Captain, I'll do my best. Thank you.'

I looked at him hard, wondering whether to suggest he should talk to Julia about my old room. I thought of the children in that house, and decided I couldn't. I felt powerless to help him.

When he left, a Tupperware pot of food in his hand, muttering vaguely about hostels, I felt I had failed him so badly that I ran upstairs, lay down on the bed, and cried.

chapter thirty-two

The first weekend of December

In spite of everything, going away was exhilarating. I had co-opted Mia into my horrible lie easily enough, by pretending I was sourcing unspecified 'special secret surprises' for Harry for our wedding.

'I'll explain all of it,' I told her. 'But for now, you just have to go along with my story, if he asks. Which he won't.'

My only fear had been that Harry might see her in Falmouth during the time when we were 'away'.

'Is there anywhere you'd like to go instead?' I had asked.

'Actually,' she said shyly, 'there is. I'd like to go to Plymouth.'

'Your mum?'

'Yeah.' After a few minutes, she had opened up a bit. 'I'm in touch with her, like I told you. Remember when she sent me those pyjamas?'

'Last Christmas,' I remembered.

'Yeah. Before that she'd been posting money. Like, I'd

just open an envelope and there'd be fifty pounds in there and a piece of paper saying *love from Mum* on it, with a row of little kisses. I didn't know what to do with it, but I didn't want to tell Dad or he'd have made her stop.'

'You gave some to the twins?'

'Yeah. It felt good, to pass it on a bit. That didn't last, anyway. I don't know where she'd got it but it stopped. And as you know, we've been talking for a bit, and now she says she wants to meet me.'

I tried to get my head round this. I knew how I would feel if my mother suddenly wanted to see me, and I felt a stab of jealousy.

'You can't go and stay with her.'

'Yeah, I don't want to. I don't want to be her ickle girl. She can't tell me when it's bedtime or any of that shit. But I do want to see her.'

In the end, we came up with the best plan we could. I had booked and paid for a hotel for her to stay in, and she was going to Plymouth with Joe, who had promised to go to the meeting with her. I had even spoken to Mia's mother on the phone.

'I just want to do the right thing,' she kept saying.

All the same, I was not completely sure whether I was making a huge mistake by allowing this to happen. There was no one I could ask.

There were so many layers to my deceit this weekend, that I was barely managing to remember who was supposed to know what. Nobody at all knew where I was actually going.

We called for Mia on the way to the station. I rang the

bell, while Harry waited in the car outside. The pavements were still icy, and I had to tread with care. I was wearing a pair of nice shoes with wedge heels that I thought someone might put on if they were going to Cheltenham on a spa weekend. I had comfortable walking shoes in my bag.

Mia was waiting just inside the front door.

'Bye, guys,' she shouted. 'Wow, look at that car. I get to ride in a red sports car!'

'Have a great time, you two,' Julia called from the sitting room. 'Have a sauna for me. Wish I was coming with you.'

'Yeah,' said Mia, eyes wide. 'So do we. Not.'

Outside, I opened the passenger door and moved the seat forward so that Mia could climb into the tiny back seat.

'Hey, Lily,' said Harry, 'why not let Mia sit in the front? I haven't really properly met her. And considering that she's going to be a bridesmaid at my wedding . . .'

I squeezed into the back. 'Sure.'

Mia looked uncomfortable as she settled herself into the front seat of the car. I looked out of the window at the frost on the trees and on the parked cars, and listened to their conversation.

'So, Mia,' Harry said. 'Looking forward to Lily's hen weekend?'

'Yes.'

'Don't be nervous of me. We're practically going to be related. So, is there a Mr Mia? I'm sure a pretty girl like you can't be young, free and single?'

She giggled and the back of her neck went pink. 'There's Joe. We've been going out nearly a year but he's moving to Newcastle.'

'Newcastle! Why in God's name does he want to move to *Newcastle*?'

I tuned out. Harry was charming her again and I was glad they were meeting properly. I hated myself for deceiving him. My stomach was churning and I ached with regret. I ought to be confiding in him, rather than creeping around behind his back. I just wanted it all to be all right.

By the time he dropped us at Truro station, I had to make an effort to look him in the face. I felt he would be able to read everything written plainly on my features. He did not seem to notice anything, however, and enfolded me in his arms.

'This is rubbish,' he said. 'Let's not be apart again, OK?'

'OK,' I agreed. I wanted to stay. Everything about him made me want to stay at his side and trust that everything was, in fact, as it seemed.

Joe was already quietly sitting at the other end of the train, and came to join us as soon as Truro was behind us. They got off at Plymouth, thinking I was carrying on to London on my unspecified secret mission. In fact, I stayed on the train as far as Reading, where I followed the signs for the bus to Heathrow, and sat on a coach for forty minutes, thrilled and horrified at what I was doing, and driven on solely by the unswerving conviction that only by doing this would I know for certain.

If I found that Sarah was alive, I would have to tell him. If she had died, however, I would discover that easily enough and I would rush home ready for my wedding. Harry would be none the wiser.

All the same, January felt a bit soon.

Emily Barr

My flight left at six. I got off the bus in front of Terminal 3, and discovered that navigating around an airport was surprisingly easy. I had dreaded this part, assuming that because I had never done it before, I would have no idea what to do, and was fully prepared to grab someone in uniform and ask for help. In fact, I found my flight listed on a screen, easily located the check-in desk, and handed over my passport and paperwork.

I smiled a nervous smile at the man behind the desk, but he just asked a string of routine questions, printed out a card and handed it to me, while looking completely bored.

There were clusters of people everywhere, crowds and queues, and I should have been trembling in fear and longing to be back in our lovely house; but as at Paddington station, I revelled in it. I loved staring at the people, listening to snatches of their conversation in all sorts of languages as I passed. I liked being just a face in the crowd, ignored and accepted.

I stood in a queue at security quite happily. When a man gave me a plastic bag and told me to put 'yer liquids' in it, I did so without question. The only 'liquids' I had in my bag were a face moisturiser, a body lotion, and a tube of foundation from Boots that Julia had given me, months earlier. The face and body lotions were taken away for being too big, but I was allowed to keep the foundation. This was baffling, but I didn't really care. I had changed more cash into Euros than I thought I was going to need, and I imagined it would be easy enough to replace them.

The departures area was full of shops, and people

sleeping across rows of seats, and noise. I loved it. There was a long queue at WH Smith, and I stood in it happily and purchased a guide book. I found my gate, where things were much calmer, bought a coffee from a little stand nearby, and sat and read, glancing out of the window at the planes more often than I glanced at the page.

Look at me, I kept thinking. Just look at me. I'm going on a plane.

There was a constant nagging guilt about the deception I was perpetrating on my darling Harry. However, I told myself that I was doing it for good reasons. I was doing it because I loved him. Even if he did discover my deceit, when I explained he would understand. It wasn't me, it was Sarah. He would understand, because I knew he loved me and would forgive me, no matter what.

An aeroplane landed, right outside the window. People came off it, and trudged out and away, into the belly of the airport. Then, all of a sudden, I was on a plane. The air was stale and it was more mundane than I would ever have imagined. I found my seat, carefully fastened my seatbelt. After a while, the steps slid away from the aeroplane. I closed my eyes, and waited, and then I was away.

Some of the people on this train had also been on my flight. When we boarded at Heathrow, they had all seemed to be speaking English. Now, suddenly, the same people were Spanish. I had been trying to study Spanish. If I focused, I could understand the odd word. Two women sitting opposite me were talking, in a desultory manner, about Michael Jackson. I could tell because they kept saying his name. Some boys, younger than me, were, I thought, discussing a woman. After a while, I began to wonder whether it was me. I looked up and caught the eye of the youngest-looking one, who blushed and looked away.

Everything was different, intense. I had been swept along by the crowd, through Passport Control, where a thin-faced man barely even glanced at my shiny passport, and onto a shuttle bus where the driver did not seem to want any cash. I got off, following the masses, at the train station. A ticket was three euros. The machine gave me change.

Now I was sitting on a train from Barcelona airport into the city, and no one apart from that boy was looking at me. My little bag was at my feet, and the train was a bit smelly and clunked loudly on its rails, and I was a part of an entirely alien scene.

I studied the map on the back of the *Rough Guide* that I bought at Heathrow. I needed to change onto the purple line of the Metro at Passeig de Gràcia. I would get out at Monumental, two stops down the line, and walk a little way to where I hoped I would find my hotel. I had not yet been on the London Underground, but I was well on my way to completing my first journey on the Barcelona Metro.

I got off at Passeig de Gràcia, and did my best to follow the signs to my next train. I walked and walked and walked. A huge corridor, its floor black and rubbery, stretched onwards, walls grimy but well lit, a man exactly halfway along it playing Bob Dylan on the guitar and singing 'Blowing in the Wind' with a heavy accent.

I stopped in front of him. He winked at me without pausing, and I put one of the euro coins that the ticket machine had spat at me into his hat. He smiled such a warm smile that I grinned all the way to my next train.

When I came out of the Metro, finally, at Monumental, I kept my head down. For a city that, according to the guide book, was busy twenty-four hours a day, it was very quiet. In fact, it was deserted.

The smell here was different. There were exhaust fumes on the air, and the indefinable smells of a city in which people ate different food and lived different lives from the ones I knew.

I found the right direction in which to walk. A few cars passed, but there were not many of them although it was a main road. Tall and broad apartment buildings, with wrought iron around tiny balconies, lined the road, but all their windows, rising up higher and higher above me in rows, were blank. I tried to imagine who was inside, but all I knew about Barcelona was what the relentlessly upbeat prose of the guide book had told me. I had been expecting people who were so cool they would not even look at me, people with asymmetrical haircuts and funky glasses, and quirky bars and clubs, and music everywhere. This quiet reality was both stranger and more mundane than anything I had expected. I tried to calm myself, and keep walking. I felt my breathing becoming more and more agitated, my footsteps faster, and in the end I ran to the hotel.

Its double glass doors slid open silently at my approach, and I walked into a lobby that had a fake marble floor, with a massive open-plan dining room off to the left, and a reception desk in front of me.

It was after midnight, and there was no one in the lobby

at all. The lighting was low and spooky. I walked over to the desk and stood there, waiting for something to happen. Almost at once, a man walked out from a glass door behind the reception desk, and smiled.

According to his name badge, his name was Dean.

'Hello,' he said in perfect English. 'Checking in?'

'Yes.' I wanted to ask how he knew I was English, but I didn't. 'My name is Lily Button.' I could not help looking around the room as I identified myself. My name is Lily Button (which is a stupid name) and I should not be here. Yet I'm glad I am because this is already the best thing I've ever done. Apart from meeting Harry, that is.

He tapped at his keyboard, nodded, and handed me a form. Soon I had a key card in my hand and instructions to take the lift to the sixth floor. The lift took me up silently, and I passed rows of identical doors. Mine was number 628, and its door was different from the others, because it was on a diagonal piece of wall, on a corner. For a long time, I tried to work out how to persuade it to open with the credit-card-style key I had been given, and in the end, it turned out that inserting and removing the card, the right way round, very quickly, made a green light come on, and if I pressed the handle down at the very instant in which that happened, access was granted.

The room was beige, brown and orange, with a window that looked out on nothing but an expanse of white exterior wall and a blank window with its curtains closed. I was slightly disappointed not to see the entire city spread out before me, but *at least it was cosy*. I giggled aloud. Grandma had said those last five words, in my head, from beyond the grave.

I switched my phone on, and watched the little screen as it worked out where in the world it was, finally settling on a network called Movistar. As I looked, it beeped, and three texts appeared.

The first was from Harry. *I'm missing you like crazy. Let's not be apart again* he wrote. My heart contracted at my treachery. The second was from Julia. *Hope you're having a lovely time at your spa, you two! x* The third was from Al. *Sorry 2 turn up like that. Got some pills. doing ok.*

I texted Harry back, hating myself, replied to Julia with a mendacious affirmative, and wrote to Al: *don't be sorry. I'm the one that's sorry. crap friend. really, everything is up in the air right now, will call you when I have news. see you in a couple of weeks? can you advise yourself about benefits and find a proper place to live again?* I brushed my teeth, and washed some of the airport grime from my feet. Then I lay down on the bed. I listened to the distant traffic, and wondered what on earth might be going to happen to me tomorrow.

chapter thirty-three

I sat on a high stool at the bar and smiled at the thin woman who handed me a coffee in a white mug and a croissant on a saucer. Every café I had passed seemed to be exactly like this one: rickety tables and chairs, stools at the bar, a few people drinking tall glasses of beer. The air was thick with cigarette smoke.

'Gracias,' I said, and the woman still seemed to understand me and said something brisk in reply.

My coffee was small but strong. I surveyed the scene. It was strange, but not at all frightening. I had imagined foreign countries to be more intimidating than this. Moving a couple of miles into Falmouth had been far more difficult than this was proving to be, so far. This city made me feel the same way my brief glimpse of London had: that there was room for everyone, that I could exhale and be myself, and no one would mutter or gossip.

The map – Sarah's map – was spread in front of me, part of it resting on the counter. I touched my current location with a finger. The closest of Sarah's places to me was four blocks away, along the main road, Gran Via de les Corts Catalanes, and two streets down. It was just marked with a red cross. I would go there first.

I sipped my drink and pulled pieces off the croissant and ate them. I drained the last drops from my cup, paid my bill, and jumped off my stool, ready to go.

It turned out that it was easy to get around this city on foot, guide book in hand. I walked to the spot marked by the red cross with no trouble at all. My heart pounded as I approached it. I had no idea what I was going to see there: if it was an apartment building, I would have a good look round, just in case Sarah herself might be there.

She would not. I knew she would not. She was dead.

It was a little restaurant, a place down some stairs with a menu on a chalk board outside it. It was closed, but I peered in through the barred windows and saw tables with white cloths on them, set for lunch with cutlery and wine glasses.

Above it was an office block, and above that, I supposed, apartments, but I was not going to bother to check them out. I pictured Harry walking down the steps, arm-in-arm with his tempestuous wife, heading to the restaurant. It was all too plausible, and I tried not to be jealous of a woman he had married, lovelessly, when I was ten.

I walked to the Arc de Triomf, and down the large paved area south of it. People rode bicycles around me, and they jogged past, and walked in groups, and laughed and talked. I just carried on. At the end of the walkway, I turned and headed in approximately the right direction.

I looked around me as I walked. I glanced at wrought-iron

window bars, the peeled paint on a light green door, a man kneeling on the pavement with a paintbrush. A black taxi with yellow doors swerved by far too fast. A small woman with short grey hair and glasses and a Mao jacket stared at me as I walked past her doorway.

I wandered down little streets with washing hanging out of all the windows, and through occasional squares with tables set out in them. I took a roundabout route to my destination, checking other places Sarah had marked. One of them was an English language school. Another was a government office of some kind. It was all just out of reach.

Half an hour later, I paused outside the police station on Carrer Nou de la Rambla. In this building, I was going to find out the answer to my question, one way or another. I would walk out of this door knowing that she was dead, almost certainly. Presuming that they were going to tell me, anyway.

It was strange to hope someone was dead, but I did. Then I would be able to go home and get married. Perhaps Harry would be amenable to moving away, to a city somewhere, and starting a new life in which no one knew our history. Maybe we could move to Paris, or New York, or Sydney. We could easily go and live in a place in which no one would ever give us a second glance.

I shook my head to dislodge the daydreams, and pushed the glass door.

It was bright and modern inside, and not at all scary. In my imagination, foreign police stations were horrific places, into which the tourist would disappear, only to emerge twenty years later, hairy and skeletal from a dirty prison.

There was a reception desk, glassed off from the lobby, and a good-looking, chunky man behind it smiled at me. His springy hair was cut short, but not so short that it lost its spring.

'*Hola,*' he said.

'*Hola,*' I said. '*Habla inglés?*'

'Little,' he said with a grin.

I did my best to explain that I was looking to speak to someone about my friend, who had died in Barcelona last Christmas Day. As an afterthought, I said that it was not actually my friend, it was my sister, because I thought they might tell me more that way. I asked, slowly and carefully, whether it would be possible for me to get a copy of whatever police report there was into her death. I looked at him, pleading with my eyes.

He frowned, then laughed.

'It's normal that someone steals your handbag,' he said, in English. 'Nobody steals your handbag?'

'Nobody.'

He went over what I had just asked him, asked for my sister's name, for my name, for the dates and locations, and he handed me a ticket with D6 printed on it, and told me to go to the waiting room.

I sat in a plastic chair in a large airy room with windows along the top of the wall, tiles on the floor, and two humming vending machines at the far end of the room. I nodded at a middle-aged couple who were sitting a couple of seats away from me, talking so rapidly that I could not differentiate the words, let alone understand any of them.

I was not even sure whether they were speaking Spanish or Catalan. A man on his own sat right at the end of the room, near the drinks machine. I took my book out of my bag and started to read, but I could not concentrate. I was scared that Harry was going to call. I was scared about what I was going to find out.

The couple went to an interview room when their number came up, suddenly quiet as they crossed the room. Two French women arrived, talking, I deciphered, about a stolen handbag. The man on his own was called to a room. Three young black men arrived and sat where he had been. I stood up and walked across the room to read the posters on the noticeboard. One of them was a series of cartoons about what to do if it snowed. With the help of the accompanying cartoons, I worked it out: only go out if you have to, run hot water through your pipes, if you need to use the car, pack the boot with spare clothes, food and drink just in case. More people arrived, and were called. They seemed to have forgotten about me.

By the time D6 came up, I was on the verge of leaving. Then the machine buzzed, and it was there. D6 to B7.

My legs shook as I walked to the waiting-room door, not looking at anyone. I went back past the man on the reception desk, who gave me a cheerful grin. Two other officers walked by me and went through a door, he a black man, she a peroxide-blonde woman. They laughed and joked and took no notice of me.

B7 turned out to be a cubbyhole, containing a desk with two chairs on my side of it and one on the other, screened off from identical spaces on either side of it, and with an open-plan police office visible behind the police officer's chair. There was a woman sitting there, not much older than me, with jet-black hair and black civilian clothes on.

I sat down and she smiled. I forced a smile back. She held her head on one side and asked me to go over all the details.

'You are completely sure about this?'

'Yes,' I said. 'Christmas Day, nearly a year ago. She died in the water.'

'In Barcelona?'

'Yes, of course.'

'Not Sitges, not Vilanova?'

'No. Here.'

Then she shook her head. 'I'm sorry,' she said, in slow, clear English. 'I have looked back over the records, but that information would be easy to find. Everyone would know. Nobody died in the water, here, at Christmas last year, or this year, or a different year. It happens sometimes when the weather is bad. I'm sorry about your sister, but this must have happened in a different place, or at a different time.'

'No one died like that here last Christmas?'

'No one.'

Next stop was the hotel they had stayed at. It was the three-star one in the back streets, not the luxurious place Harry had described. Why had he done that?

I was disorientated by my new knowledge. If Sarah had died, the police would know – and yet they had no record of her drowning. Fergus said he had watched them pulling her body out of the water. That meant he had lied. The fact that she had not died in Barcelona did not mean that she was still alive, of course. It simply meant that the story everyone had been told about her death was not true.

I stood on the other side of the narrow road. The building was painted cream, and had windowboxes with geraniums in them, the usual wrought-iron decorations around the bottom of the windows and, through the glass doors, I could see a cream lobby. The hotel's name was on the whitewashed wall in gold metal letters, and there were three discreet stars underneath the words.

The doors opened automatically as I approached. There was classical music playing in the entrance hall. I looked around, at the white sofa and wicker chairs. This was too shabby for Harry. He must have hated it.

A young man appeared and looked at me quizzically. Every single word of Spanish deserted me.

'Hello,' I said. 'Do you speak English?'

'Of course,' he said pleasantly. He was dressed in black trousers and a white shirt, as if he were going to a wedding, but not a very smart one.

'I need to ask you something,' I said. My hand shook as I reached into my bag and took out the picture of Harry and Sarah that I had stolen from their wedding album, which now lived in the bottom of a box at the back of a cupboard. 'My friends stayed here at Christmas last year. While they were here, one of them,' I pointed to Sarah, 'died. Do you remember them?'

He frowned and took the photo. 'She? No one has died at the hotel.'

'No,' I agreed. 'Not at the hotel. Out in Barcelona. In the sea.'

'Oh.' He shook his head. 'Sorry. But I did not work here.'

'OK. Is there anyone who did?'

He screwed his face up. 'No, I'm sorry.'

'No one at all I could talk to?'

'No, sorry. Nobody.'

'Oh.' I wondered what to say next. I heard the doors slide open behind me, and I saw his attention transfer instantly from me, an annoying visitor who was not paying any money but just asking stupid questions, to some more important people.

I had to keep hold of the man's attention.

'Is there anyone who was here?' I asked quickly. 'Last Christmas?'

'Come after four o'clock,' he said. Then he turned his back on me and greeted his new visitors, a smiling couple in matching slacks and raincoats.

Between now and four o'clock I had nothing to do. Since I had read the guide book, I knew what I ought to be doing. I should go to the Sagrada Familia, to Gaudí's great unfinished cathedral. It was Barcelona's top tourist sight, and Sarah had marked it, perhaps for herself and Harry, on the map.

I started walking.

chapter thirty-four

The walk to the cathedral was a blur. There were people in the way, in coats and boots and with their heads down, and as I wove my way between them, I felt invisible. Everyone was lying, and nothing made any sense at all.

I kept taking wrong turnings, because I was not concentrating. I went down blind alleys, came out on roads I had already passed twenty minutes earlier, discovered myself walking south when I felt I was walking north. When I found myself, yet again, on Las Ramblas, I decided to walk right up it.

There were flower stalls, and stalls selling poor, cold little birds in cages. There were people disguised as robots standing very still. The crowds were probably far bigger in summer, but it still felt crammed with people. They ambled around with guide books in their hands, taking photos with their phones. I pushed through the middle of groups, but no one said a word to me. I could do anything. I could walk down the middle of a road and nothing would happen. I could do a handstand at the doorway of the huge department store, El Corte Inglés, and no one would notice me.

I found my way to Gaudí's Cathedral anyway, without meaning to. It was the middle of the afternoon, and I was dizzy. I had only eaten the croissant for breakfast, and I was starving. There was a queue by the ticket counter, but since nothing was making sense, I just walked to the front of it, smiled at the people waiting next in line, and barged in. Nobody said anything; I had known it would happen that way.

I handed over some euros and walked in.

This was a cathedral that was still being built. A crane soared higher than its towers. I stared at it. Because it was called a cathedral, I had expected it to be a bit like Truro Cathedral. Instead, it was something completely different, with several gothic towers with curvy patterns on them and, as I got closer, organic shapes, the ones you saw in plants and trees and leaves, that swirled around it. I liked the soft edges. In real life, this place was overwhelming.

Around the back, there was a bench, and a group of proper tourists were sitting on it looking at the Passion façade over the door. I went inside, feeling reverent in spite of myself, and stood on the edge of the building site. Now it seemed we were back in medieval times, when cathedrals sprang up. It took my breath away. This was the inside of a cathedral, but it had all the detritus of construction work: there were bags of sand, tools, even a little digger.

They had all lied. I was lying too, just by being here. I knew that I was in the middle of something I did not understand at all. If I had had Fergus's phone number, I would have called him, then and there. But I did not. There was nobody who would help me now.

I could smell the builders' sand in the air. It was dusty and cold, and my breath was puffing out around me. When I struggled back outside, my legs gave way and the bench was empty just in time. I sat on it, closed my eyes, and wondered what on earth I was going to do.

When the man sat next to me, I ignored him. Ignoring everyone, and being ignored back, was suiting me. After a while, I could tell that he wanted to say something. I looked at him.

He had thick blond hair and cheeks that were pink from the cold.

'Hey,' he said, in an accent, 'are you OK?'

'Yes, of course.' My voice sounded crisp and very correct after his. I sounded like the Queen.

'That's good then. You looked like you might not be feeling too well.'

He was not much older than me, and he was the first person I had properly met since I arrived here. This was a strange experience that might not be happening to me anyway. What the hell? I thought. I had never thought 'what the hell?' in my life before, and I smiled at my recklessness.

'I was feeling a bit weird,' I admitted, 'but not ill. Just odd.'

'Oh, sorry to hear that,' he said. 'You better now?'

'Kind of.'

'On holiday?'

I laughed. 'Not exactly. It's a long story. I guess "on holiday" could be the short version.'

'Not a happy holiday?'

'No. Not a happy holiday.'

I looked again at his open face. I knew nothing about anything, had no idea how to read people, but this man seemed nice enough. I needed not to be on my own right now, and he was here, talking to me.

'I think some food would make a difference,' I said to him. 'Do you want to go to a café or something?'

He leaped to his feet. 'Best offer I've had all year.'

chapter thirty-five

Jack went to the cathedral because he had been living in Barcelona for months and it was the only place in the city that even Kiwis knew, and people kept assuming he'd been there, and it was getting embarrassing.

He queued for half an hour or so, even though it was December and he had expected to walk straight in. He tried to imagine a church in New Zealand that could make people stand in line for thirty-three minutes, and pay twelve euros just for the privilege of wandering in and having a look around.

It was worth it. Of course it was.

He wasn't working this afternoon, and after he'd done this bit of catch-up sightseeing, he was going to go shopping for the ingredients for a fish stew. He blew on his hands and stared up at the cathedral's façade. It was one of those cold crisp days that took the skin off your face, and something warming was going to be just the ticket.

He could see why everyone raved about this place. It was like an old cathedral that you saw in books, but it was different. The Mary and baby, for instance: they did not look like the traditional ones. Everything was very slightly different. The shapes were not at all like normal church shapes, and he liked that about it. It was a bit cheeky. You could stare at it for days. He spent half an hour walking around looking delightedly at everything, then sat himself down on a bench and took some photos.

He was going through his shopping list in his head when he noticed there was a girl next to him. He was not even sure who had been here first – it was possible she'd been there all along – but he noticed her now because she seemed to be gasping for breath. She was biting her lip and closing her eyes, and she was deathly pale. When her eyes were open, they were astonishing: enormous, a deep and soft brown.

Although she was not the girl in his head, he was drawn to her. The more he looked, the more she interested him. He tried to catch her attention, but she was concentrating on getting the breath in and out, as far as he could tell. After a while he leaned forward to where she would see him if she opened her eyes, and said: 'Hey, are you OK?'

It took her a while to answer. He thought she was ignoring him, or that she could not even hear him. Also, he had said it in English, which was stupid of him. She might be going to keel over at any moment. What did you do if that happened? He looked around for someone in uniform.

Then she suddenly said: 'Yes, of course.'

'That's good then,' said Jack, but he was uncertain. 'You looked like you might not be feeling too well.'

He tried not to stare at her too much, because it would

319

make the poor girl uncomfortable, but as well as her beautiful eyes, she had the most amazing hair. It was long and curly and there was more of it than he had ever seen on any person before. Underneath all that, her face was like a china doll's, pretty and pale. He hoped she did not think he was coming on to her. He was worried about this girl, that was all. He corrected himself: this woman. Anya, from Serbia, had said that unless a girl was a child, you had to call her a woman. She was right, he could see that.

'I was feeling a bit weird, but not ill,' she said. 'Just odd.' She was English, like Peter. She talked like one of the BBC newsreaders they sometimes watched on the telly.

They spoke a bit, just polite chit-chat. It was a surprise, and a delight, when the woman asked if he'd like to go to a café.

Jack refused to go to one of the cafés outside the cathedral, because he avoided the places with hiked prices for tourists, and these fell into that category. He led her through a few streets, over some pedestrian crossings, round corners, and into a bakery on a random quiet street. It was a place he had spotted on the way over. There was a huge counter with all sorts of bread, sandwiches and pastries behind it and a delicious smell of baking. The chairs and tables were made of twiddly iron, which he often did not like, but there were cushions on the chairs which made them comfortable enough to be acceptable.

They sat opposite one another at a little table. She pushed her hair back, and he wondered what they were doing here. Months he had lived here, and he had met plenty of people, but only by studying with them, or teaching them or living with them. He had never picked up a stranger on the street before. He hoped she wasn't after sex or anything. The very possibility alarmed him intensely.

She still looked pale and he needed to get some food into her – quick, he reckoned.

'Right,' he said. 'What do you want?'

'Coffee,' she said immediately. 'And anything to eat – I don't care what. Not a croissant though, because I had one for breakfast.'

It wasn't until they were sipping their coffee and she was eating a sandwich while he put away a couple of Danish pastries, that they even introduced themselves.

'I'm Jack,' he said.

'Hi, Jack. Are you South African? Sorry, I'm not very good at accents.'

'Nah, I'm Kiwi. A New Zealander.'

This news seemed to affect her more than it ought to have done. He looked at her, wondering whether she was going to explain her interest.

'I'm Lily,' she said instead.

'Hey, Lily. I was worried about you back there. Thought I was going to have to call an ambulance or something.'

'Oh, no.' She looked horrified. 'Nothing like that. I'm just . . . well, it really is a long story.'

He shrugged. 'Do you want to try me?' When she looked unsure he said: 'You're never going to have to see me again. You can tell me anything you like. That's the great thing about strangers. It could be kind of liberating.' He gambled on saying this, because he was pretty sure she wasn't after his body.

'It might be good just to talk about it. I haven't been able to . . .' Her voice drifted off, and for a moment she was deep in thought. Jack studied her face while she weighed up whether or not she should tell him her secrets. He liked the fact that she seemed to have no idea how beautiful she was. There was nothing fake or pretentious about her. She was troubled, and so he wanted to help.

'I'm supposed to be getting married next month,' she said suddenly. 'But it's all become a little bit complicated. I'm hoping everything's going to be OK though.' She twiddled her ring. 'I really am.'

chapter thirty-six

I told him everything. He was a stranger, who was being nice to me even though he didn't know me at all. I had a good feeling about him; it felt as though I had known him for a long time already. He was a good listener, and we were sitting in a lovely little café and he was interested. It was the fact that he was from New Zealand that swung it for me. He was the most tenuous of links to my parents, and a tenuous link was a lot better than no link at all.

I started with the planned wedding, then went right back to the beginning of the story, last December, and told it from there.

He listened carefully, occasionally asking questions. We got through two coffees each during the time it took me to tell the tale. Listening to the story, told as objectively as I could manage it, was strange. It felt like someone else's life.

'So you want to marry him,' said Jack, 'but you can't do that if his first wife's still around. Have you thought about leaving her to it and just living with him for a while?'

I sighed. 'Yes, but the wedding's all planned. The bridesmaids' dresses are being made, and the food's all booked, and Harry's paid a huge deposit for the venue. And apart from any of that, I *want* to marry him. I've never felt this way about anyone before.'

Jack looked at me kindly. 'OK, so you're here to find her. You've done a good job so far, with the police and the hotel. Want me to come back there with you? See if we can persuade anyone at that hotel to tell us anything?'

I looked at the watch on his wrist. It was quarter to four.

'Would you? Sorry, I don't know you at all, and now you know everything about me. I shouldn't even be speaking to you, should I? You're a strange man.'

'Oh,' he said, 'I'm not *that* strange. I'm at a loose end. We can walk across town and by the time we get there, I'll have filled you in on my messed-up life too, and then we'll be quits.'

We walked together, Jack and me, and he was easy company. Part of me was terrified that Harry might somehow find out that I was strolling around Barcelona with a man I had just met. Yet what, I asked myself, would be the worst thing he could do? Call off the wedding? It was not the strange man that was the problem. It was the rest of it.

I tried to put everything else from my head and concentrate instead on Jack's story. He had been married for ten years, and was waiting for his divorce papers now.

'How old are you?' I interrupted.

'Twenty-nine. Yes, I married young. Marry in haste, repent at leisure: never a truer proverb was spoken.'

'Right. And you've got children? Don't you miss them?'

He laughed. 'I miss them like bloody crazy, as a matter of fact. I can't tell you how much I miss them. I was trying to get Rachel – that's my ex-wife – to bring them out here for Christmas. Fat chance of that happening. She says she'd put them on a plane on their own if she could, but there's no chance she's coming all the way over here, just for *me*.'

'Can't she put them on a plane, though? Children can travel on their own, can't they? Airlines look after them.'

He sighed. 'Not for that distance. They'd be terrified. I did look into it, but they have to be at least five, and LeEtta, my little one, she's only just four. And the others are too young for a journey like that without a parent. Trust me, if I could, I would. Christ, that trip was pretty much too scary for me, let alone for my kids.'

We crossed to the middle of one of the wide avenues. I was warm now, from the exercise, though the air was freezing and the pavement was icy with puddles. There were little beds of stiff grass, iced into individual points. Jack was surprisingly easy to talk to. It was lovely to concentrate on the problems of a complete stranger with three children and an estranged wife on the other side of the world. No conversation had ever been more refreshing.

We walked back down the Ramblas. The human statues were putting their coats on and getting ready to leave, and the bird vendors were pulling thick cloths over the cages. When we reached the little hotel, I was yanked back to reality with a jolt.

'Oh, bloody hell,' I said, and giggled because I was not used to swearing.

Jack laughed, too. 'That was posh. You sound like the Princess of Cornwall or something.'

'I am the Princess of Cornwall,' I told him.

'Then, Your Majesty, shall we go in? How's your Spanish?'

'I do my best, but it's bad,' I admitted. 'Terrible, actually. How's yours?'

'Bad, too, considering I've been living here since the summer. But probably better than yours. Want me to give it a go?'

I handed him the photo of Harry and Sarah. He paused and stared at it. 'Hey,' he said. 'This the bloke? Wasn't he on telly?'

'He was, but ages ago. I mean, years and years ago. You couldn't have seen him.'

He nodded. 'I could. We get reruns of all your old stuff in New Zealand. Harry Summer. He was in that thing set in the doctor's surgery?'

I tried not to let my shock show too much. Then I remembered that it didn't matter, and let my jaw drop. 'That is the freakiest thing. You knowing his name. I never saw him on TV so I had no idea who he was, until I started cleaning his house.'

'And his wife, too. Was she on telly?'

'No, not that I know of.'

'Ah, right.' He stared at it. 'I've seen her, I know I have.' He shook his head. 'Someone who looks like her, anyway.'

'Really?'

He shrugged. 'Feels that way. Right – ready?'

'Ready.'

As soon as he saw me again, the young man called back through a curtain behind him, and motioned to me and Jack to sit down. A woman came bustling out, and the young man pointed at us and turned his attention to a big book on a table. He was conspicuously listening.

The woman was broad-shouldered and a bit fat: Grandma would have called her 'stout'. She was wearing hotel uniform, black and white, with thick black tights and dyed black hair in a bun. She started talking quickly, and finished with what was obviously a question, looking first at me and then at Jack, expectantly.

Jack began to reply to her in Spanish, and as she nodded, I could see his confidence growing.

She said something back to him. I strove even to differentiate the words from one another. Jack reached out and took the photograph from me, showed it to the woman. She stared for a while, and then spoke to Jack. He asked her to say it again, more slowly. I could tell that, from his tone of voice.

He turned to me. 'She remembers them. They shouted and screamed at each other. Everyone who was here would remember them. He stayed in the room for a couple of days because he was ill. She left him. Another man came to help him. But she didn't die.'

'She's completely sure?'

He asked her again.

'She's completely sure. She says she's sorry if this lady has died, but no, it did not happen when the couple stayed here. They were all glad to see the back of the pair of them.'

chapter thirty-seven

'Don't worry,' he said, and his hand was under my elbow. He thanked the woman and steered me out through the automatic doors. A biting wind was funnelled down the street outside and I pulled my coat around myself.

'She's not dead at all,' I said. 'Is she?'

'Doesn't sound like it.'

'Harry doesn't know. He wouldn't be marrying me if he knew. He has no idea. But Fergus does. He practically told me, actually, in London.'

We started walking.

'You going to tell me who Fergus is, then?'

'Harry's brother. He tried to get me to postpone the wedding.'

'And rightly so, by the sound of it. OK. It seems we're a bit out of our depth here. Can you contact Fergus? Is that an option?'

I thought about it. 'No. I'd have to call Harry to get his number, and there's no way Harry would give that to me. He doesn't trust his brother as it is.'

'Come on. Come with me. We'll make a plan.'

I followed him without taking much notice of where we were going.

'How old are you, Lily?' he asked at one point. When I told him he was silent for a while. 'I know I'm not one to talk,' he said, as we crossed the next road, 'but that is far too young. From what you've said, you've seen nothing of the world. Don't tie yourself down with some man older than your dad.'

'But I love him. We can't go through with it anyway, can we? Not now. Because he already has a wife.'

A little later, Jack said: 'You think he doesn't know she's still alive? Really?'

'He *definitely* doesn't. He'd hardly have booked our wedding for next month, would he?'

'I guess not. It just seems a bit unusual.'

'I'll say.'

I walked where Jack walked, blind to my surroundings. The fact that I was in Barcelona with a stranger was the very least of my worries. It seemed like a perfectly natural setting for all of this. I followed him along tree-lined avenues, across pedestrian streets, past children and people walking little dogs, constantly passing ranks of city bikes.

Sarah was alive. The truth, or probable truth, of this, was taking my breath away. She had seemed so lovely, the one time I met her. Now I listed all the things I knew she had done. She had made Harry's life a misery. She had had huge fights with him, thrown things around and disturbed the neighbours. She had threatened to kill herself if he left her. And then – the big one – she had actually let him, and everyone else, think that she was dead. I had seen him in the aftermath of that. He was distraught. He had scattered whatever it was that Fergus had given him in place of her ashes, up on the cliffs that she had loved. He had retreated into the back bedroom, miserable for months and months. She had done that to him, when she could just as easily have asked for a divorce.

I hoped we would find her, so that she could explain something of how she had come to do that to the man she had once, at least, loved. I hoped we would *not* find her, because she was a very frightening human being indeed.

Eventually I walked with Jack through a big front door, into a tatty hallway and up some stairs. This apartment was on the very top floor, and my legs began to ache on the second staircase. I half-tripped on a piece of loose Formica, and caught myself on the banister. Jack was ahead of me.

'You all right there, Lily?' he called down. His voice echoed off the stairwell.

'I'm fine.'

By the time we reached the flat, my legs were on fire. I fell in through the open front door, and Jack caught me by the arm, led me down a dingy corridor and into a kitchen.

In fact, it was more than a kitchen. Its windows were steamed up, and it was crammed with old furniture and people. There was a wooden table, covered in plates and cups and paperwork. Two women sat on a stained brown sofa; one of them had her legs up on its arm. A man stood at the hob, boiling a pan of water. Another man was perched on a worktop. They all looked around at us.

'Jack!' said one of the girls. 'What is for dinner?' She sounded as though she were Russian or something.

The man got down from the worktop and walked over to me. He was good-looking, with creamy skin and wide brown eyes.

'This is Lily, guys,' said Jack. I saw the two girls look knowingly at one another. 'She's English,' he added. 'From Cornwall.'

'Hi,' said the creamy man. 'A fellow Brit! I'm Peter.'

I shook his hand. The girls heaved themselves up and the first one kissed me on each cheek. The second kissed me twice on each cheek. The man boiling the water shook my hand in his huge one. I tried to be brave, not to shrink away from them. When it was just Jack and me, I had felt safe.

I reached for all my courage and smiled around at them.

'Hello, everyone,' I said.

'Oh, sorry guys,' Jack said. 'There's nothing for dinner tonight.'

'But you said fish stew,' said the perhaps-Russian woman with a pout.

'I know, but then events overtook me. Look, Pete, can you take a peek at this pic? This woman here – I reckon I've seen her somewhere. Apparently she's not from the telly. What do you think?' He handed the piece of paper over.

'She does look a bit familiar,' said Peter. 'Maybe she's a TEFL teacher? I wouldn't swear to it though.'

No one else recognised her. Peter had no idea where

we would track her down. 'You could go round all the English schools with that photo,' he said dubiously. 'Might take a while, though.'

'I've got this map,' I said. 'I don't know if it'd be any use.'

Jack and I went out again together, into the night. We had eaten pasta and drunk a beer, and I was ready for some detective work.

'You don't mind doing this?' I asked him, as we walked to the corner, in the light of the street lamps. Some of the shops were still open, and there were people heading purposefully in all directions.

'No,' he said. 'I don't. Let's find her. I'm intrigued. Let's see if you're going to have your wedding or not.'

'Not,' I said. 'Your flatmate recognised her. That means she's alive.'

We walked side by side, and it was still easy to talk to him, this stranger from the other side of the world. We checked every place she had marked off: most of them were English schools, and almost all of them were shut up. We showed her picture at the ones that were open, but although one person thought she looked familiar, no one knew her. When we ended up back at the closed restaurant I had seen that morning, it was open, and filled with well-heeled patrons.

'May as well give it a go,' Jack said, and I gave him the photo.

I stood in the doorway as he found the manager and showed Sarah's picture to him. The man nodded. He was talking fast to Jack, pointing down the road. They talked for a couple of minutes, and then Jack came back. I bit my lip and looked at him questioningly.

'He said she looks like a woman called Alicia,' Jack said, as we came back out onto the pavement. 'Apparently she does the odd bit of waitressing work for him. And Lily?' I looked at him. 'Alicia is English.'

'Does he know where she lives?'

'No.'

'Oh.'

Armed with a name, we retraced our steps to the Tower Bridge School of English, where one of their staff had recognised her. It was half an hour away, and the night was cold. I wanted to take Jack's arm as we walked, for warmth and companionship, but I stopped myself. I was betraying Harry just by being here. I could not walk around holding onto another man, even though it was purely platonic.

'You know New Zealand?' I asked, after a while. It was easier to ask this in the dark.

'Yes, I do,' he agreed.

'Have you heard of a place called Mount Eden?'

'Mount Eden? I think that's up by Auckland. Why, do you know it?'

'No. Well. I've sent a few letters there. It's where my parents live. I think.'

'Seriously?'

Our feet clopped softly on the pavement, side by side.

'I've dreamed of Mount Eden. It's like they're half-dead, living on some paradise mountain.'

I could hear the smile in his voice. 'There's a prison there, I know that much. Sorry. I shouldn't shatter your illusions.'

'A prison?' I thought of my lost inheritance. I thought of things that take a lot of money. I pushed the thought aside.

'But I'm sure it's a perfectly nice place too,' he said quickly. 'I live on the other island, the South Island. Can I ask how come you've never been to see them over there?'

'They left me behind,' I told him. 'It doesn't matter. I got over it ages ago. I just want to see them again. I'm sure they've been living happily there, the two of them. They were so wrapped up in each other. That's what my grandparents said and that's the way I remember it too. They were madly in love, in a bit of a freaky way. There was no room for me.'

'Oh,' he said. 'Right. That's like the— doesn't matter.'

'No, tell me. There's not many things my parents are "like". No one ever compares them to anything. Normally people just shuffle a bit and change the subject.'

'No, it's nothing. There's just some sick fucks, famous in New Zealand. They're called the Monsters of Auckland. They ignored their baby until he died.'

It could not be. I knew it couldn't. I would put it from my mind.

'What was their name?' I asked, instead.

'Smith.'

'Right.' I shook my head, doing my best to dislodge the distressing thought. I was relieved when we arrived at the Tower Bridge English School.

A lesson had just finished, and there were students, adults who looked like working people, spilling out into the road. Jack held me back.

'Wait,' he said. 'We need her address. They won't give it to us. When we were in just now, there was a filing cabinet over in the corner, and one of the labels said *Teachers* on it. I'll distract our guy. You find it. Are you OK with that?'

I did not hesitate. 'Let's do it.' I realised that I had never done anything like this before. I had never broken the rules and potentially been caught red-handed in someone else's stuff. It was exciting.

Jack walked up to the man.

'Oh,' he said. 'Hello again. Found her yet?'

'No joy. But mate, I do TEFL too, and I'm with Business English.'

'Oh, yes?'

'Could I have a quick word with you in private?'

The man looked interested. 'This is perfectly private,' he said, as the last few students emptied out into the street. The office was completely visible through the glass doors to the outside world.

'More private?'

The man hesitated. 'Well, it sounds intriguing. Why not?'

'I'll wait out here,' I offered, and the man took Jack off into a side room. I vaguely wondered what Jack was going to say, to keep him out of the way for long enough. The moment the door clicked shut behind them, I was in front of the filing cabinet. I did not want to think about those people in Auckland. I was going to get this right. Nothing else mattered. I would think about it later, much later, when things were calm.

It took me ages to find her, without a surname. There

was a section of the cabinet called *Freelances*, and inside it, everything seemed to be jumbled up. I sifted through the papers, awaiting their return at any moment, hoping no one was watching from the street.

At last, a sheet of paper with the words *Alicia Johns* was in my hand. As I looked at it, I heard the door click open. Jack's voice was coming through it, and I knew he was trying to give me as much time as possible. I shoved the file back into the cabinet, pushed the drawer shut, and crumpled Alicia's sheet back into my pocket.

There was no time to get back to the right side of the desk, so I sat in the chair behind the table and spun myself round.

'Sorry,' I said, breathless, as they both came through the door. 'I was just playing on your swivel chair.'

The man laughed. 'You're a much more attractive receptionist than I am,' he said. 'We should hire you.'

'Thanks anyway,' said Jack. 'Bye then, mate.'

'Bye,' I called, and we almost ran out of the front door.

chapter thirty-eight

We were outside a big building, a proper apartment block which rose high into the air. It had balconies running along the front of it, and it was at least eight storeys high. The city was all around me, people piled up on top of one another everywhere. It was a place in which to lose yourself.

But why on earth would she have stayed here? Why would she have done that, when she could have gone anywhere, buried herself in any city on earth and never been found?

I was almost convinced it could not possibly be her. Barcelona was filled with stylish people, and there could easily be someone who looked like Sarah, but with different hair. I hoped it was not her. I hoped that nobody in the world would have it in them to do something as callous as the thing that Sarah, were she alive, had done to Harry.

We stood outside and waited. The air was static with expectation.

A female voice came through on the intercom.

'*Si?*'

'Hi, Alicia?' said Jack.

'Yeah?'

And with that one word, the world shifted on its axis. Harry was not a widower. Sarah had not thrown herself into the water. I was not going to be married next month. There was a metallic taste in my mouth as I bit my lip so hard that blood trickled out.

Jack was, of course, less affected.

'Hi there,' he said. 'Alicia, it's Jack – from Tower Bridge English School? James told me where to find you. Just wondering if you need any work as we're a bit short-handed and have got a big project on.'

According to Jack, any TEFL teacher would jump at this approach.

'Oh, Christ,' she said. 'I'd bite your hand off for some work. Come on up. Fourth floor.'

The door buzzed. This was the last moment at which I could run away, pretend I did not know. I was petrified to be coming face to face with someone whom I knew to be a monster. I could not walk in through the door. I turned and looked down the street. There were shadows in doorways. I could walk away but it would make no difference. I knew the truth.

My sheltered life seemed like the biggest handicap. Jack had experience of people behaving outrageously, from what he said about his ex-wife, and indeed his father. I did not. I had no idea how to deal with a person who was likely to attack me and throw things around.

'Come on,' Jack said, in such a gentle voice that I stared into his eyes for longer than I should have done.

'OK.'

He put a hand on my shoulder and steered me into the foyer. We walked up the stairs side by side. I wanted to run away, every step of the way, but it was too late for that. As we turned the corner of the staircase, I waited to hear the sound of the front door slamming shut behind us, but it seemed to close silently.

By the time we were approaching the fourth floor, I was several steps ahead of Jack. I strode around the corner, and stopped.

She recognised me instantly. Everyone remembered me because of my hair. I was expecting that; but I had been prepared for rage and fury, and not at all prepared for what actually happened.

I had heard of people turning green, but I had never seen it happen. Likewise, I had heard of people shaking like a leaf, but now I saw it. Sarah, or Alicia, was shaking like the last leaf on a tree in autumn. The colour drained from her face so completely that she was left properly green. She stared at me, and I stared back.

Her hair was short and black, cropped in a pixie-ish cut. She was dressed differently from the way she had dressed on the one occasion on which I had met her – in a pair of faded, baggy jeans and a huge mohair jumper, and she had put on a lot of weight.

I tried to see the anger in her eyes, but there was only fear. She was, I realised, far more afraid than I was; and I was terrified.

I could not say anything. Neither could she. As I reached for some words, because insanely, I had not prepared a speech for this moment, she slammed the door.

339

Jack stepped forward and put his foot on the threshold, and the door bounced back. He barged straight in, and I went after him.

It was silent. I expected to hear her scuffling around, running away, but already, it seemed, we were too late. I looked at Jack. He appeared to be at a loss, and I tried to smile, because I had no idea how a stranger had become a friend so quickly. He was now almost as deeply into this as I was.

I ran through the months since Sarah's 'suicide'. Harry had grieved for six ugly months, and I knew that his grief had been genuine. He had no idea. I was going to have to tell him the truth, and then I would have to explain how I, too, had deceived him and come to Barcelona in secret.

This flat was different from Jack's, which was my only experience, so far, of a Barcelona home. This one was spacious and light, with plants in pots and high ceilings.

Jack motioned to me to stay by the door, but I was not scared any more, and so I walked right up to him, and past him, and into the room at the end of the hall.

Someone else lived here with her, somebody with a child. There was a brightly-coloured mat on the floor, with toys and mirrors hanging down above it. On the table, a little woollen hat and some tiny mittens waited innocently for an outing.

On the table, there was a vase of red gerberas.

Jack was no longer behind me. When I looked at him, he was back in the hallway, trying a different door, opening and then closing it. I went back towards him, and opened another door myself.

This room was a bedroom, a child's room with a cot in it. It was empty. Yet I heard a sound, a little mewing whimper, more like a cat than a person. It was so close that I gasped loudly. I stepped away from the open door, and pulled it closed again.

She was standing there, and she was holding someone's child. The child was just a tiny baby. I had no idea how old it was, but it was the sort of baby that could not do anything at all for itself. The kind that just lies there and eats and sleeps. She was holding it close and staring.

'Jack!' I yelled.

'No!' She could not attack me because she was holding the baby, but I could see it in her eyes: if she could have, she would be leaping on me right now. She would be attacking me until I could do nothing, ever again, and then she would be running away.

'Sarah,' I said, and I edged away from her, hoping that Jack was somewhere behind me. 'It's all right.'

Her voice was low and dangerous. 'Where is he?'

'Jack?'

'Where is he?' We stared at each other. Neither of us moved. 'Where is Harry?'

'Harry?'

'He's with you.'

'No! No, he's not. He doesn't even know I'm here.' She looked like a hunted animal, trying to work out what to do, how to escape. I supposed the idea of facing up to the man she had widowed was not appealing. I tried to say the right thing. 'I came here to see if you were alive. I'm supposed to be . . .' I paused. *Marrying your husband* sounded like a crass thing to say, but it was the truth.

'Marrying your husband. Next month. But I can't, can I? Because he's still married to you.'

'Oh, for fuck's sake, Lily. You've no business to be mixed up in this. When Constanza said you were marrying him, I just . . .' We stared at each other, at deadlock. With my peripheral vision, I saw Jack edging into the room, felt him standing just behind me. He was the one who spoke next.

'You have a baby,' he said. 'I remember, when you came to the language school, you had a baby then too. I hadn't realised it was you.'

Until now, I had not processed this simple truth. This was Harry's baby.

'You were pregnant?' I said.

'Yes, I was fucking pregnant. No, he has no idea. That was the entire point. But now you're going to tell him. Lily, believe me, you are in way over your head. You do not want to be doing this.'

'No, I'm fine. This isn't about me, is it? It's about you, and Harry. What happened?'

All three of us froze as the front door slammed.

'I think I left it open,' Jack said, and we exhaled.

Sarah spoke quickly. 'I can get out along the balcony. I've practised. I have a plan. Let me and the baby go. If I go, you two, whoever *you* are,' she was looking at Jack, 'can distract him for a while and we can get away. I can't believe that I was so fucking close . . .'

'But,' I said, 'you don't have to go anywhere. I can tell you don't want to see Harry, but he has no idea I'm here. He's in Cornwall. He thinks I'm on a little hen-weekend type of thing. I'll have to tell him why we can't get married, obviously, but—'

At that she shot me a look that was filled with despair.

'Lily,' she said, 'I'm glad you have no idea about any of this, because it means it hasn't started for you yet. But . . .' She tailed off. 'Anyway. Just believe this: he does know you're here. And that means I have to leave.'

Jack spread his hands out. 'Look,' he said. 'I'm new to this, but I think I have as much idea of what's going on here as anyone. There's no need for any of this. Can we just grab a seat and talk this through? Lily hasn't done anything wrong. She just wanted to be sure of the score before going through with this wedding. Turns out she was bang on the money. There can't be a wedding, because the guy's still married, isn't he?'

Jack set off into the sitting room, and we followed him, though Sarah did not seem amenable to the idea of sitting down and talking. She kept the baby held close to her with one hand, and went around picking up all his things with the other. I stood and watched as she took his play mat and dumped it into a cupboard with a pile of his clean clothes. There were three photos of him in frames on the sides, and she put them into the cupboard too. She packed a big bag with the hat and gloves from the table, and some nappies and baby wipes from the pile in the corner. When most of his stuff was in the cupboard, she locked it and put the key in the big bag. Apart from this bag, there was no sign that a baby lived here.

As she did all this, she talked, quickly.

'It's too late,' she said. 'Lily, you are young, clueless, and I know you're not streetwise. Actually it never occurred to me that you'd have the nous to do a thing like this, because if it had occurred to me I would have planned for it. If this stops you marrying him, perhaps there'll be a bright side. Tell me this, and tell the truth: have you, even for a moment, seen the real Harry?'

'The real Harry?'

'You know. The one who did this.' She rolled up her big jumper and, just for a second, gave me a glimpse of a livid red scar down her side. Then it was gone. 'I miscarried three babies because of him. I thought I'd actually like to have this one.' She stroked the baby's hair. 'This is Carlos, by the way. I gave him a Spanish name as a sort of rubbish disguise, but I just call him Charlie anyway.'

'It's not Harry's fault if you miscarried, and anyway . . .' I had been about to say that I knew she had never wanted children, but it did not seem as though she would be interested in this take on her reality.

She looked weary as she said: 'But it *is* his fault. He was obsessed with the idea that I was sleeping with Seumas from next door. I absolutely wasn't. He'd driven past me walking up the hill with Seumas once, and Seumas was carrying my shopping for me. After that, nothing I ever said was going to convince him otherwise. I almost came to believe it myself.'

I sat down. I could not listen to this. I wanted to put my fingers in my ears. But instead I said, 'I don't recognise him at all in that. But the . . .' my voice wobbled at my treachery, but I forced myself to continue . . . 'the police,' I said through tears, 'did come to talk to me – about a hit and run accident, on the night of your Christmas party. There was a man hit by someone in a silver car. He was on life-support for ages. And then he died.' My voice was shaking, however hard I tried to control it. 'But there's no way . . .'

'You know there is,' she said. 'Bloody hell. I remember that night. If I'd known . . . You know it's true, Lily, or you wouldn't have just said it. I suppose you lied to them, because "you love him".' She made quotation marks in the air with her fingers. 'Why do you think he's kept you close? You're the only one who can give him an alibi.'

'Sarah,' I said. I was spinning. 'It's not at all like th—'

'It's a horrible moment,' she interrupted, 'when you start to see the truth. But there's no time for this. If you're here, he's here. So that means I'm off.'

I took hold of her arm. She shook me off.

'He's *not* here,' I said. I could not engage with any of the rest of it. I wanted her to know that, for the moment at least, she was safe. 'He thinks I'm at a spa, on a hen weekend. I just told you that.'

'He doesn't.'

'He does.'

She stopped for a moment. 'Lily, he doesn't. OK then – call him. Not on my phone, but withhold the number on your mobile, or his mobile.' She nodded to Jack. 'And ring him. If his phone rings with a British tone, then I'll accept that he might not have followed you out here, and we can talk it through for a few minutes before I go. If it's a Spanish tone, I'm out of that window. I should be gone by now. I should be gone.'

Jack was holding out his phone.

'It's all right,' I said. 'I'll use mine.'

My hands trembled as I took it out of my bag. We all looked at it.

'God, that phone,' Sarah said. 'It was mine, wasn't it?'

I scrolled down until I had the word *Harry* on the screen. I looked at them, at Sarah jiggling her baby around, at Jack's open expectant face (I could see he was confidently expecting the British ring tone, though I could also see that he had no idea what one would sound like), at the baby, looking innocent and content.

It took a few long seconds to connect. Then it started to ring. It rang with a foreign tone. I had not heard one before, but this, I knew, was it. A long flat tone, followed by another, and another.

Nobody said a word. I hung up before he could answer.

'Oh,' I said in the end.

'Shit,' added Jack.

'See?' said Sarah. 'He followed you because he didn't trust you. He's spying on you. He knows precisely where you are. He's probably outside on the pavement, right now. I can still get away.'

Jack was staring at Sarah.

'Right,' he said. 'OK, Sarah. Let's get you out of here. I have no idea what's going on, but you need to be somewhere else, don't you? You've got a place to go?'

'Yes. Thank you. Look, I'm clutching at straws here, but he might not know *why* Lily is here. You're going to have to face him for me. Tell him anything you want but don't mention me, OK? Lily doesn't have to marry him anyway.' She had her coat on now, and a woollen hat that she pulled down as low as she could. She put a fleece hat on the baby and did her coat up so that the child was almost invisible.

She hesitated. 'Jack? He's not going to like Lily being

here with you. Help her stand up to him. Lily, if you see the real Harry, it's going to be a blessing in disguise. Good luck. I wish I could take you with me. There are no words for that man.'

'But . . .' I did not believe her. I didn't believe a word she said about him. She was mad, and bad. That scar looked nasty, but it could have come from anywhere. Harry would never have done that to her.

She shook her head at me, and left, through the window.

chapter thirty-nine

Jack

Lily was pale and tense. There were tears in her eyes as she walked over to the window and closed it.

'What now, Jack?' she asked, her face suddenly wild and panicked. 'What do we do?'

He tried to think of a sensible answer.

'Lily,' he said. 'Come here. It's OK.' He could see that Sarah was telling the truth about the man, but he feared that he would not be the one to make Lily see that, and he was scared that if he went at it too strongly, he would send her running outside the apartment into that bastard's arms. 'This is not about you,' he told her. 'It's about Harry, isn't it, and Sarah. We just have to . . .'

At that point, he ground to a halt. He had no idea what they *just had* to do. Presumably, the bloke was hanging around this building somewhere, and also, he presumably knew which flat they were in. It was only a matter of time before he would appear on the doorstep; and if he did that, Lily would let him in, Jack knew she would.

If they left, he had to assume that they would walk straight into him. On the other hand, there was nothing else to be done. Lily was looking at him with huge wild eyes.

'We have to leave here,' she said. 'Go somewhere else. I should ring Fergus.'

Jack was sceptical. 'His brother?'

'He knows about it all, I'm sure he does.' Lily was different. Maybe, Jack thought, she was in a state of shock. It was almost like a trance.

'You haven't got his number. You said that, remember? Look, this is a lot for you to take in.'

She shook her head. 'Sarah's wrong. She must be. I mean, on the one hand,' she waved her little white hand around for emphasis, 'on the one hand you have a woman who faked her own suicide and had a secret baby while her own husband, who would have been happy to give her a divorce, went through hell. On the other hand,' she spread the fingers of her other hand, 'you have a man who lost his wife, and he was genuinely devastated, I know he was because I was there. Who found some happiness again. And who then finds out that everything was a massive trick. Who would you trust in that scenario?'

Jack felt that this was a rhetorical question, but all the same, he could not help himself. 'I'd trust Sarah, actually,' he said.

Lily frowned at him and shook her head so her hair bounced around.

'Why would you though?' she almost shouted, suddenly. 'Why trust *her*? She's the liar. Oh Jack. I almost believed her, but . . . I love Harry. I do.'

'Do you really, though? What about that business with the police and the car?'

Lily's face closed. 'You're right about one thing,' she said. 'This *is* about the two of them. It's not about me, although it's all my fault that it's come to light. Let's get away. We can go back to yours or something. I don't want to be in her place any longer.'

And before Jack could say a word, she was out of the door.

He stood and stared at the door, swinging open, for a second. This morning, Lily had been a stranger to him. Now he was in rather deeper than he might have opted to be, had he been given a choice. And she had just left the apartment, to head down the stairs straight into the arms of a man whom Jack truly believed to be a dangerous bastard.

'Lily,' he shouted. 'Wait! Let's find another way out.'

He ran down the four flights of stairs, but she was running faster. Her footsteps echoed around the hallway: he could hear her, but every time he rounded a corner, she had already got around the next one. By the time he was at the top of the last set of stairs, it was too late.

There was a tall man standing just inside the front door, and Lily was standing next to him, closer than you would unless you were lovers. Jack hung back, stepping into the shadow, trying to hear what they were saying, but their voices were low.

She did not seem to be in any danger. He was talking softly, gently to her. He was wearing an expensive-looking overcoat with a burgundy scarf. Jack would not have a clue how to dress like that. This man looked powerful, and he clearly had Lily completely in thrall to him. He put a hand on her shoulder and drew her in closer.

It made Jack want to cry with frustration. A beautiful girl with the world at her feet, and she gets taken in by an idiot like that with a flash car and a nice coat.

Lily was crying. The man, Harry, was comforting her. Then, all of a sudden, their voices were louder.

'But Harry,' she said, and her voice was clear. 'You got rid of your silver car.'

'Oh Lily,' he said. 'Stop it. You're being ridiculous. Hysterical. *Where is my wife?*' The last sentence was almost shouted.

Jack's heart was pumping. He wanted to wade in and pull Lily out of there, onto the street, take her away – but he feared that if he did, things would end up worse. All the same, if this bastard looked like he was going to raise a fist, he'd be in like Flynn.

She did not reply. Jack thought of Sarah, and the baby, and just as he was poised to run towards Lily and stop her, somehow, from telling, she did it.

'Lily?' Harry said, in a tone that sounded pretty menacing to Jack.

'She went out of the window,' she said quickly. 'Onto the balcony. To the neighbour's flat, I think.'

Jack was back up the stairs in a second. He was on the fourth floor in minutes. There was no sound of footsteps behind him. He had no idea what might be going on down there. He banged on what he hoped was the right door. The landing up here was carpeted, he noticed, in mustard yellow. It must take time to locate a carpet that nasty.

'Sarah!' he called, in the lowest voice that might still be heard. 'It's Jack. She just told him you're here!'

Seconds later, Sarah was at the open door. She was trembling but she looked determined.

'Right,' she said. 'Jack, did she tell him about Charlie?'

'Not that I heard, no. But I didn't hear everything. I don't think so.'

She held the baby out. 'Take him. There's a cupboard on the third-floor landing. Wait in there till he's passed, then take Charlie away, check into a hotel or something, anything. Call Fergus. He'll get hold of me. I can face Harry. But he's not getting my son.'

'Sarah, will you . . . ?'

'I'll be fine,' she said. 'Paloma and Pedro are here. They're calling the police. It'll blow my cover completely but that doesn't matter any more. Go on. Go.' They could both hear him coming up the stone stairs. Sarah thrust the baby's bag at him.

'You've got kids,' she said. 'Look after him.'

'I promise.'

He ran, willing Charlie to keep quiet. He knew he was racing the approaching footsteps, and he tried both to walk quietly, and to get there quickly, and not to alarm the baby, who was now asleep.

The cupboard was there, and he pushed his way in, past a vacuum cleaner and some mops, stood next to a plastic bucket. He pulled the door closed, and seconds later, heavy footsteps approached.

He tensed up. Now, here was a situation he was pretty sure he had never signed up for. Hiding in a cupboard with someone else's baby, praying that a bad guy he'd never met would carry on walking. He almost smiled as it occurred to him that he had achieved his dream of living in an Almodóvar world.

Jack did not breathe. He could not even see the baby, because it was pitch dark, and it smelled of dust and disinfectant, but he prayed for Charlie's sake that he was still asleep.

The footsteps sped up again, and then they receded, up the last flight of stairs. He wanted to stay and check that Sarah was all right, but he knew he could not do that. She had entrusted him with her most precious object.

He was anxious as he pushed the door open. The coast was clear.

Lily was waiting on the pavement outside the front door. When Jack came out with the baby, she jumped and gasped.

'Jack!' she said. 'What the hell?'

'I should say the same to you.' He should not be angry with her, but he was. 'You told him! You told him where she was hiding! Lily, how *could* you?'

She was crying. 'I'm sorry. And now I know. I don't want to believe it, but I know she was telling the truth. Oh, Jack! What have I done?'

He looked at her with some suspicion. 'What?' he said. He turned and started walking, knowing that he had to get the baby away. 'One minute you're turning her in, the next moment you believe her? How does that work?'

She ran to catch up with him.

'It was something he said,' she explained, and she wiped her eyes on her sleeve, and seemed to be walking with him.

chapter forty

Nothing had ever made me this wretched. I had never done anything wicked before. Not like this. I had done a terrible thing, because Harry had ordered me to, and that glimpse I had seen of a completely different person was enough.

He had changed. He was so desperate to find Sarah that he had looked at me with an expression I had never seen before, and hissed some terrible words to me, and suddenly everything fell into place.

He had lowered his voice and said: 'Lily, if you don't tell me where she is hiding, I will break every bone in your body. I will smash your face up so no man will ever look at you again. And that's before we get started on this boy you're cheating on me with. Making a fool of me. Tell me now and make amends.'

And I was so petrified that the words came out of my mouth before I could stop them. He hugged me then, but I just wanted to get away and never go back.

I let him carry on hugging me, just in case Sarah was

getting away. I even kissed him, although I hated myself for doing it. I took his hand and asked if we could go to a hotel, but he smiled, touched my nose with his finger, and said: 'Later. You're a good girl, Lily. Wait for me right here, and then we'll do something amazing. I love you, you know.'

And he ran off. There was nothing I could do to hold him back. I thought of poor Sarah, terrorised by him, betrayed by me, and I wanted to make it right, but I was completely out of ideas.

I would shop him though, about the drink driving. I had been suspicious for months, and it was long past time for me to do the right thing. I looked at myself, and did not like anything I saw. If only Grandma was with me, or even Julia, or my parents, to help me get it right. I needed someone to stop me making such stupid, weak decisions.

The night was getting cold. A few people wandered past, and I looked at them in the artificial light of the lamp posts, and wondered where they were going. How could people be living normal lives, when my reality had just turned out to be a mirage?

He had hurt her, I did not doubt it. He had made her miscarry her babies. He had killed someone. He might be killing her right now.

I turned to go back into the building, but the door was locked. A couple were approaching, wandering down the pavement with their arms around each other, oblivious to me.

Suddenly, Jack came through the door. He had baby Charlie, and he was furious with me.

'Jack!' I said. 'What the hell?'

'I should say the same to you.' He hated me. I tried not to cry. I had ruined everything.

When we had been walking for a little while, he looked down at me. 'Lily, you'll just bring him to us.'

'I won't. I'm sorry. I did the wrong thing. I was so scared. So, so scared of him.' I fought to retain control of myself. How could I have loved him without seeing any of this? How had I allowed myself to overlook the warnings?

The receptionist thought we were a family: Jack, baby Carlos, and me. She offered us a travel cot, and Jack accepted it. She wanted our passport numbers, but I just filled in the form with random numbers, while Jack told her I knew them all by heart. We had not used our real names and I had enough of Harry's cash on me to pay the hundred euro charge.

I wanted to talk to him. It was imperative that I should speak. Yet no words were coming. The baby was crying and there was nothing I could do about that.

Jack found a little kettle in a cupboard. The hotel was a lot nicer than it had looked from the outside. It was better than the one my things were currently residing in, in a different part of the city. He filled the kettle with water from the en suite bathroom and plugged it in. Immediately it started noisily heating the water.

I stood up and tried to jiggle the baby around, but he carried on crying. He was so small, and so angry. I tried to imagine his future. He was half-Harry. Harry probably knew about him by now. When I thought of Harry, my fiancé, I felt nothing at all. I was wretched and numb.

'Just do your best to soothe him,' Jack said, 'and I'll get this bottle warmed up. That should do the trick.'

He was holding a baby bottle that I supposed he had taken out of the bag, though I had not seen him doing it. I held this baby, Sarah's baby, my stepson, I supposed, against my chest and walked around. I walked over to the window. We had taken a tiny rickety lift up here to the seventh floor, and although we looked out at the street, we were so high that it felt safe. If I stood right up against the window, by a heater that blasted warm air on my legs, I could look down to the road – but all I saw down there were indistinguishable people and cars with pools of light in front of them.

I looked back. Jack was pouring water into a small plastic jug that I supposed had also come in the bag, and then he was lowering the bottle into it.

'Lily,' he said. 'You all right? Stupid question. Sorry.'

I drew in a deep breath. 'I can't think about it. Not the important things. We need to call Fergus and I haven't got his number.'

'Yeah,' he said. 'You're going to have to find it. What can we do? Does he live in London?'

'I don't even know which part of London.' I screwed my eyes up, trying to remember. I had to get this right. 'Somewhere that you have to get a taxi to from Belsize Park.'

'You're saying that to the wrong bloke. London's on my list, but I've never set foot in the place yet.'

'Oh, Jack,' I said. 'I bet you wish you'd never spoken to me at the cathedral, don't you?'

'I don't actually,' he said. 'I'm glad I did. Though if I

hadn't, you might not have found Sarah, and none of this might have happened. Something would have happened though, wouldn't it? Hey, Lily?' I looked at him. 'Don't be too hard on yourself. We got Charlie-boy away, and Sarah had back-up. She wasn't scared. She was ready for him.'

'He was here. He was following me.' I shuddered, and held the baby closer. He was making little hiccuping sounds now. Jack took the bottle from the jug and shook a couple of drops onto the back of his hand, then nodded.

'Like riding a bike, this stuff. Here, give me the little guy, and get on the phone and find a way of tracking down this Fergus bloke.'

I watched the baby starting to drink the milk. Jack knew what to do, how to hold him, how to hold the bottle. Sarah was pregnant when she died. I corrected myself: when she pretended to die. I had known she was alive for weeks, really. But only a few months ago, she had been giving birth, in some hospital in Barcelona, all on her own.

I had very few numbers in my phone. I did not have a number for Nina, which I was almost glad about, so I called the only person I could think of who I hoped would want to help me. It was the first number in my phone's address book.

He answered on the fourth ring. I willed him to be sober and sensible. I had no idea whether I could count on him, or not. *Please be together,* I begged silently. *Please help.*

'Al?' I said. 'It's Lily.'

'Lily? Are you OK? Sorry for—'

'No, it's fine. Look, I'm in Barcelona and I need your help. It's urgent. I'm not with Harry any more, but he's

358

here and I really need to contact his brother, Fergus. I have no idea how to do it. Are you sober?'

'You know what? I am. His name's Fergus Summer? Where does he live, what does he do?'

'London. Can't remember his job. Are you in Falmouth?'

'Yes. I've got a new place. Of sorts. No internet access.'

'OK, cool. Can you get round to Constanza's house? Next door to Harry's. Number eight. She'll have it. She's part of Sarah's network.'

'OK. On my way. Look, I have to—'

I cut him off. 'It's fine. I'm sorry too. We can talk when I'm back.'

'Right. I'll call you from there. On your mobile?'

'Yes.'

There was nothing we could do but wait. Charlie drank most of the milk from the bottle, then drifted off to sleep. Jack lowered him gently into the cot, and we both stood back and admired the tiny sleeping creature.

'Jesus,' he said. 'She must be desperate, to hand her baby over. Bloody hell.'

I could hardly say the words. They came out as a whisper. 'He might have killed her by now.'

'No. The neighbours were there. They were calling the police. She's a streetwise woman.' He sighed. 'Bloody hell, Lily. I knew a guy back in New Zealand who used to batter his wife around. Everyone knew it but they'd never admit it. But I've never seen anything like this bloke. I hope he rots in fucking hell, that's for sure.'

'But it's Harry.' I could not compute this still, even though I had seen it in him with my own eyes.

'You know you can never see him again,' Jack said to me. 'You do know that?'

And in spite of everything, the reality of losing Harry, the Harry I thought I had, hit me in the stomach like a kick. What was left to me now? I could not even move back in with Julia, because she was going to be furious with me when she discovered that I had left Mia on a secret trip to visit her mother. Then I was horrified with myself about that, too. I knew nothing about Mia's mother. She could be a drug addict, could be a thief; she, too, could be violent, or a killer. All I knew was what she had said to me on the phone; but she could have said anything, could have been anyone.

'All my stuff is at his house,' I said. The stupid words hung in the air for a moment, and then my telephone began to ring. I snatched it up.

'Hello?' I whispered.

'Lily? It's Constanza. You're in Spain? What the hell?'

'I need Fergus's number.'

'I know. I called him already, as soon as your friend turned up. Lucky we were here. We were just going out. Your mate would have got a very confused babysitter.'

'You called him?'

'Yeah, he's heading out there. You need to ring his mobile and tell him what's going on. Got a pen? Speak to him, then call me back and tell me what's happening. Is she OK? Is Carlos?'

I looked at the baby. 'Carlos is fine.'

'Speak to Fergus. Call me back.'

Fergus had booked himself on a flight that left in three hours. He was in the back of a minicab on his way to

Heathrow when I spoke to him. I gave him a rundown of events. I forced myself to admit what I had done.

'Oh, Lily,' he said, in the end. 'Look, there's a lot you need to know. Wait for me exactly where you are. I'm concerned that I haven't heard from Sarah. How long ago did you leave her?'

I had no idea. 'More than an hour.'

'Right. Well, I'll keep the phone on until they make me switch it off on the plane. Then I'm coming to your hotel, OK? Stay in that room, sleep if you can. Look after that baby. Can I speak to your friend?'

I passed the phone to Jack, and heard him explain to Fergus that he was an English teacher from New Zealand who had just happened to get caught up in this. I could hear his sincerity, and I hoped that Fergus could, too. It was strange that I had only just met him, because he felt like the oldest and best friend I had ever had.

'Well, I don't know about you,' Jack said, 'but I'm not going to be getting any sleep. He just said his flight lands at half past midnight. We can expect to see him here at maybe two or so? I don't know. You lie down and get some rest, if you can.' He smiled to himself. 'It's important to sleep when the baby sleeps.'

'No way.'

'No, I thought not.' He was walking around the room, opening cupboard doors, until he found the one he was looking for. 'Minibar,' he said. 'I hoped there might be one. When I was in Singapore, all I did was hang in the room and grab beers from the minibar. Can you imagine? All Singapore out there, the gateway to Asia, and all I could do was to wait it out in my room and drink the minibar dry by myself.'

'Really?'

'God, yeah. I'd never been anywhere, and suddenly I was in Singapore, and the people there! The stuff going on! Everywhere you look, there are things happening and they're all strange. It freaked me out, I tell you that. It freaked me out so much that I wanted to go home. That was the only thing I wanted to do, to go back to my wayward wife and my wonderful, glorious kids, and say that none of it mattered. But of course I couldn't, because I'd made such a song and dance about going away. So I just waited it out to see what would happen. And that is how I came to be New Zealand's premier expert on the subject of minibars.'

He took out a bottle of beer and a small bottle of wine and held them both out to me. I pointed to the beer. Wine was what I drank with Harry: this called for something different. Jack nodded and took one for himself, too. He removed the tops from them both, and passed me a bottle. I took a sip. When I lived with my grandparents, in my funny, sheltered half-life, I'd had no idea what a lubricant alcohol was to normal people's everyday lives. I also had no idea how much I would grow to like it.

'Tell me more about Singapore,' I said. 'You must have gone out sometimes.'

'Oh, I did. It's hard to explain what it's like. And you're from England, so heaps and heaps of people all crowded in a city, that's normal for you, but . . .'

'It's not,' I assured him. 'Not for me. I've only been to London once.' I shuddered at the memories. Nina had assessed me and declared me a suitable new member of the family. Fergus had done everything he could to warn me off, short of telling me the truth about Sarah; and I had set the burglar alarm off because I'd had no idea that Harry was obediently going to sleep in a separate bedroom from me even though he was forty-four and we were living together. *Harry*. I shuddered again.

'And that was only for a weekend, and I didn't see any of the sights,' I added. 'But I liked it a lot. And I'd be loving Barcelona, if it wasn't all so . . .'

'So fucked? You're a small-towner like me? Well, in that case, Singapore would freak you out. It's the people everywhere. The heat – it's so humid it's hard work even to pick up one foot and put it in front of the other. There's spices and damp hot air, and shops and people yelling. Some of it's all modern and Western, I guess, but I only knew that because I'd read it in the book. It looked pretty *un*Western to me. It was not one bit like the South Island. That is for bloody sure.'

I thought about it. 'I'd like to go to Singapore one day. When all of this . . .' I looked at the sleeping baby, and then back at Jack, the familiar stranger. 'When it's all sorted out.' It was easy to say the words. I could still not think about it, not directly. If I had got Harry so wrong, just because he was nice to me, then what else was I getting wrong? I was in a hotel room with a stranger and someone else's baby. Anything could be about to happen. I edged away from Jack. He seemed to understand.

'Hey,' he said. 'Don't worry – all right? I'm not like him, I can promise you that. I could never have it in me to do that.'

I looked at him, into his clear grey eyes. I believed him. Yet I had believed Harry. But now that I looked back, I acknowledged that I had known some things about Harry for a long time. I had suspected for ages that his might have been the silver car that knocked down Darren Mann and put him on a life-support machine.

I put the bottle down, sick at my own weakness. I had been brought up better than this. Both my grandparents had strong morals and they had imparted them to me. We were kind to animals, we fed the birds, we gave our old clothes to charity. We recycled everything. We donated to Oxfam and bought all our Christmas cards and wrapping paper from charity shops. Yet when I had found myself the only person who was able to put a killer into prison, I had shrunk away and agreed to marry him instead.

'I believe you,' I told Jack. If he had bad intentions of any sort, he would surely have acted upon them by now. We just had to pass the time until Fergus arrived. I took a deep breath, and changed the subject.

chapter forty-one

At quarter to two in the morning, there was a gentle tap on the door. Jack was lying on the bed, dozing with baby Carlos on his chest. The two of them looked so peaceful that I tiptoed to the door and opened it as quietly as I could.

When I saw him, I threw myself into his chest. He grabbed me with both arms and pulled me close.

'Lily,' he said. I was surprised by the tears that were seeping into his shirt. I was not expecting to fall apart at the sight of him, but I let him take me by the hand and lead me into the room. He closed the door behind us and clicked it so it was double-locked. Then he sat me in the chair by the window, and stroked my hair.

Fergus looked so much like Harry. The part of me that still wanted to give Harry a chance clung on to him as the nearest thing I was going to get. He crouched beside me.

'Lily,' he whispered. 'It's all right. I'm so sorry. You were in way over your head and you had no idea what was going on. I'll explain it all to you later on. I'm just checking in on you before I go to Sarah. This is the Kiwi then?'

We looked at Jack. He and Carlos were both snoring. Jack looked younger like this, asleep and vulnerable. He was beautiful, I realised.

'He's been good to me,' I said. 'He still is.'

'Yeah, I hope he's genuine. Be careful.'

I tried to smile. 'I haven't been much of a judge, have I?'

'Oh, older, more experienced people than you have been taken in, believe me. I wanted to tell you about Harry, but he swore it was different with you. I don't know – I should have tried harder. Look, you're all right here, aren't you? Stay right where you are. I'm off to see Sarah. I'll be back as soon as I can.'

I hung onto his hand. 'I want to come with you. I can't bear just to sit here and wait.'

'I'm older than you – I'm forty-two. I'm afraid I have to pull rank. I want you here, with the Kiwi and the baby. I can't leave my nephew with a stranger. Sorry, but I just can't.'

'Jack's not a stranger any more. Please, Fergus. I made all this happen. I'm right in the middle of it and I'm coming with you.'

He was smiling at me with a funny look on his face.

'The Lily of a few weeks ago wouldn't have done this. She would have hidden away.'

'So let me come. I'm an adult.'

He sighed. 'Against my better judgement, I suppose I can't stop you. Leave a note for the Kiwi explaining that you're with me and you're fine. We're seeing Sarah, though. Not my brother. I don't want you going anywhere near him.'

*   *   *

We walked through the night, back to the very police station at which I had discovered that Sarah was alive. The air was velvety, surprisingly warm for December, and there were Christmas lights hanging between lamp posts and in people's windows.

There was so much I wanted to ask Fergus.

'So,' I said. 'Um . . .'

'Yes,' he said, smiling down at me. 'Um, indeed.'

'Tell me about Harry.'

He sighed, and the tension, which I could see he was trying to hide, was obvious on his face.

'Harry is a very damaged man,' he said carefully, as we walked up the Ramblas. There were so many people out, talking and laughing, drunk and happy. We wove our way between the groups. 'In a way it's not his fault. He and my mother were very close. When our father died, Harry and Nina were almost happy, because it had always been the two of them in their own mutually adoring world. They were a strange little unit. You could trace it back to Nina's neuroses, but let's not bother. My mother is a poisonous woman, as you must have seen for yourself. She put a lot of stuff onto Harry. He had to be her golden boy. I was barely noticed in comparison. When Father died, I was on my own.' He paused. 'And then she sent Harry away to school, and that was the undoing of him, really. From then on, his behaviour seemed to verge on, well, some might say the psychopathic.'

'He's not a psychopath!'

'Who knows? I think he is, actually, but he's not exactly going to submit himself for testing. He built a shell around himself, for protection. The woman he adored sent him away, as a child, to live in an institution. It's hard to grasp what a trauma that was for him. Far worse than our father dying, which he had actually seen as a positive.

'He hated me, for those two years when I was still at home, living in a kind of distant way with Nina, who didn't give much of a shit about me. Then when *I* got to school he bullied me like you wouldn't believe. Other boys looked to their older brothers for protection. I was the one desperately trying to avoid mine. He spread it around that I wet the bed. He would walk up to me, take my bag, and I'd be trying to explain to the masters that I had done the work, but I didn't have it, and because of the stupid code of honour thing, I couldn't say that my own brother had flushed it down the loo. I did not do well at school and I rejoiced when he left.'

I felt so sick that I had to stop walking for a moment. Fergus put a hand on my shoulder.

'You OK?'

'Yes. Then what?' We started walking again. We pushed through a crowd of students, who ignored us.

'Then he did the law for a while, presenting himself as a hot-shot lawyer. It's always been about validation from the outside world, and from Nina, so although it seemed surprising when he suddenly veered into showbiz, I was probably less astonished than most.'

I remembered what Julia had told me about his soap career ending suddenly. 'What happened?' I asked.

'Oh, he drank too much, took too much coke, spiralled out of control, got violent.' Fergus took my arm and made me wait while a taxi drove past, at a surprisingly stately pace, and then led me across the road, onto the street with the police station on it. 'Violent to women,' he clarified. 'He was on the edge. Worse than the soap character he was playing. Very mixed up with hookers, totally lost sight of the normal way to behave, but if it was ever pointed out to him, there was fury. It was never his fault. It was the woman, it was his dealer, it was the bosses, it was generally me. My wife, Jasmine, loathes him. That's why she left me. Because I wouldn't cut him out of my life.'

'Why wouldn't you?'

'Because of Sarah. And then because of you, Lily. So, showbiz and Harry did not mix well. And eventually it all went too far. He was with two girls, two escorts, in a hotel room, and he went berserk and attacked them. One managed to lock herself in the bathroom and call the police, but by the time they got there, he'd beaten the other poor woman so badly that she had to have part of her face reconstructed. It was hushed up, the series he was in paid her off so she didn't press charges, and Harry had to get the hell out of there, find himself a wife, and get respectable pretty bloody quick.'

'And Sarah married him, knowing all that?'

'Sarah married him, not knowing most of that. Lily, don't you see? You sound incredulous. If I'm not mistaken, you're due to do the very same thing, next month.'

I swallowed hard. 'I'm going to need your help, Fergus.'

There was a woman on duty at the police station this time. As soon as we started speaking to her, filling in each other's sentences in our basic Spanish, she nodded.

'English?' she said. 'Family?'

'Sí,' said Fergus. 'I'm his brother.' I was in the same building as Harry and Sarah. How, I wondered, were the police managing to untangle the threads of their insanely complex story?

'*Hermano*,' I said, remembering the pages of vocabulary I had memorised.

The woman started speaking, but it was too fast and I could not understand her. She pointed us towards the waiting room, and we shut the door and sat on the rickety chairs. No one else was in there. The vending machines hummed.

My stomach was full of acid. I tried to block out everything Fergus had told me. He could not have been talking about my Harry. Those things had been done by another man. I was scared to be close to him, now.

I looked back at the past six months. It was simply impossible for me to put the man who had made me feel that I was the most spectacular and beautiful person in the world, next to the man Fergus had just described, and to slide the two images together until they were on top of each other, one person. The person Fergus had just told me about was not the man who had come to find me at Tommy's party on the beach, who had got me a job that I wanted, who had proposed to me at Maenporth as the sun set. Yet he had looked me in the eye and threatened to break every bone in my body, and I knew that everything Fergus had said was true.

How long would it take me to be able to accept that, and what I would do next?

'Bag of crisps?' Fergus asked, searching through his pockets for change. 'When did you last eat?'

'Not really hungry.' I scooped the change from the bottom of my bag and handed it to him. 'Here you go, I've got loads of coins. Look, Fergus, you were right. I shouldn't be here. I don't want to see him. Even knowing that he's in this building . . . I shouldn't be in the same place. I need to get out of here.'

He nodded. 'Yes. I'll walk you back to the hotel. We could fix it so you never need to see him again, you know, Lily. If they're keeping him here for any reason, you can dash back and move your stuff out, and bugger off to live your life somewhere else.'

I sighed. 'It would feel cowardly, but I think it would be best.'

Just then, the screen above the door buzzed into life, and B6 was spelled out in red. At the same moment, the door to the waiting room was opened, and a police officer stood there. He was slightly overweight, and his stomach bulged against the buttons of his shirt. The large moustache that crept from his top lip to the middle of his cheeks made me smile.

He spoke to us in English. 'You can come, please? You are brother?'

'Yes,' said Fergus. 'I'm the brother.'

'Good. Is complicated.'

'Look,' I said to Fergus, stepping close to him, looking up, 'I'll head back to the hotel. I'll be fine. It's full of people out there, and we know Harry's here. It's not far. I'll see you back there.'

He looked from me to the officer, and back again, then said, 'I don't want you to go on your own. It's the middle of the night.'

'If I stay here I'll see Harry. I'm not ready to do that. And this is the centre of Barcelona. It's safe.'

'I know. I suppose we can't get the Kiwi to come by for you, because of Charlie-boy. OK, walk fast, and text me when you get there.'

I stood on tiptoes and kissed his cheek.

I had almost reached the lights and bustle of the Ramblas, when I felt a hand on my shoulder. I should have spun around in shock, but my mind was so far away from Barcelona that I barely noticed it.

'Lily,' said the voice, and for a second I thought it was Fergus. Then I knew.

'Harry,' I said, and I swallowed the bile that had risen to my throat.

'Lily,' he said again, and his voice was gentle. At least he wasn't going to attack me. 'Come on,' he said. 'Let's get a beer. Everything seems to have gone completely crazy, doesn't it?'

I shook my head and walked backwards, away from him, towards the revellers on the city's main street.

'You were in the police station,' I said. 'In a cell.'

He laughed. 'In a cell? Of course I wasn't in a cell! What have I done? It's my first wife who's got some explaining to do – not me. I didn't do a thing, but she called the cops on me anyway. Released without charge, as far as I could understand what the hell they were talking about. Now, Lily. Come on, my darling. We'll get a drink and try to work out what the fuck has been going on behind our backs.'

I wanted to get to where the crowds were. Harry was

sounding like the man I had fallen in love with, and it was confusing me.

'No,' I said. It was all I could think of.

'Hey.' He was hurt. 'Lily? It's all right. This is not about you and me, is it? It's about Sarah. She had me totally fooled. Completely. I feel like the biggest mug in the world.'

'It's not that.'

He bent towards me, as if interested, and I looked into his face without meaning to. I looked away quickly. It was too difficult.

'Is Sarah still there? And Fergus?'

He smiled. 'Not for long, I don't think. It's not as if there was a life insurance claim or anything. Though my misguided brother will, I'm sure, be in the shit back home because he committed an enormous amount of fraud last year. It's always the damsels in distress with him. I can see you're unsettled by it all, and who the hell can blame you. God knows what they've been telling you. Come on, just a drink. We'll go to the busiest bar on the Ramblas, so you won't be on your own with me, if that's what's disturbing you.'

To be with Harry, and to be going for a drink, felt so normal, that it was easy to forget that everything had changed. I was not sure that I could say no to him, anyway, because he was bigger and more forceful than I was.

'OK, then,' I told him, and he took my arm and we walked together to the corner and stepped into the nearest bar. Harry ordered two beers, and we took a table by the window.

chapter forty-two

I knew I had to say something before he did. I had to say it before I lost my nerve and everything went back to normal.

'Harry,' I said quickly, 'I don't want to get married. You told me you would break every bone in my body. You said that to me a few hours ago.'

He grimaced, as if it was a trivial error. 'Oh Lily, I'm so sorry. I was stressed in the extreme. I was just saying anything that I thought would get me to Sarah. Did I really say that? To you? I don't even recall it.'

'Why did you follow me? All the way here?'

He sipped his drink without taking his eyes off me. I looked back into his eyes, and I was scared.

'I did not believe for one moment that you were going to a spa with Mia. Lily, you are a rubbish liar. I'm sorry, but you are. I tried to work out what you might really be doing. There was nothing on the home computer. Nothing anywhere. Then I came across a map of Barcelona tucked away under all your knickers. I still had no idea why you'd want to come out here, of all places, on the sly, but I guessed that was what you were doing and that it had something to do with Sarah.

'And then, when I looked at that map, it had little circles around things and notes on it, and I could have sworn they were in Sarah's writing, so I was seriously confused.'

'I thought she was alive,' I said, hating myself for courting his approval again. 'And we were planning our wedding. I didn't want you to be a bigamist without realising it. I wanted just to see if I could find out, without telling you. So if she was actually dead, you wouldn't even have to know.'

'Hmm. I have to say, Lily, I'm a little confused. More than a little. You weren't as good as you thought you were about covering your tracks. I found your travel documentation on the morning you were leaving.'

I had been so careful. 'How?'

'You went to the loo just before we left the house. It only took a second to find it tucked into your book in your bag. I booked myself onto the next flight as soon as I dropped you and Mia off. Caught up with you again as you left your hotel the next morning. You're not as observant as you ought to be, you know, if you're going to pull stunts like this. Which you're not, are you?'

'Oh,' I said. I was still reeling. 'No.' I grasped at the smallest thing. 'You lied. You said you and Sarah stayed at the smartest hotel in Barcelona, but you didn't. You stayed at the three-star one.'

He laughed as if delighted. 'I didn't *want* to stay in it. It was a shithole. Why would I want to admit to that? Living like some scummy student? I don't think so.

'Look,' he said, leaning forward so he was in my sight-line, and smiling his old smile at me. I tried hard to resist. 'The thing is, Lily Button, this is all details. Let's leave them to it. We can go to the airport now, you and me. We'll grab a cab, swing by your hotel, you can pick up your stuff and we'll go and sleep for whatever's left of the night in a place near the airport, and get ourselves home first thing in the morning. We're happy at home, aren't we? You and me?'

'No,' I managed to say. 'I don't want to.'

'It does hurt, that you'd do a thing like that to me,' he mused. 'But I know that you didn't mean to hurt me. You were, in your funny little way, trying to do the right thing. At least, that's what I thought until you were suddenly attached to some scruffy idiot who clearly thought he was in with a chance.'

'No,' I said. 'It isn't like that. Not at all.'

'Like I said, it's all details. Let's go. If you don't want to go home, we can head to the coast, or go to France, or anywhere you like. Who cares about the rest of them? I'm glad Sarah's alive. It's always better for people one has loved to be alive than dead.'

The trouble was, it was incredibly difficult to say no to him. I was scared of him, and because I was scared, I tried to convince myself that I loved him. It would be so much easier to be his adoring girlfriend, to do what he wanted to do. I was used to him. He had never threatened me (until a few hours ago), had never raised his voice, or given, as far as I could tell, any indication that he might harm me.

I still felt that I could be the one to change him.

I thought of Sarah's livid scar. I thought of Fergus. Fergus could not have spun me a web of lies. Everything he said had made sense. I trusted Fergus more than I could ever trust Harry.

'No,' I said. 'I think we're over, Harry.'

He laughed at this, a genuine laugh, not a nasty one. It was as if he thought I had made a brilliant joke.

'Lily,' he said. 'You silly thing. You don't get to do that. I can see your head's been messed up by all this rubbish, and I don't blame you. Really, I don't. Lily, have I ever done anything in our relationship that has made you feel uncomfortable? Anything?' I opened my mouth and he quickly added: 'Before today?'

'No,' I admitted. 'Not before today.'

'When I met you, you were so sweet and naïve. You didn't know how to order a cocktail or eat a prawn. You didn't know that there were radio stations other than BBC Radio Four, and you had no idea who Beyoncé or Justin Bieber or Simon Cowell were. And I took you from that, from a shitty little life that was never going to amount to anything, and I gave you the world. I gave you the world on a fucking plate. Lily – you don't get to throw it back at me.'

'It's not like that.'

'Oh no? You do owe me a bit, you know. Whose money did you spend when you came out here to double-cross me? Whose cash took you to the arms of that backpacker?'

'Harry,' I said. I drew in a lungful of air and tried to say the right thing. There must be something, some formulation of air through vocal cords, tempered by tongue and teeth, that would get me away from here.

Everything was melting like wax and reforming into new, sinister shapes. It was true. I had been nothing. My life had been shitty. He had given me everything. I did owe him.

'I did know who Simon Cowell was,' was all I could manage. 'And Beyoncé.'

I looked him in the eye and tried again. 'But Harry,' I said, trying hard to keep my voice straight. We were the only people left in the bar. A man was sweeping the floor. We were going to have to leave in a minute.

'Yes, my darling?' His voice was utterly controlled.

'You hurt Sarah. You made her lose her babies.'

He laughed, and he looked perfectly at ease. 'She told you that, did she? Is that what she's saying?'

'Yes.'

'And you believe her? A woman you know for certain has told enormous, unforgivable lies to all of us, destroyed all our lives? You believe her, rather than me, the man you profess to love?'

I shook my head. 'But I do believe her, because—'

'Yes, she's convincing, I know. Of course she is. But Lily, I'm so deeply hurt that you can think that of me. I know I can be, possibly, a bit of a control freak. I don't want to be. I know I said something pretty nasty to you earlier this evening, but I was desperate. My whole life was upside down. Come on, darling. It's about us. You and me. All the rest is detail. As I keep telling you.'

The man finished sweeping, and looked at his watch. I stood up.

'Sorry,' I said quickly. I tried to keep my voice level, like his, so that he would see that I meant it. 'I'll pay you back all of your money that I ever spent, one day. I did love you. I was madly in love. I would have done anything for you – or I thought I would. But it wasn't you, it turns out. It was the person you were pretending to be. The person I imagined. I'm on Sarah's side. I believe her. I believe Fergus. I'm with them. I'm not with you any more, Harry.'

Tears were pouring down my cheeks. I could not stop loving him, just like that. All the same, I knew it was over, for ever.

My legs wobbled as I made my way to the door, but I stumbled out, his laughter following me. The crowds had thinned. It was nearly morning. I set off down the street, trembling, then I started to walk tall.

He did not realise it, but I had done it. I started to smile. All I needed to do was to get back to the hotel, as soon as I could. I began to run. I would run all the way through the dark streets of Barcelona, my feet pounding the pavements, the cold air reinvigorating me. I would run past apartment blocks with wrought-iron balconies and past blank windows, past closed shutters and turned-off Christmas lights. I would run and run, and I would reach the hotel and find my friends. I was euphoric.

That was all I was thinking of, when I heard the footsteps coming up behind me.

At first, stupidly, I thought it was a mugger. You had to watch out for thieves in Barcelona. I held my handbag tightly to my body; and then he grabbed me and pulled me into a dark doorway and I saw his face. He finally believed me.

'You're not doing this,' he said. 'Like a fucking Nancy

Drew, coming out here to mess it all up. You don't get to walk away. You're wearing my ring.'

My heart was pounding so hard that I could feel it through my entire body. This was danger, real danger. I tried to tug the ring off my finger, but he grabbed my wrists and pulled them back. Then he glanced up and down the alley we were on, and on seeing there was no one there, he started to hit me. I opened my mouth and screamed as loudly as I could. He punched me in the mouth to shut me up. His strength was terrifying. I felt my face throbbing. I screamed again, and he hit me again.

'I didn't want to do this, Lily,' he hissed. 'I didn't think I'd ever have to do this. You should not have pushed me. I thought better of you. You are being stupid.'

I fought him back. A part of me was detached from everything that was happening, observing from somewhere above my head, and noting with interest the vicious way I kicked him and kneed him in the groin. I had never had a physical fight with anyone, ever. Yet, in this moment of danger, I defended myself with every atom of strength I had.

All the same, my strength was not enough. He was bigger and stronger, and he had had a lot more practice. He pounded at me, and I was Sarah. I was all the women he had attacked in the past. There were women in London whose names I would never know. I wondered who I was, to him. Someone he hated. His mother, perhaps, or the opposite of his mother? I wondered whether he had always wanted to do this to me, whether he had been biding his time, waiting for this moment.

Even as he pushed me to the ground so he could kick me in the ribs, I thought he had loved me, in his way.

Then I was numb, and I stopped fighting back because I could no longer move. Then I closed my eyes. It did not stop.

Later, much later, I woke up. He had gone. I was lying in a doorway, frozen, and everything hurt. I knew I was alive because my heart was beating: I heard it. I could only open one eye, and when I spat the blood out of my mouth, something clinked onto the stone doorstep.

It was cold. So, so cold. There was nobody about. I closed my eye again and waited.

It was light, and someone was trying to make me sit up. I shook them off. This was a strange state; I was not properly in the world, nor far enough out of it. Everything I thought I had was gone. He had hurt me as badly as he possibly could, without actually killing me; had left me in a European alley all night in the middle of winter.

There was something around my shoulders. It was a thick overcoat. With my single working eye, I tried to focus. I was in the centre of a little group of people, and though I could not see their faces, I sensed that they were kind. They felt sorry for me. I probably looked like a monster. I leaned back on whatever was behind me, listened to the hissing rush in my head that might have been my own blood, or that might have been the sound of everything I thought I knew evaporating.

He had done this to me. He had done it to Sarah. He must have done it to others, too. This was what he did.

There was nothing in the world, at that moment, that I cared about, apart from this: *I was going to bring him down*. I was going to do everything I possibly could to make him pay for the things he had done to us, and to Darren Mann. Although everything hurt, I felt almost good. I knew exactly what I had to do.

chapter forty-three

Two days later

All I could think about was going back to the police, and telling them the truth – to forget everything I had previously said to them. It was not only my life that had been irrevocably changed. The very least I could do was to help Darren Mann's parents find out the truth.

'You,' said Jack, 'are like a different person.'

I tried to smile, but winced. We were walking in the sunshine, and it was hard work being resolutely oblivious to all the staring.

'Like a person with a fucked-up face?' I had never said the f-word before. I was experimenting.

'Like a relieved person with a fucked-up face. You know, I think it's fading already? You'll be back to normal before you know it.'

I touched my cheek and winced. 'You think?' I had been checked over at the hospital and, somehow, there was nothing seriously wrong. It was all bruising. But I was bruised all over, like a windfallen apple. I was missing two teeth, which would be a reminder of my former fiancé for the rest of my life, and I could not wait to get home and get them replaced, however that worked.

I looked horrific. The reflection that gaped back at me when I looked in the mirror was disfigured, which I supposed had been that man's plan. Oddly, I could not think of him by his name any more, because 'Harry', in my mind, was still next to 'love'. I called him 'that man'. It was as close as I could get. One of my eyes was still almost closed, and I was lightheaded with the strong painkillers I was taking. He thought he had destroyed me, but the strangest thing of all was that he hadn't. It was only now that I was in this broken state, that I knew, with more certainty than I had ever known it before, that I was going to be all right.

'I'll miss it,' I told Jack. I liked him. I was terribly wary, and could not contemplate the notion of anything apart from friendship, but perhaps, I thought. One day. It would be conceivable. Jack was straightforward, and good-hearted, and entirely different from that man. 'I'll miss the way everyone stares at me, and pretends they're not staring, and wonders what happened.'

'You won't really.'

'No, not really.'

'You'll get plenty of attention, Lily – I promise you. There's something about you that's changed. You're open, not guarded any more.' He hesitated. 'I think you're going to find life very different when all this is done. In a good way.'

'Yes,' I told him, with a smile that hurt slightly. I was getting good at smiling with my mouth shut, because of those missing teeth.

The man who hurt me had vanished into the night, and if I allowed myself, I would see his shadow everywhere. I was making a determined effort not to succumb to paranoia. He might be about to jump on me again, but he probably wasn't. Sooner or later, he would have to turn up, here, or back in Cornwall, or somewhere else, and he would be picked up by the authorities. For now, I was sticking tight to my group of new friends. I was never on my own.

It was nearly time to go home and deal with the wreckage of the old life. It seemed impossible that I had come out here, only a few short days earlier, with the aim of protecting my beloved fiancé from the scheming trickery of his wicked first wife. Everything I thought I knew had been wrong. As far as I was aware, my wedding was still arranged for January. And although I still ached all over, everything that happened here had been lucky.

I flashed back, without wanting to, to myself lying on the ground while my fiancé kicked me viciously, over and over again, in the ribs. It was hard to think of that humiliation as a blessing, but I suspected it would turn out to be one of the best things that had ever happened to me. If this had *not* happened, I would be on the verge of walking down the aisle to him.

It was a crisp day, and there were Christmas decorations slung between the lamp posts. People walked around in little groups, staring at me, then looking quickly away.

Children sometimes pointed at the livid bruises all over my face. I smiled at them, lips pressed together, when they did, to show that I was not scary. It did not always work.

There was a huge ferry across the harbour, in front of us.

'Jack,' I said, as we crossed a cycle path on the wide pavement. I hated the way my voice sounded, distorted by the gaps where my teeth had been, but I pressed on. 'I don't know what I would have done if I hadn't met you.'

He smiled. I could not completely trust my judgement of people, after the past year, but it did seem that I could count on Jack.

'You're welcome,' he said, 'and please stop thanking me. I've . . .' He blushed and looked down. 'Well. I've been in Barcelona half a year, now, and all that time, I've been kind of looking for someone. I knew I'd know her when I found her, and . . .'

He stopped speaking. Our eyes met. I looked away, pleased.

We caught up with the other two standing on a narrow wooden walkway that crossed a corner of the water.

'This is the spot,' Sarah said, and we all looked down. 'This is where I supposedly threw myself to my death. It would be tricky, I think. Someone would see you and fish you out.'

For a moment, I remembered myself, on the edge of the harbour in Falmouth, having exactly that problem.

'It would have been a cry for help,' I said, recalling Al's kindness that day and longing to see him. I had called him with the barest details, but I needed, now, to tell him everything. 'Not a serious attempt. It would never work.'

'Well,' she said, 'exactly. It would be a stupid way to do it.'

'What the hell actually happened?'

'Yeah,' Jack agreed. 'How in God's name did you two pull it off?'

She looked at Fergus.

'It was surprisingly easy,' she said, 'if you have enough allies. No one actually checks. Harry was out for the count, with something pretty vicious.'

Fergus lowered his voice. 'We used one of those "date rape drugs",' he said. 'Rohypnol. Scary, but it worked.'

'Fergus, you were here? All along? Without Harry knowing?'

'Yes. And the reason I was here was to get Sarah away from my psycho brother, clean away, before he worked out that she was pregnant. She wasn't going to allow it to happen this time, and neither was I.'

We all stood and looked out at the water. It was calm, and the cold winter breeze was rippling its surface and blowing straight at us. I pulled my hair across my face like a scarf, or a piece of armour.

'When he woke up, there was no one there,' Fergus continued. 'And after a bit of time had passed and he was trying to find her, I called him, told him she was dead and the police were trying to get hold of him at home, and that was how I'd been contacted. I said I'd identified the body as soon as I got here. He was a bit too cut up to question the details.'

I looked at Sarah. 'It wasn't true, then – that he'd just announced he was leaving you?'

Sarah closed her eyes and kissed the top of Carlos's head.

'He said that? He would, I suppose, wouldn't he. The master of rearranging the facts in his own favour. No, I told him I was leaving for ever, that I wasn't going back home. That was our original plan. That I would completely leave him. Just go, let him head back to Cornwall on his own. I was petrified, because I had very rarely stood up for myself, and when I did it never ended well, but I meant it, and he clearly hated me, so I thought he might have let me go. But he flipped out. Christ, I was scared. He had a knife on him, the psycho. As you've noticed, he did some damage. He laid into me, and then walked off.'

She tapped her side, and I winced. 'He didn't know there was a baby in there, obviously, or he would have aimed a little bit differently, taken Charlie out too. He wasn't going to let me walk away. He had to destroy me first.' She paused. 'You know how it is, now. I wish you didn't, Lily.'

'He didn't question it when I said I'd seen her body,' Fergus said quietly. 'I told him she'd hurt her side somehow. It was totally plausible to him that after he stabbed her, she threw herself in the sea. Or that he actually killed her and got away with it.'

'Maybe he had a sliver of doubt,' Sarah said. 'Who knows? But he decided to move on to a younger model anyway.' She put her hand over mine, on the railing.

'I took him back to London,' said Fergus, 'and got a British death certificate – you can get these things easily enough once you know who to ask – and he didn't question that, either. He embraced the role of the tragic widower pretty bloody heartily.'

'What was in the urn?' I had to ask. 'What did he scatter at Porthleven?'

Fergus looked down. 'Ash from Mum's fireplace. I took it out with me, in a Tupperware box.'

I bit my lip with the available teeth, and smiled at the absurdity.

'And then,' I said, 'I came along. All stupid and naïve.'

Fergus nodded towards a café by the water's edge, part of a beautiful development of old warehouses. We followed him in and sat at a corner table behind a screen of plants. I put a hand on his arm on the way over to the table.

'Fergus?' I said. 'The first time we met?' He grinned at the memory. 'Did you really ask Harry for my phone number after that?'

'Did he say that?' I nodded. 'No. He was probably trying to scare you away from me. Wanting to keep you to himself. With hindsight, I should have got your number. If I'd had any idea how things were going to go, I would have kept better tabs on you.'

It was early for lunch, and we were the only ones in the restaurant. Sarah ordered a few dishes and some fizzy water.

'Now,' she said. 'Lily: if he ever turns up again, there's only one thing that will properly destroy him. If I'd had any idea he mowed someone down, the night before we left, I'd have stayed and shopped him for it. Honestly, I would. That poor boy. His poor family. I had no idea. When did you find out?'

I sighed and sipped my water.

'It was all over the news,' I said, 'but it took ages before it occurred to me that it was Harry. Even when the police turned up to check his alibi, I still managed to convince myself that it was a mistake.'

'That would have given you a clue,' said Jack.

'I had to work hard to overlook it. God, I was stupid. I remembered him going out at that exact time for champagne, and coming home without it, a bit shaken up. And all the news reports were about a silver car, and he'd had his silver car locked away for ages, and then he made a big thing of part-exchanging it for a little red sports car as a symbol of his new life with me.'

Fergus and Sarah looked at each other and smiled.

'Mid-life crisis cliché?' said Sarah.

'I'd say,' agreed Fergus.

'But I had no idea why he did it.' I looked at Sarah. 'Ran the guy down. I mean, I know there can't be a reason that makes sense, but . . .'

She sighed and unhitched Charlie from the sling, as he was starting to cry. As she spoke, she casually unhooked bits of clothing and started to breastfeed.

'Oh, Lily. You know, the first few years we were together I was like you were. He can be amazing, can't he? So charming, so adoring. It's hard not to fall madly in love if he wants you to. It changed, obviously. He started by making me doubt myself, cutting me off from my friends, making me think I was going mad. Little things. He'd ruin something I was cooking by turning the oven off – or, once, I was wrapping a present for my sister and he carefully unwrapped it again, rolled the paper back up and put it away, so I thought I was losing my mind.'

I felt sick.

'Would he, say, crumple things you'd ironed and put them back in the basket?' I managed to ask.

'Yes. That sort of thing.'

'I thought it was me.'

'And you didn't want him to know you were crazy, so you didn't mention it. You just tried extra hard to get it right?'

'Yes.'

'There you go. It was beginning for you, Lily. Anyway, that progressed into beating me up for my own good. I'm sorry I can't look at your face properly, by the way. It's horrific to see it on someone else. When it was just me, I could invent all sorts of rationalisations to keep myself going. I must have provoked it, it wasn't that bad . . . but when I see it on you, nothing in the world could be more clear-cut. He kept away from my face most of the time for the obvious reason, but occasionally he allowed himself a black eye. I was so conditioned that I put up with it, year after year. And that's something I'll never quite understand about myself.

'So, that night of the Christmas party, we were at war. I was pregnant and terrified, and I was trying as hard as I could to mask the fact that I was planning to leave him, because I was sure that he could read it on my face. I was tipping my champagne into the poor gerberas whenever he was out of the room so he wouldn't see I wasn't drinking and guess about Charlie.

'You were a breath of fresh air, walking into the house, and I was so relieved to see you. Then I caught him sliming over you and I took him aside and told him to stop it. I knew I would suffer for that, but I was brave, just for a moment, because I knew I was on my way out. He was so furious. He wanted to go for me when I told him to back off from you, Lily. I could see it in his eyes, but he couldn't because you were there, and so he stormed off muttering about champagne instead. He was off looking for another outlet.'

'And Darren Mann had the misfortune to be in the wrong place at the wrong time,' said Fergus. 'I don't think he actually pointed the car at him with the intention of killing him. I think he was drunk and furious and driving like a maniac.'

'Which amounts to the same thing,' I said. I was amazed that the love I had misguidedly felt for Harry had quickly solidified into its polar opposite.

'It does,' Jack agreed, watching me from across the table with his gentle eyes.

'We flew out here the next morning,' said Sarah. 'I had no idea at all. Then I never went home, so I never knew anything about it.'

I thought about her, all this time, living in Spain, having a baby.

'If he turns up again,' I said, 'he'll know about Charlie. Won't you have to let him have a relationship with him, if he asks?'

She shrugged. 'Trying not to think about that – the possibility that he might want a son and heir all of a sudden. It's the kind of trick he'd pull.' She cuddled the baby closer into her. 'But he probably wouldn't believe Charlie's his.'

'When was Charlie born?'

'The last day of August.'

Harry and I had spent August drinking champagne and being in love, while his wife was giving birth, alone and in a foreign country.

'And why did you stay here? Why not go somewhere else to have the baby?'

'Yeah,' said Jack. 'I was wondering that, too. There's a whole world out there.'

She smiled. 'The whole reason I booked the Christmas break to Barcelona, my dears, is because my sister's husband's family have a house in Mallorca. I haven't been hanging around this city. I went straight over there, on the ferry, when I left – that big ferry, just across the harbour. Harry knew nothing about Alastair's family's house, because he cut off my family completely and pretty much got me to do the same. Rose and I had always spoken, but she was frustrated with me. She knew exactly what was going on; she never bought into the Charming Harry Summer routine, and he hated her for that. So she was only too happy to help out with this project. She was there, waiting in Mallorca, and that's where Carlos was born.

'Harry went home with my passport, because we felt it would be too suspicious for it to vanish when I "died", and I imagine he cancelled it, what with me being dead and everything. So I haven't been able to leave Spain. I came back over here to do a bit of teaching, to raise some cash, and work out whether anyone at the British Consulate would mind me applying for a new passport while being dead, or whether I needed Fergus to acquire some new paperwork for me from his shady contacts.' She rolled her eyes. 'I rented that apartment for three months. It was only meant to be a stepping stone, en route to more distant shores. It was pure chance that I was back here at the very moment when you came looking.'

'Sorry,' I said quietly.

'Hey,' she said. '*I'm* sorry.'

Fergus got up and pulled his phone out of his back pocket. It was ringing quietly. He stepped away from us.

I watched him, an olive halfway to my mouth. Although he was too far away for me to hear his side of the conversation, by the time he hung up and came back to us, I knew what he was going to say.

His face was so much like his brother's, but he was so different, so kind. I could read it all on his face.

He paused, standing next to the table. We all looked at him, none of us moving, all waiting.

'They've got him,' he said. 'Picked him up crossing the border into France. He's been arrested, and it sounds like he's going to be handed over to the British police.'

Sarah and I looked at each other.

'We'd better get back,' she said. 'And look him in the eye, and shoot his fucking lies down in court. Are you in?'

I nodded.

'Nothing could stop me,' I said.

chapter forty-four

Six months later

I ignored the letter for two and a half hours, before the things I was imagining became so bad that I decided to open it. That always happened, in the end. I took it upstairs to my little bedroom with the Barbie bed, sat down, and tried to keep my hands from trembling as I took three closely-written sheets out of the envelope.

It was written on thin paper. Prison paper, I supposed. His letters always came on it. I spread it out on my knees. It said:

> *Dearest Lily,*
>
> *What are you doing, I wonder? Where are you reading this?*
>
> *I have plenty of thinking time in here, and I am writing to remind you that I still love you, my darling. You are young and it's been easy for Sarah and my so-called brother to turn your*

*head. My heart will be forever broken by the look
you gave me as you stood in the witness box and
testified against me.*

*But it is not your fault. One day you will
realise what you have done. And when that day
comes, my sweet little Lily, I will be waiting for
you. You still have my ring: put it back on. As
you would say yourself: 'Love is not love that
alters when it alteration finds'. And in spite of all
you have done to me, I would marry you
tomorrow.*

It was the same old nonsense, and it made me feel
physically sick. I skimmed through the pages, crumpled
it up and took it downstairs. Mia was in the kitchen, tall
and stunning and sunny.

'Hey,' she said. 'You all right?'

'Letter from prison,' I said, and handed it to her.

'Jesus,' she said, with a short laugh. 'How many is that?'

'It's the third this week. I opened this one. He still loves
me, apparently. Wants me to put his ring back on. He's
pretending that he doesn't know that I posted the ring
to his horrible mother, months ago.' When I came back
from Barcelona, Nina had found my phone number and
called me day and night to scream abuse, until I discovered
that I could block her number.

'Here.' Mia put her hand out, and I handed the letter
over. She lit one of the gas rings on the hob, held a corner
of the crumpled ball in it until it caught light, then dropped
it all into the sink. We both watched it crumble into ash.

'Thanks,' I told her.

'You're welcome.'
'You revising today?'
'Yeah. You?'
'Same.'

I had nearly finished my access course. I had two more exams to take, and then I would be qualified to go to university. Higher education was the long-term plan. There were a few other things I wanted to do first.

Everyone else was at work or school. Mia and I were doing well at encouraging one another to work, and at coordinating our study breaks. We had studied together all year, since my return from Barcelona, bruised, tooth-less, and still shocked, just before one of the most bizarre Christmases yet.

'Meet for lunch at one?' I asked.
'Sounds good.'

We smiled and headed back to our rooms. Mia was suddenly an adult. She had a tentative relationship with her mother, had split up properly from Joe when he moved (declaring that 'he was too nice anyway') and was filled with a new and shining confidence. I was sure we would be friends for a long time to come.

I had moved straight back to Julia's house when I returned. Al, shaky but sober, came to the big house with me and waited while I packed up my stuff and got it out of there for ever. I had moved quickly around Harry's house, not allowing myself to think about it, forcing the memories away. I reset the burglar alarm with his egotis-tical HARRY code, double-locked the door, and posted my keys back through the letter box.

For months there was still a small, secret part of me

that pined for the Harry I had loved. I knew he was a mirage, and I hated the real Harry, but it took a long time for me to accept the full truth.

All the same, I had sent him to prison. He would be there for a long, long time to come. Causing death by dangerous driving, driving while under the influence of alcohol, a sprinkling of other charges, and he had been found guilty of all of them.

His downfall was spectacular. He was all over the papers, local and national, and the full story of his exit from the soap twelve years earlier was aired. It was worse than I thought. I often wondered how many other women there were, out there, who had encountered his dark side. Occasionally I imagined his future. Would he, one day, come out of prison, rework the past to make himself the innocent victim of malicious women, and start again? I knew he would.

I had been worried about the lies I had told the police about his whereabouts on that fateful evening, but I had resolved to take the rap for it. However, under the circumstances, I was let off with a warning.

Everyone knew that Sarah was back from the dead, as she had testified against him. They knew about the baby, though she carefully told everyone he had been born at the end of September, conceived in Spain. The town had been kept in gossip fodder for the past six months, and I was used to people staring at me and talking about me. I did not care, at all. I went to college with Mia, and spent time with her, and kept in touch with Fergus, who had been loudly disowned by his mother, and with Sarah, and Constanza, and with Jack.

Al was in Sudan, where he had gone as a volunteer at a refugee camp, as soon as he sobered up.

'The plan is, it stops me being so bloody self-indulgent,' he said, before he went. 'Makes me think about other people. I reckon it's the way forward, Lily.'

I was not convinced. Al would always be vulnerable, yet strong. I was waiting anxiously to hear his latest news, always half-waiting for a dramatic crash. So far, it seemed to be working out for him.

Best of all, I was able to make plans, thanks to a bolt from beyond the grave. In March, I went back to the grandparents' cottage to arrange, finally, to shift all the stuff out of the shed. Julia and John came with me, with a hired van. They were going to help me sell everything on eBay. Left to myself, I would not have had the faintest idea how eBay worked.

It was strange to revisit the cottage. I felt so far away from the scared girl who had grown up there, away from the world. I walked up the garden path, noticing the way the new owners had got rid of the climbing plants that had always tried to pull the place apart.

'My goodness, Lily,' said Julia. 'You moved from here to our house?'

'Glorious,' said John.

A man answered the door. He had flyaway hair and a bobbly jumper, and glasses that perched on the end of his nose.

'Yes?' he said. 'Hello?'

'Sorry to disturb you,' I said, and I saw his expression change, as he thought we must be Jehovah's Witnesses. 'I'm

Lily,' I said quickly. 'I used to live here. I sold the house to you when my grandparents died, but we never met. I'm just here to take the stuff from the shed, if that's all right, and if you haven't chucked it out by now. I'm so sorry you've had it so long.'

His face cleared. 'Lily!' he said warmly. 'Well, at last. Thank you for turning up. We've been trying to get hold of you but your solicitor didn't have a contact number. He thought you were living in Falmouth, but beyond that we didn't have a clue. Come on in!'

'Are you sure?' I introduced Julia and John. 'We've got a van. I'm happy just to grab things out of the shed and leave you alone.'

'No, no. Not at all. You have to come in. All of you.'

The cottage was the same, but different. It took all my strength to walk through the door. I skirted around the tiles on which Grandma and Granddad had both fallen, at the bottom of the stairs. I tried not to look at the new furniture. The cottage smelled of baking bread and something savoury cooking. It was homely but in a new way. A smart way.

'Cup of tea?' the man said, putting the kettle on without waiting for an answer. 'Allison!' he yelled, and a few moments later, a woman arrived, sticking a pen behind her ear. She smiled vaguely at us.

'Hello?' she said.

'Allison,' said the man. 'Guess who this is? None other than Lily Button.'

'Lily Button! Oh, have we found her?'

'She found us.'

'We thought you'd be older, didn't we?' They both nodded.

'This is Julia, and this is John,' I felt obliged to say, through my bafflement. 'Friends of mine.'

'And this is Jeremy, because I'm sure he hasn't remembered to introduce himself. Please, everyone, have a cup of tea – are we making tea? Good. Now, sit down. We've done the house up a bit as you can see, just a little cosmetic stuff. And while we were at it, we took down the wall between the two reception rooms. Little did we realise that there was a tiny cupboard in it, hidden under a picture. And in that cupboard were a couple of Jiffy bags with your name on. I'm afraid we opened them, just to check. Now, we didn't want you to get caught out with any kind of tax, as that would have defeated the whole object. So we just told your solicitor we had a few questions and wanted to know how long you'd be using the shed.'

'I'll go and fetch them.' Jeremy handed everyone a cup of strong tea, put a plate of ginger biscuits on the table, and left the room.

John nudged me. I did not look at either him or Julia. I could not. I was tense all over. Two white Jiffy bags were placed reverently on the table in front of me. I took one, and picked off the sellotape on the end with shaking fingers.

'Having taken the liberty of opening it for you,' Allison said, 'we took the extra liberty of counting it. It was exciting, like being in a TV film or something, wasn't it? Obviously it's all intact. There's a letter in there too. Bless them.'

'How much is there?'

They looked at each other. 'Seventy-two thousand,' said Jeremy.

'Five hundred and fifty pounds,' added Allison.

'And zero pence,' they finished together.

I looked at the bags. I could not say a word.

'You could have kept it,' John murmured to them. They laughed and shook their heads.

'How could we possibly?' Jeremy asked.

I had money. I had options. I had read Grandma's letter again and again, a missive from beyond the grave.

You won't get the house, dear Lilybella, when we're gone, she had written, at some point when she was still rational.

We had to free up some money for Estelle and Michael. We never told you about it, because what they did over there was so terribly, horribly distressing and they had, frankly, harmed you enough. You needed to be protected from it. But we managed to keep this aside for you, my darling. Use it well. Have some fun and see the world. You've been cooped up with us old folk for too long. Follow your dreams. Have a ball. Be happy, my darling. Be happy.

I sat on my bed and opened my books. Studying had been far easier than I had expected and I knew the exams were not going to present a problem. As soon as they were over, I was going to set off. I was going to have some adventures. My ticket was on my highest shelf, waiting for me.

I intended to follow Grandma's advice.

Epilogue

Jack went to Spain, and he met the girl. It had not happened the way he had expected. She was meant to be Spanish, for one thing, but she was English. Her hair was meant to be straight and black, not curly and brown. In his daydreams, she was definitely not engaged to another man when she met him, particularly not a violent psychopath. Almodóvar, he felt, might have liked that detail.

Yet the girl in his daydreams was nothing compared with the real woman. He had never imagined her particular mixture of vulnerability and strength. The enormous brown eyes were new to him. Everything about her was just exactly right.

Jack was surprised at how calm he was about it. She was The One. This was the reason why, all his life, he had needed to go to Spain. He had known Lily, now, for half a year, and had not even kissed her properly. That was good: the waiting, worrying, anticipating was making him see the world in glorious technicolour for the first time in his life.

He whistled as he packed up everything from the little room in his flat. He had sold most of his books, and a lot of his stuff, and all that was left was what was going to fit into his backpack. It was time to move on from Barca. He was flying home, tomorrow, to see the kids. He could hardly wait. A year, he had been away. It seemed a lifetime. The idea of going back to Queenstown was strange, but he was only going to be visiting. He was not going to be driving his ute, moving back in with Rachel. His dad would not hurt him. He would be there on his own terms.

LeEtta was four. She was going to school these days. Aidan must be quite the young man by now. And Sarah-Jane sounded almost like a teenager on the phone, though he knew she was only nine, still his little girl.

A week after he got there, Lily would arrive in New Zealand, to do the thing she knew she needed to do. Her parents, her so-called 'parents', had moved to New Zealand and had another baby, and they had left him to die because they could not be bothered with him any more than they could with Lily; and this time there was no family around to take him in. Jack had Googled and found out their real names easily enough. He wanted to murder them, but he would leave them to rot.

Jack and Lily would go to Mount Eden together. He would help her do what she felt she had to do. It turned out Mount Eden was a man's prison, so they would find her dad there. They would look him in the eye and see him for what he was. Then they would do the same with her mother.

After that, anything would be possible.

It was strange, he thought, because his best friends

should be the people he had known for all his life: Queenstown was full of them. But his best friend was a funny English girl with the most complicated life. He was looking forward to seeing his mates again, though he felt odd about it. It was strange to be the one who had left. Jack could barely compute the fact that while he had been learning to teach, and teaching, and learning to cook, and then meeting the girl of his dreams, everyone else's lives at home had been going on in the ordinary way. At least, he presumed they had. But he would only be calling in.

Rachel had said that when he found a nice beach with a hotel, in a country she approved of, she would bring the children out to visit him.

His wife had a boyfriend, someone new in town, and she had looked nervous, as well she might, when she told him, on Skype, that this bloke might be moving in with her and the kids. Jack was going back to check him over. But as long as he was a good bloke, Jack could deal with it. He could deal with anything, now.

The world had never looked as big, or as exciting, as it did at this moment. He was packing up his life in Spain, but Barcelona would always be magical to him. It was where they had met, on a bench at Gaudí's cathedral.

And now, together, they were going to go out and see what the rest of this huge, unpredictable world had in store for them. Jack smiled, and put his old guide book into his backpack.

EMILY BARR

The Perfect Lie

Venice – the perfect getaway . . .

For Lucy Riddick, Venice has always been the dream destination. A dream inspired by the pretty picture pinned to her mother's kitchen wall. To Lucy, Venice seems the ideal place to lose herself.

And now she needs to do just that. The secret she's been keeping from her boyfriend and her friends has finally caught up with her and Lucy needs to disappear – and fast. There's no better time to pack her bags and head for Italy.

But what if, when she sets foot in Venice, Lucy finds that the one thing she has been running from, the *one* thing she has been trying to escape, is already there, lying in wait for her?

Time to run away again? Or time to end the chase, once and for all?

Praise for the sensational Emily Barr:

'We can't praise Emily Barr's novels enough; they're fresh, original and hugely readable' *Glamour*

'A great read from start to finish' *The Times*

'Sleep-sabotagingly moreish' *Cosmopolitan*

978 0 7553 5134 3

headline
review

EMILY BARR

The Life You Want

Tansy Harris is a terrible mother.

The kind who forgets to pick her children up from school. The kind who drinks half a bottle of wine at lunchtime. The kind who contemplates an affair with her son's teacher.

Something must be done, and Tansy decides the answer is a trip to India – where better to take stock, sort her head out? She will leave her husband and two boys at home, and come back a better person.

India is incredible, everything – and more – Tansy hoped it would be. But when she visits an old backpacker friend who's joined a cult in the south, she lifts the lid on something terrifying. And the moment Tansy realises she's in the wrong place at the wrong time . . .

. . . is the moment it's too late.

Emily Barr's electrifying novels get under your skin. And stay there:

'One brilliantly compelling page-turner' *Closer*

'Sleep-sabotagingly moreish' *Cosmopolitan*

'A great read from start to finish . . . believable characters that are variously biting, insightful and sympathetic' *The Times*

'We can't praise Emily Barr's novels enough; they're fresh, original and hugely readable' *Glamour*

978 0 7553 3560 2

headline
review